# SUCH A GOOD FAMILY

CAITLIN WEAVER

To request permissions, contact the publisher at rights@stormpublishing.co

Ebook ISBN: 978-1-80508-613-0
Paperback ISBN: 978-1-80508-614-7

Cover design: Rose Cooper
Cover images: Alamy, Shutterstock

Published by Storm Publishing.
For further information, visit:
www.stormpublishing.co

*To my parents, who gave me my love of words.*

# ONE

## LORRIE

### *Five months before*

It was Christmas Eve and I was pleasantly drunk. At least, as drunk as I ever allowed myself to become, which meant I'd had three (maybe four) glasses of wine and could feel my control freak tendencies receding. As I stood surveying the party—my party—the generic holiday playlist I'd put on switched over to "Baby It's Cold Outside." I winced; the hosts on a popular morning radio show had recently declared the song "canceled."

As I wondered whether to skip through the song, I swayed on my feet, and grabbed the back of an armchair to steady myself.

"Do I need to cut you off?" asked a voice from behind me, with a laugh. I turned to see Eden, my best friend and neighbor. She slipped her arm around my waist and ran her other hand through her carefully styled auburn waves.

"Maybe," I admitted, resting my head on her shoulder and inhaling her familiar musky perfume.

"You really outdid yourself this year." She nodded at the crowded living room where a twelve-foot Christmas tree stood in the corner under the vaulted ceiling and garlands hung from every inch of the mantel and bookshelves. "And the outdoor lights, I mean, they're breathtaking."

"That's what Ed said about the price tag." I grinned. I'd splurged to have our exterior Christmas lights professionally installed this year, much to my husband's chagrin. I was determined to make everything extra special this last year before my oldest, Knox, went off to college and everything changed.

"God, how many years have you done this again?" asked Eden. "Ten? Eleven? I've lost count."

"It's the Thirteenth Annual Keller Family Christmas Eve open house." I raised my glass and tripped over my words only slightly. My mind traveled back to our first gathering, an impromptu potluck for the neighbors, back when the kids were just sticky-faced toddlers, some not even born yet.

"Uh-oh, you're doing that misty-eyed nostalgic thing." Eden eyed me, arching one perfectly groomed eyebrow.

"Just soaking it in," I replied. "The last Christmas with everyone home."

"Oh, come on." She shook her head. "The kids will be home from college for Christmas next year. At least Summer will, probably with a suitcase full of dirty laundry and an empty bank account."

"I know," I sighed. "But it won't be the same." Tears pricked my eyes. "How did it all go by so fast?"

"Christ, Lorrie." Eden squeezed my waist. "It's only eight p.m. You've at least got to hold it together until Santa visits." She smiled slyly. "Speaking of which, is Ed all set for his big night?"

One of the neighborhood husbands played Santa each year, passing the red suit back and forth among them like a Super Bowl trophy. They took the role very seriously, each trying to outdo the others year after year. Last year Eden's husband, Witt, had accessorized with knockoff Gucci sunglasses, a grill over his front teeth, and a large gold chain, and had surprised us all with a not-half-bad rap version of "White Christmas."

I nodded. "Ed disappeared a few minutes ago, so I assume he's getting ready for his big entrance."

"Think he can top Paul's performance?"

Though we never let on to our husbands, the wives maintained an informal ranking of the Santa performances. The overall winner was Paul Shulman, Eden's next-door neighbor.

"The Jewish Santa," I laughed. Three years ago Paul had appeared wearing a yarmulke with the red suit and had done a very entertaining breakdance routine to "The Dreidel Song." He'd spun around on the ground on his back for the grand finale, and had spent the rest of the party lying on the couch with an ice pack.

Eden gave me a sidelong glance. "I assume you didn't invite him this year."

I shook my head and grimaced. "I invited Abby but she couldn't make it." Abby Shulman had been a regular at book club and other neighborhood mom gatherings. I'd seen her a lot less, though, after her decidedly unamicable divorce from Paul last year. A professor at Georgia Tech, he'd gotten one of his students pregnant. I'd seen the girl around the neighborhood—Jules, I'd heard her name was—pushing the baby in a stroller, wearing a ring on her left hand. I did my best to avoid her, as her presence served as a sharp reminder that what happened to Abby could happen to any of us.

Eden and I stood for a minute watching the party swirl around us. It was an unseasonably warm Atlanta evening so someone had opened the French doors leading to the backyard. A breeze wafted in and sent a stack of gold cocktail napkins fluttering off the kitchen island into the air. The music, which had switched over to a jazzy version of "Deck the Halls," blended with the sound of laughter and ice clinking in glasses. The mulled wine I'd made infused the house with the smell of cloves and citrus. I closed my eyes, soaking in the feeling of being surrounded by my family and closest friends on my favorite night of the year.

"Have we lost Lorrie?" I opened my eyes to see Witt standing in front of us. Eden tilted her head up and he bent to kiss her, leaving his lips on hers just long enough for me to feel a flash of jealousy. I couldn't remember the last time Ed had spontaneously kissed me.

"Lorrie's busy imagining packing up our children's steamer trunks and sending them off to war." Eden mimed dramatic waving and swooning.

I laughed and nudged her with my elbow. "Oh please, I know you're just as sad as I am to see them go."

She sighed. "It's true. But at least you'll still have two kids at home to keep you busy. Our house will be so empty. I'm going to have to take up day drinking or skeet shooting or something."

Witt slipped his arm around her shoulder and ran his hand through his sandy-colored hair that was attractively graying at the temples. "Preferably not in that order."

My youngest, Chloé, came bounding up to me, her coltish preteen legs too long for her little girl body. She had Ed's hazel eyes and dark hair, and a heart-shaped face that made her look like a porcelain doll.

"When's Daddy coming?" she asked, hands on her hips.

"You mean Santa?" I raised my eyebrows.

"I thought I heard reindeer hooves on the roof a minute ago." Witt cupped his hand around his ear.

"Santa's not real." Chloé rolled her eyes.

Witt gasped. "What? No!" He buried his face in his hands and let out an exaggerated sob. Chloé eyed him with skepticism. He raised his face and peeked one eye open to look at her.

"You're faking," she said, crossing her arms. "I knew it."

"Jeez, when did you get so cynical?" He ruffled her hair.

Chloé pretended to duck out of the way but couldn't hide her smile. Everyone loved Witt.

"*Santa* will be here soon." I made air quotes with my fingers. "Go find the other kids, and tell them to get ready." Chloé flounced away, swishing fabric of the ballerina wrap skirt she'd insisted on wearing.

"Speaking of other kids," said Witt, "have either of you seen Summer? I found her phone in the bathroom." He held up an iPhone in a purple and black zebra-striped case.

Eden snorted. "For the amount of time she spends on that thing, you'd think she'd keep better track of it."

"Like mother, like daughter." Witt grinned.

"You're obviously drunk." Eden put her finger to his lips. I looked away as they kissed again.

"I haven't seen Knox or Archie around for a while, either." I scanned the room for my sons. "Though I bet Archie's hiding in the basement playing video games."

Eden laughed, then turned to me. "I almost forgot," she said. "I brought your Christmas present."

"No, wait, I want to give you mine first!" I clapped my hands. Eden had a knack for choosing the perfect gift, but this year I was especially excited about the one I'd gotten her. I pulled at her arm. "Come on, I stashed it in the guest room with all the other presents."

"Don't worry about me, I'll be fine," Witt called after us in a loud voice.

"I don't know why I bother hiding the gifts anymore," I said as we made our way down the hall. "The kids just wanted to pick out their own stuff this year. It was so depressing."

I opened the door to the guest room and froze at the sight of a figure writhing on the bed. I fumbled for the light, my eyes struggling to adjust in the dark. Squinting, I realized it was two people; a boy and a girl, their limbs wrapped around each other, faces pressed together. My hand found the switch and as I flipped on the light one of them gave a strangled cry. They disentangled themselves and scrambled off the bed to their feet.

"Holy shit," Eden said.

My mouth fell open. In front of us, clothes rumpled and faces flushed, stood Knox and Summer. Half of Summer's long, copper-colored hair had come out of her ponytail and she brushed it off her face. The button-up shirt I'd forced Knox to wear was mostly untucked and he had what looked to be a smear of shimmery peach lip gloss across one cheek. Both were breathing heavily.

"Well," I managed, taking a deep breath. As my nerves settled I worked to suppress a giggle.

"I'm so sorry," Summer said, her chest heaving. She looked from her mother back to me with an expression of half embarrassment, half pride. "We didn't think anyone—I mean, we didn't know—"

"How long has *this* been going on?" Eden asked, gesturing at the two of them before crossing her arms. Summer looked at Knox, who looked at the floor.

"A few weeks, I guess." He shrugged.

My mind raced back over my recent interactions with him. How had I missed this? Over the years Eden and I had joked about Knox and Summer getting together one day, but somehow it had happened right under both of our oblivious noses.

"Why don't you get back to the party." Eden gestured to the door. The two teenagers nodded and darted past us into the hall like spooked animals.

"Well," I said again, and the giggle I'd been holding back escaped. Eden looked at me and let out her own snort of laughter, grabbing me and pulling me over so that we landed flat on our backs on the bed, gasping for breath between waves of laughter.

Eden wiped her eyes. "Do you think we willed this to

happen?" she asked. "All those baths we used to give them together when they were toddlers..."

I sat up and tried to compose myself. "It would be pretty great to be in-laws, wouldn't it?"

Eden hoisted herself up next to me. "Yeah, someday! But not when they're eighteen."

"So what now?" I asked. "Do we need to... talk to them about it?"

Eden made a face. "I guess so. But I know exactly how *that's* going to go. Whenever I try to give Summer any kind of advice she just rolls her eyes and stares at me like I'm speaking another language."

I sighed. "I know. I always pictured myself as the cool mom whose kids would be totally comfortable talking to her about sex, but Knox just beelines out of the room whenever I try."

Eden's eyes widened. "Oh God. Sex..." From the living room a cheer went up.

"Sounds like Santa's here," I said, reluctant to end the conversation. "I guess we should get out there."

We entered the living room just as Ed sashayed in. He was dressed in black boots and the familiar red Santa pants and hat. His thick, dark hair had been sprayed light gray and he wore a white beard so realistic I had to look twice to make sure it was really my husband underneath. But that's where the similarities to Santa ended. Under the beard Ed was shirtless, his broad, hairless chest bare except for the red suspenders he'd hooked his thumbs through.

The crowd hooted and hollered. "Who hired the Chippendales?" someone shouted.

"Careful, Ed, there are kids here," someone else teased. The kids were mostly teenagers by now, though, and most of them were laughing along with their parents—with the exception of Knox and Chloé, who looked mortified. And Archie—wait, where was Archie?

I whirled around and got to the basement door just as it opened. "Santa's here?" Archie said, emerging. "Why didn't you come get me?"

"I'm sorry, sweetheart, I forgot."

"Thanks a lot." Archie rolled his eyes and headed into the living room. He stopped when he saw Ed, grimaced, and turned back around. "Yeah, never mind."

I started to call after him as he disappeared back down the stairs, but stopped. It was Christmas, after all. The kid deserved a break.

Ed was strutting around the room now, a large burlap sack slung over his shoulder. "Time to find out who's been naughty and who's been nice," he called, wiggling his thick eyebrows and pulling on his suspenders. He stopped in front of Witt, who fanned himself and pretended to fall backward in a faint. Laughter swept through the room.

"And now, ladies and gentlemen," Ed said, dropping his voice an octave lower than usual, "the moment you've all been waiting for..." He jumped on top of the ottoman and began gyrating his hips, swinging the burlap bag in a circle over his head.

"I am *not* seeing this." Eden covered her eyes.

"You and me both." I forced a laugh to cover my embarrassment. Once Ed had a few drinks in him he could be a bit over the top, something I dreaded on nights like these. But I knew from experience that trying to rein him in would only backfire.

Looking at him standing there, though, I had to admit he looked good. He'd always been in decent shape, but a couple of years ago he'd taken up CrossFit and stopped eating pasta and bread. It was annoying how fast his six-pack had appeared. I patted my midsection with its slight pad of fat that no amount of Pilates or Peloton rides seemed able to shift.

Ed jumped down and started handing out the wrapped gifts each family had contributed to the bag. When he stopped in front of Eden and me, he swiped his hand over his glistening brow and grinned.

"Better than Witt last year, right?" he asked.

Eden raised her eyebrows. "You know, I hear they're casting for the next Magic Mike movie."

"They'd be lucky to have me," said Ed, winking.

"You were great." I smiled and offered up my lips. He bent to kiss me but was already in motion toward the next cluster of people and instead grazed my ear with his mouth.

"I need another drink after that," said Eden, turning toward the kitchen.

"I'll be right there," I promised. "I just have to do one thing."

I returned to the guest room to retrieve Eden's gift and paused, eyeing the bed. While it was hard to think about Knox having a girlfriend at all, Summer was head and shoulders above any of the other perky cheerleader types who'd attached themselves to him in the past. To me they all looked alike and I was constantly mixing up their names—Mackenzie? Michaela?

I blinked away the movie that had already started in my head: Knox and Summer smiling at each other as they walked back down the aisle after their wedding. Eden and me, pacing the hospital waiting room together while we waited to see the baby who would have Summer's red hair and Knox's blue eyes. Our families together for Thanksgiving, Christmas, and summer vacations at the lake...

Once I found Eden's gift, I wound my way back through the party and discovered her stretched out on the patio couch outside, her drink propped up on her chest.

"Sorry"—she waved her hand—"the room was starting to spin." She turned her head toward me and caught sight of the gift bag. "Ooh, is that for me?"

I nodded. She hoisted herself to a seated position and reached for the bag, pulling out the tissue paper and tossing it on the ground until she got to the small black velvet box. Inside was a delicate gold chain on which hung a tiny, elephant-shaped charm.

A smile spread across her face. "I love it!"

Elephants were Eden's favorite animal. She said it was because, like her, they had excellent memories, especially when it came to holding petty grudges. And also because they were considered lucky.

"I have one, too," I said, lifting my matching necklace out from under my blouse. "So now we'll never forget each other, no matter what."

"It's perfect," she said, sweeping me into a hug. "It's like those matching necklaces you got at the mall with your best friend when you were twelve."

"Exactly," I laughed. "Except ours are 18 karat gold." I raised what was left of the drink in my glass. "To us," I said. "And to luck."

Eden smiled and clinked her glass against mine. "May we never need it."

# TWO
## EDEN

### *Four months before*

"I'm heading out," I announced. Witt looked up from the couch where he was stretched out with his laptop, typing with one eye on the soccer match on TV. Whenever he poked fun at the reality shows I watched, calling them "overdramatic," I liked to point out that half of soccer was just grown men writhing on the ground.

"Where are you going?" His brow furrowed and I thought for the millionth time how unfair it was that men over forty were still considered attractive without Botox.

"Oh you know, I thought I'd hit a strip club and then score some cocaine." I blew him a kiss and twirled a lock of hair around my finger.

His face brightened. "Can I come?"

I snorted. "You wish."

"Sure you don't want to stay home?" He patted the couch next to him. I swung my hips as I walked over and leaned in to kiss him, running my fingers over the stubble on his square jaw. Even after all these years the feel of his lips against mine still caused a spark deep inside me. After a minute, though, I pushed back and stood up.

"That's it?" His pale blue eyes flew open.

"Book club waits for no one."

"Did you read the book this time?"

"Though Donna Tartt was awarded the Pulitzer Prize for her novel *The Goldfinch*, critics found it polarizing," I recited.

"So that's a no."

"Oh come on, I'm known for not reading the book. I wouldn't want to disappoint."

"Off to your fans, then. Oh, remember I leave for New York tomorrow."

"Is it on the—"

"It's on the calendar," he confirmed. An entertainment lawyer, Witt was always either packing or unpacking from a business trip.

"OK. Love you."

"Love you more."

I made my way across the street to Lorrie's house and opened the front door without bothering to knock, something I must have done hundreds of times over the last fifteen years. She and Ed had moved to our Mountaindale neighborhood only a month after Witt and me, and I could still picture seeing her at the playground for the first time. She had looked at me, sitting alone on a bench at one end of the playground, and at the group of moms gathered in a tight circle at the other end. Without hesitation she walked in my direction and parked her stroller next to mine. I'll never forget that she chose me.

"Hello, hello," I called, pausing in the hallway to glance over the family pictures displayed on a narrow glass table. My stomach tightened to see one of Summer and Knox, taken at the winter formal dance they'd attended a week earlier. Lorrie had shared it on social media, side by side with a picture of them playing in the sandbox together when they were little. The likes and comments had rained in.

Awww, meant to be!
Cutest arranged marriage ever!!
Taking childhood sweethearts to the next level!

While I'd been wishing for most of high school that Summer would spend more time with boys than she did alone in her room with her guitar, what I hadn't wished for was Knox. I had a soft spot for him, of course. After all, growing up he'd spent nearly as much time at my house as he had his own. But as Knox became tall and athletic, I'd watched his resemblance to the boys from my own high school days grow—the ones with cocky grins and cheerleader girlfriends; the ones who had no problem sneaking through my bedroom window for hand jobs and sometimes more, and then ignoring me in school the next day. I told myself Knox was different, one of the good ones— Lorrie was his mom, after all. But my stomach still tightened every time I saw my daughter with him.

"In here," Lorrie called from the living room. Caroline and some other neighborhood moms were already gathered on the couch, including our newest member, Natalie. I looked for a seat as far away from her as possible, remembering her monologue at the last meeting about the pressures of parenting young children. She was the only one of us who still worked. I gave her another year before the demands of the kids' activities and school events became unmanageable alongside her career. I, on the other hand, had quit working the minute Witt and I started trying to get pregnant. Convinced I'd get knocked up immediately, I was excited to settle in and eat whatever I wanted after years of watching the scale so I didn't get booted off the modeling jobs that (barely) paid my New York City rent.

Except it turned out getting pregnant was more of a grueling marathon and less like the breezy sprint I'd anticipated.

"What are we talking about?" I reached for one of the wine-glasses set out on the coffee table. "Please tell me it's not the book."

"I really do want to talk about the book at some point." Lorrie waved her copy at me, which had color-coded sticky notes attached to various pages.

"Of course you do." I rolled my eyes and smiled.

Lorrie laughed. "We were talking about how we can't believe we all have kids going off to college in a few months—well, except for Natalie."

I poured myself a healthy glass of Merlot. "I changed my mind; I'd rather talk about the book." Lorrie shot me a sympathetic look. She alone knew how truly bereft I felt at the thought of my only child leaving the nest.

"Tom is obsessed with getting an RV once the kids are gone," said Caroline. "So we can drive to visit them and stop at national parks along the way." She had twins in Summer's grade, Violet and Jackson. Though Violet and Summer had been best friends since their Girl Scout days, I had little stomach for Caroline, who always seemed to be clutching her pearls about something.

I wrinkled my nose. "Ugh, sorry to hear it."

Caroline looked wounded. "I think it sounds fun."

I stared at her over the top of my glass. "Caroline, you do realize you have to pump out your own shit in those things, right?"

Lorrie laughed. "Ignore her, Caroline; Eden has PTSD when it comes to camping."

"Yeah, thanks to you," I snorted.

"I feel like there's a story there." Natalie raised an eyebrow.

Lorrie and I exchanged a look. *"Tent collapse!"* we cried in unison, dissolving into laughter at the memory of me swearing and flailing around under the deflated canvas structure while Lorrie tried valiantly to locate the zipped-up entrance to get me out.

"That was the first and last time I went camping," I said, though it wasn't true. The first time had been with my mom the week we'd been evicted from our trailer for getting behind on the payments—but no one here could know about that.

"You two." Caroline looked back and forth between Lorrie and me, trying to mask her annoyance that we'd derailed the conversation.

Lorrie wiped her eyes and cleared her throat, shooting me a guilty look. "I think the RV idea is lovely, Caroline," she said. "And at least Tom's acknowledging that the kids are graduating in less than five months. Ed refuses to even talk about it. I'm totally on my own getting all the housing forms in and nagging Knox to look at the fall course catalog."

"Tell me about it." I swigged the last of my wine and Lorrie automatically picked up the bottle to pour me more. "As far as Witt's concerned he's already done his part getting Summer into Princeton by being an alumni. The rest of the boring details are up to me."

"They have no idea how much we do," groused Natalie. "But then it's like Bryan expects confetti every time he unloads the dishwasher."

"Oh, Tom is very good about doing his part," Caroline said, folding her hands into a self-satisfied tent on her lap. "He really values everything I do for our family."

Lorrie and I exchanged another look; we'd both seen Caroline running around like a squirrel on Ritalin whenever they had people over, while Tom hung out near wherever the drinks were being served. But it wasn't like I was going to argue with her, especially when I had reason to feel lucky on this issue, as Witt actually *was* good about helping out. He was the one who did all the laundry, something he'd taken on right after we'd moved in together when I'd turned an entire load of his white undershirts pink.

"It's like no one ever taught you how to do laundry," he'd joked as he showed me how to sort colors and choose the right water temperature.

I'd immediately thought of my mom and how she'd only dragged herself to the laundromat once we'd worn our clothes so many times they'd started to smell. "For your information," I replied to Witt, "no one ever did."

"Well, Caroline, you're lucky to have Tom," Lorrie said, ignoring the private eye-roll I sent her way. "I thought I might at least get help from Ed with some of the other stuff, like talking to Knox about... you know, sex and stuff. But he's leaving that to me too."

Natalie's eyes widened with confusion. "But Knox already knows about sex... right?"

Caroline smirked. "He's an eighteen-year-old boy, Natalie, he probably thinks he invented sex."

"I think it's so important to talk to our kids about this stuff," Lorrie said, "but I haven't had much luck getting the conversation started. I mean, it's college. I just want him to be smart, you know?"

"Oh I know," Natalie said, cringing. "God knows I had my fair share of vodka punch and questionable encounters."

"We all did," I said, joining in, though the only college experience I had to speak of was one semester at Poughkeepsie Community College before I got scouted by a mid-tier modeling agency at my waitressing job and immediately dropped out. Most of my questionable history pre-dated that anyway.

Lorrie glanced around and lowered her voice to a whisper. "Ed said we should buy Knox condoms for graduation."

Caroline gasped. "But isn't that, like, giving him permission to...?"

"Oh for God's sake, Caroline," Lorrie said. "Surely you're not that naive. All anyone does in college is have sex. It's better that he uses protection. And dating is so complex these days... maybe I should get the condom packs inscribed with legal agreements of consent for all parties to sign before they can be used." Everyone laughed at that and Lorrie continued, "Maybe I'll require that they get them notarized before proceeding."

"Trojan Condoms, official sponsor of the MeToo movement," Caroline quipped, setting everyone off again.

Everyone laughed but me. I'd spent far too many hours in therapy healing from my own past sexual encounters to find this funny. Lorrie noticed my expressionless face and flashed me a look of concern and apology.

"But don't you think Knox and Summer will stay together?" asked Caroline. "I mean, they're just so adorable. And then the two of you can be grandmas together!"

I waved my hand as if to banish the possibility. "College is a whole new world."

"If they're meant to be, it will work out." Lorrie tucked her light brown, chin-length hair behind her ear and smiled at me.

Later that night, after everyone had left, I assumed my usual position stretched out on one end of Lorrie's couch, a pleasant wine buzz washing over me. She lay on the other end, our legs reaching out toward each other and meeting in the middle.

"I am one hundred percent going to regret this tomorrow," she said, pointing to her wine tumbler.

"You deserve some fun," I said.

"I don't even know what fun is anymore. I've become so boring."

"No."

"Yes."

"Look," I said, struggling to a seated position. "Motherhood is one long identity crisis. Just when we figure it out, like, oh, OK, this is who I am now, everything changes. Inevitably we become boring because we get biologically reprogrammed for safety and security."

"But you're not boring." Lorrie waved her wineglass at me.

"I am now. You didn't know me before I had Summer." I took a large gulp of Merlot. "Back when I was on a first-name basis with the bouncer at every club in Lower Manhattan. At one point I had two Vanderbilts and a Kennedy in my phone. Oh, and once I flashed Anderson Cooper in a coat room. Not that he was interested."

"You didn't!"

"It was a dare." I shrugged.

Lorrie groaned. "Clearly I was never that interesting to begin with—I mean, I was a nerdy kid who grew up to be a nerdy lawyer. But I think you're right about the reprogramming. Like, the other day Chloé came home in tears because a couple of the other girls were making fun of her in dance class, telling her she had ugly knees—I mean, how ridiculous! But the next time I saw those girls it was all I could do to keep myself from punching them both in the face."

"I can see the headline now: *Mountaindale Mom Arrested in Ballet Brawl*."

Lorrie laughed. "I'm sure there's a mom out there who's done it."

"Oh absolutely," I said. "If anyone ever touched Summer, I'd destroy them."

# THREE

## JULES

### *Three months before*

The warm, mid-February sunshine did its best impression of spring as I pushed the stroller down the driveway for my Sunday morning walk. Mountaindale, the neighborhood where Paul and I lived, sprang up in the 1930s as a modest commuter suburb to Atlanta's newly booming downtown. Most of the original tidy brick homes had been knocked down to make way for newer houses like ours, large structures with clean lines and big windows. It was the kind of upscale neighborhood I couldn't even have imagined living in when I'd moved to Atlanta for college. Now, as a relative newcomer, I was still getting used to living somewhere that had a luxury car in every driveway and an organic farmer's market where people didn't blink at paying fifteen dollars for a jar of hand-ground peanut butter.

I'd already turned onto the street when I saw her, a tall, striking woman muttering to herself on the lawn next to mine. Though we'd never spoken, I knew it was Eden Van Doren. I saw her in the coffee shop up the street sometimes, sitting with the other moms fresh from school drop-off, all wearing some

variation of high-end leggings and distressed T-shirts bearing
slogans like "Peace, Love and Kale," and "Namaste Y'all." They
sipped skinny cappuccinos and flitted from table to table like
birds during an insect swarm, doling out greetings and air-kisses
—all while pointedly ignoring me.

She was frowning at the lawn, clearly displeased about
something, but then she swiveled to look at me, as if she'd just
registered I was there. I was suddenly self-conscious about my
bedhead and the sweatpants I'd fished out of the laundry
hamper. Eden, on the other hand, looked fresh from a
Lululemon photo shoot in pristine white leggings and a figure-
hugging T-shirt that read "Coffee Snob" in pink looping script.
Her hair spilled down over her shoulders and I was hypnotized
by the smoothness of her milky skin.

"Hi," I said. "We haven't met yet. I'm Jules Shulman, Paul's
wife." I let my tongue linger over the last word, still getting used
to it even though we'd been married for six months. I held up
my left hand before remembering I hadn't put my ring on yet
today.

"Oh, I know who you are," Eden said. For a split second the
hint of a not-unkind smile played around her lips, then she
rearranged her face into a blank expression. I realized she was
staring at the ropy scars that crisscrossed the back of my hand. I
shoved my hand in my pocket, wanting to avoid questions that
were none of her business.

Her gaze slid back to the lawn. "Fucking Bermuda grass,"
she said. "There was a dead patch of lawn and I was very clear
with the landscaper we wanted it replaced with Zoysia." With
an exasperated sigh she pulled her phone out of her pocket and
began to dial. "Excuse me," she said, as she pressed the phone to
her ear. Then, loudly into the speaker, "Roberto, this is Eden
Van Doren. We have a problem."

She waved her arm, either expressing her displeasure with
the lawn or dismissing me, I wasn't sure. Either way, the interac-

tion was over. And while Eden hadn't turned the other way in the grocery store or crossed the street to avoid me as some of the other Mountaindale moms did, her indifference still added to the hot ball of loneliness growing in my chest.

I don't know why I kept hoping things would be different, that I'd finally be accepted in Mountaindale. Paul's ex-wife, Abby, had been one of them, after all. Still, the sting of being an outcast never lessened.

I'd worked up a sweat by the time I wound my way through the neighborhood and back to the house. I carried Audrey inside and was greeted by the smell of fresh brewed coffee and the sound of Paul whistling as he retrieved a piece of toast from the toaster and dropped it onto a plate. We'd picked out new dishes when I moved in. Although there had been a perfectly good set in the cupboard, Paul suggested it might be better for us to start fresh with certain things—dishes, towels, a new bed— that he hadn't shared with his ex-wife. He didn't say the last part out loud, but I knew he was thinking it. Neither of us wanted to deal with the daily guilt of sleeping on the mattress he'd shared with a woman who now hated us both.

"There you are," he said, smiling and stretching his arms out to take Audrey from me. "I missed you both when I woke up!" He kissed me lightly on the lips, then nuzzled his nose against Audrey's cheek and she rewarded him with a giggle.

"She just woke up so she's probably ready for a snack," I said, making a beeline for the gurgling coffee maker.

Paul nodded. "Let's get you fed, you butterball." He wrapped one hand around Audrey's chunky thigh as he strapped her into the highchair and unveiled a plate of Cheerios and sliced banana.

I grabbed my favorite mug, black with white letters that spelled out *Curtis Institute of Music*. It was the one thing I'd kept from my time there, my daily reminder that I'd been good —really good—at something before it all fell apart. I closed my eyes as I took my first sip, my brain ricocheting to the earlier scene with Eden, hearing her voice in my head. *Oh, I know who you are.*

I was surprised at the hot tears that stung my eyes and wiped them away with my sleeve, but not before Paul noticed.

"Honey," he said, his thick eyebrows knitting together in concern. "What is it?"

"I'll never be welcome here, will I?" My voice was thick. Then the tears spilled down, my loneliness pouring out despite my best attempts to keep it bottled up.

Paul sighed and pulled me toward him, one hand on Audrey's sippy cup to keep her from hurling it to the floor. "I'm sorry," he said, wrapping his arm around my shoulders. He hung his head and for a moment I worried I'd hurt his feelings by bringing it up. The only one who felt worse than me about breaking up Paul's marriage was Paul. "What happened?" He lifted his head and pressed his cheek against mine.

"It wasn't a big deal," I said, trying to pull myself together. "I just ran into Eden, that's all."

Paul sighed. "You know," he said, pulling back so he could look at me, "even Abby didn't like her all that much." He said his ex-wife's name with practiced neutrality. "Eden... she has a strong personality."

I gave a short laugh. "So I see."

"I'm just saying, you're probably better off steering clear of her anyway."

"It would just be nice to have the choice, you know?" My voice came out sounding like a bratty teenager. I couldn't tell Paul how much I'd fantasized about what it might have been like if I hadn't moved to the neighborhood with so much baggage—a twenty-four-year-old taking up residence in the house recently vacated by one of their own, treated as if infidelity was somehow contagious. I stepped closer to Paul and buried my face in his neck.

"I'm sorry it's been so hard," he whispered into my hair.

"Do you ever regret it?" I lifted my head and pointed to my chest and then to Audrey. "This?"

"Never. Do you?"

I paused and gave him a light kiss on the lips. "Only when you try to use words like 'rizz' or 'slay' to remind me that you're not *that* old."

"Hey!" Paul grabbed me and began to tickle me. "I am not old! Just wise."

I shrieked with laughter and tried to escape. Audrey joined in with her own high-pitched yelps of delight and smeared a fistful of pulverized banana on her face. Paul's arms relaxed around me and we pressed our bodies together. Then I took a deep breath and sucked the loneliness back inside where it belonged.

On Monday, after looking out the window to make sure Eden wasn't in the yard, I slung Audrey on my hip and walked down to check the mail. I glanced down the street and saw a figure loping toward me on long legs. I'd seen her before, usually in the early morning as she left for school, her narrow shoulders hunched under the weight of her backpack as she clambered into a waiting car driven by another boy from the neighborhood. Her long, red hair trailed behind her and she had the awkward gait of someone who hadn't quite grown into her body. Still, I could tell she would grow up to be just as beautiful as her mother.

She wore heavy black boots laced up over black jeans and a baggy black sweater. It wasn't an outfit I imagined Eden approved of. As she drew within a few feet of me she began singing, her mouth open wide and her eyes half-closed with her fist in the air like she was auditioning to be the next Ariana

Grande. I laughed louder than I meant to, and her eyes flew open. She tore the headphones from her ears.

"Oh my God," she said, embarrassed. "Sorry, I was really loud, wasn't I?"

"Yeah," I said. "But the good news is you're definitely ready for *American Idol*."

She laughed, and her eyes, green like Eden's, moved down to Audrey. "What a cutie! How old is she?"

"Ten months."

"Hi, peanut," she cooed, bending toward her. Audrey clapped delightedly. "Let me know if you ever need a sitter," she said, straightening up. "You can ask anyone in the neighborhood about me. I've babysat for everyone, basically. I'm Summer, by the way."

"I know," I said. "I've met your mom."

Summer rolled her eyes. "Lucky you."

# FOUR

## EDEN

### *Three months before*

Summer sat at the kitchen island, her shoulders squared as if on a throne and her laptop open in front of her. Witt and I flanked her on either side like loyal courtesans. Her finger hovered over the link in an email bearing the Princeton logo.

"I think I'm going to pass out," I said, drawing in a shallow breath and leaning forward to clutch the countertop.

"Honey..." Witt shot me his best *it's not about you* look and reached out to grip my free hand. But I really did feel woozy as I watched my only child prepare to meet her future.

"OK." Summer pursed her lips and inhaled sharply. "Here goes." She clicked the link, which opened a Princeton-branded login screen and then a second screen filled with words. I leaned in closer to read over her shoulder but the letters blurred together. Either I was fainting for real or it was time to finally admit I needed reading glasses.

"We are pleased to inform you that—" Witt began reading aloud, but was interrupted by a shriek from Summer.

"I got in! I got in!" She hurtled sideways off her chair into the arms of her father, who took up her chant.

"You got in, you got in!" They jumped up and down with their arms around each other and shrieked like tweens at a Taylor Swift concert. So many feelings collided inside me that I couldn't decide whether to laugh or sob.

"I'm so proud of you," I managed to choke out, somewhere between crying and laughing. I pulled Summer into a hug, and then the crying kicked in for real and I heaved great sobs, my nose running uncontrollably as I tried to wipe the tears and snot from my face.

"Mom!" said Summer, looking in disgust at my snotty face. "I am *so* glad we didn't make a reaction video," she added, referring to the trend of high schoolers filming themselves learning their college admission status.

"Hey," I defended myself, blowing my nose on the tissue Witt handed me. "It's not every day you learn your brilliant daughter got into Princeton—early decision no less."

"I mean, we kinda knew I would, right?" Summer looked between Witt and me. "Because of Dad?"

Witt reached out and ruffled her hair. "That helped, for sure, kiddo. But they're not just going to accept any slouch whose dad went there. All your hard work in school was definitely the deciding factor."

Bittersweet tears filled my eyes again and I sent up a silent—impossible—wish that nothing would ever change and the three of us could just live in this moment forever.

I'd harbored a secret hope Summer would choose somewhere closer to home. Princeton was a universe away—which was the point, of course. Princeton was part of her *trajectory*, a word Witt made fun of me for using.

"She's not a rocket ship," he liked to tease.

He didn't understand the power of momentum because he'd never needed it—though he was easily wounded by the suggestion that privilege had played any role in his success, and quick to credit his hard work and intellect. I had no problem indulging his fantasy. While it was true that he was both smart and industrious, in the end I didn't care how he'd gotten everything we had. I cared that we had it.

Whereas I'd spent my childhood in thrift store clothing, the smell of which never completely washed off, Summer's closet featured only the latest brands. I edited her weekend sleepover invitation list to ensure they were girls from good families, most of whom lived in our same quiet, tree-lined neighborhood. I let them try on my makeup and stay up as late as they wanted, and turned a blind eye when my expensive lipstick or nail polish went home the next morning in the monogrammed backpack of Madison or Annabelle or one of the Charlottes. From tennis lessons to girlfriends, Summer had grown up with the best of everything. Including, now, a ticket to the Ivy League and a future I wouldn't be part of on a daily basis. My heart clenched at the thought.

"Where's my phone?" Summer scrambled to her feet. "I promised Violet I'd text her as soon as I found out."

"It's next to the coffee maker," I said. "What about dinner at Lombardo's to celebrate?" Witt nodded with enthusiasm. Lombardo's was our neighborhood Italian spot which both he and Summer loved for its homey red-and-white checked tablecloths and tradition of putting a candle in a giant meatball on your birthday.

Having retrieved her phone, Summer clutched it to her chest and blushed. "I kind of told Knox I'd celebrate with him tonight," she said.

I pushed myself up to stand next to her and crossed my arms. "But it's a school night."

Witt got up and put his arms around me from behind and I leaned against his broad shoulders. "Relax, honey. This is a big deal; I think we can cut her some slack for one night." He winked at Summer, who rewarded him with a wide, goofy smile.

"Fine," I sighed, though I didn't like being usurped by a boyfriend. "But be home by nine."

"Nine thirty," Witt said, and I swatted his arm.

As Summer bounded upstairs to get ready, he nuzzled his face into my neck. "But that doesn't mean we still can't celebrate," he said. I relaxed back against him. "I just need to send one work email. Meet you upstairs in five?"

"OK," I nodded, my body already responding to his touch. As he walked toward his office I grabbed my phone and texted:

> She got in.

Lorrie replied immediately with confetti and champagne bottle emojis.

> AHHHHHHHHH! Congratulations! How are you feeling?

> Ecstatic? Terrified?

> Ha, sounds about right. I mean, weren't we just potty training them yesterday?

> Exactly. What am I going to do with myself once she's gone?

> Hang out with me more!

I laughed. Between driving Chloé around to her million activities, running the Westwood Parents Association, and now her new volunteer position on the board of a non-profit, Lorrie was the busiest person I knew.

Seriously though, it's a whole new chapter for both you and Summer. It's going to be amazing, I promise.

Love you

Love you more.

I clicked my phone off and went upstairs to check on Summer and wait for Witt. I hoped Lorrie was right.

# FIVE

## JULES

### *Three months before*

Summer rang the doorbell promptly at six o'clock. She had a ring of angry black eyeliner around her eyes and wore a black T-shirt and cutoff jean shorts over a pair of ripped black tights. I felt an immediate kinship with her; it was exactly the kind of outfit I had dreamed about being able to wear to high school. Instead I'd spent every school day in a navy blue skirt and white collared shirt for class at the Victory Baptist Academy, where my belief in the Almighty Creator was valued far more than my musical talent.

"Hi!" Summer said, her bubbly voice standing in stark contrast to her outfit. Audrey smiled and reached her arms out to Summer.

"Oh good," I said, relieved. "She's been having some separation anxiety and she just got comfortable with our other sitter, so..." I shrugged.

For the past three Tuesday nights I'd left Audrey with Sonya, a grandmotherly woman who'd babysat years ago for Paul's now teenage son. Unfortunately Sonya had badly sprained her ankle, leaving me without childcare for my night class, since Paul had a class of his own to teach that night. I'd considered missing it, but it was my first return to college since pressing pause on my education when I got pregnant, and it had taken a considerable number of self-pep talks for me to register in the first place.

"It's cool, babies love me." Summer scooped Audrey into her arms and blew a raspberry on her cheek. Audrey shrieked with laughter.

I gave Summer a quick rundown of the bedtime routine and started on a tour of the house.

"Oh, I've been here before," she said. "My mom used to make me have playdates with Ari." She laughed. "I'd get so mad because he never let me play with any of his action figures; he just kept them in boxes up on the shelf."

"That sounds like Ari," I said dryly. Paul's son Ari was a senior in high school like Summer and had a genius IQ—his mother had had him tested and made sure to work that into every conversation. He stayed with us every other week, and he did his best not to talk to me or make eye contact. I hated those weeks, when I felt like I was walking on eggshells in my own home. Which, in fairness, had been Ari's home first. Paul liked to remind me how hard the divorce had been on Ari and that I should cut him some slack. I got it, but I also wondered when everyone was going to start cutting me some. "Anyway," I said. "Let me at least show you the nursery."

Summer followed me upstairs, and as we passed Ari's room his door opened and he nearly ran into us.

"Whoa, sorry," I said, jumping back. I tried to give him a wide berth when we were both home, mostly because we had very little to say to each other.

"Oh, hey Summer," he said, looking past me and straightening up out of his usual slumped posture.

"Hey Ari." She waved.

"What are you doing here?" He frowned at me like I might have lured Summer to the house for some kind of witchcraft.

"Babysitting."

"Oh, right." Ari's eyes focused on Audrey in my arms, who smiled and blew a spit bubble for him. I thought I caught a glimmer of a smile, then he turned back to Summer. "Um, I should get going."

"Have fun at Mathletes," I chirped, my voice too high and bright.

"It's Robotics Club tonight," he replied, his eyes still on Summer. "Bye, Summer."

She gave another wave as he headed downstairs.

"Whoa, are those, like, drones?" she whispered and pointed to the shelf in Ari's room where menacing-looking winged electronic devices of various sizes were lined up like a fleet of evil insects. Ari treated them with great care, dusting them and taking them out regularly for "exercise" as he trained for his drone pilot license. They gave me the creeps, and even though they were powered off I still felt like they were watching me when I walked by.

"Yep," I said.

"Why does he have so many?"

"You know, he explained all the differences between them to me once but I don't have a PhD in mechanical engineering so..." I made a motion like a plane soaring over my head. Summer giggled.

When I finished showing her around upstairs, we headed back down to the kitchen and I gathered up my backpack. "I'll be in class at the Georgia Tech campus but just text if you have any questions. I'll keep my phone on vibrate."

"Like a college class?" Summer cocked her head. "I thought you were, like, older."

"I'm finishing my degree." A flush crept up my neck at having to state my open secret out loud.

"Oh, right," She slapped her forehead. "My mom told me about what happened with you and Dr. Shulman. So like, what kind of class?"

"I'm majoring in business," I said. For lack of a better idea I'd picked a major as far from music as I could get. "But I'm still trying to figure out what I want to do for like, a job."

"I wish my mom would get a job." Summer heaved a sigh. "Outside of telling me how to live my life."

"She seems very passionate about your lawn." I tried to hide my smile.


When I got home after class Audrey was asleep and Summer was engrossed in the season finale of a hospital drama I'd already watched. She hit pause when I came in.

"How did bedtime go?" I bent down to peer at the baby monitor on the couch next to her.

"She was an angel." She smiled and moved to turn off the TV.

"Stay and finish the episode if you want," I said. "The ending is crazy." She nodded and turned back to the TV. "I deserve ice cream after sitting through the world's most boring class," I said, heading for the kitchen. "Want any?"

Summer's eyes lit up. "Sure!"

I sat on the couch with her, and by the end of the episode we were both teary-eyed, even though I'd seen it before.

"I can't believe she just walks out on him like that!" Summer sniffled. "After everything they went through."

"I can't believe I cried *again*," I said, scraping the last bite of ice cream out of my bowl.

"Can I ask you a question?" Summer said, looking at me curiously.

"Sure."

"What happened to your hand?"

Reflexively I covered my damaged hand with my other one. I knew how ugly the scar tissue was. "An accident," I said, reciting the line I'd trained myself to say. Nine out of ten times it shut down the conversation.

"What kind of accident?" she asked.

I closed my eyes and was transported back to the Philadelphia street outside the Curtis Institute where I'd been getting out of a friend's battered Honda Civic. I never saw the car door before it crushed my hand, slammed accidentally by a near-sighted bassist. The following months passed in a haze of surgeries after I'd reluctantly retraced my path back to my childhood bedroom in north Georgia. The doctors tried to be kind but it didn't take much reading between the lines at my appointments to know my music career was over.

"Oh my God, that sucks," Summer said when I finished the story, looking stricken. "I can't imagine not being able to play guitar anymore."

"Well, I can still play, I just won't be at Carnegie Hall anytime soon. So, what kind of stuff do you play?" I groped for a change of subject, fighting back the tears that still came when I thought too long about what I'd given up.

"Covers, mostly. Like Olivia Rodrigo and Billie Eilish. But I also like old stuff, like Blondie and Joni Mitchell. She looked up at me shyly. "I wanted to go to music school but my parents told me I had to get a degree I could get a job with first."

"Let me be your cautionary tale." I'd meant to sound jokey but it came out much darker.

"My mom said you were Paul's student." Summer hesitated. "And that it's a total cliché for a professor to sleep with his student."

"Did she?" I raised my eyebrows, caught off guard by her directness.

"But I think it's totally romantic how you met," she added.

I suppressed an eye-roll. Romantic was the last word I

would have used to describe the messy university investigation Paul went through after we took our relationship public, or his even messier divorce. He'd been my assigned advisor when I transferred to Tech after three years of music school. I shivered, remembering the bolt of lightning that had gone through both of us at that first meeting in his office. I'd registered for his class the next day; unaware I was about to destroy a marriage.

"Do you have a boyfriend?" I asked Summer, changing the subject again. Her cheeks went pink and her lips stretched into a wide smile. "I'm going to take that as a yes," I laughed.

"We've been hanging out together for like, two months," she said.

"Wow. That's like, an eternity in high school, right?"

She laughed. "Kinda."

"So?"

"So what?"

"So tell me about him!" I poked her playfully.

Her smile stretched even bigger. "He's, like a big baseball star. And super popular. Unlike me." Her smile faltered.

"What do you mean?"

"I'm, like, a music nerd, so we have totally different friend groups."

"Oh, high school," I sighed. "You couldn't pay me enough to do that again."

"I don't know." Summer's eyes were dreamy and unfocused. "Everything feels pretty perfect right now."

# SIX

## LORRIE

### *That Night: Sunday, 3 a.m.*

Knox was late for his curfew for the third time this week. It had been thirty minutes the first time, then forty-five the next. Both times Ed refused to let me get out of bed when I heard my son's footsteps on the stairs.

"Let it go, Lor," he'd said. "It's his last week of high school for Christ's sake. He deserves to have some fun."

Both times I bit my tongue in the morning as I watched Knox groggily pour milk over his cereal, leaving the carton on the counter for someone else to put away. His bed-tousled dark blond hair fell in a perfect wave to his chin in a way that mine never would despite my best attempts with the blow-dryer. His eyes were the same light blue they'd been on the day he was born. All three kids had the same eyes originally, but Knox's were the only ones that hadn't darkened to some shade of brown. As I watched his man-sized hand gripping the spoon I felt uncharacteristically nostalgic. It seemed like only last week he was padding into our bedroom in the middle of the night, teddy bear in tow. Now in one short week he would be graduating from high school.

Tonight, though, he was undeniably late. As the clock hit three a.m., I lay awake on the living room couch where Ed had suggested I relocate unless I was going to stop tossing and turning with worry. The front door creaked and I sprang up, smoothing my hair.

"Hi," I croaked as Knox appeared in the hallway.

"Jeez, mom." He jolted backward. "You scared the shit out of me."

"Language," I said automatically.

"Sorry."

"Late night?" I tried to keep the scolding tone out of my voice. All the parenting books I'd read told me that was the quickest way to shut down communication with your teen. He zipped up his hoodie as I approached, but not before I saw the scratch on his collarbone. "Ouch, what happened?"

He shrugged. "Someone's stupid cat."

"Did you wash it out? Here, let me see." I took a step toward him.

"Don't," he said sharply. I rocked back on my heels, startled. "Sorry," he said, shaking his head. "I just meant—I can take care of myself. I'll put some Neosporin on it."

I nodded and cleared my throat. "So, it's pretty late."

"I know, I'm sorry," Knox said quickly. "I, uh, fell asleep at Jackson's house."

I frowned. "I didn't know the Doyles had a cat. I thought Caroline was allergic."

"They don't. We were... somewhere else before."

"Oh," I nodded, resisting the urge to probe further. As much as I struggled with the concept, Knox was almost an adult and it was time to start letting go a little. "Try to keep a better eye on the clock next time, OK?" I said instead. "You still have a curfew for now."

"I will." Knox gave a small nod and turned to head upstairs.

As I climbed back into bed I heard the shower turn on in the bathroom Knox and Archie shared, something he didn't usually bother with at night. I hoped my comment about his curfew would do the trick. I was the stricter parent, concerned about broccoli and bedtimes. My worst fights with Ed happened when I tried to correct his lackadaisical parenting. They would start in tense whispers and end with him banging his fist on the table, yelling, "Goddamn it, Lorrie, stop micromanaging me!"

I used to yell back, but over time I'd perfected my mask of acquiescence. This allowed me to go about quietly parenting the way the books said I should. The fighting also got us to the sex faster.

There was something about fighting that wound up Ed in a way that only one thing would release. It took me by surprise at first, how quickly he could go from anger to lust. Where our usual lovemaking was sweetly predictable—lights off, him on top followed by ten minutes of cuddling—our sex after a fight was hungry and impulsive. He would take me against the wall with my dress yanked up or bent over the dresser with my hands held behind my back. There were smacks on the butt and language so foul it made my face burn even while I begged for more. After, we lay entangled wherever we finished, a rare moment of inhabiting the same spatial and emotional plane. I'd tell myself that the next time he put down his iPad and turned to me in the bed on a normal night I'd talk dirty or ask him to do those same things to me that happened when things got heated. Always, though, my prudish Midwestern upbringing would get the better of me. I'd submit to the process while we checked all the boxes in the same order we always did, leaving each other efficiently satisfied and not one touch more.

I heard Knox's shower turn off, then after a few more minutes I heard the sound of his feet in the hallway, then his bedroom door opening and closing again. Easing out of bed I padded into the dark hallway and performed my nightly ritual of placing my hand on the doorknob of each child's room, reassuring myself that all three were home and safe.

Some days I was jealous that Eden had only one child. I loved my children, but if someone had told me when I met Ed that one day I'd be coordinating car pool instead of cross-examining witnesses, I'd have laughed. Back then I pictured myself effortlessly juggling motherhood and career like a Cirque du Soleil performer in heels and a pantsuit. But I hadn't anticipated the disapproving stares of the partners I worked for as I left the office "early" at seven p.m. to relieve the nanny, nor how little I would care about drafting courtroom briefs once there was a small person with my eyes and Ed's smile who depended on me.

Now, though, my identity was wrapped up in being president of the Parent Boosters and the mother of Knox, Archie, and Chloé. And sure, I'd recently been asked to join the board of Free Motherhood, an organization that supported women who gave birth while in prison, but they'd wanted me for my connections to wealthy potential donors, not my law degree. As I stood in the quiet, dark house I felt the familiar tug of war between gratitude for the life I'd built, and longing for the one I never got to have.

I glanced at Knox's door and wondered where he'd been that night, and with whom. I turned in the direction of Eden's house, as though I could see it through the walls. I wondered if Summer had also just gotten home.

I remembered how Eden and Summer used to sleep over if both our husbands happened to be traveling for work at the same time.

"This must be what living in a commune is like," she'd joked after we worked together to feed, bathe, and read bedtime stories to all the kids.

"Sign me up," I said. "It's nice to have some help, for once."
Back then Knox was scared of the dark so Summer slept in a
sleeping bag on the floor next to his bed. In the morning we'd
always find him on the floor next to her, both of their heads
squeezed together on one pillow.

I shook myself out of the memory. How strange it was that
Knox and Summer were nearly adults now—and that they'd
been dating for over five months. As much as I didn't want to
think about it, the realist in me knew they were probably having
sex by now.

Now that he was older I wanted Knox to be able to talk to
me about relationships, but I'd exhausted all my parenting
strategies with no luck. I'd sent him articles and bought him
books. I'd tried talking to him while in the car, and while
watching TV. They were all met by the same mortified silence
and one-syllable answers.

I told myself I'd done what I could, but as I padded back
down the hallway to my bedroom, I couldn't shake the nagging
feeling that I'd somehow failed to raise the kind of boy I
intended to.

# SEVEN

## EDEN

### Sunday, 9 a.m.

The spinning studio had a strict no electronic devices policy, which I almost always ignored.

"This is your time to leave the outside world behind," the instructor intoned before every class, as if the outside world didn't assault my mind with every pedal stroke. *Are Witt and I having enough sex?* Stroke. *I think I'm out of Ambien.* Stroke. *I wonder if the caterer could still add the sushi bar for Summer's graduation party.* Stroke. *Have I always had that weird mole?* Stroke. Halfway through class I wiped the sweat out of my eyes and snuck a glance at my phone. There was a kissy emoji text from Witt before he'd boarded his plane earlier and a message from Lorrie confirming she'd stop by with a bottle of wine to keep me company later. There were also three missed calls and a text from an unknown number. I clicked to open the text.

> At University Hospital ER with Summer. This is Jules.

My hands shook as I tried to reply, my fingers fumbling over the tiny keyboard.

> What's wrong is she OK what happened?

I held my breath and waited for the three gray dots to appear but nothing happened.

I blew through two red lights on the way to the hospital, muscling cars out of the way with my Escalade. I'd needed the third row of seats to drive car pool when Summer was younger and now I felt vulnerable in anything smaller, as if the need to ram through a police barricade or bump some entitled prick's Tesla out of the way could arise at any moment. I gripped the steering wheel with one hand and my phone with the other, waiting for Jules to respond.

I pictured Summer bleeding and motionless on a hospital bed, surrounded by a team of doctors and nurses frantically pumping on her chest and yelling orders at each other. When had she come home last night? Why hadn't I waited up instead of falling asleep to bad TV? My heart felt like it would explode from beating so fast.

At the hospital I left the car in a tow zone with the hazards flashing and rushed through the wide bank of glass doors that led to the emergency department, my feet skidding across the slippery floor as I realized I was still wearing my spinning shoes. Yanking them off, I ran up to the desk in my sweaty socks.

"My daughter, I need to know where she is."

"Your daughter's name?" asked the expressionless woman behind the desk.

"Summer Van Doren."

"ID?" I pulled my driver's license from my wallet, spilling the contents in the process. She plucked the piece of plastic from my fingers with one hand and punched at her keyboard with the other. Squinting at the screen, she looked back up at me. "OK, she's expecting you. Exam room 3, through those double doors, make a left." I swept my credit cards and cash off the counter into my purse and sprinted for the doors.

The floor seemed to drop out from beneath me as I saw Summer sitting on a metal exam table in the small, chilly room, a paper gown hanging loosely off her narrow shoulders. She looked small and frail with her long legs dangling above the floor and her elbow wrapped in gauze.

Jules had pulled a chair up next to the table, exactly as I would have. She was squeezing my daughter's hand with one hand and cradling her baby with the other. With her dark hair pulled back into a ponytail and her face bare of makeup, Jules looked more like an organic shampoo ad than the husband-stealing siren the other neighborhood moms made her out to be.

"Mom!" Summer's voice was hoarse. Her pale face had purple smudges under her heavily lashed eyes. The effect made her look as if she hadn't slept in years, which I knew wasn't true because I'd been personally prying her out of bed every morning for her last month of high school. Her long, coppery curls were tangled and matted down on one side like when she was a little girl and refused to let me comb out the snarls. That struggle seemed like just yesterday. How was it possible that her high school graduation was only a week away?

"Sweetheart!" I staggered across the room, stepping between my daughter and Jules and wrapping my baby in my arms. She smelled like alcohol, stale vomit, and the expensive shampoo she regularly swiped from my bathroom. With Summer pressed against me, the thudding of my heart inched upward until it felt like it was in my throat. My relief at seeing her in one piece mixed with anger at myself for ever letting her out of my sight. I no longer cared about college; I'd sooner keep her tethered to me for the rest of our lives.

Summer buried her face in my shoulder. "I'm sorry, Mom,"

she whispered, her voice catching. I felt the wetness of her tears mingling with my sweat.

"Shh, it's OK." I rubbed her back, refusing to allow any space between us "I'm here now." Summer's shoulders heaved as she kept her face pressed against me. I shot a pointed, questioning look toward Jules, who was jiggling and shushing the baby. "What happened?"

"I found her passed out in your bathroom this morning," Jules said in a low tone.

"In my house?" I asked, louder than I'd intended to. My head was buzzing with confusion.

"She was checking on me," Summer said, her shoulders caving in on themselves. "I was supposed to babysit this morning." Her voice was small and sounded younger than her usual exasperated teenage tone.

"I tried texting and calling when she didn't show up." Jules ran her hands through her dark hair. "I was late for something important." She said it as if it was an apology. "When I didn't get a response I went over and knocked on your door."

Unlike most of the other neighborhood moms, I didn't technically have a problem with Jules. As far as I was concerned she seemed like an upgrade from Paul's smug, perpetually stressed-out first wife who never failed to bring up that she'd gone to *Harvard* and been on the *partner track* at her accounting firm before she decided to stay home with their son. I felt compelled to snub Jules on principle, though, out of some twisted sense of loyalty to women my own age.

"Who let you into the house?" I tightened the grip on Summer's shoulders.

"Witt."

"Witt?" I repeated my husband's name like he was a distant cousin I'd forgotten about.

"I talked to him through your video doorbell. I think maybe he was at the airport? He told me where the spare key was."

I turned my gaze back to Summer, whose eyes were rimmed with red. "Baby, please talk to me," I pleaded. "What happened to your elbow? You can tell me anything. You're not in trouble, I promise."

Summer drew in a deep, hiccupy breath. "I was at—a party. With Knox, and some other people." She closed her mouth and pressed her lips tight together as she was afraid of what might escape.

"She was foggy when I got there, but she said some things..." Jules shook her head, unable to form the rest of the words.

Summer's face crumpled in on itself as she rocked forward against my chest. "Mommy," she whispered.

The wave of relief I felt seeing my daughter intact was replaced by a hard nut of dread forming in my stomach. Nothing bad could happen to Summer, not now, when her future was within grasp. Graduation was a week away and she'd already started sleeping in a T-shirt with Princeton's black and orange shield on the front. Her future stretched out in front of her like a glittering, endless runway.

"Shh," I whispered as I stroked my daughter's hair. "It's going to be OK."

The baby was crying now and clutching at Jules's shirt. "I'm sorry," said Jules, "She needs to eat." I caught a flash of her already-flat postpartum stomach as she lifted her shirt and resisted the urge to suck in my own.

There was a staccato knock at the door, symbolic in nature only as it opened immediately. Summer disentangled herself from my embrace as a man with a stethoscope looped around his neck strode in. He was a decade younger than me with spiky, gelled hair and a disturbingly bronzed face. His extreme level of fitness was obvious under his closely tailored clothes and white coat. I wrinkled my nose as I caught a whiff of his cloud of cologne.

"I'm Dr. Tucker," he said. "You are"—he consulted his clipboard—"the patient's mother?" I nodded. He gestured to an older woman hovering in the doorway behind him. "And this is..."

"Maureen Adams, trained sexual assault nurse examiner." The woman's frizzy gray hair formed an unflattering halo around her face.

I stared at the nurse. "I'm sorry, why are you here?"

The doctor cleared his throat. "Ms. Adams is trained to perform the forensic exam to gather any... evidence."

My stomach lurched. "What kind of evidence?" I whirled my head toward Jules. "What's going on here? What happened?"

Jules looked stricken. "I—"

The nurse stepped forward as if she was about to touch my arm, then thought better of it. "I know this is hard, but I'll talk your daughter through the whole process. We'll start with some pictures, to document any bruises or lesions. Then we'll sweep her body for any foreign DNA, including an internal exam."

"Can you give us a minute?" My voice came out strangled. "Alone?" The nurse nodded and filed out, the doctor following her. Jules hesitated as she lifted the baby to her shoulder, looking at Summer.

"I'm here if you need anything," she said, getting up and heading for the door, which she pulled shut behind her.

I turned to my daughter, my heart pounding. "Summer—" Her eyes were filled with tears. "What—who—"

She hung her head and her voice came out in a whisper. "Knox."

My vision narrowed into a tunnel, blackness closing in. I grabbed the exam table to steady myself. "Knox?" I croaked. "He...?" I couldn't say the word.

Summer nodded.

Adrenaline surged in me and my survival instincts roared to life. I gathered Summer into a tight hug, squeezing her fiercely.

When I felt her breathing slow I pulled back to look at her. "Let's get you home," I said.

She looked at me, wide-eyed. "But what about the exam?"

"You don't want it. Trust me."

"I don't?"

"I promise I will take care of this. I won't let anything else bad happen to you."

"But the nurse—"

"The nurse is doing her job. And I'm doing mine. You know that I always do what's best for you, right?"

"Yes." Her voice faltered.

"Then, baby, it's time to go home."

# EIGHT

## LORRIE

### *Sunday, 10 a.m.*

I frowned at my phone. It had already been a couple of hours since I'd texted Eden. Usually she replied within seconds. She was my on-call dressing room consultant, my late-night husbands-just-don't-get-it venting partner, and my first stop with any good news that came my way. I'd told her I was pregnant with Chloé before I even told Ed.

We'd promised to be each other's "one call" should we ever find ourselves in a holding cell—which we agreed was a much more likely scenario for Eden than me.

"What would you get arrested for?" she'd snorted. "Breaking into someone's house and organizing their sock drawer? Overusing Robert's Rules of Order at a Parent Boosters meeting?" I'd thrown a decorative pillow at her to defend myself, but we both knew she was right.

I rechecked my phone and shook my head. Eden had probably lost her phone again. My beautiful, perpetually disorganized friend.

*What time is good tonight?* read my text, followed by two

wineglass emojis even though Chloé had explained to me that emojis weren't cool anymore. At age twelve she was brimming with confidence. I wished I could bottle it up for her and dole it out over the next few years when she would need it most.

With Ed and Knox off at Knox's baseball game and Chloé at a sleepover, the house felt quiet. Yawning, I poured myself another cup of coffee. I was groggy from waiting up for Knox the night before. Even though I'd had the chance to sleep in, the anxiety-inducing length of my to-do list had my eyes open long before I wanted them to be. Today's priorities: get the last invitations out for Knox's graduation party, finalize the catering order, label all of Chloé's dance camp gear with her name, and take Archie shopping for something other than a black T-shirt to wear to his brother's graduation.

"Archie!" I called up the stairs for the third time. "Last call for breakfast, honey." I wanted to get to the mall before it got crowded with Sunday shoppers.

After a few minutes he shuffled into the kitchen wearing pajama bottoms with one of the hems ripped and trailing on the ground, and a wrinkled black T-shirt with Einstein's face on it. Rubbing the crusts of sleep from his eyes, he pulled out one of the kitchen bar stools and sat down.

"Pancakes?" I asked.

He shook his head. "Just cereal. I can get it."

"I don't mind," I said, pleased he'd even offered. I poured him a bowl, along with a glass of orange juice, and leaned against the opposite side of the kitchen island. "I'd like to leave for the mall by noon."

"The mall?" he slurped a bite of cereal, a trickle of milk escaping from the corner of his mouth. Teenage boys were hard to love, sometimes.

"We're getting you something nice to wear to Knox's graduation, remember?"

His shoulders slumped. "I really have to go to that?"

"Archie! It's your brother's graduation, of course you have to go." I clucked my tongue.

"It'll be so long," he groaned. "And boring."

"Knox would be crushed if you weren't there." I reached for my most frequent weapon: guilt.

Archie made a scoffing sound in the back of his throat. "Yeah, right."

I crossed my arms. "What's that supposed to mean?"

He shrugged. "Nothing," he mumbled, slurping more cereal.

I uncrossed my arms and softened my voice. "The two of you don't really... hang out anymore, do you?" I tried to remember the last time I'd seen both my sons in the same room other than for our required family dinners. Archie shrugged and kept his eyes on his bowl. "Oh, I almost forgot," I said, going to the pantry to retrieve his pill bottle from inside the canister of dried beans where we'd agreed to keep it. "Here." I handed him a small green pill.

He swallowed it with a swig of orange juice, then looked up at me. "Do you think I'll always have to take those?" he asked.

"Well," I said slowly. "You seem like you're feeling better these past couple of months, so I think it's helping. That and seeing Dr. Frank."

It was true. For the first few months of high school Archie had spent most of his time alone in his room or in the basement with his video games. It became nearly impossible to pry him out of bed in the mornings, though the dark circles under his eyes made it clear he wasn't sleeping. And while he'd never been an A student like Knox, when I found out he was failing both English and Algebra I knew something was deeply wrong.

Eden's therapist had recommended Dr. Frank, who worked specifically with teenagers. As far as I was concerned, he was a miracle worker. Archie seemed to be coming back to life, like an inflatable decoration slowly filling with air. His eyes were brighter and his face less drawn. He'd even made a friend at school who came over sometimes to play video games with him.

"Are you seeing Tadpole this weekend?" I tried to keep a straight face as I said the girl's nickname. I'd asked Archie repeatedly what her real name was but he claimed not to know. Her older brother was on the baseball team with Knox, and neither sibling was gifted with height.

He shook his head. "Naw, her family went to the lake." He took another bite of cereal and was quiet for a minute. "So, will I, like, need those pills forever?" he asked again.

"I don't know, honey," I said, careful to keep my face neutral. "Some people's brains are just wired differently. Yours might be. But it also might just be current circumstances."

"What do you mean?"

"That high school sucks."

His eyes widened and then he laughed. I was pleased I'd been able to shock him with as close to a curse word as I'd ever uttered in front of him.

His eyes flickered over to a large, circular refrigerator magnet made from a photo of Knox in his baseball uniform. "Not for everyone."

"Your brother has his challenges, too," I said, though I couldn't name any off the top of my head. Everything seemed to come easily to my outgoing oldest child.

Archie slurped up the last bite of his cereal and gazed down at the counter. "Dr. Frank said it's weird Dad doesn't know I see him," he murmured.

I tensed. "Well, your father has strong feelings about... what Dr. Frank does."

"I know, I know," said Archie. "Dad doesn't think they're real doctors like he is."

I hesitated. Over the years Ed had worked his way up to being the top physician for the Atlanta Braves baseball team. It was a huge accomplishment, but sometimes I worried about all the time he spent in such a testosterone-fueled environment. "We can tell Dad if you want to," I said. I held back a grimace, picturing Ed's reaction and the argument that would follow.

Archie considered this, then shook his head. "Not right now, anyway."

I nodded, relieved. "Your dad loves you very much, kiddo." My phone buzzed with an incoming call. I looked down to see if it was Eden but saw the caterer's name displayed on my screen. "I need to take this," I said. "We're leaving at noon, OK?"

With the phone to my ear, I stepped outside to grab the prior day's mail. "Let's do 200 sliders instead of 150," I said, walking to the end of the driveway. "And more steak kebabs than chicken."

The caterer read through the rest of the order. I nodded along, catching sight of Eden's Escalade pulling into her driveway. Summer got out first and vanished into the house. "Mm-hmm," I said, trying to wrap up the call. "Yes, perfect. Thanks. Bye." Eden walked around the car toward the door, carrying her gym bag. "Eden!" I called, waving. "Hey, Eden!"

She looked up and raised her arm as if to wave, then jerked it back down to her side. Her eyes met mine for a split second and goosebumps rose on my arms despite the warm day. Then, without a word, Eden turned and walked inside.

# NINE

## EDEN

### *Sunday, 10:30 a.m.*

Summer was silent as we drove home from the hospital, her face turned away, forehead leaning on the passenger side window.

"It's going to be OK," I said. The words seemed ridiculously small as they came out of my mouth, like an army of toy soldiers facing down a real-life battlefield.

"Whatever." Summer's voice sounded small and far away.

I concentrated on the road in front of me, on my speed gauge, on making full stops at all the intersections. Anything to keep my brain from returning to the scene at the hospital. Anything to keep from thinking about the questions I needed to ask my daughter. I knew firsthand once she said it out loud there was no way to take it back. Nothing would ever be the same.

I signaled and turned onto our street, slowing as we passed a lemonade stand run by two young girls, their mother part of the new guard that would soon replace me on the Parent Boosters when Summer went off to college.

"So," I said, taking a deep breath. "Knox." I flicked my eyes toward her. She gave the smallest of nods.

I gripped the steering wheel and tried to keep my voice level. "When?"

"Last night."

"Where?"

"The park."

"The *park*? You told me you were going over to the Doyles."

"We left." Her voice was flat.

"And you went to the park? After dark? Do you have any idea how dangerous that is?" The words spilled out of my mouth before I realized the irony of them. Shaking my head, I tried to backtrack. "So you went to the park. With Knox."

"Yes." Her tone rose in annoyance. She continued to stare out the window.

"And you... he..."

"We had sex."

I flinched and exhaled sharply. "Did you want to?" She gave the tiniest shake of her head. "But he... did it anyway," I confirmed. She nodded.

As I pulled into our driveway I weighed my words carefully. "Did you say no?" There was a long pause.

"I think so." Her voice was muffled against the window and I strained to make out each word, afraid I would miss the critical one that would tell me what I should do.

"What do you mean you think so?"

"We had a fight."

"Summer—"

"I don't want to talk about this anymore." She sat up and turned toward me. Her eyes were swollen and her face was blank.

"Summer, did you say no?"

"I said I don't want to talk about it." She wrenched open the car door and slammed it behind her. I let her go.

I sank forward and rested my head on the steering wheel for a moment. My heart hammered like the techno music from spin class. Steeling myself, I pushed the car door open. A familiar voice called my name as my feet hit the driveway.

Turning, I saw Lorrie waving to me from across the street. My arm rose instinctively to wave back, then I froze and dropped it back to my side. Until that moment I'd been thinking solely about Knox and how much I wanted to snap his neck with my bare hands. I hadn't considered what this meant for my friendship with Lorrie... for our intricately intertwined lives.

Judging by the smile on Lorrie's face she hadn't heard the news. I lowered my gaze and hurried into the house.

Inside I was greeted by a small pile of dog poop on the kitchen floor. "Damn it, Bailey," I cursed. Our ten-year-old miniature Dachshund was paralyzed from the waist down after an unfortunate jump off the couch. It happened only a year after we got her, so I'd spent the better part of the last decade changing her diapers, which she wriggled out of with Houdini-like regularity.

I cleaned up the floor and grabbed last night's bottle of Chardonnay out of the refrigerator, my body still buzzing with panicked adrenaline. There was one glass left, if filling a tumbler to the rim and then slugging the remaining swallows counted as one. I walked into the living room, feeling the relief of the cold wine hitting my stomach.

My shoulders were bunched up around my ears from tension and my head felt in danger of exploding from the sheer volume of thoughts spinning around in it. My eyes landed on the row of silver-framed photographs lining the mantel. Most were of Summer. She'd been a cherub-like baby who'd grown into a beautiful child. As a teenager, she was a striking young woman, the kind who would get noticed by a boy like Knox Keller. I gripped my wineglass tighter.

I dialed Witt and his phone immediately went to voicemail.

"Damn it," I cursed again, hurling my phone onto the couch in frustration. I paced the living room and caught a whiff of something overripe. After a minute I realized it was me. I was still in my workout clothes, my sweat dried and sticky on my skin and my underarms rank.

Taking the steps two at a time, I went up and knocked on Summer's closed door. When there was no answer I opened it slowly. The room was dark and her body was curled into a ball on the bed. When I got closer her slow, regular breathing told me she was asleep. I hesitated, then left her alone. She needed to rest. And I needed to calm down and focus on what to do next.

In my bathroom I stripped down and stepped under the stream of hot water. It was good I couldn't reach Witt, I reasoned. His fatherly instincts would kick in and he'd go crazy with anger and would want police and lawyers involved—a subject I didn't want to broach with him. It was better to delay telling him until I had a plan. I understood his reflex to call the authorities for help, to summon uniformed men with guns or expensive leather briefcases and important titles. But men like that could not solve this problem, this *situation*, as they would call it—or worse, *misunderstanding*. No, they would only make it worse by asking the same calculated questions many times over, retraumatizing my daughter by forcing her to repeat which body part was put where and when, subtly searching for inconsistencies in her story. Seeking anything that would reveal this was just another case of a nice boy from a good family victimized by an overwrought teenage girl.

The whispers would start, the crowds parting around her as she walked through the halls at school, invitations to parties rescinded, lunch tables closed off. That was the best-case scenario. She might also arrive at school one day to find unspeakable things scrawled across her locker in permanent marker; to feel a million invisible hands reach out to grab her breasts, her ass, and between her legs as she passed through a group of boys on her way to the bathroom; to be summoned to the principal's office and told she had become a "distraction" and that she'd be better off finishing the school year elsewhere. Or, worst of all, she might come to believe the whispers and words on her locker, and lean into her new identity, doing things that would ignite a burning shame inside her that she'd spend the rest of her life trying to extinguish.

I knew how these things went. And now that the worst had happened, there was no way I was going to put my daughter through more trauma. No one was going to shame my daughter.

"It wasn't my fault," I whispered to myself as the shampoo swirled into the drain at my feet, practicing the mantra my therapist had given me. *She leaves for college soon*, I thought. *I can protect her until then. We'll get her a great therapist. She'll start fresh at Princeton.*

I toweled off and pulled on a pair of leggings and a recently worn Atlanta United T-shirt of Witt's that smelled like him. Pausing at Summer's door, I cracked it open. She'd rolled over onto her side and was making small snuffling sounds in her sleep like Bailey did.

Back downstairs I paced some more, starting and then deleting text after text to Witt. Finally I gave up; I couldn't bear to see the words I had to tell him typed in black and white on the screen. I threw myself on the couch and pulled Bailey up next to me. She curled up against my leg and was soon snoring. I picked up my phone again and instinctively started to text Lorrie before I realized what I was doing. I always reached for her, whatever the situation. She'd talked me through three miscarriages as Witt and I tried to have a second child, dropping off dinners and taking care of Summer for long stints during the day when depression pinned me to the bed. When my mother died of lung cancer it was Lorrie who'd flown home with me to help me clean out and sell her trailer, emptying an endless number of ashtrays and defrosting a freezer full of Stouffer's boxed meals. Now, though, when I needed her most, she was the last person I could speak to. Overwhelmed, I dropped the phone back on the couch and closed my eyes as a wave of exhaustion swept over me.

I startled awake to the sound of the doorbell. Bailey gave a loud bark beside me. "Fucking Jehovah's Witnesses," I muttered, scrambling for the door. If they woke Summer, then they were about to meet the devil. I wrenched open the door to find two men standing on my welcome mat. One was a head taller than the other and wore an off-the-rack suit jacket several sizes too big. The other wore a neatly pressed police uniform and his broad shoulders nearly took up the whole doorway.

"Mrs. Van Doren?" the tall one said. "We're here to talk about your daughter."

# TEN

## LORRIE

### *Sunday, 12 p.m.*

"We're leaving for the mall in five minutes!" I shouted down the stairs into the basement where Archie had his gaming systems set up. Though I hated video games on principle, by now it was clear that my fifteen-year-old had few passions outside them. And given that so few things seemed to make him happy these days, I let him have this one.

Eden was the only one who knew about Dr. Frank, Archie's therapist. She was the only one outside of Ed who knew how worried I'd become when Archie had faded into a shell of the goofy, creative kid I loved, earlier that year. She was the only one who knew about his pills.

"He's going to be fine," she'd assured me on the way to the pharmacy. I'd wanted moral support when I went to fill Archie's prescription the first time. "I mean, who knows where I'd be without Lexapro, you know? Probably addicted to daytime television and living in your basement with Archie."

I'd laughed so hard I missed the turn into the CVS parking lot.

After I called down to Archie I started back to the kitchen to grab my purse. The sound of a soft knock on the front door stopped me. Strange. The UPS driver usually rang the doorbell, as did the young, hopeful canvassers for the Sierra Club who came by regularly to follow up on a donation I'd made five years earlier.

Peering through the window, I saw it was Eden.

"Finally," I said, opening the door. "I've been trying to get ahold of you all day. Are we still on for tonight? I'm definitely going to need a drink after forcing Archie to go the mall with me. Also, did you see the latest passive-aggressive email from Grace Kinley to the Parent Boosters listserv? I swear, that woman makes a full-time job out of complaining."

Eden's hair was damp and pulled back from her face, her skin uncharacteristically free of makeup. I marveled at the marble-like smoothness of her face as I thought of the deep creases between my eyebrows and the tiny lines that feathered out around my eyes. At forty-seven I'd only recently begun dying my light brown hair to cover the growing colony of grays. I'd felt vain sitting in the stylist's chair, concerned I was on a slippery slope to extreme plastic surgery.

"Hi." Eden shifted on her feet on the welcome mat. I caught sight of the gold elephant necklace I'd given her, the twin of the one around my own neck.

"Come in already," I said, gesturing to her. "I'm just trying to pry Archie out of the basement but I've got a few minutes."

Eden hovered in the doorway for a moment, then stepped inside and shut the door behind her.

"What can I get you?" I asked. "Coffee? LaCroix? Is it too early for a shot of tequila? God help me, there's no way I'm going to be able to get through the kids' graduation week without copious amounts of alcohol."

I turned toward the kitchen but Eden remained rooted in the entryway. She was staring at the photo of Knox and

Summer at winter formal. While Eden continued to dismiss their romance as a passing high school fad, almost five months had passed since we'd walked in on them on Christmas Eve. They seemed to be going strong. Knox drove Summer to school every morning that he didn't have early baseball practice, and I often saw her in the stands at his games, sitting alone, or sometimes with Violet Doyle from next door. Her red hair and black clothing were easy to spot in a sea of blond highlights and baseball caps. Personally, I thought she'd be much prettier without her black eyeliner and combat boots, but at least she wore shirts that didn't look like sports bras, which seemed to be all the rage these days.

"I need to tell you something." Something in Eden's tone caused the hair on my arms to prickle. "The police are going to call you."

"What? Why?" I wheeled to face her.

"It's Knox."

"What happened?" Adrenaline surged through my body and I reached for the wall to steady myself. Eden put her face in her hands as she drew a long breath. When she lifted her head every muscle in her body seemed to tighten.

"Knox... took advantage of Summer last night."

"I don't understand." I tried to process her words. Separately they all made sense but strung together in the sentence she'd uttered I couldn't grasp their meaning. Her face, so familiar to me, was unreadable. It was as if it belonged to someone else.

She sighed heavily and looked behind her at the door. "Look, the police asked me not to talk to you—to anyone. But I wanted you to know."

"You called the police about my son?" My voice rose.

"It wasn't my choice to involve them," Eden said flatly. "I know how this goes. But I guess the hospital was obligated to report."

"Hospital? Wait, what? Report? What are you talking about?"

"Please don't make me say it again." Her voice wavered.

"Eden, if someone hurt Summer—"

"She says it was Knox."

"That's impossible! Did she tell you that? Did you see it? I mean, come on, you know Knox."

"And I know my daughter."

I furrowed my brow in confusion. "We'll figure this out. I'd be happy to talk to the police, explain that there's been some sort of mistake. Clearly there's no way Knox could have done something like this—to his girlfriend, no less."

"Are you accusing Summer of lying?"

There was a weight to her tone that made my stomach lurch. "I'm saying there must be another explanation you haven't considered." I stepped toward her, my hands open at my sides. She backed away. I eyed her closely, a kernel of dread lodging in my throat that made it hard to get the next words out. "Wait, you really think this happened, don't you? That my son—"

"Why would Summer lie?"

I sucked in my breath, a flicker of anger roiling my usual calm. "Look, this is serious, Eden. You can't play around with this kind of thing."

"Why do you think I'm here?" The sharpness in her tone matched mine. She shook her head. "This was a mistake. I shouldn't have come over." She took a step toward the door, then turned back around. "This is bad, Lorrie. For everyone involved. I'd like to... keep it private. For everyone's sake."

"Of course," I said. It would make no sense to spread such a ludicrous rumor around. I squeezed my hands together to quell the tremor that had suddenly appeared in them.

Eden slammed the door behind her and it echoed through the house.

# ELEVEN
## ARCHIE

### *Three months before*

Dr. Frank and I have an agreement; he lets me win at Rummy and I don't tell my mom that all we're doing in our weekly sessions is playing cards. And really he doesn't have to let me win because he's terrible. You'd think someone with a PhD wouldn't suck so much at card games, especially the ones that involve strategy. I asked him once if all child psychiatrists played cards, like if it was a "get kids to open up" tactic they learned in school. He'd looked at me through his wire-rim glasses and raised an eyebrow.

"Don't you think I'd be better at it if it was?" he asked.

When Mom took me to my first appointment with him she said it was because my brain didn't work like everyone else's. That most people didn't have a nonstop scrolling ticker in their head, like the kind you see on the bottom of the screen in all caps when you're watching the news. Mine lists things like climate change, my geometry quiz, and why my parents fight so much lately. When high school started it was like someone turned up the volume on all my worries. Trying to hear anything else going on in my brain was exhausting. So Mom brought me to see Dr. Frank.

Some weeks I don't have much to say, so we just play cards. Other times, like today, I surprise myself with how many words spill out of my mouth.

"I have, um, a friend coming over after school tomorrow," I said, clearing my throat. I tried not to sound as excited as I felt. Dr. Frank nodded. He'd already figured out that, with my wardrobe of all black and my tendency to eat lunch by myself in my history teacher's classroom, I wasn't exactly the most popular kid in school.

"Nice," he said. "How did you meet him?"

"Her," I corrected. "She came to eat in Mr. Avery's classroom last week. I guess they kicked her out of the cafeteria for having a peanut butter sandwich. She liked my drawings so she started eating in there with me." I carried around a notebook full of sketches of dragons and intergalactic street fighters and worked on them while I ate lunch. "Anyway, we're going to play Mortal Kombat—it's her favorite game, too. By the way, thanks again for that."

I'd spent months trying to convince my mom to buy the game for me but she said it was too violent. Which I get, but the reason I wanted it didn't have anything to do with that. It's because the graphics are so good you feel like you're right there in the game—which made it impossible for me to think about anything else, like nuclear war or whether I'll get into a good college. It's hard to explain, but to me blowing up buildings and mowing down bad guys is relaxing because I'm not worrying about anything else.

I told Dr. Frank all that one week and he wrote something down on his little notepad. The next week I came home from school and the game was sitting on my bed. Before I was allowed to play it, though, Mom gave me a lecture about how sexist and violent toward women video games are and how that's not how she was raising me, blah blah. I nodded along, not wanting to tell her I wasn't the kid she should be worried about.

"You're welcome," Dr. Frank said. "So tell me more about your friend."

"Well," I said, thinking about Tadpole's dark blond hair buzzed close to her head and her backpack covered with ironed-on patches bearing the names of heavy metal bands. "She just, like, seems cool. But I think my mom thinks she's my girlfriend." I made a face. Mom had been way too excited when I'd asked if Tadpole could come over.

"Do you want her to be your girlfriend?" Dr. Frank asked. He laid down a pair of threes.

"Nah. And anyway, she likes girls."

"Ah," he said. "What about you?"

"What do you mean?"

"Do you know if you like girls or boys?"

"Oh. Girls. But I'm not, like, obsessed with them like my brother and his friends." I thought of the loud, smelly baseball players that piled into our kitchen a few times a week after practice, eating all our good snacks and sticking me with the boring, healthy trail mix Mom always bought.

"What makes you say they're obsessed?" Dr. Frank looked up at me.

"Well for one they're always, like, talking about girls. What they look like, what they're wearing, who did what with which girl." I frowned, remembering a conversation I'd overheard Knox's friends having, about whether tits or asses were more important.

"How do you feel when they talk that way?"

"Just, like, kinda gross inside, I guess. Like, who made them the judges? Plus, I wouldn't want anyone talking about Chloé that way. Or Tadpole."

"Have you told your brother you don't like it when he does that?"

"No way. He already thinks I'm weird."

"Why is that?"

I paused and gripped my cards. I wasn't sure I wanted to tell Dr. Frank why. I felt sick every time I thought about it, so I mostly tried not to. But now that he'd brought it up, the memory came zooming back into my mind.

A couple of months ago my iPad had died while I was doing an assignment and I couldn't find my charger, so I'd grabbed Knox's tablet off the coffee table to finish. His passcode was easy —he was the idiot who used his birthday. When the screen fired up, though, a video started playing where he'd left off. A woman was naked and blindfolded, down on her hands and knees. A man with his pants down had his thing shoved in her mouth and it looked like she was choking on it. Another man was rocking back and forth behind her, slapping her backside and calling her names that would get me grounded for eternity if they ever came out of my mouth.

"What the hell?" A voice startled me so bad I dropped the iPad on the floor. I turned to see Knox standing behind me.

"I didn't mean to—" I stammered.

"Don't touch my shit," he said, swiping his arm down to retrieve the device. His face was flushed and he looked like he wanted to punch me.

"I'm sorry." I scooted to the opposite end of the couch.

"Spencer sent that to me," he said, unclenching his fists. "I didn't know what it was." Spencer was Knox's best friend, a blond version of the Hulk who roamed the halls at school in a cloud of body spray.

"OK," I muttered. Knox turned on his heel and left the room.

In Dr. Frank's office I ran my fingers over the smoothness of my cards and avoided meeting his eyes. "Knox and I just, like, aren't super close anymore," I said.

I didn't want Dr. Frank to think Knox was a bad person if I

told him about the video. I'd seen porn before, but mostly the kind with cheesy music and a half-naked housewife answering the door for the "delivery guy." Plus my dad had a collection of old *Playboys* he didn't exactly keep hidden, but in those pictures the women frolicked in fields or rode horses and generally looked pretty happy.

The video on Knox's iPad, though, was different.

The woman hadn't looked like she was enjoying herself, and the men didn't seem to care. Somehow I knew that video would cause real trouble if I ratted him out. So, I kept my mouth shut, and so did Knox. If we passed each other at school we didn't make eye contact. If he was doing homework or watching TV in the family room I stayed in the basement with my games. If we were ever in the car together we stared out the windows or at our phones, avoiding conversation. All of sudden my brother felt like a stranger.

"Were you and Knox close when you were younger?" asked Dr. Frank.

"Yeah, we were like, best friends." I tried to swallow the lump that had suddenly grown in my throat. "At least he was mine." I thought of our blanket forts and bike rides. "But things change, I guess." I tried to sound nonchalant.

"I'm sorry," said Dr. Frank. "Losing a friend is hard."

"Yeah, I miss the old Knox. Still, even though he's a total dick these days, I'm weirdly proud of him, you know? Like, he's probably the best athlete at Westwood. Even all teachers know who he is. It's like on game day everyone is rooting for him, high-fiving him in the halls and stuff. That must feel good."

"Maybe it does," said Dr. Frank. "But I guarantee your brother has problems, too."

"Knox?" I shook my head. "No way. His life is perfect."

# TWELVE

## LORRIE

### *Sunday, 12:30 p.m.*

Ed answered my call from in the stands of Knox's baseball game, the last of the season.

"You need to bring Knox home immediately," I said. I tried to keep my voice steady, aware he was sitting with other parents.

"What happened? Are the kids OK?"

"They're fine. I'll explain when you get home."

"Lor, Knox is pitching right now. I don't know what's so important that—"

"It's an emergency," I said. "I think." What Eden had said made no sense, but I'd also never seen that haunted look in her eyes before.

"It's either an emergency or it's not."

"Eden was here saying some crazy things, and—"

"So far that sounds like Eden being Eden, not an emergency." In the background I heard the crack of the bat and the roar of the crowd. "Shit, there goes Knox's no hitter," muttered Ed. "Would've been a nice way to close out the season."

I took a deep breath and tried to sound calm and rational. "I really need you both to come home right away."

"Lor, I'm not pulling him out of the last game of his high school career. He'll remember this forever. Besides, there're only a couple of innings left."

I sighed, rubbing the back of my neck to soothe away the goosebumps that had arisen. "Fine. Just don't let him talk to anyone. Come straight home—and don't bring anyone else." Ed was notorious for inviting the whole team back to our house after games. He'd make a big show of ordering a towering stack of pizzas and cracking open a beer for himself. After I'd seen Knox cringe more than once when his dad started to tell one of his lengthy stories about his exploits with the pro ball players, I'd gently suggested to Ed that he should let the boys hang out on their own.

"Aw, it's fine," he'd said. "They like having me around."

I directed my attention back to my phone conversation. "I mean it," I said. "Straight home."

"I heard you." Ed sounded annoyed.

"See you soon." I hung up and turned to see Archie standing behind me.

"Mom, what's going on?" He'd put on a fresh T-shirt, this one black with the number 3.14 on the front. I felt a rush of love for my quiet, brainy child who never ceased to frustrate his father with his lack of interest in playing catch or hitting golf balls.

"Nothing, sweetie." I attempted a smile. "We just have to delay our shopping trip, all right?"

He eyed me skeptically. "Is everything OK? Was Eden here?"

"Everything's fine," I said. "Why don't you go play video games for a little while longer and then I'll come get you."

"Um, sure." His face registered surprise but he didn't argue as he disappeared back into the basement.

After what felt like an eternity I heard the rumble of Ed's car pulling into the garage. It was followed by the sound of the side door opening and the clatter of Knox's gear bag hitting the mudroom floor, right where I would have to step over it later. He burst through the door, sweaty and streaked in the reddish dust from the baseball field.

Ed was on his heels. "Another win to close out the season!" He clapped Knox on the back.

Knox was unsmiling, and he glowered at me. "Why'd we have to leave right away? Everyone was celebrating."

"Yeah, what was the big emergency? Or should I say, non-emergency?" Ed and Knox exchanged a look.

At that moment Chloé barreled in the front door, having been dropped off from her sleepover. "Mom, I'm home! What's the emergency?" she said, dropping her bag in the middle of the entryway. I flashed my daughter a wan smile, then turned back to Knox.

"I'm so glad you won," I said, but it came out in a high-pitched squeak. I cleared my throat and turned to Knox. "I just —I just needed to ask you something."

"So ask," he shrugged. "I'm starving, I'm gonna make a sandwich." He started toward the kitchen.

"Ooh, can you make me one, too?" Chloé asked. "With peanut butter and banana and potato chips?"

"Wait," I said. This was not how I'd planned to have this conversation.

"Lor, enough already." Ed shook his head and followed the kids into the kitchen, opening the refrigerator. "What's up?"

"Wait!" I said again, the force of the word echoing through the room. Everyone turned to look at me.

I inhaled deeply. "Chloé, you can have a sandwich later. Right now I need to talk to your brother, so go upstairs please."

She crossed her arms and frowned. "But I—"

"Upstairs," I said sharply.

She stamped her foot and made a scoffing sound, but turned to go. "Fine," she huffed.

Turning to face Knox, I tried to swallow the lump that had formed in my throat. "What happened with Summer last night?"

He blinked, then crossed the room and flopped down on the couch, his face turned away from me.

"No dirty uniforms on the couch," I said.

"Is that what this is about?" Ignoring me, he grabbed a pillow and stuck it behind his head.

"Up!" I said through gritted teeth. Ed closed the refrigerator and started to speak but I waved him off.

"How do you know about it, anyway?" mumbled Knox, sitting up.

My body turned to lead. "So... it's true?"

"Wait, what's true? What are we talking about?" Ed demanded.

"Eden was here." I felt my calm facade slip.

"Eden was here? To talk about this?" Knox's face wrinkled in confusion.

My voice began to waver. "Knox, it's very important that you tell us about last night."

"About the fight we had?"

"The fight?"

"Yeah, me and Summer, we had a fight—that's what you're talking about, right?"

"That's... it?"

"I think so... yeah. Why, what did Eden say?" Knox furrowed his eyebrows as if trying hard to remember something.

"Someone want to fill me in here?" Ed frowned.

"What did you fight about?" I pressed, ignoring my husband.

Knox shrugged. "I don't know, relationship stuff."

"I need you to be more specific."

He rolled his eyes. "Mom, it's none of your business."

"While you're under my roof everything is my business."

"It was no big deal."

"Are you sure? Where were you last night?"

"I told you, at Jackson's."

"And then where?"

He looked at the ground. "With Summer."

"And you had a fight?"

"OK, enough with the cross-examination," interjected Ed, wearing an exasperated expression. "You're not a lawyer anymore, remember?"

"It was no big deal," repeated Knox, looking away.

"I'm afraid it was," I said, looking past him at Ed. "Because Summer says you raped her."

There was a moment of thick silence.

"She said what?" Ed exploded. "What the—"

I cut him off. "Knox, you need to tell us what you fought about. Eden said the police are involved."

"The police?" Knox's head snapped toward mine.

I nodded. "It's possible they'll want to talk to you, so we need to understand your story."

"My story? I didn't—"

"What happened," I corrected myself. "Please, it's important."

"The police?" interjected Ed. "Are you fucking kidding me?"

"I didn't rape anyone!" Knox's face had gone pale. "Look, I don't remember everything, but it definitely wasn't that."

"Why don't you remember everything?"

Knox hung his head. "We were drinking," he mumbled.

I inhaled sharply. "Both of you?" He nodded.

"Yes."

Knox nodded again.

"Were you drunk?"

"A little, maybe."

"Was she?"

He looked at the ground. "Yeah, I'm pretty sure she was."

"Knox!" I cried. "We've *talked* about that." Or at least, I'd tried to.

"Jesus, Knox, you couldn't have waited until after graduation to party?" Ed shook his head.

"I'm sorry." Knox's shoulders slumped forward.

"Look, I'm sure this is some kind of misunderstanding." Ed cleared his throat. Knox nodded, looking like he might throw up.

"Knox, we just want to understand what happened." I kept my voice low and soothing like I had when he was a toddler in the throes of a tantrum.

"Yes." Knox looked away and chewed on a hangnail. "With protection and everything, like you guys told me."

"Good," Ed nodded. Whether he was referring to the sex or the protection, I wasn't sure.

I felt behind me for a kitchen stool and sank onto it, feeling faint. Had I even had breakfast, or just coffee? My palms turned sweaty. "And while you were... I mean... what happened?"

Knox sank back down onto the couch and this time I didn't ask him to get up. "We had a fight," he said. "About relationship stuff. Summer wants to stay together next year at college. But I don't know if that's what I want."

"That's wise," said Ed. "Lots of fish in the sea."

"So, we broke up," Knox said.

My stomach dropped. "Before or after?"

"After."

I willed my head to clear. "Last night, you and Summer, you weren't at Jackson's that whole time, were you? Until three in the morning?"

"No, after a while we left the party and went to the park."

"What did you do at the park?"

"What is this, like, the third degree?"

"Just answer your mom's questions," said Ed. I looked up, surprised and grateful he wasn't going to force me to play the bad cop role all on my own.

"We talked, and... you know." Knox averted his eyes.

I swallowed hard. "Knox, did Summer want to have sex last night? How drunk was she? Is there any chance you... misunderstood her?"

He looked up, startled. "What? No! I mean yeah, of course she wanted to. We'd done it a bunch of times before."

"Then why would she—"

"Look, they broke up, she got pissed and made up a story." Ed pursed his lips. "It'll be embarrassing for her, but we'll straighten it out."

I nodded, but had trouble imagining the sweet girl I'd known since she was in diapers acting that way. It just didn't sound like Summer.

"What happens now?" Knox stood up and shifted on his feet. "Do I really have to talk to the police?"

"I don't know." I glanced at Ed. "Maybe it would help if you just talked to Summer. Apologized."

"Apologized for what?" Ed narrowed his eyes.

"For..." I waved my hand, realizing I was unsure. "The fight, I guess."

"No way." Ed pointed a finger at Knox. "No apologizing, you hear me? An apology means you did something wrong, which you didn't. This will all blow over, I promise."

Knox nodded, looking anything but convinced. I walked over and gave him a quick hug. "It'll be OK," I said. To my surprise, he returned my hug, something he hadn't done voluntarily since middle school. And while the feeling of my son's embrace should have felt good, a prickling arose along my spine.

After Knox left the room to shower I sank down onto the

couch. Ed paced the living room, his jaw clenching and unclenching in quick, tight motions.

"Eden said the police are going to want to talk to us," I said.

"I'll handle the police," he said.

"I just keep thinking this has to be some kind of misunderstanding."

Ed waved his hand. "Maybe. It's sad, but this shit happens."

"What does?"

"Women lying about this stuff."

"It doesn't, actually." A flash of annoyance shot through me at his uneducated assumption. I'd read up on the statistics back when I used to volunteer for the Atlanta Women's Shelter where many of the women who came in had been victims of sexual violence.

"What's that?"

"I read that only a small percentage of rape allegations are false."

Ed turned to me, his face darkening. "Are you saying our son is a liar?"

"Of course not." I didn't know exactly what I was saying.

The sound of the doorbell pierced the tension, causing us both to jump. Exhaling sharply, Ed grabbed his phone and checked our home security camera app.

"That was fast," he muttered, smoothing his hair, which was still thick in his late forties with only a hint of gray. I watched him square his shoulders and stride toward the front door.

"Jim, hey man, good to see you," he said in an upbeat voice.

"Ed, hi, sorry to disturb. Can we come in for a minute?" I recognized the voice of Jim Evans, or Officer Jim, as he was known by the neighborhood kids. He was a regular at Career Day at the elementary school. As the team physician for the Atlanta Braves, Ed had access to complimentary tickets and once or twice a year made sure to pass a handful of them along to Jim to give out at the precinct, always good seats close to the field.

"Sure thing," I heard Ed say. "Can we get you anything to drink?"

"No, thanks Ed, we're good."

The two men rounded the corner into my view, followed by a short, brick-like woman with dark, bluntly cut chin-length hair. She was in uniform like Jim, a pair of handcuffs dangling from her belt. I had a brief vision of my son being led away in them and blinked it quickly away.

"Lorrie, hi, sorry to disturb you," Jim repeated. "This is Officer McBride."

The woman nodded to Ed and me.

"Look, I'll get straight to it." Jim shifted uncomfortably. "There's been a report of an... incident, and, well, we're gonna need to talk to Knox."

"Yes, we've heard," said Ed.

"Oh?" Jim looked surprised.

"The girl's mother was here this morning to talk to Lorrie."

"We're best friends," I offered. Officer McBride frowned.

"Ah, OK then." Jim looked relieved.

"So you know what happened," said Officer McBride.

"We know what the girl says happened," said Ed.

"Summer," I said, adding her name.

"Right, yeah," nodded Jim.

"My understanding is that they had a run-of-the-mill argument and the girl got upset," continued Ed. "Classic teenage girl drama."

"Sir, how old is your son?" asked Officer McBride.

"He turned eighteen in January," I said.

"Then we're going to need to talk to him directly, take a statement," she said, turning to me. "At the precinct."

"Now Jim, that sounds awfully formal." Ed spoke as if Officer McBride wasn't in the room, his voice taking on an edge.

"Afraid so, Ed." Jim held up his hands in apology. "Any hint of sexual misconduct these days and we have to follow strict procedures—lots has changed. But you all can drive him over if you want."

"Jim, while I'm sure this is a misunderstanding we can clear up quickly, I'm thinking we should have our lawyer there." Ed spoke slowly, his tone friendly. "Can you give us an hour or so?"

"We'll need—" began Officer McBride.

"That'll be fine." Jim cut her off and she shot him a look. "We'll see you at the station soon."

# THIRTEEN

## EDEN

### *Sunday, 3 p.m.*

I heard the click-clack of Witt's rolling suitcase on the front walkway, then his key in the lock. I met him at the door, falling into his arms before he was even inside. My tears surprised me. I wasn't a crier, except when it came to those Humane Society commercials with the Sarah McLachlan music and the sad-eyed animals staring out at you from their cages. Those got me every time—and my credit card.

"Shhh," he said, stroking my hair and kicking the front door shut with his foot. "I'm home now." I could tell he was surprised by my emotional state. "Where is she?" he asked.

"Upstairs. She's been asleep all day, except to shower."

He shook his head, his face pale. We walked to the couch and sank down on it, still clinging to each other like a life buoy in a riptide. "Tell me everything," he said.

"I haven't forced her to talk." I leaned my head on his shoulder. "I wanted to let her rest. All she's said is that..." I swallowed hard. "That she didn't want to have sex. And that Knox went ahead anyway."

I told Witt about the text I'd gotten from Jules, my sprint to the hospital, and, crucially, the visit from the police.

"They need to ask her some questions," I said. "But I didn't want to do anything until I talked to you. They gave me a number to call as soon as you got home." I pulled a creased business card from the pocket of my joggers.

Witt nodded. "I'll call them. We should have her talk to them as soon as possible, while the details are fresh. I assume the hospital did some sort of exam, but those results will likely take a while to process." He had switched over to what I called his lawyer voice. I could always tell when he was on the phone with a client because his voice became lower and his words more enunciated.

I looked down. "They didn't do an exam."

"At the hospital? But I'd think it would be standard—"

"We decided we didn't want one." I lifted my head and met his gaze. The room went so quiet I could hear the faint beep of a neighbor locking their car outside.

Witt spoke slowly, his handsome face darkening with confusion. "Eden, please tell me I misunderstood—please tell me you made her do the exam."

I gave a small shake of my head. He pulled away from me as if I was radioactive, scrambling to his feet. "Why the hell would you do that? That's evidence, Eden—evidence we'll need." He glanced at his watch and began pacing. "OK, it's only been, what, seven or eight hours since you took her this morning? We'll just go back to the hospital now. I'll get the car."

"Witt—" I put a hand on his arm to stop him from charging out of the room. He shook it off. For a moment I wavered, my mind flooded with the memory of a conference room that smelled of stale coffee and the row of old, balding men who sat across the table from me, one of whom was my school principal. The others never bothered to introduce themselves. I remembered one in particular. He had a large, red nose and heft that strained the buttons of his starched shirt. He made me repeat details while his eyes grew glassy and the corners of his mouth started to glisten with saliva. Where exactly had the teacher put his hands, how far had his fingers been inside me, did I enjoy it?

While Witt thought a hospital exam—*evidence*—would protect Summer, I knew the truth. The only real protection would be to get her as far away as possible from Knox and anyone else who would call her a slut behind her back—or to her face—and tell her she was worthless over and over until she believed it. I was not about to let history repeat itself.

"No," I said. "She's not doing it. It's too late, anyway," I added, hoping that would somehow make it all right. Witt shot me a look of such poisonous disappointment that I felt my soul shudder.

"We'll talk about this later," he said. "Right now I'm going upstairs to see my daughter."

As his footsteps receded up the stairs I sighed and sank back down onto the couch, my hands resting on the expensive brushed suede material. Our five-bedroom house was a far cry from the double-wide I'd grown up in, with a father who stopped in on a biannual basis and a mother who smiled and washed her hair regularly when she was on her meds, and locked herself in her room for days when she wasn't. Mostly the latter.

Summer didn't know how lucky she was. I hadn't had anyone to teach me how to dress to fit in or behave around boys. Instead I'd opted for push-up bras and blow jobs in exchange for someone's—anyone's—attention.

I picked up the framed family photo sitting on the end table. It was taken when Summer was twelve, the last year she was still willing to smile for the camera. In it we're sprawled on the grass in the backyard. Summer's head is on my shoulder and her arm is linked through Witt's. She's gazing at the camera with a look of pure contentedness.

That fall she started middle school and stopped smiling. She also stopped spending hours on the phone every night with her friends Annabelle and Charlotte, or stopping off at their houses after school.

"Nothing *happened*," she'd shrugged when I'd asked. "I still see them at school. They're just different now."

"Different how, baby?"

"Kind of... snobby, I guess," she said, lowering her eyes. "They sit with this other girl at lunch, Ella. It's like, Ella's table. All they do there is talk about people behind their backs."

*Baby, that's power*, I'd wanted to say. That's what you want. To be the owner of the lunch table, the talker and not the talked about. I ached to give her the guidebook to teenage girl politics, the one I hadn't had at her age. I wanted to sit her down and to hand over the secret formula to being loved and a little bit feared. *Just listen to me*, I wanted to beg. *I can make it easy for you. I could make you queen of them all.*

Setting down the photo, I pushed myself up off the couch and went to the window, pulling back the curtain. Across the street the white brick of Lorrie's house caught the late afternoon sunlight. The flower beds in the front yard were bright with freshly planted pansies and the hedges neatly trimmed. Everything appeared in order.

I smiled, remembering how Lorrie's flowerbeds had suffered the year she potty trained Knox.

"He'll only go outside, and only on the flowers." She'd thrown up her hands. "In the front yard, for anyone to see!"

"At least he'll go," I said. Summer had refused to part with her Pull-Ups. Then one day she'd seen Knox pull down his pants and aim into the flowerbed. She'd charged over next to him and pulled down her own pants, releasing a stream of pee down her legs into her shoes, then looking up at me with wide, dismayed eyes. Lorrie and I had howled.

. . .

As I stared across the street the garage door cranked suddenly upward. I darted back from the window even though I doubted they could see me. The three of them entered the garage, Ed striding with purpose, Lorrie behind him with her fists clenched at her sides, and Knox with his head down and his hands shoved in his pockets. Knox got into the back seat of their Mercedes SUV but Ed and Lorrie stood behind the vehicle for a minute, framed under the open garage door. Their lips moved rapidly and Lorrie pointed an accusing finger at Ed. He crossed his arms and jerked his head in the direction of the street. Lorrie dropped her arm and glanced around, her eyes lingering on my house. I let the curtain fall closed and forced myself to take three deep breaths before I looked again.

They were gone.

# FOURTEEN

## LORRIE

### *Sunday, 3 p.m.*

We made the drive to the police station in silence after Ed and I argued about what Knox should wear. I'd wanted him to swap his T-shirt for a button-up shirt.

"No way," said Ed. "He can't look like he's trying too hard to make a good impression. He needs to look like a normal kid whose Sunday was interrupted."

"But he *is* trying to make a good impression," I said, exasperated.

Ed sighed and gripped the steering wheel tighter. "Can you just trust me for once? I know how this works."

"And so do I," I snapped. "I was the lawyer in the family, remember?"

"Are they going to arrest me?" asked Knox from the back seat, his voice shaky.

"They don't arrest people for bullshit like this," said Ed. I glanced back at Knox, who didn't look comforted.

"Of course not." I tried for a more soothing tone. "They just want to talk to you."

"But if I need a lawyer then this is, like, serious, right?"

"It's just a technical thing; it's going to be fine." I reached back and squeezed his knee. He didn't move away.

"How will I know what to say?" he asked.

"Beau will tell you want to say," said Ed. I shot him a glare, then tried to soften my face as I looked back to Knox.

"You just tell the truth, OK sweetheart?"

Knox met my eyes, then looked away and nodded.

In the parking lot Ed shut off the car and nodded at a tall, broad-shouldered man with a thick head of white hair in a dark suit leaning against his Lexus. "There he is."

"How do you know him, again?" I asked, but Ed was already climbing out of the car and waving the man over.

"This is Beau Sykes," he said. Beau wore dark glasses despite the overcast day, which he didn't remove as he looked past me to shake hands with Knox.

"All right then," he said in a heavy Southern drawl. "Here's how this will work. Be yourself, be natural. Be specific when you answer their questions but don't offer additional information. Tell the truth when you can, and I'll take care of the rest."

"Meaning what?" I asked, hands on my hips. His head swiveled toward me like he'd already forgotten I was there. He pushed his glasses down his nose to peer at me. His face was just shy of handsome, like someone had taken a movie star and slightly blurred all the edges, weakened the chin and pushed the eyes too far apart.

"Meaning I'll tell him when to shut up," he said.

"I don't know," I said to Ed. Something about Beau made me think of a shark circling its prey. "I think it should just be you and me there with Knox."

"I'm afraid that's not possible," said Beau.

"Wait, my mom and dad can't come?" Knox asked.

"Knox is eighteen and therefore an adult in the eyes of the

law," continued Beau. "Y'all won't be allowed in the room. Only his lawyer—me."

Knox turned to me, his face pale and frightened. "But I want you to come, Mom."

I flashed back to dropping him off at kindergarten for the first time, his tiny hand gripping mine, holding on until the last possible second as his dad pushed him forward into the waiting arms of a teacher. "Surely if we talk to Officer Jim he can—" I began.

"Not possible." Beau cut me off and glanced at his watch.

"You're in good hands with Mr. Sykes," Ed said, patting Knox's shoulder. "There's nobody better for this, I promise."

"So, what happens exactly?" I pressed, feeling ill at ease. "Knox answers some questions, and then?" I felt my long-dormant lawyerly instincts rumble to life.

"Then it's up to the state attorney general's office," said Beau. "They'll decide whether to press charges based on the evidence, though I believe that to be unlikely in this situation."

"Why is that?" I asked. My voice had taken on a cool, clipped tone I remembered from my days in the courtroom.

Beau glanced at Ed, who nodded. "I have it on good authority that there is a lack of forensic evidence," Beau said. I stared at him blankly. He cleared his throat. "Mrs. Keller, perhaps you've heard the rather crude term 'rape kit?' Well, in this case, for whatever reason, one was not collected. Meaning that unless there was a witness, which it seems there was not, there is a lack of corroborating evidence."

Ed leaned forward. "I believe what Beau is saying is that it's Knox's word against Summer's."

"Indeed," said Beau. "And that is very much in our favor." The relief that flooded my body only lasted an instant. Almost immediately an oily slick of guilt settled over the top of it. *Because no one ever believes the woman,* I thought.

Inside, Ed and I sat in a pair of vinyl-covered chairs outside a conference room. A knot of helplessness rose in my throat as I hugged my firstborn and watched him disappear through the heavy door with Beau.

Ed squeezed my hand as we sat side by side. I stared at the dingy concrete wall in front of us, remembering how I'd hugged Knox to my chest in the hospital delivery room, overcome with a love so fierce it left me breathless with joy and overwhelmed by responsibility. Now my sweet baby boy was on the verge of adulthood and the moment I feared most had arrived; he was alone without my protection.

"This is a bad idea," I whispered tersely to Ed as we sat waiting. "Tell me again what you know about this Beau character?"

"I know him through work." Ed's eyes darted to the side and something in my stomach dropped.

"What do you mean? He works for the team?" My voice grew louder, my tone more aggressive.

"Sometimes. He's more of a consultant, as needed."

"Needed for what? Who does he work for specifically?" It came out sounding like an accusation. Something didn't feel right.

"Calm down," Ed hissed, glancing around. "We can talk about it later." His phone beeped and he squinted at the screen. "I've got to take this," he said, standing.

I watched him cross the lobby and push through the glass doors as a fire of resentment ignited in my belly. I'd had enough of Ed's self-important way of excusing himself for "emergency" work calls at all hours of the day and night. These were baseball players we were dealing with, not soldiers on the front lines.

Sitting alone, I pushed my chair back until it was touching the wall, as if Knox might be able to feel my presence through the concrete. A stack of old magazines sat on a side table nearby, as if anyone sitting in this waiting room would be able to focus on reading. I stared at my watch, observing the minute hand was making its way around at a desperately slow pace.

I remembered the days when time to myself was so rare it came in ten-minute increments, snatched in the parking lot at soccer games or hiding in the laundry room on the nights Ed was home to corral the kids into pajamas and clean teeth. Lately I missed the days when I was so urgently and constantly needed that even leaving the room for a minute would result in fat, sloppy tears from at least one of the kids.

"Go to the gym, or a movie or something," Ed had said when I fretted about my waning usefulness. "You've raised three amazing kids; you deserve some time to yourself."

When the kids were younger, I would have given a small fortune to sit alone in a dark movie theater for an afternoon. Now, though, I was searching for more. My kids' lives were changing and moving on and I didn't want to be left rooted and forgotten in the same spot.

I pulled my phone from my purse and tried to calm my racing thoughts with one of the word games I liked to play. Distracted, my thoughts kept jumping from the word scramble in front of me to Eden. Surely once we got to the bottom of what had really happened things would go back to normal between us.

I unlocked my phone and scrolled to yesterday's text to Eden.

> I wish Knox was interested in going to college somewhere that didn't revolve around baseball. I worry he's going to be that pathetic guy who peaks in high school and then spends the rest of his life talking about the good old days. Am I terrible for thinking that?

I winced, wondering what she must be thinking of Knox now. But surely she couldn't really believe he'd do something so awful, could she? I reread her reply to the text.

You couldn't be terrible if you tried. xoxoxo

Ed's phone call outside the police station seemed to last forever. He had just stepped back inside when the conference room door heaved open. Knox walked out, followed by Beau and two uniformed officers.

"Hi, sweetheart." I went to hug him and he slumped against me, his arms hanging at his sides.

"Outside," Beau muttered, motioning for us to move forward and out the door. In the parking lot he led us away from the building. Glancing around, he clapped a hand on Knox's shoulder. "All things considered, I'd say it went well."

"What does that mean?" I asked, narrowing my eyes. I wanted facts, not slippery, vague reassurances.

"It means we are asserting the sexual contact in question that night was consensual. I believe the attorney general's office will find no evidence to the contrary and thus will choose not to pursue this further."

I turned to Knox. "What was it like? What did they ask you? What did they ask Beau?"

"I—" began Knox.

"Who else is giving statements?" interrupted Ed.

"Well, the girl, clearly, and there's apparently a neighbor who took her to the hospital in the first place, a young woman she babysits for."

"Jules Shulman," I said.

"But given that there were no actual witnesses on the night in question, I predict they will quickly close the books on this one."

"What happens next?" I asked. "What do we need to do?"

"Hopefully, nothing." Beau shrugged, looking past me at Ed. "Right now, go about your usual business. Don't discuss these proceedings outside of your family." He eyed Knox. "Especially you, young man. No locker-room talk with friends or anything that could be a setback." Knox nodded. He looked pale and tired.

"Thanks again, Beau." Ed held out his hand. "We really appreciate you coming on such short notice."

Beau shook his hand. "I'll let you know what I hear."

We drove home in silence with Knox slumped against the window in the back seat. Resentment buzzed around my chest looking for a place to land—like on the way Ed had abandoned me for his phone call, how he'd accepted the way Beau talked past me, or the casually confident way he drove with only one hand on the wheel.

The house was exactly as we'd left it, with baseball equipment littering the entryway, the loaf of bread on the counter, and my sections of the *New York Times* weekend edition and empty coffee cup on the kitchen island. It felt strange returning to find everything in the same place, ready for us to pick the day back up where we'd left off. I wanted to dismiss the events of the morning as a meaningless blip in an otherwise normal Sunday and to busy myself with loading the dishwasher, going for a run, and taking Archie shopping. But I couldn't shake the feeling that everything had changed. I turned to face my son.

"It's time to tell us exactly what happened."

# FIFTEEN

## JULES

### *Two months before*

Audrey started to cry the minute I put the shampoo in my hair. *Of course you'd pick this exact minute to wake up*, I thought, hurrying to lather and rinse and then to swipe the bar of soap over my body so I'd be at least marginally clean. Shaving my legs would have to wait—again. Then, miraculously, her cries stopped. I cracked open the shower door, straining to hear any fussing, but there was nothing. She must have gone back to sleep. Unable to believe my luck, I celebrated by applying a conditioning hair mask and waiting the full five minutes the bottle recommended, luxuriating in the hot steam and silence.

When I got out of the shower and dressed, Audrey was still quiet. I pressed the button on the baby monitor to get a view of her crib, which was empty. Panic shot through me as I dropped my lotion back onto the counter and sprinted to her room. Flinging her door open, I found Ari sitting in the rocker, a sleeping Audrey in his arms.

"She was crying," he said. "I didn't think you could hear her in the shower."

"I heard her," I said, my tone defensive. "I just thought..." I trailed off and tried to backtrack. "I mean, thanks."

He nodded and stood up slowly, transferring the still-slumbering Audrey into my arms with surprising gentleness. "I better get going," he said without making eye contact as he left the room.

When Summer arrived to babysit a half hour later I was surprised to see her wearing a light gray T-shirt, cutoff jean shorts, and Converse sneakers instead of her usual all-black ensemble. The T-shirt, which had *Property of Westwood Baseball* printed on the front, was baggy on her slight frame and she'd knotted it at the waist.

"Hi," I said. "New shirt?"

She blushed. "It's Knox's. I just came from his game."

"Ohhh." I raised my eyebrows and smiled. Her blush deepened.

Inside Audrey crawled over to her and held out her arms to be picked up. Summer buckled her into her highchair while I packed my backpack. We had a routine down now.

I looked forward to Tuesday nights, not because of my economics class, where it took me copious amounts of caffeine to stay awake, but because I got to see Summer.

"Um, what's on the menu tonight?" Summer held up a spoonful of a chunky brownish substance from Audrey's bowl.

"Kale and turkey purée," I said, searching under the couch for my shoes. Audrey's newest game was pushing them under different pieces of furniture. "But I think maybe I didn't blend it long enough. Oh, and before I forget, Ari's staying with us this week but he's at a friend's studying. I have no idea when he'll be back, though."

Summer shrugged. "No problem." She sniffed the purée and made a face. "You know you can buy baby food at the store, right?"

I folded my arms across my chest. "Are you negging my homemade baby food?"

Summer eyed the brown slop on the spoon, then looked back at me. "Definitely."

I groaned. "OK fine, I admit it's a little... brown. But doing it myself makes me feel like a good mom."

"You *are* a good mom."

The compliment sent a wave of warmth through my body. "Aw, thanks." I smiled. "So, what's new with you?"

"Ugh." Summer sighed as she wiggled the spoon in front of Audrey's mouth. "It's promposal season."

"Prom... what?" I fished one shoe out from under the couch and located the other under the coffee table.

"You know, like filling someone's locker with balloons or getting the band on the football field to hold up a sign for you to ask them to prom."

"That seems like a lot of trouble."

Summer rolled her eyes. "You sound like someone's crabby old grandma."

"Well, I do feel like one most days." I slipped my shoes on and stuck my tongue out at her.

"Here." Summer pulled her phone out of her pocket. "Someone just sent me this."

She clicked on a video and handed me the phone just as Audrey sneezed, spraying kale and turkey all over Summer.

I tried to keep from laughing. "Knox, like, doesn't want his shirt back, right?"

Summer rolled her eyes at me and pinched Audrey's round cheek. "It's a good thing you're so cute," she said to her.

I set the phone on the counter and watched it with one eye while I balanced on one leg to tie my shoes. A shaky video of what looked like the high school gym played. There was upbeat music in the background and a woman's voice yelling, "Two, three, four, and kick!"

"Here they come!" breathed whoever was holding the phone. The music cut out and a line of high school boys trotted into view, all with the same shaggy hair and plaid button-up shirt.

"That's Knox on the far right." Summer pointed. I zoomed in on the screen. Knox was the tallest of the group, with broad shoulders and dark blond hair. When he flashed the camera a quick smile and tossed his hair out of his eyes he looked like he belonged in a boy band or on the cover of an Abercrombie catalog.

"Wow, hottie." I clucked my tongue. "But what's he doing?"

"Helping his friend, Spencer. Just keep watching." My watch dinged, telling me it was time to leave.

"Wait for it…" narrated the phone holder.

On cue the boys quickly unbuttoned their shirts, one struggling with the buttons for a few seconds, momentarily causing the sentence spelled out on their hairless chests to be "WILL YOU PROM ME EMILIA?" The blond boy in the middle of the line produced a single rose from behind his back.

"Emilia, will you accept this rose and go to prom with me?"

The shot panned to a petite, shapely girl in black leggings and a Spartans Dance Team T-shirt knotted at her tiny waist. She squealed and ran to the boy, letting herself be scooped up and spun around.

"I mean, can you believe it?" asked Summer as I handed the phone back to her. Despite her best efforts at pretending the spoon was an airplane, Audrey kept her mouth clamped shut.

"Yeah, it did kind of look like a casting call for an early 2000s boy band," I said.

Summer rolled her eyes. "I know! It's like, so fake! Knox told me Emilia basically, like, told Spencer they were breaking up if he didn't do a promposal."

"Did Knox do a promposal?" I glanced at the kitchen clock. I was already late but was in no hurry to leave. Over the weeks

Summer had morphed from babysitter into something that resembled a friend—which I desperately needed. It had been too painful to keep in touch with any of my music school friends after my accident, and the loose relationships I'd formed in the one year I'd spent at Georgia Tech had unraveled fast once I became the girl who got knocked up by her professor. And clearly I'd been naive to think I'd be accepted by any of the other moms in the neighborhood.

Summer looked down at the counter and shook her head. "No, Knox didn't do one."

"But you're going to prom, right? Wait, is it still cool to go to prom?"

She sighed. "He says he doesn't want to go. That prom is stupid. And he's right, for sure. It's just that, like, I've never had anyone ask me to anything like that, you know?"

I looked over and caught the wistfulness on her face. "And you want to be asked," I said.

She nodded and scraped the purée off Audrey's highchair table back into the bowl. "Lame, huh?"

"I thought prom was stupid, too," I said. "But I still really wanted to go."

"You did?"

"Yeah. With Ricky Spaulding. He sat next to me in orchestra. He played the oboe and he was double-jointed so he could twist his arms around into all these weird shapes."

"So did he ask you?"

"Nope. I was too much of a nerd to even get asked out by a fellow nerd."

Summer laughed. She grabbed a cloth and tried to wipe off Audrey's face and hands. "I think she's done eating."

I eyed the gelatinous mound of brown purée. "She wasn't really into it, was she?"

Summer shook her head. "She definitely was not. Anyway, prom would probably just be weird if we went together."

"Why?"

"Because we'd be with Knox's friends, and I don't really belong with that crowd."

"So hang out with your friends instead."

"Yeah, they kinda all think Knox is a brainless jock."

"The joys of high school." I smiled wryly.

"Yeah," she sighed. "It sucks." She waved the spoon in the air and pointed to Audrey's bowl. "Almost as much as this baby food. Maybe just buy it next time?"

I sighed and nodded. "OK, fair."

When I got home later Summer was on the couch with the baby monitor, moving her fingers up and down a long rectangular pillow she cradled in her lap like a guitar, pausing to scribble in a notebook next to her.

"Hey," she said, looking up when I came in.

"What are you doing?" I dumped my backpack on the couch and plopped down next to her. Picking up the monitor I saw Audrey was curled up asleep on her stomach, her knees under her like a bullfrog.

"Oh, nothing. Just working on a song I'm writing."

"You can write a song without an instrument?"

She shrugged. "I can hear the chords in my head."

"Wow." I was impressed. I'd taken my share of composition classes and there was no way I could come up with a melody unless I was in front of a piano.

The front door opened and shut. A minute later Ari emerged from the foyer in a hooded sweatshirt, his shoulders slumped under his weighty backpack.

"Hey Ari," I said in an effort to be friendly. "How's it going?"

Ari had Paul's large brown eyes, and they stared at me now

out from under his aspiring unibrow. "Oh," he said, ignoring me. "Hey Summer."

"Hi Ari," she said.

"How are you?" he asked.

"Good," she nodded.

"I heard you got into Princeton. Congratulations."

"Thanks. What about you?"

Ari straightened his spine proudly. "MIT. They have an excellent robotics department."

"Cool," Summer said.

Ari stood there for another minute until the silence became awkward. "Well, see you around." He gave a half-wave.

"See ya." Summer waved back.

"Wow," I mouthed to Summer once Ari had headed up the stairs. I looked back to check he was out of earshot, then whispered, "He must really like you. That's way more than he's ever said to me at one time."

She rolled her eyes.

"Anyway," I said, "bring your guitar over next time. I'd love to hear some of your songs."

The hollows of her cheeks reddened. "I don't really play them for anyone."

"Why not? Writing music is *hard*. If I wrote a song I'd be belting it out in, like, the middle of Target."

Summer considered this. "I'm not sure I'd want anyone to hear mine. They're kind of personal, you know?"

"Do I at least get to hear what it's about?"

She looked back down at the pillow and continued to move her fingers around on it. "Falling in love." I knew her well enough by now to notice the shadow that flitted across her face.

"Hey," I said. "Everything OK?"

"Yeah," she said, but she didn't raise her head to meet my eyes. "Of course."

# SIXTEEN

## ARCHIE

### *Sunday, 5 p.m.*

My brother might be a rapist.

When I heard my parents and Knox get back from the police station, I crept out of my room and stayed out of sight at the top of the stairs.

"We'd done it before." Knox's voice sounded weird and tired. "I don't know why things were different this time; why she acted different."

"What had you done before?" asked my mom.

"Gone to the park together. The same spot."

"Where?"

"The gazebo by the jogging path."

"Why?" Silence. "Knox, we need to know." I heard the frustration in my mom's voice. I moved down a step so I could just see into the room. Knox was leaning against the kitchen counter, staring at the ground.

"OK, jeez," he sighed. "It's just, I never thought I'd be telling my parents about my sex life. It's embarrassing."

"I understand it's embarrassing. But we're trying to help." That was my mom's I'm-losing-my-patience voice.

"We'd gone to the gazebo and... had sex. This time, though, she got mad after. I think maybe because she hurt her arm, twisted it or something."

"While you were... having sex?"

"I guess. She was making such a big deal about it, like it was my fault. I said she needed to calm down. Then she got really mad. I said maybe we should take a break, and that's when she went nuts and scratched me. Then she started crying and ran out of the gazebo."

"Knox, did she... ask you to stop? At any point?"

"No." His head jerked up, his face pale. "I would never—I didn't know her arm was hurting. She was making a lot of noises, but I thought—" His voice sounded faint. "I thought she liked it." He pulled on his eyebrow like he did when he was nervous. There was another long silence.

"What's going to happen?"

Even from where I stood hidden, I could see he was trying not to cry.

"We'll wait to hear from Beau," my father's voice cut in. I hadn't realized he was even in the room. "But I trust him when he says it looks good."

My mom's phone dinged and she looked down at the screen. "Chloé!" she called in the direction of the stairs. "Leila's mom will be here in two minutes to pick you up for ballet so get a move on, honey!"

Knox looked from Mom to Dad. "Can I go now?"

"Yes." My dad stepped into view and put his hand on Knox's shoulder. "But we're keeping this in the family right now, all right? Not a word to anyone else."

"Especially Summer," my mom added. Knox nodded and turned away from them.

I had plenty of time to run up the stairs and disappear, but I stood rooted to my spot. Knox nearly ran straight into me as he started up the stairs. He looked scared, something I hadn't seen him look in a long time. When he saw me, though, his face turned mean.

"What the hell are you doing?" he said.

"Is Summer hurt?" I said the words before I could stop them.

Knox's face got tight and his mouth turned into a straight line. "You don't know what you're talking about."

"But I heard Mom—"

He poked two fingers against my chest. "I said, you don't know what you're talking about. Stay out of it, OK?" As he lowered his hand, it trembled—with fear or anger, I didn't know. Then he barged past me to his room and slammed the door.

"Chloé!" my mom called as her phone dinged again. "They're here!" She sounded tired and annoyed.

"Coming!" yelled my sister as she barreled toward me on the stairs. I squeezed myself to one side and she rushed past like I wasn't even there, leaving a trail of sweet vanilla body spray in her wake that nearly made me gag.

"Do you have your water bottle?" my mom asked.

"Yeahseeyoulaterbye," Chloé called as she rushed out the door.

After a beat my parents started talking again, but their voices were quieter now. As I tried to hear what they were saying I thought about Knox and Summer. I could tell Knox really liked her when he'd started going out to lunch with her instead of his friends. Seniors were allowed to leave the school grounds for lunch, and they left together almost every day. Though that was probably easier than trying to figure out where to sit together in the cafeteria. Summer definitely wasn't popular like Knox, so I couldn't imagine him sitting with her band friends any more than I could imagine her grabbing a seat next to Spencer and the rest of the baseball bros.

I also saw the way Knox looked at her, like he'd been handed the winning lottery ticket and couldn't believe his luck. I'd seen him with other girls, looking past them while they talked and giggled into his face. With Summer, his eyes followed her every move.

I wondered if Knox and Summer were in love and what that felt like. I knew they were having sex because I'd found the box of condoms hidden in the back of his drawer in the bathroom we shared. I wondered what it was like.

I thought about Jemma Lee, my biology lab partner and wondered what it would be like to kiss her. She wrote the Arts & Culture column for the school newspaper, the *Westwood Watermark*, smelled like cherry Chapstick, and had a killer collection of Vans sneakers in all different colors and patterns.

"I started collecting them when I was twelve," Jemma had told me proudly. "I'm lucky my feet stopped growing then." She didn't seem to mind getting me as a lab partner, even though everyone else scooched their desk away from mine when the teacher announced we had to pair up. She also wasn't squeamish when we had to dissect a frog together, and didn't make fun of me when I got dizzy the first time we cut into it.

"Put your head between your legs and breathe," she said, putting her hand on my back and tipping me forward. "That's what our soccer coach tells us when we get the wind knocked out of us." I bent over and breathed, trying not to think about her hand touching my shoulder blade, which only made the dizziness worse.

"OK, I think I'm all right," I said after a minute, lifting my head and propping myself up on my lab stool. She smiled and flashed me a thumbs-up. "I really hope you weren't planning to be a doctor."

"No, a mortician," I said. "Except I hear it's a dying business."

"That's terrible," Jemma groaned, smiling.

"I know," I admitted with a grin. I smiled to myself the rest of the day and even forgot to worry about my carbon footprint or domestic terrorism for an entire class period.

Downstairs I saw my dad walking back toward the staircase where I was still sitting. I scrambled to my feet but he passed by without noticing me and headed toward his study. Only when I heard the door shut behind him did I head down into the living room.

My mom was sitting on the couch, staring into space.

"What's going on with Knox and Summer?" I asked. Her eyebrows rose just slightly. "I'm not stupid, and I'm definitely not deaf," I added.

She sighed, which she'd been doing a lot lately. "I know you're not, honey. I'm sorry. I just thought we'd wait and talk about it as a family once we had more information."

"What information? What happened?"

She patted the couch next to her. "Sit with me for a minute?"

I lowered myself warily onto the couch.

She tucked her legs up under her. "There seems to have been a... misunderstanding between your brother and Summer. They had a fight last night, and, well, Summer says your brother... took advantage of her." She glanced at me to confirm I understood what she was trying to say.

"Like he raped her?" The word tasted horrible on my tongue, like when you drink orange juice after you've brushed your teeth.

"We're not using that word," she said sharply, waving her hand as if to brush away my question. "Knox says they were drinking and they had a fight." She took a deep breath and said gently, "So that's our story."

"Our *story*?"

"That's what happened."

I had a sudden memory of standing in the backyard with

Summer one night when she was babysitting. The air was thick and lightning bugs dotted the dark grass. I'd never seen so many of them all at once. Chloé and I ran around scooping them into glass jars, catching so many that the containers glowed like flashlights. Summer stood in the middle of the lawn, her curls wild, twirling around against the twinkly backdrop. Every time she twirled by me I could smell her familiar scent of sugar and mint.

"Isn't this the most amazing thing you've ever seen?" she kept saying. At one point she reached out to squeeze my hand. "We have to remember this forever!" That was the night I fell in love with her.

Looking my mom in the eye, I couldn't stop myself from asking the question. "So we believe Knox instead of Summer?"

"Archie." It sounded like a warning.

"I'm just saying, you're the one always talking about how we should believe women. Like remember the R. Kelly documentary? And all that creepy stuff with the Hollywood guy? How is this any different?" I didn't add that lately I'd felt a weird darkness around my brother, like a trail of dark smoke that hung in the room even after he'd gone. Still, Knox was my brother. I wanted to believe him.

"Archie, Knox might not admit it, but he needs your support right now." Mom's tone was pleading, and for the first time I noticed how red her eyes were.

"OK," I said.

But it wasn't OK, not at all.

# SEVENTEEN
## KNOX

### *Sunday, 5:30 p.m.*

I closed the door to my room and flopped face down onto my bed, trying to ignore the sick feeling in my stomach and the tangled-up thoughts in my head. I couldn't believe I'd had to share the details of my sex life twice in one day. It had been bad enough at the police station, with Beau interrupting me every time I tried to talk about me and Summer until finally I just stopped trying and started answering all the questions with as few words as possible. But then to also have to talk about it with my parents—so awkward.

I picked up my phone and scrolled through the missed texts from Spencer, Jackson, and the rest of the team.

> wtf dude? where'd you go after the game?

> bro where u disappear to?

> hit me up later dude, having people at my house tonight

I sighed and swiped them away, opening up my last exchange with the only person I wanted to hear from. Summer:

> see you at Jackson and Violet's in 15?

> yup, but don't wanna stay too long. hang out just us after that?

She'd sent a row of xo's in reply.

I'd answered as many questions as I could at the police station, but there was a lot that was fuzzy. Normally I didn't drink because Coach had a zero tolerance policy and no way was I risking my spot on the team. But at Jackson's I'd let Spencer fill my water bottle with vodka and Gatorade. I figured the season was basically over, so what was I holding out for? I hoped it would help turn down the volume on that voice in my head telling me what a piece of shit I was.

I sighed and rolled over on the bed, facing my shelf of baseball trophies. Despite how many there were, I had had enough of baseball. I used to get this feeling whenever I'd walk out onto the field, like a weird sense of quiet in my head. I felt tuned in, like I'd found a frequency no one else could hear. I could size up a batter and know which pitch would knock him off balance, or sense when a runner was cheating a half step too far and pick him off before he had a chance to blink. I was unbeatable.

Then halfway through this year's season, all of a sudden I couldn't find that frequency anymore. I stepped onto the field and waited for the quiet *click* in my head as I tuned in, but all I heard was static. I'd squint and try to focus but my mind was crowded with the noise of my thoughts and secrets.

Downstairs my parents' voices rose and fell and I knew they were fighting. I could hear fragments of the conversation as their voices got louder.

"—being unreasonable... our friends... all I'm saying... talk to them... no lawyers..."

"—*you* listen... naive... if you think... know what's best, damn it..."

Then all of a sudden they got quiet and I knew they'd remembered we were all upstairs. The same old shit.

Honestly, I didn't get why they had even ended up together. They seemed so different. I mean, I'd seen their wedding pictures where they looked young and happy and my mom even looked kind of pretty. But these days she always seemed tired and stressed, and even when she was asking me about school or baseball it only ever seemed like she was half listening while the other part of her brain ran through some kind of checklist. And when my dad was around she just kind of... faded.

I got it, I mean, it was hard for anyone else to get a word in when my dad was around. And these days he seemed to *always* be around, mainly when my friends were over. He'd walk in and give Spencer and Jackson fist-bumps and slaps on the back like he was one of us. Then he'd kind of take over the room with some embarrassing dirty joke or stupid story about how buddy-buddy he is with this famous baseball player or that one. So desperate. The worst part was that my friends seemed to think he was cool.

On the shelf below my trophies all my yearbooks were lined up in order. I grabbed the one from seventh grade, my first year of junior high, and paged to Summer's picture. Her green eyes smiled up at me. I traced my finger over her long curls in the photograph. Even back then I'd sometimes wondered what it would be like to run my hands through them.

She'd signed the yearbook under her picture in small, neat handwriting. *To Knox, Thanks for being a good friend. Have an awesome summer. Your friend forever, Summer.*

I felt like I'd swallowed something rotten. I hadn't really been a good friend. When we were younger, sure. I'd memorized the Goosebumps scary stories from my books because she loved the shivery feeling she got when I told them to her, and smuggled cookies into her backpack at car pool because her mom was always on a diet and wouldn't allow them in the house.

Once junior high started, though, everything was different. It was crazy how fast the rules of who got to sit where in the cafeteria got established. Because I was tall and athletic I landed a spot at the table everyone else seemed to want to be at. But Summer ended up at the misfit table, the one made up of kids who didn't have a place anywhere else. She didn't seem to care, though, and went on painting her nails black when all the other girls did neon pink, and wearing her wild hair in a pony-tail when everyone was doing French braids.

Spencer elbowed me in the hall one day after I'd said hi to her. "Dude," he said. "Are you into that weird girl or some-thing?" From his voice I knew what the right answer was.

"Our families are friends or whatever," I said, trying to make it sound like I had nothing to do with it.

But my secret was that I liked hanging out with Summer. Whenever our families got together to barbecue, the two of us would listen to music and trade playlists. She always had the best ones, even if some of it was kind of old, like R.E.M. and Jane's Addiction. At school, though, our lives were like a failed Venn diagram with no overlap.

I put down the yearbook and stared at my iPad at the end of the bed, calling to me like it always did. I gave it a swift kick onto the floor like it was a bomb about to go off. It landed several feet clear of the bed with a dull thud. For a second I pictured taking it downstairs and smashing it on the concrete of the driveway outside.

Maybe I needed to become a monk. Monks didn't have internet, right? Or maybe I could go live somewhere where they didn't have Wi-Fi, if such a place existed. Antarctica, maybe?

My head throbbed. I lay back on my pillow and closed my eyes, but my head immediately filled with fuzzy fragments of memory from the night before. Summer and me kissing in the gazebo at the park. Me saying maybe we shouldn't date in college next year, all the while trying to keep from throwing up at the thought of being without her. The startled, wounded look on her face. Summer crying. More kissing. Me rolling on top of her. More crying, then no sound at all. The bolt of shame that went through my body like it always did after we had sex. The silence as we walked home.

I shook my head and tried to think about something else, something that didn't make me want to cry. I thought back to the day in early December when I'd watched her perform with the band at a school assembly. She'd done a solo number on the guitar while they reset the stage risers behind her for the next part of the program, an acoustic version of an Imagine Dragons' song, and she'd killed it, gotten a standing ovation and everything. I mean, it was like something you'd hear on the radio.

When the last bell of the day rang my feet took on a life of their own and propelled me toward her locker. There was a small group of kids already there, clustered around Summer. Two freshman girls gushed about her performance. Summer was super nice to them with all their squealing and carrying on. I stood nearby trying not to look awkward until everyone had left.

"Totally star-struck," I said once they were gone, shaking my head.

"Them or you?" Summer asked, tucking a ringlet behind her ear and smiling up at me.

In that moment, standing between her locker and the boys' bathroom, I realized what I should've known all along: I was in love with Summer Van Doren.

"You were amazing," I said, taking a step closer to her. She smelled sweet and minty, just like I remembered.

"Thanks." She leaned against the locker next to me. "That

means a lot coming from someone who knew me before I was famous."

I laughed. "I'm happy to be able to say I knew you when."

"You know I wasn't even supposed to perform? They were supposed to have Twinda McClary do her baton twirling routine."

"No way! They were going to make us sit through Twirling Twinda again?"

"Actually, she had a new routine and it was pretty good." Summer raised her eyebrows. "It was set to 'Party in the USA.'"

"That's my favorite song." I deadpanned. Summer laughed again and her arm brushed mine, leaving my skin tingling.

"I guess she sprained her ankle during rehearsal and they had to stick me in at the last minute."

In the quiet hallway I could hear my blood pumping in my ears like when I was on the pitching mound with the bases loaded. "Hey, um, do you want to, I mean, like, are you doing anything this weekend?" I asked.

"Yes," she said, almost interrupting me. "I mean, no. But yes to whatever you're asking. That is, if you're asking."

I smiled. "I'm definitely asking."

A noise from the corner of my bedroom snapped me back into the present. I shot to a seated position as I looked around. Archie was standing in my doorway.

"Would you stop spying on me?" I snapped. He flinched, and I immediately felt like a jerk, but I didn't soften my face or say I was sorry.

He stared at me for a long moment, like he was trying to see inside me. "Mom said to tell you dinner's ready." Then he turned and left me alone.

# EIGHTEEN

## EDEN

### *Sunday, 5:30 p.m.*

I stepped away from the window to see Witt descending the stairs, followed by Summer. Her pale face was scrubbed clean and without her usual black eyeliner she looked younger than her eighteen years. Her long curls had been twisted into a bun, several of them already escaping and trailing down her back. She wore black leggings and an old Princeton sweatshirt of Witt's that was baggy on her narrow frame.

"Hi," I said, my voice catching. She stared at the floor.

Witt cleared his throat, looking past me. "I'm going to take Summer down to the police station to give a statement." He paused, and I knew he was waiting for me to say something; to react, or insist on going along.

I closed my eyes and pictured the dirty linoleum and faded yellow walls of the room in my hometown police station where I'd sat waiting for help that never arrived. My mom had insisted we report what happened to me, her maternal instinct surfacing for the briefest of moments. Giving in to her wishes was my biggest regret.

I opened my eyes and looked at Witt. "Do we need a lawyer or something?"

His eyes met mine for a split second before he looked away. "I am one, remember? At least enough of one for this situation. Then we'll see." His tone was not unkind, and relief flooded my body. I wasn't used to fighting with Witt.

We'd met in New York at one of the parties the modeling agency sent me to, a plum assignment because of the cocaine in the bathrooms and the rich guys at the bar. And though I was used to pretending I had a more sophisticated pedigree than community college dropout, with Witt I never pretended to be anyone other than who I was. I'd freely shared the details of my colorful childhood with him, from the cans of Vienna sausage I'd eaten cold when our utilities were turned off, to the time I'd gotten detention for setting off the school fire alarm while smoking in the janitor's closet. Though through all my story-telling I'd alluded only in broad strokes to what happened with my teacher. And even though I'd often thought about telling him, somehow I could never get the words out. As much as Witt loved me, there were certain pictures I wasn't ready to paint for him.

"You're really not coming?" he asked, his gaze evaluating me in a way I hadn't felt before. Like it was some kind of test.

I looked at the ground as the familiar mix of guilt and self-loathing began to swirl in my chest. "I—I'll wait here."

Witt made a terse sound in his throat and he and Summer turned to leave. My chest went hot and I had the urge to grab them and pull them back to me, like I was saving them from boarding a plane I knew was going to crash. But when I looked back up they were already out the door.

I watched from the window as the car backed down the driveway and turned onto the street. I started at Lorrie's house again. I'd never had a female friend before her, not in the true sense of the word. The only bridesmaids at my wedding were

Witt's two sisters and my roommate at the time, a fellow model who stole twenty dollars from my purse from time to time but also did her own dishes and didn't bring guys home, so I never brought it up.

In my experience women were either jealous of me or they wanted something from me, like an introduction to one of Witt's rich friends or clients, or to borrow the clothes I was sometimes gifted on gigs. I thought things might be different when we moved to Atlanta for Witt's job, but the moms I met at the playground were just the same—smiling with their eyes while asking pointed questions to help them figure out where I fit in the Mountaindale hierarchy.

Lorrie was different. She wore me down with her frankness and self-deprecating humor. Also she made great margaritas. Before I knew it we were spending every day together at each other's houses. We fed the kids an infinity loop of snacks and counted the minutes until we could put them down for naps and collapse in the living room to greedily catch up on the decades of each other's lives we'd unfairly missed.

Staring at the ceiling it dawned on me that I might no longer have a best friend. An empty ache started in my chest, radiating outward until it filled my whole body. Outside of my family, Lorrie was the only person I truly trusted. Or had trusted. Was it already past tense?

The emptiness inside felt like it might swallow me. I tried to take slow, deep breaths the way Dr. Wright had taught me in therapy. When that didn't work I grabbed the remote and turned on Bravo to zone out instead.

The sky outside had turned dark when the sound of car doors slamming in the garage made me sit up. I looked up in time to see Summer walk in and disappear up the stairs to her room.

Following the sound of clinking glass to the kitchen I found Witt at the counter pouring himself a Scotch.

"How did it go?" I asked softly.

His eyes were red-rimmed and wet when he turned around. "I'll kill that piece of shit if I ever see him," he said, his free hand balled into a fist. "What he did to her—"

"Stop." I held my hand up to my ears. "I don't want the details."

He stared at me. "What is wrong with you, Eden? This is our daughter we're talking about. We're the adults here, and you're acting like you're the one who's too fragile to deal with it?"

"You don't understand," I said. I felt the bile rising in my throat the same way it had every time the teacher had locked the classroom door and beckoned to me.

"No, *you* don't understand. Half the detective's questions were about the hospital and why Summer didn't get the exam; why she didn't want any evidence gathered. Basically he made it clear that, if it's a case of he-said-she-said, we have almost zero chance of prosecuting."

I felt the tears start again and shook them from my eyes, disgusted with myself for being so weak.

"Look," said Witt, and I heard his voice soften a shade. "It's been an awful day. I'm still angry about the way you made a decision—a huge one—without consulting me. But right now we need to figure this out together. For Summer. I made some calls while we were waiting and found out Ed hired this guy, Beau Sykes. He specializes in sexual harassment, assault, domestic violence, anything shady, really. Mainly for high-profile people, like athletes. I don't know how Ed would know him other than through working with the pro baseball players. I'm guessing at least one of those guys has a lawsuit hanging around. Anyway, they apparently call Beau "the Python" because he suffocates the accuser with threats and blackmail—

anything he can use for leverage—until they sign an NDA. Nothing ever goes to court."

I shuddered. "That doesn't sound good."

Witt set his jaw. "It's not." *And it's your fault*, I could tell he wanted to add.

"I'm sorry." I bowed my head and backed away. "I'm going to check on Summer."

Witt gave a frustrated sigh and turned away from me.

Upstairs, Summer lay face down on her bed, her face buried in a pillow. Her room still looked largely as it had when she was a little girl, with the pale pink valances and matching skirted vanity table I'd picked out. The posters on the wall had changed over time, most recently a picture of Lin-Manuel Miranda and the rest of the cast from *Hamilton*.

She lay facing away from me. "I told the police everything," she said, before I could even ask. "How we went to a party and then walked to the park." Her tone was flat. "And that we were drinking."

"At the Doyles? Where was Caroline—Mrs. Doyle?"

"She was there, but they were upstairs like usual. We were in the rec room downstairs like always, and they never come down."

"So this wasn't the first time you were drinking at Violet's house, unchaperoned."

She turned her head briefly to look at me. "I don't want to get anyone in trouble."

"No one's getting in trouble, I promise." I tried a calmer tone. I would deal with Caroline later. "How much did you drink, sweetheart?"

She gave a sharp laugh. "You sound like the police. They only asked me that like, ten times."

I sank down on the bed next to her and felt her flinch at my nearness. "Summer, did you tell him no?"

"They asked me that, too."

"But did you?"

She was quiet. Then when she turned her face to me for the first time I could see the tears on her face. "I tried, Mom," she whispered. "I promise, I tried."

I gathered her against my shoulder. "It's not your fault," I said. I needed her to know from the beginning what I'd spent years learning in Dr. Wright's office.

As I rubbed my daughter's back I felt a rush of rage surge through me like a levy bursting. Fucking Knox Keller. I knew the type. Mr. Baseball, Homecoming Court, the golden boy who's had everything handed to him and has never heard the word no. But I would make sure this didn't take my daughter down. I just needed to keep it from getting out, to keep her safe from anyone using it against her in any way.

"Summer, have you told anyone else what happened? Violet? Any of your other friends?"

She lifted her head and gave it a small shake. "Mom, what's going to happen?"

"Shh," I whispered. "I'm going to take care of everything."

# NINETEEN
## LORRIE

### *Sunday, 6:30 p.m.*

The only one who seemed to be eating was Chloé. Everyone else's plates were mostly still full, the salmon and lentils I'd made pushed around into various piles.

"Chloé, how was swim practice today?" I asked, my voice falsely bright. I'd been encouraging her to branch out and focus on more than just dance in the interest of being well-rounded.

"Good!" she said, snapping the hot pink scrunchie on her wrist. "I beat Madison in the two hundred freestyle." She looked around the table for approval from her father and brothers and was met by blank faces.

"Good for you," I said, louder than I'd meant to, a smile pasted on my face. "I know you've been working hard, sweetheart."

"I need to be at school early tomorrow for a thing." Knox spoke without looking up. "So someone else needs to give Archie a ride."

My breath caught in my throat. "I wasn't thinking you'd be going to school."

"Why wouldn't he?" Ed looked up, uttering his first words of the meal. "He should do everything just like he normally does. Just like Beau said."

"Who's Beau?" asked Chloé. Her bottom lip poked out in concerned curiosity as she looked from me to Ed with wide eyes.

"Yeah," echoed Archie, his eyes on his brother. "Who's Beau?"

"No one." I waved my hand and gave Ed a sharp look. "And regardless of what anyone else says, I don't think school is a good idea."

Ed set down his fork, his face growing dark. "He's going to school."

Knox looked back and forth between the two of us. "Mom, it's OK," he said, sensing the tension. "I want to go to school, really. I don't want to miss out on the last week of senior year."

"He's going." Ed turned his attention back to his plate, his tone final.

I choked back an angry retort, knowing I'd been defeated. But why? When had we decided Ed had the final say in our family? I reached over and squeezed Knox's arm. All I wanted to do was keep him right next where I could protect him, for the rest of his life if I could. If I could have swaddled him in a blanket and rocked him on my lap, I would have. Knox had been the cuddliest of my children when he was younger, snuggling on the couch with his head on my shoulder right up until he became a teenager. Now the most I could hope for from him was a half-smile and a shoulder bump from time to time. These days his face had become an impenetrable mask, and I spent a lot of my time wondering what was going on inside his head— and his heart.

"I'm volunteering at Chloé's school tomorrow morning so you'll have to drive Archie," I said to Ed, more aggressively than I needed to. I set my napkin down and waited for him to protest. Our eyes met for a split second and he pressed his lips together.

"Fine," he said, his voice curt.

"I need two big pieces of poster board for tomorrow," announced Chloé. "For science class."

"Chlo, it's almost seven p.m. on Sunday night," I said, unable to hide the irritation in my voice. "Why didn't you tell me earlier?"

"I forgot," she shrugged, snapping her scrunchie again.

"Can you take her?" I asked Ed. The last thing I wanted to do was get in the car and leave the warmth and safety of my house. That suddenly felt akin to poking my head out of my cave into the dangerous jungle. Also, I was tired of everyone assuming I'd take care of their every last-minute need, like my time belonged to them.

It pained me that none of the kids ever remembered me working. They'd never seen me dressed in a suit going head to head with a judge, or celebrating a victory for a client. The death of my career had happened in small increments that added up quickly while I was busy soothing tantrums and packing lunches. An extended maternity leave with Archie had turned into two years, then add another baby, because what's one more, and in the blink of an eye I had found myself with a fifteen-year stint as a stay-at-home-mom.

"I promised I'd check in on one of the guys who had his ACL done last week," said Ed, pushing back his chair. "In fact, I'm late." Wiping his mouth, he dropped his napkin on his chair and headed for his study. My fingers tensed like they wanted something to strangle and I started to call after him.

"Can we go to Target?" Chloé interrupted me. "Isabella just got these cool tights there. They have glitter on them!" She bounced in her chair with excitement.

"I've got homework," Knox said. He stood and pulled his phone out of his pocket.

"Remember, no texting anyone about anything from today, OK?" I said, rubbing my temples where a headache had begun. "You too." I nodded at Archie.

"Like he has any friends to text," Knox muttered.

"At least I'm not wanted by the police," Archie retorted.

"Who's wanted by the police?" Chloé asked, looking from one brother to the other.

"Only in your lame video games," Knox shot back at Archie.

"Oh, like you're so—"

"Enough!" I shouted, banging my hand on the table hard enough to make the silverware rattle. Three sets of eyes widened and turned in my direction. "Enough," I said again. Standing, I surveyed my children, all in various states of shock at my outburst. A wave of fatigue crashed over me and I felt a sudden urge to be somewhere very far away where no one needed anything from me.

I pointed to the table. "Tonight," I said, "you can wash your own damn dishes." I grabbed my phone off the kitchen island and stomped into the living room. I'd silenced the ringer during dinner and a glance at the text notification on my screen made me freeze.

Eden.

I swiped open the text.

Hey, it read. Have you told anyone?

My hands trembled as I responded, feeling every emotion at once. Angry at her for believing Knox could do something so terrible. Overjoyed to hear from my friend. Unsure what to say to her. Scared to think about the future.

The police talked to Knox. But otherwise no.

Three dots appeared.

> They talked to Summer too. But we're still
> trying to keep it private. For her sake.

> Of course. Can we talk?

Despite the trip to the police station I still held out hope that if Eden and I just sat down together, somehow we'd figure out how to make this all go away. Three gray dots appeared and remained on the screen for a long time. I held my breath.

> I'll be outside in 5.

A dizzying relief fizzed through my body. Everything would be OK.

Five minutes later I pushed open my front door and walked across the street. There was no sign of Eden. Then her garage door rumbled open.

"In here," a low voice called. I walked toward the garage but still didn't see her. "In *here*," she said again, and I saw she was in her Escalade, motioning for me to join her.

"Are we going somewhere?" I said, climbing up into the passenger seat. She sighed.

"No, I just don't want anyone to see us together. You know how people talk."

"Do we need code names or secret hand signs?" I said, trying for a lame joke. She didn't smile. I cleared my throat and tried again. "How are you?"

She looked at me, disbelief and anger on her face. "How *am* I? My daughter was just subjected to ninety minutes of police questioning about what she was wearing on Saturday night, how many times she'd had sex before with how many people, and how much she'd had to drink that night and whether that could have 'confused' her. And you want to know how I *am*?"

My shoulders slumped forward and I shook my head. "I'm sorry. I just meant—"

"You know what? This was a bad idea," she cut me off and reached for the door handle. "You should go."

"No." I reached my hand toward her arm but stopped just short of touching her. "Please. I mean it, I'm sorry Summer had to go through that. That's awful, it truly is. But I asked how you are because I'm your friend and I care. I will always care."

She let out a short, bitter laugh. "I'm really fucking shitty," she said, turning to look at me. "That's how I am."

I sighed and tipped my head back against the seat. "Yeah. Me too."

We sat in silence for a minute. A torrent of words swirled through my head but I couldn't form any of them into a sentence. At least not the right sentence.

"You should go," Eden said again. She leaned her head back against the headrest and closed her eyes, her face tired. The last thing I wanted to do was leave her, but I nodded and reached for the door handle.

My body was most of the way out of the car when I turned back. "Wait," I said. "What happens now?"

"I don't know," she said. She didn't turn her head and her eyes remained shut. I hesitated, then closed the door behind me.

# TWENTY

## SUMMER

### *Sunday, 7 p.m.*

I stared up at the dark ceiling in my room, barely able to make out the crack I'd always thought looked like a rabbit with one ear flopped over. I rolled over to check my phone again. Two more texts from Violet.

> up for a run tonight?

Then an hour later:

> hello?? did u lose ur phone again?

There were also a slew of messages from Jules, all pleading for me to let her know how I was doing, but I couldn't bring myself to reply—mostly because I didn't know what to say.

There were no texts from him. I didn't expect any, but it still made my heart ache, for some reason.

Though I'd been in love with Knox as long as I could remember, I never thought I'd actually be his girlfriend. We were close as kids, whispering scary stories to each other on the floor of his room late at night when I slept over, and holding lemonade stands together whenever we wanted money for new stuff (Pokémon cards for him, rainbow loom supplies for me.) Knox always did our sales pitch while I took care of the money. But then we got to junior high and everything changed.

My phone dinged with an incoming text.

> Do you need anything? I'm right downstairs if
> you need me.

I sighed and tossed the phone aside. My mom had literally *just* checked on me fifteen minutes ago when Dad and I got home from the police station. It had been beyond awful to have to have him in the conference room with me while I recounted as many of the humiliating details as I could remember from last night. I'd wanted to ask him to leave, but he had that look on his face—his Papa Bear look, I called it. I saw it a lot when I was younger and someone would foul me on the soccer field, and once when a guy whistled at me on our family beach trip, not realizing my dad was two feet away. It was a look that said he would do anything to protect me. I didn't have the energy to take that away from him at the police station.

I pulled my guitar up off the floor. I always slept with it next to my bed in case I got a song idea in the middle of the night. I was first violin in the school orchestra, but guitar was what I really loved.

I started strumming the song I'd been working on, then stopped. Was it weird that I was just sitting here in my room with my guitar like I'd be doing on a normal Sunday night? My eyes were puffy and dry from all the crying I'd done earlier, but right now I just felt... blank. Like I was only killing time until... I didn't know exactly what. It was like I was a cardboard stand-in for my own life.

I didn't want to think about Knox, but my brain was used to

him taking up ninety percent of my mental space so it went there automatically. What was he doing right now? Was he thinking about me, too? Did he hate me now? Had he heard me last night when I'd said no, or had I only whispered it while I cried with his body on top of me, my lungs emptying as his weight pinned me down.

I felt a dull pressure in my head, like being on an airplane coming in for a landing. I put my hands over my ears and pressed, hoping to make it go away but it only got worse. I was breathing fast now, and sweating even though my skin felt clammy. Being alone in my room no longer seemed like such a good idea.

I picked my phone up from where I'd tossed it and paused, my finger hovering near Knox's name in my recent texts. Then I tapped on Violet's name.

> really need to talk. can you come over?

A minute later my phone dinged. with a response.

> be right there.

Ten minutes later there was a soft knock at my door and my mom poked her head in. "Violet is here, sweetie. I told her you weren't feeling well but she said you asked her to come over?" I nodded and my mom inhaled deeply, as if trying to be patient. "Sweetie, your father and I agreed it would be best to keep things, um, private for now, so I don't think—"

"I need to talk to someone who isn't you." I hadn't meant my voice to sound as cutting as it did. My mother flinched. She stood in my doorframe for a moment, her eyes fixed on me but focused far away.

"All right," she nodded finally. "That makes sense. I

just... please ask Violet not to... share anything you tell her. It's a legal issue."

I nodded and pulled my knees into my chest, wrapping my arms around them. A minute later I heard Violet's feet on the stairs and the door opening.

"Whoa," she said, taking in the darkness of my room. "Are you like, holding a séance in here or something?"

I laughed in spite of myself and reached over to turn on the bedside lamp. Violet definitely wasn't the best friend my mom would have chosen for me—she would have preferred someone who was more focused on being elected to Homecoming Court and less concerned with dismantling the patriarchy and getting into law school. But we'd been friends since junior high, and despite our different friend groups—I hung out with the orchestra nerds and she ran with the kids who wore statement glasses and spent her time running the *Westwood Watermark*, school paper—we'd slept over at each other's houses at least once a week for years. Or we used to, until I got so busy with Knox. I felt a pang of guilt.

"Thanks for coming over," I said. "I'm—I'm sorry I've been such a bad friend." Tears stung the corners of my eyes where the skin was now raw.

Violet looked mystified by my sudden attack of emotion. "What in the world are you talking about, Van Doren?" she said in her no-nonsense way.

I sucked in a shuddering breath. "Knox and I broke up last night."

Violet's eyes went wide. "What? Why? What happened?"

I shook my head, unsure where to start. "We also—I mean he—" The words caught in my throat and my breath sped up again until I was panting the way Bailey did after she hauled herself across the living room floor.

"Summer? Are you OK?"

I shook my head. "At the park, he didn't stop when I... I didn't want to, but..."

Understanding swept across Violet's face. "He *raped* you?" She whispered the word.

I blinked and forced myself to nod. "The police said it's a serious accusation to make."

"The *police*? Oh my God, Summer, why didn't you call me?"

"I didn't really know what to do." I felt like I was shrinking, becoming so small I might vanish into the tangle of my bedclothes.

Violet reached over and hugged me so fiercely I ended up with a chunk of her long, dark hair in my mouth. My arms felt limp around her, though. The tears had stopped and I slipped back into being my blank self, empty and exhausted from my revelation.

Knox and I had gotten friendlier again once junior high was over and the dust had settled from the scramble for popularity that felt like a game of musical chairs. I'd catch a ride to school with him once in a while if Violet couldn't drive me, and sometimes we'd talk if we found ourselves in line together in the cafeteria or at a school assembly. Those interactions always left me flushed and with a fizzy feeling inside, but I assumed he just saw me as his childhood friend. Until the day he'd asked me out.

It had happened just like I always imagined it would: him coming toward me in the hall and everything else fading away. At first I wondered if it was another one of my daydreams, but I could smell the faint odor of leftover fish sticks wafting up from the cafeteria and feel the pimple forming on my chin so I knew it was real.

Violet was pacing my room now, her fingers fluffing her blunt bangs like she always did when she was thinking. Two scarlet circles had formed on her cheeks. "Have you talked to the police?"

"My dad took me to the police station earlier," I said.

"And you're pressing charges, right?"

"I'm not sure that's how it works?" A small pit had formed in my stomach. Talking to Violet about it made everything feel so real. "I guess it's the attorney general who decides whether to press charges? Like, if there's enough evidence, or something like that." I felt hazy on the details. Toward the end of the police interview I hadn't felt like I was even present in the room anymore, like it was just my body sitting there in the hard plastic chair but my mind was somewhere else.

"Got, it." She continued her pacing. "So we need to focus on other things in the meantime. Immediate action. We'll petition the school for an assembly on toxic masculinity and rape culture. Write letters to the attorney general. Hold a rally. We can reach out to our state congressional representatives. Maybe we can even get your name on some sort of bill they could propose. Let me do some research on—"

"No." The word came out louder than I meant it to.

Violet stopped ticking things off on her fingers and looked at me as if for an instant she'd forgotten I was there.

I wrapped my arms around myself in a tight hug and sank down onto my bed. "I don't want to do any of that. I just want to pretend it never happened. I'm sorry I even told you." And I was. The relief I'd felt at telling her what happened had vanished. Now I just felt suffocated.

She put her hands on her hips. "Summer, you can't just let him get away with this."

"Enough, Violet!" The sharp, guttural growl of my voice stunned both of us into silence. We stared at each other for a second, then she crossed the room and sat next to me on the bed. She wrapped her arm around my shoulder and tipped her head to touch mine.

"I'm so, so sorry, Sum-Sum," she whispered, using my childhood nickname. "I'm so sorry this happened to you. Are you OK?" She pulled back to look at me.

I was silent for a minute, considering. "I don't actually know," I whispered back.

I'd told Violet what I could remember about the night before, but there was a lot I wasn't ready to share about everything that had come before.

# TWENTY-ONE

## JULES

### *One month before*

When the doorbell rang at five thirty I assumed it was an Amazon package. Summer wasn't due to babysit until six. Then it rang again. Glancing out the window, I saw it was Summer.

"I'm early," she said when I opened the door. "Is that OK?"

"You know you can always come over whenever," I said, leading her into the kitchen where Audrey was sitting on the floor, busy unloading all the Tupperware from a drawer.

"Phew," Summer said. "I had to get out of the house. My mom is making me mental." I made a sympathetic noise and perked up my ears. I loved hearing Summer complain about her mom.

"Do tell," I said, rubbing my hands together like an evil witch in a fairy tale. Summer slung her backpack over a chair and sank onto the floor next to Audrey and poked her belly. Audrey rewarded her with a giggle and handed her a plastic lid.

"She keeps trying to take me shopping for college."

"And that's a bad thing because you... hate having new clothes you don't have to pay for?" I confirmed, puzzled. "You know when you're an adult you have to, like, take yourself shopping, right? It's super lame."

Summer ignored my sarcasm and sighed. "She won't shut up about how I probably want to 'update' my wardrobe for college. To have some things that are, you know, a little more 'chic and stylish.'" She made air quotes with her fingers and imitated Eden's throaty voice. "It's *Princeton* after all. And you never get a second chance to make a first impression." She made a face and gestured to her black shirt and black cutoff jean shorts. "She's basically positive I'll never make any friends looking like this. Oh, and she also told me she'd pay for one of those Brazilian hair straightening treatments and a makeup tutorial." Her shoulders slumped and I thought I saw tears in her eyes as she looked down.

"Hey," I said, patting her shoulder. "I'm sure your mom thinks you're beautiful just the way you are. I mean, I think Audrey's perfect even when she has boogers smeared on her face—which is basically like, all the time."

Summer rolled her eyes. "My mom was a model, did you know that? Before she met my dad. There's a box under their bed of all the magazines and stuff she was in."

"Oh, wow, I didn't know."

"She must be so disappointed to have gotten me for a daughter." Her voice caught. "Here, let me do that." She stood up and moved toward the kitchen island where I was cutting a pear into small bites for Audrey. I waved her off.

"I'm sure she doesn't think that." I had an odd sensation of feeling motherly toward Summer for the first time.

Audrey crawled after Summer and held her arms up to her. "Oh she does," Summer said, bending to scoop up my daughter. "Like, when will she accept that I'm never going to fit into some Homecoming Queen Barbie mold?"

"There's no way your mom is disappointed in you." I

couldn't believe I was defending Eden. But, like me, she was a mom, and I knew how deep that love ran.

Summer sighed as she held Audrey close. "I know she thinks I'm wasting my time with the violin and the guitar. Like I should be trying out for cheer squad instead."

"So really, Cheerleader Barbie, not Homecoming Queen Barbie," I said.

Summer managed a weak smile. "Same thing, right?"

I cocked my head. "Does your mom go to your orchestra concerts?"

"Yeah, she never misses that stuff."

I raised my eyebrows. "Then maybe she isn't so disappointed after all." It was the first time I'd felt closer in experience to Eden than I had to Summer.

Summer allowed another small smile. She picked up a piece of pear and Audrey opened her mouth to be fed like a baby bird. She giggled and her face brightened.

Summer focused on feeding Audrey while I packed up my textbook and laptop. After a couple of minutes she cleared her throat. "Hey, um, when did you lose your virginity?" she asked.

I choked on the sip of water I'd just taken. Summer and I had covered a lot of ground hanging out the past few weeks, but this was definitely new territory.

"Um, I'll take extremely personal questions for four hundred dollars, Alex," I said, but Summer didn't laugh. I cleared my throat and turned to face her. "I was nineteen," I said. "Why?"

"Because sex is like, the *thing* this year. Like, I mean, people have been doing it forever but no one talked about it because then you'd get called a slut. But all of a sudden it's like you're lame if you're *not* doing it."

"And you're... doing it? Not doing it? Blink once for yes, twice for no."

Summer looked down as if she was studying the bite-sized

pieces of cheese and avocado in Audrey's bowl. "No. But I'm *thinking* about doing it."

I breathed a sigh of relief. "You have lots of time," I said. "You don't have to rush into anything."

Summer rolled her eyes. "I swear my mom has said that exact same thing to me." She wiped a smear of avocado off Audrey's cheek. "Were you in love your first time?"

I snorted, thinking of the fumbled encounter with my music school roommate's friend. "Not even close. But I guess I kind of wish I had been."

"Why?"

I paused, thinking about how being with Paul had changed my whole definition of what good sex was. "I think it would have been more fun that way."

"Oh." She twisted the earring in her right ear, a tiny skull and crossbones. "So, how do you know when you're in love?"

I chewed my lip and considered the question. "I think if you have to ask the question, you're not."

When I got home from class later I saw the TV on through the window but I didn't see Summer's head leaning back onto the cushion. I hoped she hadn't had to go upstairs to soothe Audrey. She was in the middle of a particularly exhausting sleep regression.

When I entered the house I heard a faint grunting noise. Turning the corner into the living room, the couch came into view. On it lay a boy with his pants around his ankles, his eyes closed and face contorted. Above him on all fours was Summer, wearing only her underwear, her head moving up and down over the boy's crotch. His fingers were buried in her hair, pressing her face to his body.

The boy grunted. "That's how you do it. You know you like being my little slut."

My keys slipped from my hand and clattered onto the wood floor and my hand flew up to half cover my eyes. Summer's head shot up, her body following.

"Ow!" cried the boy. "What the—"

"Jules!" Summer grabbed for her shirt, nearly tumbling off the couch in the process. I took a step backward, almost falling over myself.

"Shit." The boy scrambled to pull up his pants. Both of them shot to their feet and Summer tugged her shirt down over her midsection. The boy stood silent and motionless as she thrust one leg into her pants, then hopped on one foot while struggling with the other.

"This is, um, Knox." Finally getting her second leg through her pants, she yanked them up and gestured to the boy.

"Hi." I wondered what I was supposed to do in this situation. Introduce myself and get out a third ice cream bowl? Grab a kitchen knife and run him off? I was definitely leaning toward the latter.

"I should go," he muttered.

I stood mutely as he walked past me to the front door. I heard it creak open and close again with a thud. I turned to Summer. "Um, what the hell—"

"Please," she cut me off, her eyes filled with tears. "Don't tell my mom."

# TWENTY-TWO

## KNOX

### *Sunday, 8 p.m.*

I bounced the basketball twice, then bent my knees and let it arc through the air toward the hoop. It clanged off the rim, the third shot in a row I'd missed. I swore under my breath.

"Get it together, Keller," I muttered, feeling a surge of anger. About what, I wasn't exactly sure. Maybe the fact that my mom had forced us to sit down and have dinner like nothing was wrong, like we were still the perfect family she wanted us to be. Maybe about the look Archie had given me on the stairs earlier when he'd asked me if Summer was OK, like he already thought I was some kind of criminal. Maybe that I'd fucked everything up last night with the only person who really mattered to me. Maybe all of it.

I tried so hard to get my head straight. What the hell had happened between me and Summer? I knew she'd be hurt when I brought up seeing other people in college, which is why I'd been putting it off. I couldn't tell her it had nothing to do with her. That sounded so lame. But it was true. *I* was the problem. I didn't even want to see other people, I just wanted to figure out how to stop being so fucked up.

Now, though, I wanted to tell her everything. I needed her to know the truth.

I had to see her.

I set the basketball down and glanced through the large picture window at the living room. It was empty. I made my way down our driveway, hoping I looked like I was going out for a casual stroll. Summer's house was across the street but her bedroom was around the back. I glanced behind me as I crept up the dark driveway. A motion light went on and I bolted for the shadows, my heart thudding like a machine gun.

Keeping my footsteps light, I walked through the open gate and into the backyard. Flattening myself against a big tree at the side of the yard, I looked up at her bedroom window. It was dark.

My heart deflated. I pulled out my phone. I wanted to text her, but it felt like a wall had gone up between us and I didn't know how to break it back down. The screen glowed for a second, showing a red battery icon, and then went dark. Shit. I tried to power it back on it sat lifeless in my hand.

I stared back up at her window. "Summer!" I whispered hoarsely. "Summer!"

It sounds cheesy, but once we started hanging out for real it felt like we had always been meant for each other. Spending time with her was like finding a release valve on the pressure cooker of my life. I realized for the first time how exhausting it was to be the Knox Keller everyone else knew. But with Summer I could relax and let down my guard.

The problem was that she thought I was a good person. Which meant there were certain things I could never tell her. For starters, that I was jealous my brother got to see a shrink and talk about whatever was bothering him. I wasn't supposed to know about that or the pills, but my parents' late-night fights about Archie weren't exactly quiet. Hearing them trade insults through the wall sealed it for me; there was only room in our family for one damaged child. No matter how bad things got, no matter how much I tossed and turned at night or felt sick with shame about my secret, I knew I had to keep pretending everything was fine.

"Summer!" I called more loudly in the direction of her window. I looked around me for something I could throw at it. I grabbed a stick that was by my feet. Drawing my arm back behind me like I was going to throw a pitch, I released it in a perfect arc upward. It bounced off her window and fell back to the ground.

The creak of a door opening startled me. I jumped back, hugging the tree. Mrs. Shulman walked out of her back door holding a bag of trash. She headed for the garbage bin, which was only feet from where I stood on the other side of the low fence, crouched behind the tree. I held my breath. No doubt she already thought I was a total creep after catching me on her couch with my dick out. I could feel my face burn with shame even thinking about it now.

Summer had started kissing me the minute I got to the Shulman's house that night. She pulled me down onto the couch, pulling her shirt over her head and unhooking her bra. Warning bells went off in my head and I scooted away from her.

"What is it?" she asked, crossing her arms in front of her bare chest. I tried not to stare at her perfect boobs. "What don't you like about me?"

"That's not it," I said.

"Then why don't you... want me? Am I bad at this?"

"What? Oh my God, no. Just, no." I groaned and put my face in my hands.

"I mean, I know you have a lot more experience than me, but if you could just tell me what you want me to do... I just want to do it right."

"Hey." I grabbed her hand. "You're doing everything right, I promise."

"Then why don't you want to... be with me?"

I stared at the creamy skin of her naked shoulder and her bright green eyes, now full of tears. I knew I didn't deserve her. I also knew that if she knew about the dark things I did, the way watching naked women on their knees and backs be told what to do by men who called them sluts and other names turned me on, she'd think so too.

"It's complicated," I said, squeezing her hand. "I just... I'm nervous, I guess." It was as close to the truth as I could get.

"Well, let's be nervous together." She smiled and her fingers inched toward my zipper. I felt myself harden and a moment later her head was between my legs. Fear washed over me and my erection began to wilt. And then the shame came as I focused on the images that normally helped; women being held down, their hair pulled as they were called dirty names. I pushed my hips up against her face and grabbed for her hair as I let myself fall further into the fantasy.

"Deeper," I groaned. I felt her gag slightly but I kept my fingers laced through her hair and her face pressed close to my body. I ground against her face, picking up speed. I screwed my eyes shut, unable to look at her while I repeated the awful words I'd heard in the videos. And then Mrs. Shulman showed up.

I'd sprinted home from the Shulmans' house like someone was chasing me, terrified of what would happen next. Mrs. Shulman would call my mom, or Summer's mom, or some face-less authority and report me for being a sicko. Or maybe she'd tell the whole world. What was wrong with me? Why did I need the dark, dirty thoughts to feel good?

Mrs. Shulman let the lid of the trash bin fall closed with a loud thud and brushed off her hands. The light came on in Summer's room and her face appeared in the window. I wanted to call her name again but strangled the word in my throat as Mrs. Shulman looked around. Then slowly she turned and walked back inside.

The light went back off in Summer's room. I cursed under my breath and hunted for another stick. My aim was off this time and it bounced off the siding of the house next to the window. I threw another, which grazed the windowsill. Then another, which hit the very bottom of the window.

I held my breath and waited, but her light stayed off.

# TWENTY-THREE

## EDEN

### *Monday, 7:30 a.m.*

Witt and I moved around the kitchen in silence, him grinding coffee beans and me measuring collagen powder into the blender for my smoothie. Our normally well-choreographed morning routine felt stilted. We kept bumping elbows or both reaching for the refrigerator door at the same time. At our feet Bailey scooted around on her two good legs, knocking us both off balance.

He'd come to bed late but I was still awake, staring into the darkness, my mind whirring despite the Xanax I'd taken. I'd thought about reaching for him, but just as I stretched out my fingers he rolled onto his side away from me. Minutes later I heard the deep rhythm of his breath.

When I woke up my Apple watch informed me I'd gotten a mere five hours and fourteen minutes of restful sleep. Disgusted, I took it off and tossed it into a bathroom drawer.

Now, in the kitchen, Witt held out a mug of coffee. "Here," he said.

Looking up, I realized I'd been staring into space, my hand

poised over the blender, holding the measuring cup. I reached for the mug. "Thanks," I said, hopeful that maybe his anger toward me was abating. Unlike me, Witt didn't hold grudges.

The alarm on my phone sounded, letting me know it was time to wake Summer up for school.

Witt looked at my phone. "She's not going, right?" he asked.

"No chance in hell," I said, silencing the alarm. He nodded.

Lately Summer had been riding to school with Knox, or on mornings when she didn't I drove her since student parking at Westwood was limited. For a moment I wondered what the scene at Lorrie's house looked like this morning. Did everything feel as confusing and awkward as it did at mine? Our conversation in the garage had left me feeling drained and hopeless. It was the first time I'd ever not known what to say to my best friend. The first time I'd ever questioned whether she *was* my best friend.

"I set up a couple of legal consults for this morning," Witt said. "To make sure we're fully informed about our options. The first one is at ten."

I suppressed a shudder at the idea of sitting across from a lawyer discussing the one thing I'd promised myself would never happen to my daughter. "I just—I don't think I... can you just fill me in later?" I said.

Witt flattened inward like he'd just taken a punch. "Really, Eden?" he asked. "This is important." He never called me by my name, preferring "baby" or "sweetheart." The formality of it stung.

I brought the coffee mug to my lips and let the hot steam hit my face while I tried to find the right words. "I know it is," I said. "But I can't. I just can't."

"So I'm on my own here?" His eyebrows knit together in angry confusion.

"It's not like that."

Witt's forehead creased and he opened his mouth to

respond, then shook his head and stayed quiet. He took a final swig of coffee and, setting his mug in the sink, sniffed the air around him. I smelled it the same time he did. "I'll go change her diaper," I sighed, set down my coffee and picked up Bailey.

Witt shook his head. "Seriously, how many more years are you going to do this?"

I petted Bailey's silky head. "It's not her fault. But she's not going to last forever. Then I promise we'll get a dog with a fully functioning bowel system. A puppy, maybe."

"No more dogs." He shook his head and checked his watch. "I need to get going. I have a meeting at the office and then... well, let me know if you change your mind about coming, OK?

"OK," I said. The disappointed expression on his face hurt more than angry words ever could have.

"Bye, love you," he said, leaning forward to kiss me.

"Love you, too."

Both the words and the kiss were perfunctory but we both knew they still meant something.

I popped in my earbuds while I cleaned up the kitchen. Clicking away from my usual true crime podcast, I selected a celebrity gossip one instead, losing myself in the world of multi-million-dollar divorces and rehab meltdowns.

After that, I walked back and forth outside Summer's room, willing her to wake up, but the room stayed quiet. Finally I dared to open the door a crack. Peeking inside I saw she was still burrowed under her comforter, one of her long, pale arms dangling off the bed.

I continued my pacing in the living room. It was clear I needed to find a purpose for the rest of the day or I was going to lose my mind. Walking to the window I peered out. Outside, people got in their cars for work or school, walked their dogs, or headed out for a morning jog. Meanwhile inside it felt like the world had stopped turning and gravity no longer applied.

Then, driving up the street I caught sight of a police car. I watched it roll along, willing it to stop at Lorrie's. I pictured Knox in handcuffs being loaded into the back. I'd record the whole thing and watch it over and over. The car slowed and for a split second I thought my fantasy might come true. Then it flicked on its turn signal and pulled into the Shulmans' driveway.

It parked there and for a long minute no one got out. Then both front doors swung open at the same moment and two men emerged. I drew in a sharp breath as I realized what was happening.

# TWENTY-FOUR

## JULES

### *Monday, 8 a.m.*

The doorbell sounded as I was searching for my keys; it was probably Amazon delivering the baby gate I'd ordered. I'd have Paul bring it in when he got home later.

I checked my phone. If I didn't leave in the next ten minutes I was going to be late for the baby "Move and Groove" class at Gymboree. The description said I would "boogie down with my baby" and "meet new friends." I wondered if Eden had taken Summer to things like that when she was little; if we would have been friends if we'd met while boogieing down with our babies. I knew we probably didn't have a lot in common, but I was starting to realize maybe I didn't exactly have a lot in common with Summer, either.

I located my keys on the coffee table under the pile of laundry I'd meant to fold the day before. Audrey giggled as I jingled them triumphantly.

"Come on, dance partner," I said to her. "Time to go."

The doorbell sounded again. Sighing and glancing at the time again, I carried Audrey to the front door. On the other side stood a squat, broad-shouldered man in a police uniform and a tall, thin one in a dark suitcoat that looked like it might have fit him one hundred pounds ago.

"Can I help you?" I said, opening the door.

"Mrs. Shulman?"

"It's Jules," I said. "I'm not eighty."

His eyebrows twitched but his face remained blank. "I'm Officer Acosta and this is Detective Keenan." They flipped their badges open like they do in the movies. "We were hoping to ask you a few questions concerning Summer Van Doren."

"Summer?" My stomach lurched. "Have you talked to her? Is she OK?"

The men exchanged a look. "Ma'am, could we come in for a minute?" asked the uniformed officer.

Sitting in the living room with them, I did my best to recount what had happened when I'd found Summer doubled over in her bathroom. I didn't want to make her look bad so I didn't mention that she'd smelled like a bar at closing time, just that she didn't seem to be feeling well.

"Had she been drinking?" asked the officer. I'd watched every single season of *CSI* while I was recovering from hand surgery and tried to remember what the tip-offs were that someone was lying. Looking down? Or was it looking up? Too much eye contact or not enough?"

"I couldn't really say," I shrugged.

"Have you spoken with her since?"

"No," I said, my jaw tightening. It had been over twenty-four hours since I'd brought Summer to the hospital and she hadn't returned any of my texts or voicemails checking on her since then.

"What's your relationship to her?"

"We're... friends." I hesitated over the word.

Detective Keenan consulted his notepad and spoke for the first time. "It says here she was your babysitter."

"Yes, that too."

"She ever talk to you about boys?" The detective raised his eyes from his notepad to meet mine.

"Sometimes." I shifted uncomfortably as Audrey squirmed in my arms.

"Anyone in particular?"

"Um, mostly her boyfriend."

"And who was that?"

I glanced out the window where I could see Lorrie's house across the street. "Knox Keller."

"Did she ever say anything about him?" asked the detective. "Any strange behaviors on his part, did she ever indicate she was scared of him?"

"Scared? No. Nothing like that." The blow-job scene flashed through my mind. Every time I thought about I got a sick feeling, and for a second I considered telling the police about it. But it felt disloyal to be talking about Summer like this, like I was going behind her back. "Look, I'm supposed to go to a —I'm supposed to be somewhere."

"Sure, we understand," said Officer Acosta. He glanced at the detective, who nodded. "I think we have what we need. Thank you for your time, Mrs.—Jules." They stood to go, the detective buttoning his billowy jacket.

"Wait." I scrambled to my feet, hoisting Audrey along with me. "What happens now?"

"We'll contact you if we need anything else. But I doubt we will."

"No, what happens to Summer? And Knox? Will he be charged?"

The men exchanged another brief glance. I wondered if they had some kind of code with the number of blinks they gave each other. "I'm afraid we're not at liberty to discuss that, ma'am," said the detective.

After I closed the door behind them, I darted a look at the

clock and grabbed the diaper bag. If I left now I could still make at least part of the class.

The doorbell sounded again. "Seriously?" I muttered, shaking my head. "I told them I had to be somewhere." I wrenched open the front door, expecting to see the two men, but Eden stared back at me.

"Hi," she said, her eyes shifting back to the street as the police car disappeared around the bend. Her hair was pulled back in a lumpy, misshapen bun and there were smudges of mascara under her eyes. It was the first time I'd ever seen her looking less than perfect.

"Hi." I drew back in surprise. Audrey waved and a small smile spread across Eden's face as she waved back.

"I'm, um, sorry to drop by," she said. "I hope I'm not... interrupting anything?"

"Just the universe conspiring to make me late for Baby Move and Groove," I said with a sigh.

"Ah, OK." Eden backed away from the door. "I didn't mean —I'll come by another time."

"No," I said, pushing the door open wider. "It's fine. I was only going because Paul wanted me to. He says I need to get out of the house more, like see people and do stuff." Make friends was really what Paul had suggested I do, but I wasn't about to admit to Eden that I was friendless.

Eden nodded and stepped through the door, casting another look over her shoulder. "Gymboree, right?" she asked. I nodded. "I always hated those classes." She shrugged. "I mean, for starters the music is usually enough to give you a migraine."

"Right," I said. "And you may have noticed I'm not the greatest at, like, small talk."

Eden blew out a dismissive puff of air. "It's overrated anyway."

For an instant she surprised me by smiling, then her face shifted back into blankness.

"What did the police want?" she asked, catching me off guard. Jeez, did anything in this neighborhood go unnoticed?

"Just, uh, for me to answer some questions about that morning. Yesterday morning." God, how was it possible this had all happened only the day before?

"And what did you tell them?" Eden crossed her arms.

"What I told you—that I found Summer and brought her to the hospital." I leaned forward. "Is she OK, by the way? I've been texting her and I haven't heard back. I worried—I just wanted to make sure she's OK." Audrey wiggled in my arms and I set her down. She speed-crawled back down the hall. "Do you mind?" I pointed and Eden tailed me as I followed Audrey.

We stopped in the living room and Eden glanced around. I saw it as it must look through her eyes; a mound of wrinkled laundry spilling off the coffee table onto the floor, Audrey's toys lying around, pieces of yellow foam duct-taped to the sharp edges of the armchair.

"Sorry about the mess." I swept some of the laundry into my arms and looked around for somewhere else to put it.

A smile played around the edges of Eden's lips. "I miss those days." She nodded at the teething rings on the floor. "But don't worry," she continued. "I'm not going to tell you how fast it goes and to enjoy every minute. I always hated when people did that—even more than Gymboree."

I surprised myself with a laugh and dropped the laundry back onto the coffee table.

"So." Eden's near-smile disappeared and she narrowed her eyes. "Seriously, what did you tell the police?"

"Like I said—"

"Did you tell them she'd been drinking?"

"No," I replied, still wondering if I should have. Audrey squealed with delight as she discovered a Cheezit under the couch and popped it in her mouth. I sighed, defeated, and sank onto the couch. Then a bolt went through me—should I tell

Eden about the scene on my couch with Knox? She would know what to do, right? Or if there was even anything to do.

Eden paced in front of me, her fingers buried in her hair, massaging her scalp and further destroying her bun. "Beside the police, have you talked to anyone about... last night?"

I was distracted thinking about whether to tell her, whether to betray Summer's trust.

"Hey, Jules." Eden saying my name snapped me back to the moment. "Did you talk to anyone else?"

"Uh, only Paul." Though he agreed it was an awful situation, he'd again urged me to steer clear of anything involving Eden.

Her shoulders relaxed and she locked eyes with me. "Can I ask that you keep it that way?" I cocked my head and considered her question as I studied the dark circles under her eyes. "The reason I ask," she continued, "is that graduation is next week. And then she'll have a chance at a fresh start, away from here."

"You mean Princeton."

Eden nodded. Audrey had picked up my keys where I'd dropped them when the door rang and had my car key fob in her mouth. "But what happens to Knox?" I asked. In that moment I made the decision to stay loyal to Summer and not share what I'd seen. I'd known her first, after all. And even if she wasn't truly a friend, she was a hell of a lot closer to being one than Eden was. I pried the keyring out of Audrey's mouth and she started to cry.

"Does it matter?" Eden asked.

I looked up to see if she was joking but her face was cold and serious. "How could it not matter?" I asked.

"Nothing's going to happen to him. That's not how the system works." Her tone was flat.

"But surely—"

"Jules." She put her hand up. "Look, you have a daughter,

too." She glanced at Audrey, who had replaced the keyring in her mouth with the corner of a throw pillow. "What if this happened to her someday? What would you do?"

I recoiled from the thought and pulled Audrey and the pillow up onto my lap. "I'd make sure he ended up in jail."

"But what if that was never going to happen?" Eden persisted. "Would you let lawyers and police officers make your daughter relive it over and over with their questions? Would you put all the details out into the public where people could say whatever they wanted about them, and about her? Or would you do everything you could to protect your daughter from having her life destroyed through public humiliation?"

I squeezed Audrey tighter and bit my lip. "I don't know, I guess," I said finally. "It just doesn't seem right that nothing happens to him."

"Of course it's not right." Eden closed her eyes for a long moment. "But that's how it works. And all I'm asking is that you help me do what's best for my daughter." She opened her eyes and looked at me. "Please."

# TWENTY-FIVE

## ARCHIE

### *Monday, 8 a.m.*

On Monday morning at school I scanned the hall for Summer. I could see her friends standing in a circle by their lockers, whispering and looking over their shoulders, but she wasn't with them. Down the hall, Knox's friends were weirdly quiet, standing around with their chests all kind of puffed out and their arms crossed.

I hadn't seen my brother that morning. I'd heard his alarm sound multiple times but he hadn't come out of his bedroom by the time my mom honked the car horn for me to get outside so we could leave for school.

"It's like a funeral in here," Tadpole said, looking around as we walked through the hall to get to the freshman lockers. "What's going on?"

"Um, I think I might know," I said. I knew I wasn't supposed to tell her, but it wasn't fair to keep me from talking to my only friend. Then I saw Knox cutting through the crowded hallway toward his crowd. He wore his AirPods and stared at the ground. He walked fast, but Violet Doyle was faster, separating herself from her friends and planting herself in his path. Knox stopped in front of her and looked up at her.

"How could you?" she said, narrowing her eyes. Tadpole gripped my arm. People were looking their way and it had gotten weirdly quiet in the hallway.

"It's not his fault your friend's a slut." The voice came from the direction of Knox's friends, though I couldn't see who'd said it. There was a collective gasp in the hallway and Violet's eyes got big. The bell rang, and Knox's mouth twisted as he brushed past her.

By late morning the rumor had spread. Everyone in my classes was staring at me and talking in hushed tones. My stomach hurt and I wished I could pull my hoodie down over my face and disappear.

"Holy shit," said Tadpole as she burst into the class we shared.

"Ms. Fisher, watch your language," the teacher said, frowning at her.

"Sorry Mr. Tolbert!" she called, scurrying to her desk, which was next to mine.

"Is it true?" she whispered, scooting her chair closer to mine.

"I don't know," I muttered, sinking lower in my seat. "We're waiting on some kind of police report, I think."

"Like *Law & Order SVU* or something?" Tadpole was a television freak. She wanted to be a TV critic one day, so she watched everything. Between that and video games I don't know how she ever got her homework done, but somehow she still made honor roll.

"I honestly don't know." My stomach lurched and I stared down at the doodles in my notebook.

"OK I get it; you can't talk about it. It's cool."

"I can't because I don't know anything. No one's telling me *anything*." I almost yelled the last word and Tadpole jumped.

"Is everything all right, Mr. Keller?" Mr. Tolbert looked over at me.

"Yeah, everything's great," I mumbled.

Tadpole flashed me a look of concern. "Sorry," she mouthed.

I got to biology class right as the bell rang. Heads snapped in my direction as I walked through the door and the whispers started. I slid into my seat next to Jemma, who had already taken our half-dissected frog out of the industrial refrigerator and set it up for today's "operation."

"Hey," she said as our teacher, Ms. Anderson, launched into a detailed description of the kidneys and liver.

"Hey," I said.

Out of the corner of my eye I saw Miranda Canley hand a note to the girl behind her. Miranda's older sister, Mackenzie, hung out at our house a lot. I watched the girl read the note and glance my way. She made a mark on the paper and handed it to the boy sitting behind her. After hesitating a minute, he also made a mark, then folded the paper back up into a tight square. I watched it make the rounds of the classroom until someone handed it to Jemma. She smoothed the note open on her desk and her expression immediately changed as she looked over at me. I raised my eyebrows. Biting the inside of her cheek, Jemma moved the paper to where I could see it. Two headers were spelled out in big block letters, TEAM KNOX and TEAM SUMMER. Someone had drawn a heart around Knox's name, and there were checkmarks in each column, several for Summer but way more for Knox. Jemma shot a death glare at Miranda as she crumpled the paper.

A gurgling noise escaped my mouth and my breakfast rose up into my throat. I took a deep breath but the smell of formaldehyde hit me and I knew it was too late. I tipped my chair backward as I stumbled toward the classroom door.

"Archie!" I heard Ms. Anderson calling to me as I burst into the hallway and doubled over, spewing the contents of my stomach onto the concrete floor.


In the nurse's office I was handed a Dixie cup of water and told to lie down on a cot with a thermometer in my mouth.

"Normal," the nurse said after it beeped. "How long have you been feeling sick?"

*Since I found out my brother might be a rapist*, I wanted to say. "Since this morning," I said.

She nodded. "I'll call someone to pick you up. Drink lots of fluids when you get home and only eat bland foods if you feel up to it; toast, bananas, those sorts of things."

At home Mom fluffed my pillows, set Gatorade and Saltines on my nightstand, and asked me about a million times if I was sure I was OK on my own.

"I have a meeting with the Free Motherhood founder, but I can cancel," she offered, smoothing the hair off my forehead.

"It's fine," I mumbled, climbing into bed. "I just want to sleep."

"OK. I'll be home in a couple of hours. Call me if you need anything," she said, squeezing my hand.

I nodded and pulled the covers up over my head.

I woke later to my stomach grumbling in hunger, which I took to be a good sign. Downstairs, I poured myself a bowl of cereal and went outside to the front porch. The sun was strong and it had gotten warm. I liked the porch because our house was set just far back enough from the street that I could sit on the porch swing and watch people walking and driving by without anyone noticing me. It was like being in the world without having to, like, participate in it.

I was halfway through my cereal when a familiar figure came jogging down the street. Her long legs moving fast and her red ponytail swishing behind her. Before I knew what I was doing, I'd abandoned my bowl and started down the front steps, my heart racing.

"Archie?" Summer stopped in front of our walkway and took off her headphones. She looked smaller than usual in her oversized T-shirt which had *Property of Westwood Baseball* printed across the front. I wondered if it belonged to my brother. Her face was pale under her freckles.

"Hey," I croaked.

"Hi. Um, isn't it a school day?"

"I'm sick."

"Oh, sorry."

"Yeah, I threw up in biology class."

"Let me guess," she said, "the frogs?" I nodded. "Yeah, they're pretty gross. You know you can get a note from your parents so you don't have to do it, right? A girl in my class did that and they gave her worksheets or something for a few weeks."

"Really? I'll have to ask about that." What I didn't say was that as much as I hated slicing up that frog, I wasn't sure I wanted to give up the time I got to spend with Jemma.

We stared at each other for a minute and then I coughed and said, "So, you're home, too. How, um, are you?"

She lowered her eyes. When she looked back up at me, they were filled with tears. "I don't think I'm really supposed to be talking to you, Archie," she said softly.

I scrunched up my forehead and nodded. "I get it."

"Anyway, I'll see you at school tomorrow."

"You're coming back?" I thought about Miranda's note and all the checkmarks under Knox's name. I wanted to tell Summer about it but I didn't know how.

"I have to come back eventually," she shrugged. "And it's

only a few days until graduation. How bad can it be?" She gave me a small, sad smile and put her earbuds back in. I felt like my heart physically ached as I watched her jog away.

*Bad*, I thought. *It can be very bad.*

# TWENTY-SIX

## LORRIE

### *Monday, 12 p.m.*

My meeting with Keisha Tyson, one of the Free Motherhood founders, was ostensibly for her to prep me for my first official board meeting the next day. But mostly I just sat there in a daze, nodding as I tried to push the image of my son being led away in an orange jumpsuit out of my mind.

"Are you OK?" Keisha asked at one point, genuine concern on her face.

"Of course," I said, forcing my eyes to focus on her. "Just a little under the weather, I think. My son came home sick from school today."

Keisha made a show of scooting her chair away from me, the many long, tiny braids her hair was woven into swinging. I forced a laugh. "Just make sure you're well for the board meeting," she cautioned in a friendly voice. "We really need someone with your skills, Lorrie." I flushed at the compliment, though I knew what she really meant was that they needed someone with my connections to other women like me, with time on their hands and money to spend for charity. But I really believed in the work the organization was doing and I'd been thrilled when they asked me to join the board. Ed, less so.

"Look, you're already really busy with all the Parent Boosters stuff. How are you going to fit this in and still be around for the kids?" he'd said, visibly irritated.

"I'll figure it out," I'd promised, though he didn't look convinced.

When I got in the car to head home after meeting with Keisha I scoured my phone for updates from Beau, even though the thought of him made me shudder, but there were none. I sighed. Back to the waiting game.

At home Archie's bedroom door was closed and his room was quiet so I let him be. I showered, grabbed some hummus and veggies and sat at the kitchen island. Usually I would savor a moment like this, a rare instance of peace and quiet with no one asking me for anything. Today, though, quiet was the last thing I wanted.

Quiet was when you started thinking.

I stared down at my hummus and felt a wave of queasiness. Pushing it away, I reached for my laptop. Though I'd diligently decorated each room of our house, somehow I'd neglected to designate any one of them as mine. The kids had their rooms and Ed his study, but I usually worked at the kitchen island, available to be interrupted by anyone who needed a snack or a ride somewhere.

In my inbox were requests for the final payment for Archie's sleepaway camp and Chloé's dance camp, a reminder from Westwood about picking up Knox's graduation cap and gown, and the pre-read materials for the Free Motherhood board meeting.

I opened the file and began to scan through it. But after five minutes of reading over the same paragraph without absorbing any of it, I groaned and closed the laptop again. Then it occurred to me maybe Ed *had* heard from Beau and that I'd been left out of the loop. The familiarity I'd witnessed between then had given me a sour feeling in my stomach. What was I missing? Grabbing my phone, I fired off a text to Ed, asking if he'd had an update. I watched the delivery notification change to "read" but no response came.

Annoyed, I set the phone back down on the counter. Dealing with both Ed and Beau inspired the same maddening feeling: powerlessness.

I headed back upstairs to see if Archie was awake. On the way I passed Knox's room. I put my hand on the doorknob and hesitated, feeling the pull of curiosity. We'd always respected the kids' privacy. Then again, I'd never had any reason not to trust them.

The need to go in became unbearable, like an itch I couldn't reach. If I couldn't get information out of Beau or my husband, I could at least do this. I pushed open the door. His bed was unmade, the sheet and comforter flung back. The pile of clean, folded clothes I'd handed him days ago was spread across the surface of his dresser. A hoodie was draped over the bedpost and the smell of his body spray lingered in the air.

Crossing the room, I sat down at his desk and my pulse sped up. *It's no big deal,* I told myself. *It's your house. You have every right to be in here.*

I pulled open desk drawers, unsure of what I was looking for. They were filled with old school notebooks and worksheets, a jumble of medals from various youth sports, and a dusty calculator. Nothing that would indicate my son had done anything wrong. But also nothing that would indicate he hadn't.

Closing the drawers my eyes landed on his iPad. Swallowing hard I touched the screen to bring it to life. A password request appeared. Guilt swelled up in me as I tried a few words or numbers I thought might work, but I was rejected each time. I sighed and set the iPad back where I'd found it. I had friends who tracked their kids' devices with various programs and apps but that kind of surveillance had always felt invasive to me. Ed and I had done our best to educate the kids about the pitfalls of technology, and we told each other we could trust our kids to make good decisions.

I hoped we'd been right.

Pushing Knox's desk chair back in I cast a last lingering look around the room and then left it as I'd found it.

Back downstairs I found myself walking toward Ed's study. I opened the door and stepped inside, my eyes roaming over the leather armchair and built-in bookshelves filled with medical texts and the biographies of U.S. presidents he liked to read. While I'd helped him plan it all out with our interior designer, the dark wood and leather now struck me as cliché—like the set of a movie about robber barons and titans of industry. And why did he need so much space when for years I'd been asking for a bigger laundry room? For God's sake, he had a full-size couch in here. I thought of myself perched on a kitchen stool with my laptop and felt a hot bubble of resentment in my core.

Surveying the room, I realized it would be easy to cross the room to his desk, to open drawers and see what secrets they contained. Maybe I'd finally find an explanation for the layers that seemed to exist in Beau and Ed's relationship.

I shook my head. Ridiculous. Ed and I may not always see eye to eye, but we didn't hide things from each other. Or at least we never used to. He seemed so unreachable to me lately, even before the nightmare of this weekend. I felt a wave of shame at the snooping I'd done in Knox's room, and what I was standing there in Ed's study considering. Turning on my heel, I closed the study door behind me.

# TWENTY-SEVEN

## SUMMER

### *Monday, 3 p.m.*

My mom wouldn't stop hovering. I could hear her outside my door every time I took out my earbuds, pacing the hall like she was keeping guard, or sometimes just standing there breathing. She's a loud breather.

She knocked every fifteen minutes, offering snacks or to "talk about it." As if. We hadn't "talked" about anything since I was thirteen and my best friends ditched me to sit at Emilia the Queen Bee's lunch table. My mom's response had been to offer to take me shopping and get a haircut, like some stupid teen makeover movie where the nerdy girl suddenly becomes gorgeous and gets noticed by the hot guy and becomes popular.

That was not my movie.

I waited until I couldn't hear my mom pacing anymore, then picked up my guitar. I ran my fingers along the smooth wood and hugged it to my body, inhaling its special smell of sawdust and something metallic. My fingers hovered above the frets but I couldn't bring myself to touch the strings. Usually I reached for it first thing in the morning to try out the chords that had been rolling around in my head all night. Last night though, my mind had been full of the events of yesterday replaying in my mind like I was stuck in some kind of sick torture chamber. The hospital, the drive home with my mom, the humiliating trip to the police station with my dad. When I woke up after finally getting a couple of hours' sleep I felt both wired and exhausted.

I kept thinking about what Violet said when she'd come over. About the word she'd used to describe what happened to me. I rolled it around on my tongue but didn't say it out loud. If I did I felt like I'd be breaking the last fragile thread that tied me to Knox. And despite everything, I wasn't ready for that.

"Summer?" came my mom's voice.

*Back already?* I gritted my teeth and closed my eyes.

"Can I come in?"

I had no more strength to send her away so I set the guitar back on my bed and braced myself. "Sure."

The entire contents of our refrigerator and pantry looked to be stacked on the tray she carried. "I wasn't sure what you'd be in the mood for," she said. "You should really try to eat something." She set the tray on my bed and perched next to it. "I know how hard this is. And how devastated you must be."

*Devastated.* An emotion I hadn't considered. Humiliated, yes. Furious, sure. Feeling totally pathetic for going along with Knox the whole time and believing he loved me? Abso-freaking-lutely. But devastated? I looked over at my lonely guitar. Maybe.

"How could he?" I looked around to see who'd said the words and realized it was me. "How could he do this to me?" I said again, a sudden riptide of heartbreak threatening to pull me under.

My mom laid a tentative hand on my shoulder. "He did a terrible, *terrible* thing. But it wasn't your fault, OK? I need you to know that. And this isn't going to define you. Dad and I are going to get you the best help to move forward. And you will move forward, even if it doesn't feel that way right now. You're stronger than you know, Summer."

I laughed and it came out as a high-pitched cackle, like a soap opera actress playing a crazy person. "Strong?" I said. My body went rigid with an anger that came out of nowhere. My vision blurred until all I could see was a sea of black dots. "Why do I have to be strong? What if I don't want to be? I never asked to be strong. What if I want to just dig a hole and bury myself in it for the rest of my life? And Knox, why doesn't he have to be strong? Why does his life just get to keep going like normal?"

My mom had tears in her eyes and I realized I was yelling, my throat raw with the effort. The helpless look in my mom's face made me want to pitch myself forward into her arms and sob, but instead I collapsed backward onto the bed.

"I just want everything to go back to normal," I whispered. I closed my eyes and tried to erase the images of the last forty-eight hours from my mind. I pictured walking into school the next day like nothing had happened, savoring the feeling of my last week of senior year. I pictured throwing my hat up into the air at graduation. My graduation party. The summer road trip out West that Violet and I had promised each other we'd take before we each left for college. Why should I sacrifice any of that? And Knox, was he worried about any of this? Probably not. The unfairness of it made me want to claw the walls, except I was way, way too tired to do anything but just lie there.

"The old normal is gone," my mom said, her tone resolute. She reached out and took my hand with a firm grip, as if to keep me from floating away. I tilted my head up to look at her. The tears in her eyes were gone, replaced with an unflinching steeliness. "But you get to choose what the new normal looks like," she continued. "You get to chart your own path and it's going to be fucking amazing. I'm not going to let anyone take that away from you. I promise."

Her words stirred something in me that felt like it could be hope and I squeezed her hand back. For a minute I almost believed what she was saying.

# TWENTY-EIGHT

## EDEN

### *Tuesday, 7:30 a.m.*

I woke bleary-eyed after a night of tossing and turning. Even my usual combination of Ambien and a glass of wine hadn't been enough to result in any restful sleep.

The nightmares had returned. It had been two years since my last one. Progress, Dr. Frank had said. But last night I'd had both of them. First the one about Aaron Pratt, the second-string football player who, although he wouldn't make eye contact with me at school, would regularly give me rides home from school in exchange for hand jobs. In the dream I realize I'm naked in his car. I try to get out but the doors are locked. I slam my shoulder into the door until it finally opens and I tumble out, only to realize I'm standing in the middle of the football field, the stands filled with students screaming all the names they usually only called me under their breath when I passed them in the halls.

I woke up from that one gasping for breath. The next one was about my teacher, his heft pinning me down, the sour smell of his breath in my ear as he whispers, "You know you like it."

That one left me drenched in sweat and shaking when I jerked awake.

I heard voices as I pulled on my bathrobe and made my way downstairs, surprised to see Summer already awake.

"Good morning." I smoothed my hair as I entered the kitchen. Summer and Witt were sitting side by side at the kitchen island, each with a bowl of cereal. "Here, let me at least make you some eggs, or something with protein," I said, heading for the refrigerator.

"I don't have time." Summer looked at her dad. "We need to leave in ten minutes or I'll be late for first period."

"Late—for school?" I asked. "What—no." My brain felt slow to catch on, either from the Ambien or the lack of coffee. I shook my head. "No."

Summer's chin jutted out like it always did when she wasn't getting her way. "I'm going. Dad's driving me."

"No he's not," I replied, looking at Witt. "Right?"

"I was going to, yes," he said. He was dressed in his usual work uniform of a dark-colored suit over a white button-down shirt open at the throat, but his face looked paler than normal and I could see he'd nicked himself shaving.

"We need to talk about this." My voice rose with urgency.

"What's there to talk about?" Summer shrugged. "I have to go back at some point."

I gripped the countertop and took a deep breath. "Summer, you just had a very traumatic experience. You're probably in shock and—"

"You told me I get to choose what the new normal is." Summer stared me down. "And this is what I want. It's my last week of high school. I don't want to miss it. I'm not going to let him take that away from me." Her jaw was tight as she tried to smile.

"Your father and I are going to speak privately about this," I said, trying to slow my breathing.

"Fine," Summer rolled her eyes and heaved a sigh. "I'm going to get my backpack."

When I heard her feet stomping up the stairs I turned to Witt. "Are you insane?" I asked. "Our daughter was raped less than forty-eight hours ago and you're sending her back to school?"

"She wants to go," Witt said. "And she seems fine. At some point we have to start trusting her, don't we? I mean, she's going to college in a few months and you won't be there to monitor her every decision."

"She seems *fine*?" A hysterical laugh escaped from my mouth. "Her life has been irreparably damaged and she will spend the rest of her life trying to piece it back together. I can assure you—she is not fucking *fine*."

"I meant she seems fine right now," said Witt in a low voice. "As in this very minute when she is asking to go to school so she doesn't miss out on the memories of her last days of high school."

"The memories that will be forever tainted by having been raped." I practically spat the words.

"Eden, if she wants to come home I'll go get her," he said, inhaling deeply like my spinning teacher always did at the end of class before she shared her daily inspirational quote. "But right now she wants to go to school, so I'm taking her."

"Like hell you are."

Witt narrowed his eyes and set his jaw. "You know, at some point you're going to have to start showing up for our daughter. I feel like I've been flying solo on this."

"Excuse me?" A shock of anger radiated through me. "That's all I've *been* doing. But you—you have no idea how she's feeling."

Witt threw his arms up in the air in anger. "And neither do you!"

My ears began to ring like a bomb had just exploded in

front of me and I stepped back to prop myself up against the wall.

"Summer!" Witt called up the stairs. "It's time to go, sweetheart."

This time he didn't kiss me goodbye.

# TWENTY-NINE

## ARCHIE

### *Tuesday, 8 a.m.*

As much as I wanted to stay home again the next day, after I had two helpings of spaghetti for dinner Mom said clearly I was feeling fine and that I could ride to school with Knox because she had a meeting in the morning. I glanced across the table at my brother, who was pushing his pasta around on his plate. He didn't even bother to complain. Other than Chloé, who was talking nonstop about her summer dance camp, it was deadly quiet.

"They said I need seven leotards, but I only have five I really like, and Lily said she's bringing ten, so, Mom, can we go shopping this weekend? Also, I still want those glitter tights—"

"Knox, I talked to Randy today and he said he's looking forward to having you around this summer at the stadium." My dad attempted to change the subject. Randy was the general manager of the baseball team and he'd given Knox a summer job in the office. "I told him you were thinking about majoring in business."

"Yeah, maybe," mumbled Knox. "Can I be excused?"

"Sweetheart, you hardly ate anything." My mom's forehead wrinkled in concern.

"I'm not hungry, OK?" he snapped, pushing back his chair. "And if I have to hear any more about Chloé's stupid dance camp then I'm going to be the one who pukes." He grabbed his keys off the counter and stomped across the room to the front door, slamming it behind him.

Chloé's face turned a mottled pink color. Then she started to cry and bolted upstairs, slamming her door with equal gusto. I watched my parents exchange a look. Without a word my dad followed Knox and my mom got up to go after Chloé. I sat alone at the abandoned table surrounded by everyone's half-empty plates. I wondered if my family would ever go back to being normal.

In the morning Knox was already in the car waiting when I walked outside, my shoulders tight with tension. The late spring day was warm, but I kept my hoodie zipped up to my chin and my hands stuffed in my pockets as I climbed in. I glanced at Summer's house across the street. I imagined her upstairs in her room brushing her teeth and getting dressed. I thought maybe I should tell Knox she was coming back to school today, but I didn't know how without letting on that I'd talked to her yesterday. Somehow that felt disloyal. Anyway, I figured he probably already knew. Gossip traveled fast at Westwood.

Knox was quiet most of the drive, switching the radio back and forth between sports news and a morning show where the host made fart noises with his hands. As we sat at the stoplight near school, he cleared his throat.

"You think I did it, don't you?" he said, looking straight ahead.

My fists clenched inside my pockets and I stared at the light, willing it to turn green. "I don't know what to think," I said finally.

"You honestly think I could do that to someone, to Summer

of all people?" His voice caught, and when I looked over I saw the hurt on his face. All of a sudden I wanted to grab his hand and squeeze it like I used to do when I got scared in the middle of the night during our backyard campouts.

I wanted to tell him that I loved him because he was my brother, but that I might also love Summer. That ever since I was a kid I'd drifted off to sleep imagining the feeling of her hair brushing my cheek as she hugged me good night, or the pink of her cheeks when she was out of breath from playing tag with us in the backyard. But that now, lately, I also wondered what it would be like to kiss Jemma. Whether she'd kiss me back, and if she did, what I was supposed to do next. What did it mean to be someone's boyfriend?

More than anything, though, I wanted to believe my brother.

The light turned green and the car rolled forward. I stayed quiet. As we pulled into the school parking lot, Knox paused to put in his earbuds and pull up the hood of his sweatshirt. He got out of the car without looking at me and disappeared into the stream of kids headed up the stairs into the building.

The main hallway was louder than usual as everyone bubbled over with end-of-the-school-year energy. I fought my way to my locker and found Tadpole leaning against it.

"You're late; I thought you might still be home sick," she said.

"Yeah, I had to ride with Knox." I opened my locker and grabbed my biology textbook.

Tadpole widened her eyes. "Did you talk to him? About—"

"Hey, Archie."

I turned to see Jemma heading toward me. Her locker was at the far end of the hall and she'd never come over to mine before. "Hey, Jemma."

"Are you feeling better?" She bit her lip like she did when Ms. Anderson announced one of her famous pop quizzes.

I nodded. "Yeah, lots." I felt a goofy grin spread across my face.

"I'm glad." She grinned back.

Tadpole raised her eyebrows at me. "Well, aren't you two adorable?" she said. Her voice echoed as we realized the hallway had gone quiet. I looked up to see everyone's head had turned in the same direction. At the far end of the hall stood Summer. Alone, she took a step forward and the crowd parted around her.

I scanned the corner where Knox usually stood with the other baseball players. I didn't see him, but I watched his friends standing shoulder to shoulder in a kind of wall of bodies. Summer would have to walk right by them to get to her locker. My knees wobbled and I braced myself. Why was she by herself? Where were her friends? She was like a wounded animal on one of those nature shows and the hyenas were about to rip her apart.

I tried to will my feet to unfreeze and move toward her but they stayed stuck to the ground. Suddenly Violet appeared next to Summer and linked arms with her. Behind her was another girl, and a boy I recognized from Summer's orchestra friends. They bunched around her and started down the hall together. I tried to catch Summer's eye but she kept her gaze on the ground. They had almost passed Knox's friends when I heard it.

"*Slut.*" The whisper whizzed through the air. Summer's head snapped up. Then there it was again, louder.

"Slut." It was impossible to tell who said it, but it had definitely come from Spencer's direction.

"Slut." This time a girl's voice. Violet stepped toward Mackenzie Canley, who was standing next to the boys with her hands on her hips.

"You want to say that again, Mackenzie?" Violet raised her chin. Mackenzie uncrossed her arms and the two girls stared each other down.

"Sllluttt," Mackenzie said again, sliding her tongue across her perfect white teeth as she drew the word out long. Jemma grabbed my arm as Violet lunged for Mackenzie, knocking her to the floor. One of the baseball players tried to pull them apart but fell to the floor with a thud as a boy from Summer's group tackled him at the knees.

"Fight!" someone yelled, and suddenly the hallway was a mass of bodies pummeling each other. I broke from the crowd the same minute Summer did, tears streaming down her face. Jemma called my name as I shot after Summer. Spencer stepped into my path and I felt rage bubble from every pore in my body. My arm shot forward as if it had a mind of its own and my fist skidded across his face. He jerked back and held his hand to his eye at the same moment a jolt of pain rocketed down my arm. Spencer lunged back toward me and caught the corner of my eye with his fist. I doubled over from the pain, then heaved myself back up and grabbed Summer's elbow. I pulled her out of the crowd and steered her toward the stairwell that led out to the student parking lot. All the color had left her face and her shoulders were heaving.

"I think I'm going to pass out," she whispered.

"Put your head between your knees," I said, putting my hand on her back and folding her over. She stood for a minute, gripping her knees and leaning back into me as she gulped for air.

"Oh my God, oh my God," she breathed. I rubbed her back with one hand, unsure what else to do. I flexed the fingers on my other hand, the one I'd punched Spencer with. My whole hand throbbed. I'd never punched anyone before.

Unsteadily Summer drew herself back up and looked at me, a fresh round of tears on her cheeks. "Everything is so messed up, Archie."

"I know. I'm sorry," I said.

"Stop right there!" thundered a voice. I looked up to see the principal, Mr. Ellison, hurrying toward us.

"We're not—"

He put up his hand to silence me and his face twitched as he recognized Summer. "My office, both of you."

"But we didn't do anything!" I protested.

"That's enough," he said curtly. "Move it."

As we left the alcove, Summer reached out and gave my hand a quick squeeze. Her palm was cool and smooth in mine, and then it was gone.

# THIRTY

## LORRIE

### *Tuesday, 9 a.m.*

There was already a gentle murmur of conversation when I stepped into the conference room. Some of the people milling around the room and sipping coffee I'd met before, the others I'd done enough internet research on to recognize and recite their résumés. Mine was by far the least impressive.

"Lorrie, good morning." Keisha walked toward me, wearing a navy blue sweaterdress and a thin gold necklace with a small, sparkly letter I for her daughter Imani, who she'd given birth to while in prison at age nineteen. It was her moving TEDx about experiencing firsthand the deplorable lack of pre- and post-partum care in prison that had inspired me to start volunteering for Free Motherhood in the first place.

"Welcome to your first board meeting." Keisha's smile was warm. "Meredith and I are thrilled you're joining us." Across the room her co-founder, a willowy blond woman in a crisp, expensive-looking suit waved to me. Meredith Price was a well-known Atlanta criminal lawyer with a long history of pro-bono work in the prison system. Keisha nodded at the coffee urn across the room. "Go ahead and grab some coffee if you want, then we'll get started and introduce you to everyone."

Everyone sat as Keisha called the meeting to order. "Our first order of business is to say hello to a new face around the table," she said. "We're so pleased to have Lorrie Keller joining us." She nodded at me. "Lorrie went to NYU Law and has a background in litigation. She's volunteered for Free Motherhood the past two years, helping to coordinate outreach to our legislators in support of key prison reform bills."

I smiled at Keisha's generous description of my now decade-old litigation experience.

"Lorrie will be helping us with fundraising," added Meredith. "To that end, she's agreed to head up our first annual fall fundraising event."

Everyone else around the table introduced themselves. Hearing about their impressive backgrounds was a welcome distraction from the mess happening in the rest of my life. There was only one man on the board, another lawyer from Meredith's firm. And among the women there was a pediatrician, a political science professor from Emory, the pastor of a large area church, the communications director of a non-profit, and a high school teacher. I was the only one without a real job.

After a review of the prior month's meeting, we turned to the topic of fundraising. "We'd been thinking along the lines of an email appeal with a link to participate in an online raffle," said Keisha. She nodded at the board member who was a communications director. "Sheila offered to help us put together some testimonial videos from women who've participated in our programs."

"A raffle could be a good idea," I said tentatively. Keisha had brought me up to speed on this idea before the meeting and I'd come prepared with my own thoughts. "But I'm thinking we should go bigger."

"Bigger?" Meredith cocked her head.

I nodded. "I was thinking of an auction, a live, in-person event. We'd get local businesses to donate things—spa treatments, golf lessons, restaurant gift certificates, that kind of thing. People could buy a ticket to come bid on them. Of course we'd need to make it worth their while, have drinks, food, a nice venue. Something to get excited about attending. We could play the testimonial video, or better yet have a speaker. Your story is very powerful, Keisha," I turned to her. "Or maybe one of the women out on probation who's been reunited with her baby."

"No offense, Lorrie," cut in Meredith. "But our supporters aren't exactly a spa treatment and golf lessons kind of crowd."

"No," I said. "But they could be." I looked around the table. "I know a lot of mothers who love a good fundraising auction—not to mention spa treatments. And they'll want to help as soon as they hear about the work you're doing."

"You mean the work *we're* doing." Keisha smiled at me.

When the meeting concluded Meredith walked over to me. "A fancy auction, huh? That's a big promise for your first meeting. You think you can pull it off?"

I laughed, thinking of the countless hours I'd spent on the Westwood Parent Boosters annual auction. "I know I can."

"Well, I love your confidence. Sounds like you should quit your day job and go into corporate development full-time."

I smiled. "Maybe I will." My phone buzzed in my purse. "Excuse me."

Pulling it out I saw three missed calls and a voicemail from Westwood. Fear gripped me and my heart accelerated as I envisioned Archie and Knox crouching hidden in a classroom as an active shooter stalked them, or a chaotic evacuation from a bomb threat.

I hit the callback button. Trying to appear calm I waved to Keisha and pointed at the phone, then I stepped out of the conference room.

"This is Lorrie Keller," I said when they answered,

breathing fast. I paused, listening to the voice on the other end. "I'm sorry, what? That can't be right. You must mean Knox, my oldest son, not Archie. Archie would never—you can't be serious! Yes, OK. I'll be there as soon as I can."

I lowered the phone and tried to calm my breathing. *My children are safe*, I thought, though something about that word rang hollow.

# THIRTY-ONE
## KNOX

### *Tuesday, 9 a.m.*

I was already in my first-period Spanish class when other kids started coming in. I'd gone straight there from the parking lot, not even stopping at my locker. I couldn't stand the thought of seeing any of my friends, most of whom had been texting me fucked-up stuff about Summer. By the end of the day yesterday it seemed like everyone knew.

The classroom was always noisy in the morning with everyone settling in and Mr. Villanueva playing Mexican pop songs or whatever Broadway musical soundtrack he was currently obsessed with—today it was *Mamma Mia!*, the West-wood spring musical he'd just directed. Today, though, even beyond the music there was a weird energy in the room that made me sit up and look around. People's faces were flushed and everyone was talking in loud voices.

"Can you believe—"

"Holy crap—"

"—the look on her face—"

I waited for Spencer to walk in and take the seat next to me so I could ask what was going on. But the bell rang and his seat stayed empty.

"Hey," I whispered to the girl in front of me, Olivia Lombardo. She was president of the Westwood Model UN team, not exactly my crowd. Though she'd sat in front of me all semester we'd never exchanged more than two words. When she turned around and saw it was me talking to her, her eyes widened. "What's everyone so worked up about?" I asked.

"You missed it?" she asked. "Oh my God, there was a *huge* fight."

"What about?"

Her face reddened. "Um, maybe you should ask someone else."

"Like who?" I gestured to Spencer's empty seat next to me.

She sighed. "OK, fine. Mackenzie Canley called Summer Van Doren an S-L-U-T. Then Violet Doyle, like, took her down. Everyone went totally bonkers."

"Olivia? Knox? *¿Hay un problema?* Something you'd like to share with the rest of the class?"

I looked up to see Mr. Villanueva's eyes on me. "No," I mumbled, sinking lower in my seat. I felt a rush of heat to my face but the rest of my body went cold and clammy. I watched everyone around me follow Mr. V's instructions to open their books to a certain page but I was frozen in place, my head thick like the oatmeal my mom had tried to get me to eat that morning.

Who the hell did Mackenzie think she was? Was Summer OK? Did the whole school know? How did this happen?

I raised my hand.

"Si, Señor Keller," said Mr. V.

"Could I have the bathroom pass?"

He sighed and checked his watch. "Class just started. *¿Està necessario?*"

"It's, um, kind of an emergency," I said. Someone snickered.

"*Bien, ándale*," Mr. V. waved his hand toward the miniature Spanish flag hanging next to the classroom door that doubled as his hall pass.

Outside the classroom everything was quiet. I leaned against the wall, suddenly lightheaded. I bent forward with my hands on my knees. Everything felt like it was spiraling out of control.

I thought of Archie in the car that morning, how he refused to look at me when I asked if he thought I did it. Something inside my chest clenched, like a rubber band tightening around my heart. My own brother thought I was a bad person. All of a sudden my eyes were hot with tears. I swiped the back of my hand across them as I stood up and leaned against the wall, grateful for the coolness of the cinder blocks through my shirt.

Down the hall, a locker banged, and Spencer came walking toward me with his backpack slung over one shoulder. The tang of his body spray reached me before he did and my stomach turned.

"Hey bro," he said, fist-bumping me. "You missed all the fun." The skin above his left eye was swollen and purplish.

"What happened to you?"

His eyes narrowed. "Dude, Violet's such a bitch. She started it and now I'm suspended for the rest of the week. I'm gonna miss senior prank day and everything." He rolled his eyes. "It's messed up. My mom tore Mr. Ellison a new one but he wasn't having it."

"That sucks, man," I said. "Did, um, like... what happened to Summer?"

Spencer shot me a look. "What do you care, man? That chick majorly screwed you—so to speak. What a bitch."

"Don't call her that."

He tossed me a look of disgust. "She's old news, dude."

"Just, don't," I said. I looked down at my feet but not before I saw him smirk and roll his eyes.

"Whatever, bro."

I shifted on my feet and swiped my hand across the back of my neck where I was sweating. I nodded at his eye. "So Violet did that?"

"No, dude, it was your fucking brother."

"Archie?" I couldn't keep the disbelief out of my voice.

"Yeah," Spencer said. "But don't worry, he got his. Anyway, I gotta go. They gave me five minutes to get my shit and meet my mom in the parking lot."

A bolt of anger shot through me. "Are you saying you hit my brother?" I took a step toward him.

"Hey, bro, he started it," Spencer held up his hands. "You need to tell him to rein that shit in." I gritted my teeth and brought a finger up near Spencer's face, so close I was nearly touching him. My whole body vibrated with a rage I wasn't sure I could contain. A look of uneasiness rolled over Spencer's face.

"If you ever touch my brother again," I spat, "I'll kill you."

# THIRTY-TWO

## LORRIE

### *Tuesday, 9:30 a.m.*

Twenty minutes after leaving the board meeting I pulled into the Westwood parking lot. As I stepped out of my car I heard my name. I turned to see Caroline Doyle smiling and waving at me as she approached from the other side of the parking lot. I resisted the urge to leap back into my car and hide under the mountain of abandoned sweatshirts and empty seltzer cans the kids had left in the back seat. Instead I forced my arm up to wave back.

"Lorrie!" she trilled as she drew close, slightly breathless from her speed-walk.

"Hi, Caroline." I braced myself for what was surely to come. Caroline was ground zero for all Westwood gossip; surely she'd already have heard about Knox's situation.

"Hi," she said. "I was just dropping Jackson off from a dentist appointment. How are you holding up?"

I forced a smile. "Well, I've been better."

She nodded. "I know, it's all so surreal, isn't it?" She gestured toward the sprawling, two-story brick building that

housed Westwood High. "Freshman year feels like just yesterday, doesn't it?" I blinked, not understanding. "And now I have
Jackson and Violet's graduation robes hanging in my closet."
She sighed. "I mean, they say it all goes so fast, but this is
ridiculous!"

"Right," I nodded, wondering when she was going to get
around to probing for details about Knox and Summer. Or did
she not know? Was that even possible?

"Anyway," she continued. "At least you've still got Archie
and Chloé coming up through Westwood. And God forbid Mr.
Ellison would have to figure out how to raise money without
you." She laughed. "Speaking of, what are you wearing for
Casino Night tonight?"

I blinked again. I'd forgotten all about Casino Night, Westwood's final Parent Boosters event of the year. It was a
fundraiser open to all parents, but specifically designed to celebrate the parents of seniors. This year's theme was the Golden
Years of Vegas. But while I was the chair of the event, I hadn't
even bothered to open the emails the committee had sent out to
the volunteers, double-checking the details of room setup,
vendors, and ticket sales. I'd normally be all over it.

"Lorrie?" Caroline waved her hand in front of my face.

I shook my head. "I haven't decided yet. Anyway, I should
go, I'm..." I trailed off, not wanting to mention my reason for
being at the school, especially since Caroline still seemed in the
dark about whatever it was that had transpired.

Caroline nodded and flashed a knowing smile. "I'm sure
Mr. Ellison is keeping you busy up until the last minute."

I managed a weak smile and waved as I turned to go.

Inside, the familiar smell of industrial cleaner mixed with
cafeteria food put me at ease. I wondered how many hours I'd
spent here at meetings of the Parent Boosters or overseeing
fundraising events for the school foundation.

I pressed the buzzer outside the office. Inside, Archie sat

slumped in a chair near the window. The waiting area was crowded with other kids, which was unusual.

"Archie?" I approached him. He turned to me and lowered the ice pack he had pressed against his face, revealing a swollen cheekbone that was turning from red to purple. "Oh my God!" I gasped.

"Mom." He shot me a warning look and glanced at the other kids.

"Mrs. Keller, a word?"

I turned to see Mr. Ellison, the principal, standing in the door to his office. "Of course," I said, following him inside. He perched on the edge of his desk while I sat in a chair. I immediately regretted my choice of seat as I adjusted my gaze to look up at him, feeling disadvantaged.

"Mrs. Keller, as you know, we have a zero tolerance policy for violence. And I'm sorry to say that this morning Archie was involved in a fight."

"That must be wrong." I shook my head. "Archie doesn't have a violent bone in his body. And it looks to me like he was the one injured." I straightened my shoulders. "I'd like to know who's responsible for that."

"I'm not at liberty to name names," Mr. Ellison said. "And I can assure you, Archie was very much an instigator of the... incident. Very unfortunate, of course. Now, I realize Archie's never been in any kind of trouble before. But rules are rules."

"What do you mean?"

"I'm sorry to say we have to suspend Archie for the remainder of the week," he said.

"The rest of the week?" I frowned. "You can't be serious."

"Again, I'm sorry."

I pursed my lips. "Can you at least tell me what happened?"

Mr. Ellison cleared his throat with discomfort. "Mrs. Keller, I only share this with you given our long history of working together and your significant involvement in the Westwood community." He sighed. "It seems word has traveled about something that took place between your son, Knox, and... a girl." Red splotches appeared on his neck. "Do you, uh, know what I'm referring to?" I nodded, unable to speak. "Right," he said, relieved. "Well, then, some of the students—as you can imagine —are upset about what they've heard. I believe that all came to a head this morning."

"Was Knox there?"

"No," Mr. Ellison shook his head. "He wasn't involved."

I exhaled with relief. Mr. Ellison kept speaking but his words faded into the background as my mind raced. I had to tell Ed. I had to talk to Archie. I needed to see Knox. Then suddenly I snapped back to attention. "Wait, I'm sorry, what?" I asked.

Mr. Ellison looked stricken. "I hope you can understand why this is necessary," he said.

"Why what is necessary?"

"Why we need to ask you to step down from your position as president of the Parent Boosters, effective immediately."

I sucked in a breath and dug my nails into my palms. "Why would you do that?"

He cleared his throat again. "In delicate matters such as these, it's important that the school appear neutral. So we need to... distance ourselves. A bit. For now. In fact, it might be better if you elected not to attend tonight's event at all."

"Not attend Casino Night?" I blanched, thinking of the hours of work I'd put into planning an event I'd been looking forward to as a chance to celebrate getting my oldest child to the finish line of high school. Or nearly to the finish line.

"Yes," he nodded, averting his eyes and picking at an imaginary piece of lint on his shirt. "Given the circumstances, it could be a... distraction to have you there. It's your decision, of course."

The anger that had been on a low boil inside me threatened

to explode. My fingers tingled and I felt my face go splotchy. I did everything in my power to tamp the rage back down as I stood to meet Mr. Ellison's eyes.

"Of course," I said. "Now, if we're finished here, I'm going to take my son home."

# THIRTY-THREE

## EDEN

### *Tuesday, 10 a.m.*

"Mrs. Van Doren, thank you for coming," said Mr. Ellison, swinging open his office door on which hung a large brass plate that read PRINCIPAL. Summer rose in her chair and he waved a hand in her direction.

"Summer, the adults are going to talk first, all right?" he said.

"She'll come with me," I said flatly. "She already called and told me what happened. I won't have her sitting here with the same animals who did this to her." I glared at the boys waiting their turn in the row of plastic chairs outside his office. "Entitled little pricks."

"Mrs. Van Doren, please," protested Mr. Ellison. Inside his office he motioned for me to sit. I stayed standing to remind him that I was taller than he was. That he was nothing more than a miserable little man with no real power.

"Now, as I mentioned on the phone," he began, "there was an unpleasant incident this morning. A fight, in which your daughter was involved."

"She wasn't part of the fight," I said, my tone icy. "Get your facts straight."

"Yes of course. To clarify, when I say involved, I mean, well, that she instigated the fight."

"Excuse me? In what way did she instigate this fight?"

Mr. Ellison cleared his throat. "Ah, well, there were some words exchanged between her friends and another group of students, and things escalated from there."

I pointed to Summer, who was staring out the window tugging at one of her curls. "My daughter didn't exchange any of those words. In fact, if I understand correctly, those words were directed *at* her."

Mr. Ellison glanced at Summer, looking like he'd rather be anywhere else. "Mrs. Van Doren, I'm aware that there was an incident between your daughter and another student. I'm aware that Summer has alleged some... misconduct on the part of that student."

"I believe 'rape' is the word you're looking for, Mr. Ellison." It was the first time I'd said the word out loud. As it left my tongue I felt the weight of it. My body suddenly felt like it was encased in cement and I struggled to remain standing. I glanced at Summer again but her face was unchanged. "My daughter was raped," I continued. "We are dealing with the matter legally and *privately*." I raised my eyebrows in emphasis. "This is her first day back at school and I would have hoped to have your full support."

"Yes, of course," he said hastily. "Our primary objective is to support our students however we can. It's just, given the circumstances, and her involvement in today's incident, well, we think it's best she spends the rest of the week keeping up with her studies at home."

"At home? And miss the last days of her senior year?" A roaring began in my ears, like a train bearing down on me.

"It's a policy, I'm afraid." He folded his hands on the desk in front of him.

"What policy?"

"Any involvement in physical violence on school grounds is a minimum three-day suspension."

"I'm suspended?" Summer sat up in her chair.

A laugh escaped my mouth before I could stop it. "You've got to be fucking kidding me," I said. "I just told you, she wasn't involved in the fight this morning."

"I'm afraid my hands are tied, so to speak." His smile was tight. "The boys in question will be suspended too, of course."

"Including Knox Keller?"

"To my knowledge Mr. Keller was not present at this morning's incident."

"This is outrageous," I said. "My husband is a lawyer."

"I'm aware, Mrs. Van Doren." He raised his eyebrows. "But a policy is a policy." He cleared his throat again and looked down at his hands.

"No, I don't think you are aware, Mr. Ellison," I said. I felt the hot pit of rage in my stomach bubble out through my veins like lava. "I don't think you're aware of my husband's influence in the legal community. I don't think you're aware of the extent to which we've contributed to the school's foundation and how quickly we'll withdraw that support. And I sure as hell don't think you're aware of how fast we'll sue you for trampling on our daughter's rights while letting her rapist freely walk the halls of your school."

"It's an unfortunate situation all around. Really, I wish there was another option." Mr. Ellison took off his glasses to rub his eyes and sat back in his chair, looking tired.

"Fuck you," I said, standing. I grabbed a tissue off his desk and handed it to Summer, whose eyes had filled with tears that were threatening to spill onto her cheeks. "Let's go," I said. "And no one gets to see you crying."

· · ·

My tires screeched as I accelerated out of the school parking lot, narrowly missing the security tower at the exit.

"Mom!" protested Summer, gripping her seat.

"Sorry," I muttered. I knew I should pull over, that I shouldn't be driving. My vision had narrowed to a pinhole. I suddenly understood why they called it a blind rage.

Motherhood was such a mindfuck. If it had been me in Summer's place I could have risen above the petty school politics, setting my eyes on the future where I knew my life would involve none of these people, and focused all my strength on delivering me there. Hell, I had done exactly that. I'd succeeded despite my slimeball teacher and all the other men who'd treated me like I had no value. Despite the names thrown at me in the hallways at school and the invisible hands that reach out to grab parts of my body whenever I passed through a crowd. Despite the lewd graffiti the janitor regularly washed off my locker.

As a mother, though, I had one job: to keep any of that from ever happening to my daughter.

And I'd failed.

I managed to get us home, running two stop signs and then accelerating up the driveway as adrenaline continued to pump through my body.

"Mom, are you OK?" Summer asked as the car came to a stop. That she could be worried about me in this moment was the final tap of the hammer that shattered my heart.

"I'm fine, sweetheart," I said, forcing a smile. "Just upset. About all of it." She nodded. "You go on inside," I said. "I'll be right there."

I leaned back in the car and focused on the feel of the

leather steering wheel between my hands, the sound of the birds outside, and the smell of fresh-cut grass. It was a technique Dr. Wright had taught me; grounding myself in the present moment through my five senses whenever anxiety began to overtake me.

It helped a little, but I was still breathing fast. My plan to protect Summer by keeping things quiet and whisking her away after graduation was ruined. Everyone knew what had happened. And if what had taken place at school was any indication, their judgment of her would be swift and harsh. It was time for a new strategy.

I got out of the car and paused, savoring the warmth of the sun on my face.

"Eden, hi!" I looked up to see Natalie from book club pulling her car to a stop and waving through her open window. I painted on a smile and waved back. "Will you be at Lorrie's on Wednesday?" Natalie asked. "I haven't finished the book yet but I'm planning to stay up all night if I have to!"

Fucking book club. As if I had time for that right now. Yet just then another thought bloomed in my head, the seed of an idea. I walked down to the street as slowly as I could, giving it time to germinate. "Unfortunately, we've had a family emergency and I won't be there," I said when I got close to her car.

"Oh gosh, I'm so sorry. I hope everything is all right."

"Thank you." I lowered my voice and looked around. "Between you and me, I'm surprised Lorrie's still hosting it at all. I mean, I'm sure you've heard." I leaned forward and told her the whole story. I felt a pit of dread in my stomach as I talked, but I told myself that really it was only a matter of time before the story spread through Mountaindale. Better that I controlled the narrative. If the neighborhood was going to choose sides I was going to make damn sure they chose the right one. I'd felt so alone all those years ago, like no one was on my side. My daughter was *not* going to feel like that.

When I finished talking I was rewarded by the expression on Natalie's face, half horrified, half looking like the cat who'd swallowed the canary. "Oh, and please don't say anything to anyone," I added, all but ensuring she would.

Your move, Knox Keller.

# THIRTY-FOUR
## SUMMER

### *Tuesday, 10:30 a.m.*

When I finally got up to my room after the humiliating conversation in Mr. Ellison's office I threw myself onto the bed, buried my face in my pillow and screamed. How could this be happening to me? It's a cliché, but when they talk in books about how "I kept thinking I would wake up from this nightmare," right now I really did feel that way. Like, Knox couldn't have broken up with me. And he couldn't possibly have done what he did. And Mackenzie Canley—witch that she was—definitely couldn't have called me a slut in front of the whole school. And absolutely, positively *not* could I be missing my very last days of high school, the culmination of my life up until this point.

I screamed again. It was such a mess. How could this have happened?

Only a few weeks ago, I was the one who wanted to have sex. First off, because I didn't want to go off to college as a virgin, because how embarrassing. But also because it was Knox

—I mean, what could be more perfect than having your first time be with the guy you've loved your whole life?

The problem was that he didn't seem that... interested. I knew he liked me; he was always touching me, playing with my hair or caressing my cheek, but we'd make out for a little while and then he'd pull away and take me home, almost like he'd had a mini freakout or something.

It made me think of the American Girl doll I had when I was little. My mom had her custom made for me with red hair, green eyes, and freckles. I loved her so much; she was so beautiful and perfect that I never wanted to play with her for fear I'd get her dirty or break her somehow. I kept her in the box and only took her out once in a while to look at her.

That's how Knox treated me.

More than once I'd put my fingers on his zipper but he stopped me each time. That night at Jules's, though, he didn't. And I was so focused on doing what he told me that I never heard the key in the door. The most humiliating part wasn't getting caught but how fast he left—and having to beg Jules not to tell my mom.

I understood that our friends didn't exactly mix well, but sometimes I got tired of it being just the two of us. I tried to get him to go to Nic's Pies on Friday nights sometimes, where half our class hung out, ordering pizza by the slice and grouping at tables and booths in the same formation as the cafeteria. I liked the idea of being snuggled in a booth with him for everyone to see.

"Why do we need to hang out where everyone else is?" he'd groaned one night as we lay entwined on a blanket in Piedmont Park on a warm, early spring evening, waiting to hear a lineup of local bands. "You're the only person I really want to be around." His arms tightened around me. "You're the only person who really knows me."

We had sex that night for the first time, moving our blanket into an empty gazebo in a deserted area of the park after the concert ended.

"You've done this before, right?" he had murmured as he kissed me and rolled on top of me on the hard wooden floor.

"Of course," I'd lied. Nervous butterflies swarmed my body as I closed my eyes and waited to feel his lips on mine. Instead, as if a switch had flipped, his hands moved roughly over my body and his voice became curt and robotic.

"Like this," he said.

My eyes flew open as he directed me onto my hands and knees and unzipped his pants behind me. I twisted my head around to look back at him as he yanked down my underwear; his eyes were unfocused and he was muttering softly. In one sharp movement he lifted his hand and brought it down on the right side of my naked bottom with a loud thwack. A strangled yelp escaped from my throat and my body froze.

"Yeah, you like that, don't you?" he said in his robot voice.

"Y-yes?" I whispered, because while I hadn't liked the pain and surprise of it, his tone implied that he wanted me to.

"Good girl," he said.

*Thwack!* I flinched but forced myself not to move away. After all, maybe I did like it—no one had ever done it to me before so maybe it just took some getting used to. His muttering became louder as I felt his nakedness press against me. There was the crinkling of a wrapper and then a prodding between my legs that became more insistent until in one sharp movement he was inside me. I ground my teeth and let out a gasp as I absorbed the pain, my head spinning with how fast everything was happening.

As he moved against me I could hear him repeating the same phrases over and over, almost like a prayer—except they were no words I'd ever heard in a church. They were dirty, and not in the vague, untargeted way that words scrawled in restaurant bathroom stalls or tossed at you from construction sites were. The names he called me flew at me with a speed and ferocity that left me unprepared to deflect their poison. They pierced my mind and settled in my body like lead, forming a hard lump of shame in my stomach. I stayed frozen as Knox's words and movements picked up speed, the muscles in my legs trembling as I worked to keep from collapsing under his thrusts. Then with one final shudder he slumped on top of me, pulling me close as small tremors ran through his body.

"Summer, Summer, Summer."

In my haze of shock it took me a minute to recognize my own name. It seemed impossible that it could come from the same lips that only moments earlier had voiced such unrepeatable things. He ran his fingers across my cheek and held my hand to his chest.

"I love you," he whispered.

I let my body relax into his. This part of the scene I had imagined, the way he'd hold me after. I let his caresses erase the rest of it. I was loved. That was all that mattered. The rest I could overlook, at least for now.

My phone buzzed with a text from Violet, bringing me back to the present moment—the present nightmare.

> i heard you got suspended too??? wtf?????

>> yeah. wait, you too?

> yeah my mom is so pissed. but like I'm supposed to be suspended bc I tackled Mackenzie. you didn't do anything!!

>> wanna come over?

> lemme check w my mom

Ten minutes later she knocked on my bedroom door, breezing through it and throwing herself dramatically down on the bed next to me. "This is, like, insanity," she said.

"And you know who's not suspended?" I asked. "Knox."

Violet sat up. "*What?* Oh no way." She shook her head and waved a finger in the air. "We can't let him get away with this." I stared at the ceiling. "I'm pretty sure he already did."

"No." She crossed her arms, her face stormy. "You can't just give up."

Violet's response detonated another bomb of anger in the minefield of my brain, and I rolled over and pounded my fist into my pillow. Why was getting revenge, or justice, or whatever you want to call it, my responsibility? Like, what was I supposed to do about it? Wasn't there a whole system that was supposed to take care of that? Hadn't that been the whole point of involving the police?

Except when I thought about sitting in the overheated police conference room with my dad, across from the detective who had asked me the same questions over and over, worded slightly differently, like he was trying to trip me up, I didn't feel anything resembling hope or relief. Instead the awful truth dawned on me.

Knox really was going to get away with it.

# THIRTY-FIVE
## EDEN

### *Tuesday, 12 p.m.*

After talking to Natalie I walked back up the driveway, noticing the landscaping in our front yard that Witt and I had done the year before. It had been a fun project; we'd been partners on redesigning our lackluster front lawn into a space filled with brightly colored flowers and bushes that birds and butterflies flocked to. And that was how we usually operated—as partners. Now, though, I felt increasingly disconnected from him.

Inside I went upstairs to check on Summer, who was lying in bed with her iPad.

"Did Violet leave?" I asked.

"Yeah," she said without looking up. "Her mom's making her help clean out the garage."

"Yikes," I said. "So, so you want to order some lunch? Anything you want."

She kept her eyes glued to the screen. "Maybe later."

I stepped tentatively toward her bed. "I've been thinking," I said, struggling to keep my voice steady, "about how we might want to handle this."

"Handle what?"

"The fact that everyone knows."

"Mom, I don't really want to talk about this right now, OK?"

She looked exhausted, with purple circles under her eyes, her skin almost gray, but I pressed forward. This couldn't wait. "Summer, what happened at school—Knox's friends, well, assholes stick together. But I think a lot of people will be on your side, too."

She lowered the iPad and narrowed her eyes. "What do you mean?"

"Just that you're not alone. And that if we control the narrative—"

"Control the *narrative?*"

I shook my head, trying to order my jumbled thoughts. "Look, I thought we could keep everyone from finding out and that you could go off to college with a fresh start." I blinked back tears. "What happened to you at school is exactly what I was afraid of. I don't want you to ever believe—" My voice broke. "None of those things people said are true, you know that right?" I said hoarsely. Summer gazed up at me, expressionless. "Once they know the truth, people will be on your side," I continued. "And I want the world to see that. I want Knox to see that."

Summer flinched at the mention of his name. "I said I don't want to talk about it. Besides, he already got away with it." She turned back to her iPad.

"That's not true."

She set down the iPad and met my eyes. "Oh really? Then tell me you believe the police are going to do something about it. That they're going to arrest Knox and he'll go to jail or something."

There was a sharp twinge in my chest. "Sweetheart, I..." I sighed and shook my head.

Summer rolled her eyes and went back to her screen. "Yeah, I thought so."

I fought the urge to scream and pound the mattress with my fists. How was it that I was at such a loss for what to say to her? I of all people should know how to help her.

I left her alone again and paced the house. I could feel the beginning of a headache and finally flopped down on the couch while I waited for Witt to come home. I'd dialed his number on the way to pick up Summer from Mr. Ellison's office, my tone accusing as I pointed out that he'd been the one to insist she go to school that day. He'd promised to come home as soon as he could. Even though things were strained between us and we'd never before been so far apart on how to deal with anything in our lives, I couldn't wait to see him, if only to feel less alone even for a minute.

More than Witt, though, I wished I could talk to Lorrie. Or better yet, I wished I could go back in time and refuse to let Summer go out with Knox, heading off the whole disastrous pairing—for Summer's sake, but also for mine. I fingered the elephant necklace I wore every day. It felt cosmically unfair that on top of my entire world going to pieces, I'd also lost my best friend.

A cold vise of loneliness tightened around my heart. I tried for a minute to put myself in Lorrie's shoes; to imagine myself as the mother of a child who'd done something so horrific. I wondered if deep down she knew the truth about what Knox had done. If I was her, would I be able to acknowledge my child's actions or would my drive to protect him win out? I shivered at the thought of being faced with that choice.

Restless, I knocked on Summer's door again, determined to do a better job with my pep talk this time. She was glued to her phone now, scrolling as the light from the screen flickered against her face in the dark room.

I cleared my throat. "Is social media really the best idea right now?"

"There's a hashtag," she said, bewilderment on her face. "#justiceforsummer. Violet just sent it to me."

I walked over and squinted at the screen. "Really?" I'd have to pass that along to Natalie, too. "I'm not surprised people are on your side," I said. "They're angry about what happened, just like you are."

"I don't know what I am." She tucked her body into a tight ball, arms wrapped around her knees and her face buried between them. When she finally lifted her face again her cheeks were shiny with tears. "He's always gotten everything he wants," she said. "Ever since we were kids, it was like the rules didn't apply to him. I used to think it was so cool the way he just did whatever he wanted all the time. But really it was always just selfish. He just uses other people to get what he wants." She started to cry. I reached out to touch her hair and she jerked her head away. "Don't."

"Oh sweetie," I said, trying to hold back my own tears.

"I just want to be alone."

Curled in on herself she looked so small, like she was trying to shrink herself. My heart broke. I wanted to hug her and keep her from disappearing. I'd never felt so powerless. I hesitated for a moment and then turned toward the door. "I love you so much. Try to rest and I'll come check on you again in a little while."

Once I was downstairs I sent a text to Violet.

> She said there's a hashtag. Can you send it to me?

Violet responded immediately with links to Twitter.

> we should do something with this. but she won't listen

Leave it to me.

Summer slept most of the afternoon, and as evening rolled around, I busied myself making homemade chicken pot pie, her favorite, hoping the aroma would lure her downstairs. This was the real, full cream kind, not the stingy WeightWatcher's version. And since I was already going to blow through my points I figured I might as well also open a bottle of wine. I was on my second glass when I heard Witt's car rumble up the driveway. Summer entered the kitchen the same time he did, her backpack slung over her shoulder.

"Hi, baby, how are you feeling? Are you hungry? Where are you going?"

"Easy with the inquisition, Mom."

"Hi pumpkin," said Witt.

"Hi Daddy." I watched as she let him fold her into a hug and kiss the top of her head.

"Where are you going?" I asked again, eyeing her backpack.

"I'm babysitting so Jules and Mr. Shulman can go to Casino Night. Aren't you guys going, too?"

I glanced at Witt, who shrugged out of his suit jacket and hung it on a kitchen chair. He looked like he did when he got home after taking the red-eye from the West Coast, rumpled and with dark circles under his eyes. I willed him to look my way, to walk toward me and pull me in for a kiss like he usually did when he got home, but he stayed where he was.

Leaving the house for Casino Night was the last thing I felt like doing. But I also knew I'd see many of the moms I'd emailed; a good chance to stoke the fire.

"Are you sure it's a good idea to babysit?" I asked Summer. "I mean, are you feeling up to it?" I looked to Witt for backup.

"I told Jules I would and I don't want to let her down," said Summer. "Plus," she added in a softer voice, "I'd just like to do something that feels normal."

"You've been through a lot—"

"I think it could be a good idea," Witt said, with a tentative glance at me, like he didn't want to rock the boat.

I paused, then sighed. "Fine. Just—keep your phone nearby so we can check on you, OK?"

"And we're just a call away if you need us," Witt said. "I'll keep my phone glued to me." He pressed his phone to the side of his face and made a show of trying to pull it off. "I love you, pumpkin."

Summer rolled her eyes but smiled. "I love you, too, Daddy."

After she left Witt and I stared at each other across the kitchen island where I'd already dished up three plates of pot pie.

"So are we going to this Casino Night thing?" he asked, running his hand through his hair. I'd had his tuxedo dry-cleaned earlier that week and it hung in a plastic bag over his closet door.

I opened the kitchen cabinet, pulled out a bottle of ibuprofen and swallowed three with my wine. "I think we should," I said.

He nodded. "Then let's eat something first. We don't want a repeat of last year." He raised his eyebrows. The year before we'd gotten so drunk with Ed and Lorrie that we'd all ended up at a 24-hour Waffle House off Cheshire Bridge eating chicken and waffles with the statuesque women (and men dressed as women) who were headed to and from work in the nearby red light district.

"I never would have made pot pie if I'd known Summer wasn't eating with us," I said, pushing my plate away. "Do you know how many points this has? And anyway, I can't eat right now."

"Sit," he said softly, pulling out a chair for me. The kindness of the gesture nearly broke me. "You know, she's more resilient than we give her credit for. She takes after you, at the end of the day."

"She's not supposed to have to be resilient, at least not yet." I closed my eyes. "You know, I have moments when I want to kill him."

"Me too." Witt fiddled with his fork but neither of us started eating. "But there's a better option. I did some research, and even if the attorney general declines to press charges, which is likely, we could still pursue a civil case."

"What's the difference?"

"The burden of proof is lower, for one, so even without evidence from the exam we might have a chance."

"Would he go to jail?"

"No, but he'd have to pay damages—or rather, probably Lorrie and Ed would, since I'm guessing Knox has no assets to speak of. I think we should at least talk to a lawyer about it."

"I don't want their money. What he did to her—" My voice broke. My skin burned hot with long-buried rage finally erupting to the surface. I felt dizzy from its potency, caught off guard by the magnitude of my shame even after so many years. I'd put in the time with Dr. Wright, practicing my lines until I mostly believed the new narrative I'd created for myself. *It wasn't my fault.* The final test, however, was whether the rest of the world would believe it.

"Honey, you're shaking." Witt's voice seemed to be coming from far away. Still, its warmth and familiarity reminded me of all the years he'd made me feel safe and loved. It was time to know if that love was conditional.

"I need to tell you something," I said.

When I finished, I forced myself to look up at him. His face was pale and he leaned back in his chair, increasing the distance between us. My stomach clenched. Our silence grew heavy and uncomfortable, but I'd spent my strength on the telling of my story and had none left to break it.

"Why didn't you tell me?" he whispered.

"I wasn't ready to," I said. "Until now."

He pushed his chair back and walked over to mine. Pulling me to my feet, he wrapped his arms around me. I felt the wetness on his cheeks as he pressed his face to mine. "I am so sorry that happened to you," he murmured. "And I'm so glad you told me, no matter how long it took."

Burying my face in his chest, I thought of Lorrie. Though I was grateful to have Witt in my corner, she had always been my fiercest defender. Now, though, her win was my loss. Still, I missed her like you miss a lost limb, my brain still registering her presence, unable to accept she was gone.

But the fact remained that Summer would wake tomorrow with the same shame and anger pressing down on her chest that I'd carried around for decades, while Knox would be free to go about his life as if nothing had happened. There was no amount of history with Lorrie that could erase what had happened.

# THIRTY-SIX
## JULES

### *Tuesday, 6:30 p.m.*

Slowly I became aware of Paul's voice.

"I'm sorry, what did you say?" I looked up from my phone to meet his gaze.

"I said, is she coming? We need to leave in ten minutes."

Despite my misgivings, Paul had convinced me to attend a Westwood High fundraising event with him.

"I'm not excited about it either, but we should at least make an appearance," he'd said. "Abby will be all over me if we don't, accusing me of not being supportive of Ari's education. And you're his stepmom, you should be there with me." I nodded, considering the two sentences I'd managed to get Ari to exchange with me the week before. I would definitely not be winning Stepmother of the Year any time soon.

I'd been on the verge of telling Paul we couldn't go because I couldn't find a babysitter. Summer, who'd said she would do it weeks earlier, had been radio silent since I'd taken her to the hospital—nearly three days—not responding to any of my texts or calls to check on her. "I can't stop worrying about her," I'd told Paul.

"She already has a mother to do that, Jules."

"Well, she's really more of a friend," I said, though in the last couple of weeks I'd felt more motherly toward Summer than anything else. "And at the hospital—"

Paul had frowned. "Summer is not a friend! She's our teenage babysitter." The sharpness of his tone had startled me.

"I'm sorry," he sighed. "It's just, I know Eden, and I think it's best to steer clear of anything involving her." I was quiet, relieved I hadn't told Paul how Eden had come over to talk to me. I was still processing that conversation. Since then I'd spent a lot of time staring at Audrey, wondering what I'd do in the same situation. I still wasn't sure.

Then that afternoon Summer had finally texted, a short message saying only that she'd still be there to babysit.

*Are you OK?* I'd replied immediately. But she hadn't responded.

The doorbell rang and Paul's shoulders relaxed as he glanced at his watch. "I'll get it," I said, smoothing the front of the simple black wrap dress I was wearing.

Paul nodded. In his arms Audrey rubbed her eyes and fussed. "I'm going to take her upstairs and put her down. She's exhausted."

"Hi," I said, yanking open the door. "How are you?" I moved to hug her but she was staring down at her phone. "Summer?" I said.

"Oh, hi," she said, glancing up from the screen. "I'm trending." She held up the phone. Her freckles stood out on her pale face and her mouth was pinched into an expression somewhere between anxiety and excitement.

"What do you mean?" I squinted at her phone.

"Everything's happening so fast." She shook her head and

stepped into the foyer. "For starters, everyone knows what happened."

I bit my lip, remembering my conversation with Eden about keeping things quiet to protect Summer. "I'm sorry," I said.

"But lots of people are actually on my side," she continued, looking up at me with an amazed expression that made my heart twinge. "I guess there's even a hashtag—#justice-forsummer."

"Wow." I was out of my depth here. "OK. So that's good?"

She shrugged. "I'm not exactly sure." She bit the inside of her cheek and looked down. "There was a huge fight at school this morning after someone called me a—" She took a deep breath. "A slut."

I gasped. "Oh my God!"

"And now *I'm* suspended. Which is like, so unfair." She blinked back tears.

"Oh, Summer." I put my hand on her shoulder. "I'm so sorry. That sounds awful."

She closed her eyes as if trying to erase a thought from her mind. When she opened her eyes the tears spilled down her cheeks. "I feel so stupid," she whispered.

"You're not stupid."

"I *am*." She nearly spat the words. "I believed everything he said to me. I did everything he wanted. Everyone thinks he's so great, you know?" she continued. "But he's *not*." Her face was wet with tears now but she didn't seem to notice.

There was a clatter behind me and I turned to see Ari with a duffle bag over his shoulder. "Summer," he said, dropping the bag to the floor in surprise.

"Oh, hey." She wiped her face with her sleeve.

"I didn't know... how, um, are you?" He cleared his throat and I died a little at his awkwardness.

"Oh you know," she waved her arm and gave a choked laugh.

"Jules?" Paul called to me from the kitchen. "We really need to get going."

"Coming!" I called. "I'm sorry," I said again to Summer, feeling helpless. "We're not going to stay out long." I gave her shoulder a squeeze and she forced a smile.

Ari cleared his throat. "I—um, I'm headed to Robotics Club, but I could stay... if you, like, need anything."

My head snapped back over my shoulder at Ari and this uncharacteristic display of compassion. And I'd thought he was devoid of all emotion.

Summer made a soft noise in her throat. "Thanks, Ari. That's really nice. But I'm fine."

She straightened her shoulders and pressed her lips together. Ari nodded, then slung the duffle back over his shoulder and disappeared out the door.

I was underdressed for Casino Night, that much was clear. All around the swanky midtown event space women wore long dresses with plunging necklines and no shortage of sequins. Many of the men wore tuxedos, or at least tailored dinner jackets. "Why didn't you tell me this was fancy?" I murmured to Paul as we made our way inside. He glanced down at his khakis and wrinkled blue button-down.

"Since when do you rely on me for fashion advice?"

I sighed and tried to find it funny, to tell myself I was above such displays of Mountaindale excess and self-centeredness. I mean, there were wars and starving children in other parts of the world and these people were focused on drinking champagne and dressing up like Marilyn Monroe. But the problem was it looked... fun.

All around us stood knots of well-dressed couples, their chatter and laughter swirling up into the air to create a sound bath of lighthearted enjoyment. The lighting was warm and low, and on one wall of the space hung a backdrop as large as a bedsheet replicating the iconic WELCOME TO *fabulous* LAS VEGAS sign, perfect for photo ops.

Around the room there were what looked to be roulette and blackjack tables staffed by men and women in white shirts and black vests. On the far side of the room a bartender with a full beard and a sleek ponytail was pouring champagne and mixing drinks behind a wooden bar where people crowded several feet deep. The silky voice of Frank Sinatra singing "Luck Be a Lady" drifted from a nearby speaker and I had to bat away a rogue gold balloon that had escaped its place as a table center-piece where it was supposed to be weighted down by a pile of poker chips and was now drifting around the room.

"Wow." I turned to Paul. "Is this, like, a normal Westwood parent event?"

He shrugged and gestured around the room. "I mean, is any of this *normal*? I wish I could just write them a check and be done with it. But I thought I—*we*—should show up. That it might be, you know, good to be less of a pariah." He gave a small smile and squeezed my arm.

I raised my eyebrows. "Well, here goes nothing."

We crossed the room to the bar and joined the fray. I kept a neutral smile plastered on my face, though it was directed at no one in particular. As we neared the front Paul put his hand on my shoulder and leaned close to my ear.

"I just spotted Abby," he said. My jaw tensed at the mention of his ex-wife. "I'm going to go say hello and just get the awkwardness over with. It'll just take a minute. Do you mind getting us drinks? I'm going to need one."

I nodded and gave him a sympathetic smile, though the last thing I wanted was to be left alone in what felt like shark-infested waters. I focused on taking deep breaths and edging my way up to the bar. When I got there my mind suddenly went blank with anxiety and I ordered two glasses of champagne, mostly because the bottle was sitting right there. Neither Paul nor I really even liked it.

Standing off to the side I scanned the room for him as people jostled me from all directions as if they didn't see me standing there. Then a woman in a bright green dress and bizarre hat and boa caught my eye. "Oh thank God," she said, breaking into a smile. "Just who I was looking for."

I smiled back, caught off guard by her friendliness. "Hi," I said.

She looked at me expectantly, then motioned to the champagne flutes in my hands. "May I?" she said, reaching for one.

My smile froze. "Um, sure?"

"On second thought, I better take both," she said, extending a hand for the second glass. "The bar is so jammed and you're the only waiter I've seen circulating with drinks."

The flush began on my neck and spread over my body, heat radiating from my face like a glowing hot coal.

"Grace," hissed a voice as another familiar-looking woman glided up to her wearing a long, strapless blue dress that was too tight around the chest and dug into her underarms, leaving an angry red line when she raised her hand to point at me. "What are you doing?"

The green-clad woman looked miffed. "Getting a drink, Caroline. Obviously."

The other woman grabbed her elbow and pulled her back as if I was contagious. "That's Paul Shulman's new wife," she said, as if I wasn't standing right there. "The one who, *you know*." She jerked her head toward me. The woman in the green dress stared at me and then down at the champagne glasses in her hand.

"I see," she said, her face rearranging itself into a look of condescending pity. "Well, then, thanks for the drinks." She turned and let herself be led away as the woman in blue scolded her.

"Well, how was I supposed to know? It's not like I've ever *seen* her," the green dress woman retorted. She glanced back at me over her shoulder. "She's not even that pretty."

I felt a hand on my elbow. "Hey," said Paul. "Thank God that's over." He shook his head. "Should we grab some appetizers and find a place to sit? I heard they got an Elvis impersonator for later."

I closed my eyes and drew in a deep breath. I had not asked to end up here in this neighborhood, in this life. But here I was. And it was time people knew I wasn't going anywhere.

"Sure." I opened my eyes and looked at Paul. "Let's go find our place."

# THIRTY-SEVEN

## LORRIE

### *Tuesday, 7 p.m.*

Ed went ballistic when I told him about Mr. Ellison's request that we not attend Casino Night.

"Who the hell does that troll think he is?" he'd asked, slamming his fist down on the counter. "We're damn sure not listening to him."

By that point I actually wanted to stay home. I wanted to be where my children were—albeit all in separate rooms—and pretend the minefield of the outside world didn't exist. But Ed wasn't having it.

"It's not a good idea," I countered through gritted teeth. I pictured being escorted out of the event by armed security guards while everyone looked on. "Besides, you weren't the one who had to deal with Ellison earlier."

Scorn swept across Ed's face. "Well, if I had we wouldn't be in this situation because I would have put him in his place."

"Mom, can I help you get ready?" Chloé bounded in, her face lit with excitement. Enthralled by the idea of a grown-up party with costumes, she'd helped me pick out a shimmery pink drop-waist gown for the occasion. "You said I could do your makeup, remember?"

"Perfect timing, Chlo," Ed said, nodding in my direction. "Mom was just about to head upstairs."

"Oh goodie!" She clapped her hands and bounded up ahead of me. With one last glare at Ed, I followed.

On the way I sat silently in the car next to Ed and reread the email Mr. Ellison had sent to the Parent Boosters, thanking me for my service and announcing that Caroline Doyle was taking over as president and chair of Casino Night. My stomach churned with anxiety. I considered feigning illness once we arrived so we could make a quick escape before anyone noticed we were there.

Inside it was already crowded. Ed made his way to the bar, leaving me hovering on the outskirts of the crowd. Was it my imagination, or were people staring at me? I pulled my lavender silk scarf tighter around my shoulders and scanned the crowd for the one face I was simultaneously hoping to see and dreading the appearance of. But Eden, usually easy to spot with her mane of hair and long legs, was nowhere to be found.

I stood by myself, certain everyone was taking note of my isolation. Usually by now someone would have rushed up to me to compare notes on summer plans or humble brag about their child's choice of college; *"I was hoping he'd follow in my footsteps at Vanderbilt, but he just had to go to UPenn,"* or *"I mean, what's not to like about the UCLA weather? But she wanted the Columbia experience."*

Across the room I spied a group of fellow Parent Boosters moms and began making my way to them. When I got closer one of them saw me and leaned into the group, her hand over her mouth. Several heads turned my way, but when I gave a friendly wave those same heads snapped back away from me. I froze midway across the room, the heat of humiliation rising up in my face.

I picked up one of the evening's programs from an empty table and pretended to be busy reading it. I'd designed them myself and had had them printed weeks ago. The program fell open to the acknowledgments page which listed the event's sponsors and the Parent Boosters volunteers. Except it was no longer a page but a loose insert. A closer look told me that the original page had been removed. On the new insert my name had been removed as chair of the Parent Boosters, replaced by Caroline's.

Lifting my eyes from the program, I spied Mr. Ellison frowning at me from across the room. A jolt of anger ricocheted through my body like the recoil from a gun. How dare he erase all the work I'd put into this event?

Someone jostled my elbow and I turned, grateful for the attention. "My apologies. It's so crowded this evening." Mr. Villanueva, Knox's Spanish teacher, shook his head and smiled. He was my favorite of all the kids' teachers, and with his heavy brows and swoop of dark hair he was also popular with many of the female Westwood students—despite the known fact that his husband was a math teacher at the middle school down the street.

"Mr. Villanueva, how nice to see you," I said, hoping my relief at having someone—anyone—to talk to wasn't evident.

"You are looking absolutely radiant tonight, Señora Keller." He smiled. "What a lovely dress."

"Please, call me Lorrie." I waved his words away while I enjoyed the compliment. "Congratulations, I heard you outdid yourself with *Mamma Mia!* this season." Directing the mostly mediocre musical talent who aspired to be Broadway performers in the school musical every spring was a thankless task, but Mr. Villanueva, who'd once trained as an opera singer in his native Mexico, seemed to enjoy it.

He gave a warm, solicitous smile. "Yes, well, the kids deserve all the credit. They worked so hard."

"Lorrie!" I looked over to see Caroline beelining toward me, her face pinched with anxiety.

"Hi," I said.

"You have to help me," she said, grabbing my elbow.

"I'm so sorry, please excuse me," I tossed over my shoulder to Mr. Villanueva as Caroline practically dragged me away from him. "What on earth?" I said to her.

"It's a disaster, a complete disaster." She covered her face with her hands.

"Caroline, you're in charge now, remember? I'm not supposed to be—"

"Please!" she tightened her grip on my arm, her desperate eyes filling with tears. "I don't know what to do."

Wordlessly I let myself be led to a side room. There, slumped in a chair in the corner was a dark-haired man in a white, bedazzled polyester suit, fast asleep. I gave Caroline a questioning look, but then it hit me; the sharp, piney tang of alcohol. A lot of alcohol.

"I had contingency plans for if the sound system went out or if we ran out of poker chips," Caroline said, wringing her hands. "But I didn't plan for drunk Elvis." The man's chin dipped further toward his chest and he gave a loud snore.

"Oh," I said.

"He had excellent references." Caroline fought back tears. She'd been in charge of booking the entertainment for the evening and had been crowing for weeks about securing what she called "a five-star Elvis impersonator." Now, though, she looked on the verge of a nervous breakdown.

Elvis shifted in his chair and smacked his lips. One of his dark sideburns had come unglued and crept across his cheek like a fuzzy caterpillar. I fought the urge to laugh.

"The whole night is ruined!" Caroline was breathing fast and I worried she might pass out.

"Caroline?" a voice called from the hallway. "Let's get the music started already, people are getting restless—" Eden entered the small room and stopped short. "Oh," she said, seeing me.

I gestured toward the snoring man. "It appears Elvis is indisposed."

Caroline wrung her hands. "I didn't know what to do, and Lorrie always knows what to do," she said to Eden, her tone apologetic. "Oh my God, it's a disaster." She plunged her face into her hands.

"Caroline, breathe." I exchanged a look with Eden. We needed to get rid of Caroline and her hysterics. "Why don't you go find the caterer and bring back a cup of coffee," I suggested. Caroline nodded and hurried out of the room.

Eden took a step closer to me and regarded the drunk man in the white onesie. "Well," she said, "at least he's in character."

A giggle escaped my mouth before I could stop it, then another. It was all so ridiculous. Eden glanced at me, her mouth twitching, and then she cracked, too. Before I knew it I was shaking with laughter and wiping my eyes. As Eden was trying unsuccessfully to compose herself, a snort of laughter escaped through her nose.

"What the hell are we going to do?" she asked, trying to catch her breath.

"I think I might have an idea," I said, something occurring to me. I smoothed my hair. "Can you wait here for Caroline and try to keep her calm?"

Eden raised an eyebrow. "Gee, thanks for giving me the easy job," she said.

I smiled and shook my head. "I'll be right back, I promise." I floated back out into the crowd, buoyed by the moment with Eden. It had felt so normal, so *us*. Was I crazy to think there was still a chance I wouldn't lose her after all; that maybe we could work through everything that had happened?

"Excuse me, I'm so sorry to interrupt," I said, touching Mr. Villanueva's shoulder and nodding at the group of parents he'd been chatting with. "But I'm wondering if I might ask you a favor." He gave a puzzled nod and followed me. "We're having a small... challenge with the evening's entertainment," I explained as I escorted him out of the room. "But you may be able to help."

I opened the door and Mr. Villanueva's eyes traveled from Eden to the sight of the snoring man in the rhinestone suit. Eden looked from Mr. Villanueva back to me with a questioning look.

"As you can see," I said, drawing a deep breath, "this evening's musical guest is incapacitated."

"OK... yes, I see." Mr. Villanueva nodded with confusion. "I'm sorry, but what did you want my help with?"

I shook my head and summoned my most charming smile. "Well, I was hoping you'd be willing to step in." I gestured toward Elvis. "It's just, everyone is expecting some kind of entertainment tonight."

A look of panicked understanding swept over Mr. Villanueva's face. "Oh no." He put up his hands and took a step back.

Eden jumped in. Persuasion was her art, not mine. "As an artist, I'm sure you can understand how important music is to the ambiance of the evening. It loosens people up, they start having fun, which means they spend more money to support the school. Which means you have a bigger budget for the musical next year." She raised one finger in emphasis.

"Please," I pleaded. "Just one song. Maybe two. You'd be saving the entire night, and helping Westwood."

"You know," Eden twirled a lock of her hair. "I've always thought you looked like a young Elvis Presley—back before all the banana splits and quaaludes."

"And just picture Mr. Ellison's face when he hears you salvaged the biggest Westwood fundraiser of the year," I chimed in.

Mr. Villanueva closed his eyes, our tag team strategy clearly wearing him down. "Fine," he said, opening them. He pointed a long, graceful finger at the snoring man. "But I'm not wearing that ridiculous costume."

"Of course not," Eden said as I exhaled with relief. "We're going to make you look so much better than that."

"Here's the coffee!" Caroline flew back into the room clutching a mug, sloshing most of the liquid onto the floor.

"Perfect timing," I said. "I think we've found a solution." Mr. Villanueva groaned.

Eden raided the coat check and found a long-forgotten denim jacket and coaxed Mr. Villanueva into undoing a couple of his top shirt buttons and draping the jacket over his shoulders. I pulled up a few karaoke background tracks on Caroline's phone and helped her plug it into the sound system near the stage.

Once Caroline had introduced Mr. Villanueva to scattered applause and he'd taken the stage, Eden and I stood together off to the side.

*Please don't walk away*, I thought. She didn't. Sensing a détente, I took a deep breath. "It's good to see you," I said. She stiffened and remained silent, staring straight ahead at the stage. Just as quickly as it had come, the sense of normalcy between us disappeared. I tried again. "I heard what happened at school, to Summer. I'm so sorry."

She whirled to face me, her face a mask of hurt. "Don't," she said. "Just don't."

"I'm sorry," I said again. "I just thought—"

Her eyes blazed. "She's my little girl, Lorrie." Her voice was a hoarse whisper, her anguish undisguised. "How could you let him do that to my little girl?"

Anger rose up in me for an instant but wilted just as quickly into defeat. "I'm sorry," I whispered. They were the only words I had.

In the low lighting the tears in her eyes gleamed. "Me too," she said. "But that will never be enough." Then she turned and walked away.

# THIRTY-EIGHT

## KNOX

### *Tuesday, 9 p.m.*

The outdoor light over the driveway reflected in the mist, making everything look kind of eerie, like the set of a horror movie. It fit my mood. The basketball felt slick in my hands as it flew from my fingers to clatter off the rim. I'd been outside shooting baskets for the better part of an hour, the sweat gathering on my neck. Anything to distract myself.

I'd made it two days. Forty-eight excruciating hours.

Ever since that night with Summer, the idea of going on any of my usual porn websites made me feel sick. But that didn't mean I didn't still want to do it.

I glanced up at my bedroom window, the room I was trying to avoid. I felt ashamed that even with everything that was going on, that's where I wanted to be. Alone with my iPad. I'd installed a blocking software and logged every website I thought I might be tempted to access. Still, I was the one who set it up, so it would be just as easy to uninstall it and disappear down the familiar rabbit hole.

It was better to stay outside, as far away from my room as

possible. Better to keep shooting baskets until I was too exhausted to do anything but fall into bed, even if that took all night.

It started back when I was thirteen, when one of the kids on the baseball team pulled up a video on his phone in the back of the bus on our way home from a game. I watched it over someone's shoulder as it got passed around. The woman's boobs were so large she looked like she might topple forward. She was supposed to be a nurse but she wasn't dressed like anyone I'd ever seen in a doctor's office. I laughed because everyone else did, and then pulled my backpack onto my lap to hide my hard-on.

It was easy to find the websites on my own. After I finished watching I always had the same guilty feeling in my stomach, but not enough to stop. Soon I'd honed in on my favorite kinds of videos. Girls who acted shy and needed to be convinced, sometimes forcefully, to take off their clothes. In the end they always liked it.

I kept my viewing sessions to two or three times a week until high school. Then everything got so stressful. School was hard for the first time, plus I landed a spot on the varsity baseball team as a freshman. Which meant the only time I had to study was on the bus late at night on our way home from games, or after practice when I was so exhausted I could barely keep my eyes open during dinner. On the outside everything looked great. Inside, though, I felt like I was pinned under a giant boulder that got a little heavier each day.

The older guys on the team started inviting me to parties where I was the only freshman. I felt like such an impostor. I'd wander around, dipping in and out of conversations, trying to act cool. I could never think of much to say, especially around the older girls. They talked in a language I didn't speak yet about Adderall and SAT scores. Everyone seemed like they had high school all figured out.

Most of the kids drank—beer or vodka and Red Bull hidden in their water bottles—but I never did. Mostly because I was too afraid of getting busted and kicked off the team, and also because I didn't like the way it made people act. Usually I tried to go home before the girls grew loud and silly, laughing in an exaggerated way and letting their T-shirts slip off one shoulder.

Then one night I stayed too long.

I was sitting on the couch when a girl dropped down next to me and leaned her head on my shoulder.

"You have such strong arms." She wrapped her fingers around my bicep and giggled. Her name was Quinn, and while she was usually at the parties I could tell she hovered on the outskirts of the group. She was always laughing and would stand too close to you while talking, tugging at some piece of her clothing that was too short or too tight. At school I would see her standing off to the side while the other girls clumped together passing around lip gloss and touching each other's hair like a circle of grooming monkeys.

One of the boys leaned down close to my ear. "She's hitting on you, bro. You should get some action." I froze as Quinn smiled up at me and brushed her fingers across my chest.

"Check it out," another voice behind me said. "Knox is about to get himself an older girl." I felt a hand clamp down on my shoulder. "Go for it, man. Hey Quinn, Knox is cute, right?"

"He sure ish," she purred.

"You should take him to the other room and, uh, show him how much fun you are, you know?" There was a round of laughter as Quinn struggled to stand up.

"OK," she said, looking at me through half-closed eyes. "Let'sh go." She swayed slightly and I felt the whole room watching as we crossed it and stepped into someone's guest bedroom. Pulling the door shut, she kissed me and I tasted the sticky sweetness of Red Bull on her breath. Lying down on the bed, she lifted her shirt over her head and patted the mattress next to her.

"You're so nice," she mumbled, her boobs spilling out of her push-up bra. She wriggled out of her jeans, which had left an angry red band around her midsection where they'd cut into the roll of flesh just above her hips. I lowered myself on top of her and she moaned theatrically as we kissed. I thought I heard laughter outside the door as she tugged at my pants until they slid down over my knees.

*Holy shit*, I thought. *This is really happening.* It wasn't at all how I thought it would go, or even how I wanted it to, but as I picked up speed rubbing against her through my underwear I also didn't exactly want to stop. She let me pull down her underwear and I was surprised to see a tuft of hair. The women in my videos were usually bare down there.

"Mm," she moaned faintly, her eyes closed. I hoisted myself up to get a better angle and her body went still, her jaw slack. As her breathing slowed and deepened, I realized she was passed out. I froze. Was this normal? Was I supposed to keep going? Wake her up? I flopped down hard next to her, hoping the bounce of the mattress would rouse her. Nothing.

"Quinn," I whispered, but she remained motionless. My erection poked up stiffly through my boxers as the naked girl next to me let out a soft snore. I put a hand on one of her boobs and squeezed. She didn't move. It was warm and heavy in my palm. I slipped my other hand between my legs and frantically jerked off while I groped her. Terrified she'd wake up before I finished, I ran through the library of porn scenes I'd cataloged in my mind until I found one that worked to get me off fast. When I finished I wiped myself off with her shirt. Shame bubbled in my stomach. Unsure what to do next, I pulled a blanket up over both of us and closed my eyes while I waited for her to wake up.

I woke to the sound of voices. As my eyes opened a group of guys came into focus. I realized they were looking down at the bed where I was still lying with Quinn. She was awake now, too, trying to wriggle into her clothes while she kept the blanket wrapped around her.

"Hey," I said, confused by the look of panic on her face. "Are you OK?"

"Way to go, freshman," said one of the boys. Everyone laughed. A senior named Kirby held up his phone, recording Quinn as she pulled her shirt on over her head inside out. Scrunching up her bra in her hand, she swung her legs unsteadily onto the floor, keeping her head ducked down.

"Where the hell are my shoes?" she muttered.

"Over there," I pointed to the corner near the door. Kirby followed her with his phone as she wobbled toward the door.

"Bro!" he bellowed, turning the camera back to me once she'd gone. "Nailed it!" A wall of hands reached out to me in triumph. In my daze I high-fived them all while Kirby filmed.

"Is she OK?" I asked. "She seems kind of out of it. Shouldn't someone drive her home?"

"Naw, don't worry about it." Kirby shrugged, pocketing his phone. "She'll be all right."

Except on Monday I didn't see her standing with the other girls before class, or later in the cafeteria when I slid my tray into an open spot at the baseball team's table. I did see, though, that an awful lot of kids were looking my way and whispering. A couple of upper classmen I didn't know well even offered me passing high fives in the hall.

"Dude, you're a legend," said Kirby, slapping me on the back as I bit into my overcooked hamburger on its limp bun.

"What do you mean?" I asked, and the guys all laughed.

"Bagging Quinn, man! Everyone's seen the video by now."

Sweat sprang up on the back of my neck. "Oh no, we didn't even—"

"Quinn, on the other hand..." Kirby shook his head. "I

mean, boning a freshman? That's like putting up a billboard that says, 'I'll do it with anyone.'"

"But we didn't—"

"Mad props, bro," chimed in another kid, folding a piece of pizza in half and stuffing it in his mouth. "Wish I could've pulled off something like that as a frosh."

I saw Quinn the next day walking to class alone, her eyes glued to the floor. My stomach flip-flopped. I knew I should say something, set the record straight, but too many people had heard (and seen) the fake story by then and I didn't want to look stupid. Plus, I'd be lying if I said I wasn't enjoying all the attention. So I let her walk right by me, all the while feeling like the worst person in the world.

After that I got really popular. At the same time I worked up to two or three hours of porn a day, staying up way later than I should under the glow of my iPad. I'd wake exhausted in the morning with that same sick feeling in my stomach. Still, girls flipped their hair when talking to me and went out of their way to sit next to me in class. Instantly I was one of the most popular guys in school, but the few times I tried to cash in I could barely make it happen. I had to squeeze my eyes shut and summon to mind the dirtiest videos I could think of just to stay hard enough to get over the finish line. A couple of times I didn't make it, one of them with Mackenzie. I didn't want that to start getting around, so I stopped hooking up with girls altogether.

Until Summer.

But now I'd gone and messed that up, too.

The mist had turned to rain and it was coming down harder now, pelting the driveway. I clanged another shot off the rim, retrieved the ball and slammed my fist into it. I was furious with myself for what I was about to do, but unable to stop.

Inside the house was quiet. No one saw me go up to my room. I closed the door and grabbed my iPad. I found the blocking software in my Settings and clicked Uninstall.

# THIRTY-NINE

## SUMMER

**Tuesday, 10:30 p.m.**

"But you have to," Violet said. "You have a responsibility." Jules and Dr. Shulman had come home early and Violet had been pacing my bedroom for ever since I'd gotten home from babysitting, twirling pieces of her long, increasingly tangled hair around her index finger.

"I don't have to do anything," I mumbled. I was so tired. I lay on my bed staring at the ceiling, not sleeping but also not awake. I'd been in the same position as long as Violet had been pacing the room.

She came over and sat down on the bed next to me. "Look, you already have a lot of support—more and more people are tweeting with the #justiceforsummer hashtag. You need to capitalize on that. What about writing something for my blog? Like about your experience."

"My experience?" I frowned. "Experience with what?"

A look of sympathy crossed Violet's face. "I mean what happened to you," she said gently. "With Knox. Your side of the story."

When I realized what Violet meant, my first thought was *How could I ever do that to Knox?* My second was how pathetic it was that I could react that way.

"I don't know if I can do it." I bit my lip with hesitation. My stomach felt sick at the thought of people reading what I had to say. Then again, why shouldn't they? I had something to say.

"Don't know if you can do what?" I looked up to see my mom standing in my doorway holding a tray laden with brownies and a box of Thin Mint Girl Scout cookies. She and my dad had come home early from Casino Night, saying they were tired but really I knew it was to check on me.

"Hey, last month you told me we were all out!" I sat up and pointed an accusing finger at the Thin Mints.

"I hid some in the freezer in the garage," she said, giving me a guilty smile. "Here, take the whole box." She set the tray down on the floor and held the green box out toward me.

I couldn't tell if my stomach was churning with hunger or nausea. "No thanks." I let myself fall backward onto my pillow and closed my eyes.

"But they're your favorite," Violet said. I didn't need my eyes to be open to know the look she and my mom would be exchanging. Suddenly united in purpose, she and my mom had spent most of that time ganging up on me; cajoling me to eat something, to take a shower, to do anything but lie in my bed.

"So what is it you don't know if you can do?" my mom asked again, looking suspicious.

"Everyone has heard what happened by now," Violet explained. "But no one has heard the truth straight from Summer. I want her to write something for my blog. Then we can amplify it on Twitter, get the conversation going."

"I don't want a *conversation*," I snapped, yet another flash of anger searing through me. "I want..." I trailed off, suddenly stumped. What did I want? To disappear from the face of the Earth? To erase that night from my memory? For Knox to go to jail? I closed my eyes and listened to my breath reverberating in the back of my throat like waves. A nearly imperceptible thought whispered through my head, gathering strength until finally I could hear it over the rest of my mental clutter.

What I wanted was to be *believed*. Not just by my parents and my friends, but by people who'd heard what I had to say and recognized it for what it was: the truth.

"OK fine," I said, opening my eyes. "I'll do it."

"Whoa," my mom eyed me with surprised concern. "Slow down. This is not a good idea."

"Why not?" I snapped. Why did everyone keep questioning my ability to make my own decisions?

My mom held up her hands in defense. "I just think you've been through a lot, and it would be rash to—"

"Stop treating me like I'm so fragile," I cut in. "It's not like if you drop me I'm going to break." As I said it, though, I wondered if maybe I would. I hated how unpredictable my feelings had become. Was there such a thing as sudden onset bipolar disorder? The therapist my mom had made me an appointment with this afternoon probably could have told me, except that I'd refused to get out of bed to go see him.

"OK," Violet said. "So you'll write something, I'll put it on my blog, and we'll tweet it out." She snapped her fingers. "Or better yet, I'll publish it in the school paper. The last edition of *Watermark* goes out to all the students and teachers this week. I'll just, like, slip it in at the last minute, after all the other content has been approved."

"I said *no*." My mom turned to face Violet, ending their alliance with one sharp glance. Turning to me, she softened her tone. "If it's on the internet, it's there forever." She looked at me. "When people google you, like for job interviews, that's not what you want them to find."

"But Summer didn't do anything wrong." Violet crossed her arms. "So who cares?"

"*She* might," replied my mom, giving Violet a withering look. "And so do I."

"But I don't care," I assured her. And, saying it, I realized I really didn't. If no one else was going to come for Knox Keller, then maybe it was time I did.

"No." My mom reached out and grabbed my hand in a kind of plea. "Sweetheart, this absolutely isn't happening. Your father and I won't let it."

I stiffened and drew my hand back. I was tired of being told what to do.

"Sure, Mom," I said, pasting on a smile. "I understand. You're right." Behind her, Violet gave me a look of disappointed confusion. "You can leave the cookies," I added, nodding toward the door. "I think I might be hungry after all."

Once my mom had left the room I turned to Violet. "OK then, I guess I better get writing."

# FORTY

## KNOX

### *Tuesday, 11 p.m.*

After the euphoria of the release came the crash. I'd never been surfing, but I imagined it must be like cresting the top of a mega wave, the water, beach, and sky stretching out before you, on top of the world for one perfect instant, then toppling off your board and finding yourself submerged in the water with a mouthful of sand.

I lay sweaty and guilt-stricken on my bed, my iPad propped up on my bare thighs, my boxers pulled down around my knees. Frozen on the screen was the last frame of the video I'd been watching, someone's cum smeared on a woman's stomach, her head cut out of the frame.

I wiped my own stickiness away with the hand towel I always kept nearby. I always rinsed it out before tossing it in my clothes hamper, so that that my mom wouldn't come across any evidence in my laundry.

The digital clock on my nightstand told me it was 10:58 p.m. Realizing I'd been at this for nearly two hours, my body glowed with the hot guilt of my weakness—but not enough to keep me from navigating back to the video thumbnails on the main page of the website I was on.

*Just one more,* I told myself, beginning to click around to find a video I liked.

There was a knock on my door and it cracked open. Shit, I'd forgotten to lock it. My heart leapt into my throat as I tossed my laptop to the side and yanked up my boxers.

"Oh, jeez, sorry," my dad said, averting his eyes as he stopped in the doorway. "I didn't realize you were, um, busy."

"I forgot to lock the door," I mumbled, pulling a pillow over my lap.

"Nothing we all haven't done," he shrugged and leaned against the door jam, grinning at me. "When I was a teenager I used to 'borrow the copies of *Penthouse* my brother, your uncle Ben, kept under his mattress." He made air quotes. "Man, I remember one time I made the mistake of dropping one in the toilet. I put it back all wrinkled and damp, trying to pretend nothing had happened, but he knew it was me. Boy did he beat the shit out of me." He laughed like it was a good memory. "Anyway," he continued, his face growing serious. "I saw your light was still on so I figured you should be the first to know; I just got an early heads-up from a friend at the attorney general's office. They're not planning to press charges."

I frowned as I processed his statement. "So, like, I don't have to talk to any more lawyers? Or police?"

"No," he shook his head. "That's all over." I waited for the relief to hit me, but nothing happened. "Anyway," my dad continued, "I know the last few days haven't been easy on you," he said. "On any of us." His face creased into an expression I hadn't seen before, something between sadness and remorse. "You know I love you, right? That I would never let anything bad happen to you?" His voice broke slightly and his eyes grew red. "I know I haven't been the most touchy-feely dad, but I'm always here for you, son, whatever you need."

His uncharacteristic display of emotion cracked something open inside me. "I think I might... do it too much," I blurted, then covered my mouth with my hand like I could scoop the words back in.

"Do what?" he asked, furrowing his brow. I pointed to the laptop and my father's eyebrows raised, then he shook his head. "Nah, it's normal. You know that, right? I guess I should have talked to you more about it. Like I said, I'm not the greatest at that stuff."

I almost laughed. The last conversation I'd had with my dad about any of this "stuff" was when he and my mom sat me down at age eight to tell me how babies were made—which I already knew by then, of course.

"But, like, how much is normal?" I asked. Now that I'd broached the topic I couldn't stop the words from flowing out of my mouth. I felt something in my chest expand, as if I'd just been cut loose from a tight band wrapped around my ribs.

He flushed, then shrugged. "You're a teenage boy, Knox. You kind of... grow out of that phase. I wouldn't worry about it. Plus, between you and me, once you get to college you'll probably be doing it a lot more with actual girls—safely, of course." He raised his eyebrows. "I'm not ready for grandkids yet." He chuckled, then pursed his lips. "But you know you could come to me, right, if anything like that did happen? I'd help you take care of it. You can come to me with anything, you know that, right?" I nodded. "Good," he said. "And listen, I don't want you to worry about anything, OK? It's all been cleared up. Everything's going to be fine."

"OK," I said, my voice catching. I felt my ribs compressing again.

"It's a shame about the girl, of course," he continued. "She seemed sweet, but there are a lot of crazies out there. You have to be careful."

*Don't talk about her like that*, I wanted to say. "Summer," I said.

"What's that?" My dad took a step toward me.

"You said 'the girl.' Her name is Summer."

"Yeah," he said. "Well, OK. Get some sleep." Then he tapped the doorframe twice with his knuckle and left.

# FORTY-ONE

## SUMMER

### *Tuesday, 11:30 p.m.*

"Just write about what happened like you're talking to me," Violet had advised before she left my house. "Like you're telling me what happened and how it made you feel."

Which would have been easy, if only I knew.

One minute I'd be laughing at a TikTok and feeling normal, and the next I'd be sobbing in the shower, trying to scrub off my shame and stupidity at believing Knox had really loved me. I'd catch myself missing him as I drifted off to sleep, then I'd wake up on fire with rage, having fantasies about taking his perfect life and burning it to the ground.

I'd always thought of rape as a sudden, isolated incident with a well-defined beginning and end. Like, if you're jogging and someone jumps out of the bushes and attacks you, the minute he wrestles you to the ground the rape is in progress. But what if you're dating someone, someone you really like or maybe even love? And you want to have sex with that person. In fact, you've been waiting for the day when you stop kissing and holding hands and finally get to the important stuff. Then you have sex, and you don't like how it happened or how you feel after. But you love the person, so you do it again, almost like an experiment, hoping it will be different. And then another time, and maybe another, each time hoping for something different. Each time afterward your stomach feels queasy as you replay the things he said to you and the things he sort of asked, sort of demanded you do. All of which you do, because you love him and you're afraid of losing him, but you feel ashamed of later.

But you tell yourself it's worth it for the way he drives around with one hand on the steering wheel and the other gripping yours, and the nights you stay on the phone until you both fall asleep, talking about a future where high school doesn't exist, or, on the best days, the way he puts his arm around you in the hall at school for everyone to see. You don't want to give any of that up, so you keep doing the other stuff. And now it's a pattern; it's just how things go. It's what you do. You tell yourself it's no different than slipping into character while rehearsing for a play. Except in this case my part was that of someone who liked being treated that way, moaning when he asked me to moan and repeating what he wanted me to say. After you've done that for a while you're past the point of no return; it feels impossible to double back and say, "Hey, wait, actually can we try something different? I mean, I know I've been acting a certain way and repeating all the stuff you want me to say, but that was all just pretend and really it makes me feel bad and a little scared of you."

Then one day something inside you gives way, and you don't want to have that sick feeling anymore. So you say no but things are already in motion. You don't want to do it anymore. You say no but your voice seems so small. It happens anyway.

Violet was the only one I had talked to about Knox when we started dating, but even with her I was careful not to stray outside the lines of the love story I'd spent my whole life writing; the one where the handsome boy finally realizes the girl next door (or across the street, in my case) is The One and they live happily ever after. She'd spent years listening to me fan the flames of my crush, so no one was more excited for me than her when my fairytale came true. I didn't want to ruin that for her, especially when I was still confused about what was happening. I mean, how do you explain to someone that ninety percent of the time your boyfriend rubs your shoulders and tells you how perfect you are or surprises you with your favorite candy bar when you're studying for your AP History final, and the other ten percent of the time he transforms into a stranger who says things you'd never repeat to anyone and handles your body in a way that feels more like anger than love.

Hearing Violet use the word "rape" so confidently about what happened to me pulled me from the quicksand where I'd been slowly disappearing. I stayed up for hours, trying to get my feelings down on paper. I wrote in circles, unsure whether the words on the page made any sense at all. In the end, around three a.m. I took a deep breath and emailed it to Violet.

I didn't think much about what would happen after and who might suffer.

I was just tired of it being me.

# FORTY-TWO
## JULES

**Wednesday, 7:30 a.m.**

"I'm running late, any chance you can drop Ari off at school?" Paul asked as he sloshed coffee into his favorite travel mug, the one with *Economists do it on demand* written on it.

"Sure," I said, careful to keep the annoyance out of my voice. This happened at least once a week, which meant I had to stop what I was doing, wait for Ari to locate his shoes from wherever he'd stepped out of them the night before, and remove Audrey from her highchair and load her into the car. But all that wasn't even what I minded so much. It was the awkwardness of being alone with Ari, who usually spent the whole ride in silence, as if acknowledging me would somehow make my presence in his life permanent.

I'd tried, of course. When Paul and I got engaged I took Ari to dinner one night at his favorite sushi restaurant. He didn't seem like he was one for small talk, so I steadied my trembling hands on the table and laid it all out for him.

"Look," I'd said. "I know you must be angry at your dad for what happened, and probably at me, too. I want you to know I totally understand and respect that. But, we're going to be in each other's lives now, so I'm hoping we can figure out how to have some kind of relationship."

"I'm not mad at my parents for splitting up," he said, heaping wasabi into his soy sauce. "Or you."

"Oh," I said, taken aback. "OK."

"Yeah, they fought all the time anyway. But it's just annoying to live two different places. Like, I keep forgetting stuff at the wrong house."

I frowned, having not considered the logistics of his situation. "That does sound annoying."

"Anyway Mom wouldn't let me get my drone pilot's license because she said it was a waste of time. But now Dad's letting me. So." He shrugged.

"Cool," I said with what I hoped sounded like great enthusiasm. "Drones."

After that he answered most of my questions about school, his friends, and whatever else I could think to ask him in monosyllables.

"Ah, don't worry about it, honey," Paul had told me later when I'd confessed what a failure the lunch had been. "That's just Ari. He doesn't even talk to me that much."

In the car with him now, though, I felt buoyed by a sense of reckless don't-give-a-damn that lingered from Casino Night. *I will not be ignored,* I thought. *I'm here to stay, so everyone better get fucking used to it.*

"So, high school graduation!" I said, turning a bright smile his way. "That's a big deal." His body twitched as though I startled him by breaking our unspoken pact of silence. He nodded. *Nope, not today,* I thought. *Today you are going to talk to me.* "What are you most excited about?" I pressed.

"MIT." *OK, verbal acknowledgment. Progress.*

"What about MIT, specifically?" We stopped at a red light and I looked over at him. He stared straight ahead.

"The robotics program."

"Robotics, yes!" I cried, gleeful at his full-sentence response. "Tell me more about robotics." His eyes flickered toward me like I might be losing my mind. Which I had to admit was possible.

"Their robotics faculty is world-renowned. Whereas at Westwood the classes are so basic I could teach them." He said it not with scorn, but as if stating a fact.

"I'm sure you could," I said. And I didn't doubt it. *Keep it going,* I told myself. *We're on a roll now.* But I didn't have to.

"Is Summer OK?" Ari asked suddenly, still staring straight ahead. Caught off guard, I pressed too hard on the gas as the light turned green. Our car shot forward through the intersection.

"Oops, sorry," I said, braking. "Uh, what do you mean?"

"I saw what happened to her at school. And I know you two are, like, friends."

"Right," I said, overwhelmed by the amount of words coming from his mouth.

"She's always been nice to me," he said. "At least, she doesn't totally ignore me at school like everyone else."

The way he'd lingered in the foyer the other night suddenly made sense. A surprising ache formed in my heart for the awkward boy with the genius IQ sitting next to me. "You know," I said. "Maybe you should ask her how she's doing. She could probably use some people on her side."

The faintest flush crept over his face as he turned to look out the window. "Maybe I will," he said.

# FORTY-THREE

## EDEN

***Wednesday, 8:30 a.m.***

A ringing phone woke me from a deep sleep. I squinted at the incoming call from a number I didn't recognize.

"Hello," I mumbled.

"Mrs. Van Doren?"

"Yes."

"This is Lorena Gomez calling from the attorney general's office." The woman's voice was crisp and formal. My senses roared to life as I scrambled to a seated position.

"Yes," I breathed.

"I'm calling to inform you that in the matter of Summer Van Doren's alleged sexual assault, the attorney general's office will not be pressing charges."

"I'm sorry, can you repeat that?" I cleared my throat and rubbed my eyes.

"After a review of the evidence, we are unable to in good faith move forward with the case."

I slumped back against the headboard. "Of course you fucking can't," I muttered.

There was a long silence on the line.

"I'm sorry, ma'am," the woman said, lowering her voice. "I really am. I have a daughter, too. But unless something else comes to light, our hands are tied. We'll be mailing you a formal notification of our findings for your records."

Closing my eyes, I hung up the phone and slid back down into the bed and waited for relief to flood my body. No charges meant Summer wouldn't have to sit across from detectives and lawyers while they tugged at every thread of her story, asking what she was wearing, how much she'd had to drink, and submitting her sexual history for the public record. No charges meant no court proceedings that would surely drag on into the start of her first year at Princeton, pulling her away from her new life and back into this mess.

And yet, relief didn't come. Instead a toxic mix of guilt and anger burbled in my chest. I'd known there hadn't been any point in going to the police; that no justice would result from a system designed for and by the men who made up most of it. What's more, I'd helped orchestrate this exact outcome that day in the hospital when we'd left without doing the exam. But had that been the wrong decision? I shook the doubt from my head. No. I was certain the outcome would have been the same, just with more humiliation along the way.

I lay flattened in bed, my body humming with the reality that no one was left to fight for my daughter but me. I thought of Violet's plan from the night before, which, like most teenage ideas, had seemed reckless and half-baked. Now, though, I wondered if I'd missed the point. Because while the attorney general wasn't pressing charges, no charges did not mean no justice. There were plenty of ways to accomplish that.

"Hey."

My eyes snapped open to find Witt standing next to the bed, holding out a mug of coffee. He wore sweatpants and a T-shirt from the one time he'd run the New York marathon that I often stole to sleep in because it was so old and soft. "Jesus," I grabbed my chest. "You scared the shit out of me. I thought you'd left for work already."

"I took the day off."

"You did?" Greedily I reached for the steaming mug. Witt never took vacation days. Even when we were *on* vacation he was on his laptop or taking calls at least some of the time.

"Yeah." He shrugged and sat down on the edge of the bed. "With everything going on I thought it would be good to be around." The slight wrinkles around his eyes deepened as he gave me a slow, sad smile.

Tears sprang to my eyes. "You're a good man, Wittman Van Doren."

"Aw." He leaned forward to wrap his arms around me. "When did you become such a softie?"

I nuzzled into his embrace. I'd made up for a lot of bad decisions by marrying Witt. "The attorney general's office called," I said, my face buried in his neck.

He pulled back to look at me. "And?"

I shook my head. His body stiffened and moved away from mine. "We basically knew this would happen," I said, sitting up taller as I prepared for another battle.

"You were," he said curtly. "I wasn't given a choice, remember?" He rose from the bed and paced to the window, the tenderness between us vanishing.

"You have no idea what it's like," I said in a tight voice. "It follows you; it's never over. Every time you think it is, there you are again, sitting across from a fat detective who's already made up his mind that you're trash, while he tries to get you to say that really, you liked it. That you couldn't get enough of being fucked by your teacher. That you're known for blowing half the football team, so you must like it, must be asking for it. I mean, look at the way you dress. Of course a grown man would be confused and unable to control himself."

"Listen, Eden—" He put his fingers to his temples.

"No, you listen. Everybody knew and no one believed me. People called me names at school, boys backed me into corners and—" I shuddered at the memories. "And now the same thing is happening to our daughter." I flung the bedclothes off and stood. "And you think a bunch of old men in uniforms are going to be able to help her? Please."

Witt reached for me but I crossed my arms. "Honey, I'm so sorry that happened to you." His voice caught with emotion. "I don't even have the words to say how sorry I am. But this is different. Your mom had no idea how to protect you. We have resources. We have everything we need to fight for our daughter."

"Yes, we do." I swung my feet to the floor. "And that's exactly what I plan to do."

As Witt retreated downstairs I marched into Summer's room to find her asleep with her laptop next to her and her pillow over her head to fend off the morning light streaming through her window. Gently I shook her awake.

"Mom?" she rubbed her eyes and squinted at me, the same thing she used to do when I woke her from a nap as a baby. In that moment I saw her in three dimensions; the baby with the tangle of red curls who I'd nursed and rocked to sleep, the beautiful girl before me who wrote music in her head, and the fierce woman she would become. I leaned into her, wrapping my arms around all the versions of this astonishing person I'd brought into the world.

"We're doing it," I said. "We're making sure everyone knows your story."

Summer sat up straighter, fended off a yawn and gestured to her laptop. "I already did."

# FORTY-FOUR

## LORRIE

### *Wednesday, 9:30 a.m.*

I sat in the Starbucks waiting for Keisha, who had emailed last night asking to meet. I'd chosen a place close to her office where I knew I was unlikely to run into anyone else I knew.

I'd taken care with my clothes that morning, eschewing my normal "mom on a coffee run" outfit of leggings and a long T-shirt. Instead I'd chosen a geometric patterned wrap dress and black sandals with a small wedge heel. While my closet was well-stocked with athleisure and other casual clothes, only a couple of outfits could pass as business casual. I'd need to do some shopping now that I had more official duties at Free Motherhood.

I hadn't told Ed, but I was hoping this role would be a springboard for me, a way to dip my toe back into the profes-sional world. Now that the kids were older I'd been mulling over the idea of going back to work. Maybe not right away—Chloé still needed to be driven to all her activities and I wanted to see how the next year of high school went for Archie—but sometime. I knew it would take planning, anyway, since I'd been out of the workforce for so long. I hoped the connections I made through Free Motherhood might help lay the groundwork.

The door opened and I looked up. Keisha walked in; a black laptop bag slung over her shoulder. I stood up and waved. She smiled when she saw me, but there was a tightness in her face.

"Lorrie, hi," she said, approaching. "Thanks for meeting me."

"No problem." I gestured to my coffee cup on the table. "I'm sorry, I would have gotten you something but I didn't know what you'd want."

She shook her head. "That's fine. I can't stay long, anyway."

We sat and I pulled a printed list from my bag. "I've been calling around to possible auction venues. I know it seems early, but the good places book up. Fall is a popular time for events—everyone's back from summer vacation, people want to get things on the calendar before the craziness of the holidays, that sort of thing." Keisha stared down at the list. "The ones high-lighted in green are our best bets." I looked up at Keisha but her eyes remained on the table.

"This is... great," she said. Then she shook her head and sighed. "Lorrie, I need to talk to you..."

"Sure." Something in her voice made me grip my coffee cup tighter.

"We can't have you on the board. I'm sorry."

I blinked. "What? Why?"

"Look, you know I think the world of you. And I'm so grateful for the work you've already done for us. It's just, Meredith's niece goes to Westwood High." My stomach clenched. "And apparently she told Meredith there are some... rumors. About your son."

I stiffened in my seat. "That's a private matter. It has nothing to do with my work for Free Motherhood."

Keisha sighed again. "So it's true."

"No, of course not," I felt a twinge as I thought of Summer's freckled face and wide smile. "It's a baseless allegation, that's all." I curled my hands into fists and dug my fingernails into my palms to keep from screaming with frustration and anger. One by one, everything I cared about outside my family was disappearing from my life. First my best friend, then the Parent Boosters, now this.

"I understand, believe me." Keisha held up her hands. "But you have to understand our position. Free Motherhood is a justice-adjacent organization. It wouldn't look good to have one of our board member's family members under investigation for... this."

"The attorney general's office isn't pressing charges," I said quickly.

Keisha shook her head. "Regardless, it's too sensitive an issue." She gave a small shrug and smiled sadly. "I'm sorry, Lorrie, I really am."

I straightened my shoulders and forced a smile in return. "Of course. I understand."

After Keisha left I dumped the rest of my latte in the trash and walked out to my car. Once I was inside I made sure the windows were rolled up. I gripped the steering wheel and let out a scream.

Then another.

And another.

# FORTY-FIVE
## ARCHIE

### *Wednesday, 3 p.m.*

I've never been in any kind of trouble. I make my bed, do my homework, and send thank-you notes at my birthday and Christmas. So being suspended from school for a whole week was a big deal.

I could tell Jemma was impressed when she texted me on that night as I lay on my bed doing some of the calming breathing exercises Dr. Frank taught me.

> you're such a rebel. have you ever punched anyone before?

> > nope

> what did it feel like?

> > my hand hurts

> lol, you're a lover not a fighter.

I stared down at the phone, deciding how to respond. Why

was she talking about love? Did she know how nervous I felt
when I was around her?

> what'd I miss in Bio?

> talked about our final project. wanna try to
> finish after school tomorrow? i could come
> over.

I sat bolt upright as I tried to think of a response that didn't
give away the cartwheels I felt like doing. The best I could come
up with was:

> cool

While I waited for her response my phone pinged with a
text from Tadpole.

> heard you're suspended

> yeah

> damn. u in trouble?

> not really

It was true. When Mom had come to pick me up she'd gone
into Mr. Ellison's office while I sat in one of the uncomfortable
plastic chairs outside with my ice pack. By the time she came
back out the ice had melted and my head ached from the punch
I'd taken. We drove home in silence while I waited for the
lecture I knew was coming. Instead, when we reached our
driveway, I looked at her and saw that tears were streaming
down her face.

"I'm sorry, sweetie," she said, wiping her eyes.

"It's, uh, OK," I said, unsure of what she was talking about.

"No, it's not OK. It's not OK that you've been dragged into this."

"Mom, I'm fine. Anyway, I started it." I was oddly proud of the way I'd lowered my head and plowed straight into the crowd after Spencer, rage pumping in my veins.

My phone pinged with Jemma's reply.

kk. see you tomorrow

I put the phone down, a grin spreading across my face.

"What do you look so happy about?" I looked up to see Knox standing in my doorway. He was the last person I wanted to talk to about Jemma. "I heard you got suspended," he said.

"Yeah." I wondered what else he'd heard.

He took a step into my room, and shifted on his feet. "Mom said I should check on you." He peered at my face as he got closer. "So who punched you?"

"I don't know," I mumbled. "It was pretty crowded."

"I know it was Spencer," he said, his tone flat. I kept my eyes down and picked an imaginary piece of lint off the bedspread. "Anyway," he said, "Mom said to tell you dinner's in ten minutes — once they finished arguing about going to Casino Night." He rolled his eyes. "Oh, and it's lasagna." He made air quotes with his fingers.

I groaned. My mom's lasagna used thin slices of squash instead of noodles and subbed low-fat yogurt for the thick, creamy ricotta. On the nights she made it I usually ran into my dad and brother in the kitchen later as we all quietly made peanut butter sandwiches and hustled them off to our rooms.

Knox turned to leave and then looked back at me. "By the way," he said. "Good for you. Spencer had it coming."

I spent most of the next day staring wistfully at the basement door. Before Mom left to drop off Chloé that morning, she'd given me strict instructions not to play video games or watch TV.

The hours crawled by. I did all my worksheets and even cleaned my room just in case Jemma saw it. I changed my shirt a couple of times, finally settling on a clean black T-shirt and my best black jeans. When the doorbell rang later that afternoon I was waiting and yanked open the door. Jemma stood on the front porch next to a petite Asian woman who could have been her twin except for a few lines around her eyes and the handful of gray strands in her dark hair.

"Hi," I said, unable to stop a giant, goofy grin from spreading across my face.

"Hi," Jemma crossed her arms and rolled her eyes at her mom. "Um, my mom wants to meet you. Mom, this is Archie."

"Alice Lee." The woman extended her hand.

"Pleased to meet you, Mrs. Lee." I said it the way I'd been taught at the etiquette classes my parents forced me to attend in junior high. I'd also learned the foxtrot and how to hold a plate of food and a drink in one hand while at a cocktail party, two skills which so far I'd had zero use for.

"So polite!" Alice smiled at me, though her eyes lingered on my bruised cheek. Jemma turned a deep scarlet. "Is your mother home?"

"My mother?"

"She wants to make sure we're, you know, supervised." Jemma rolled her eyes.

Panic gripped me. I was the only one home and I hadn't thought to tell my mom anyone was coming over—would Jemma's mom make her leave? Luckily, at that moment Mom's car rolled up the driveway.

"Hello," she said, climbing out, looking confused to see us all on the front steps.

"Mom, this is Jemma from my biology class," I said.

"Remember she was coming over tonight to finish our project? And this is her mom, Mrs. Lee."

"Please, call me Alice," Jemma's mom said to mine.

"Hi," Jemma waved.

"Lorrie Keller, nice to meet you," said my mom as she reached the steps. "I'm sorry, sweetie, I must have forgotten," she added with a puzzled glance at me.

"Well, perfect timing that you're home," I said. "To, you know, supervise." I raised my eyebrows in her direction, hoping she'd get the hint.

"Why yes... of course." Mom nodded, then smiled at Jemma.

"All right then," said Mrs. Lee to Alice. "I'll pick you up in an hour or so?"

Jemma nodded, still blushing.

"Sorry, I forgot to tell you," I whispered to Mom as we went inside.

"She seems nice," she whispered back.

Once we'd grabbed snacks and headed downstairs, Jemma looked around at the oversized screen and L-shaped couch where I sat to play my games.

"Cool setup," she said. "Do you watch movies down here?"

"Mostly video games." I shrugged. "It's kind of, like, my part of the house. No one else is ever down here."

"That's awesome. It must be nice to have some privacy. I swear my mom follows me around from room to room at home, trying to feed me or ask me about my day." She shook her head. "The curse of being an only child."

"Ha," I said. "I have the opposite problem. My parents are so busy with Knox and my sister they forget about me half the time. The curse of being the middle child." Jemma laughed and I couldn't help grinning. "So where should we start?" I asked, gesturing to the poster board and papers we'd spread out on the floor.

Jemma stared at me. "Does it hurt?" she asked, reaching her hand toward the bruise on my face. She dropped her arm before her fingers could graze my cheek and my heart began to race.

"Not so much anymore," I said.

"That was really brave, defending Summer like that." I shrugged, my face suddenly hot. "Do you like, *like* her?" Jemma asked.

The question shot through me and I hesitated. "No," I said. "At least, not anymore—not like that."

She nodded. "OK, good."

"Why good?" A feeling of hope bloomed in my chest.

She glanced up shyly. "Just, you know, good to know you're not, like, taken."

"Definitely not taken." I smiled back, a big, stupid grin, my face burning with pleasure. The idea that I would be unavailable to Jemma Lee with her shiny hair, cool shoes, and pink, cherry-ChapStick-flavored lips was so preposterous I wanted to laugh. Instead I cleared my throat and looked back down at my drawing.

"That was awful what happened to her," Jemma said. "But weren't those your brother's friends you went after? Like, isn't Spencer his best friend?"

"Yeah," I sighed.

"So, um, does Knox know you were the one who punched Spencer?"

"Yeah," I shrugged.

She grimaced. "Awkward."

I laughed. "I think it's OK, actually."

We worked in silence for a few minutes, labeling pictures of frog organs and gluing them to the poster board.

"Can I ask you something?" Jemma asked after a while.

"Sure." My heart leapt into my throat as possibilities raced through my head. She needed a glass of water. She wanted to be my girlfriend. She'd forgotten what the spleen does.

"Did your brother do what they're saying he did?" I swallowed hard. "I'm sorry," Jemma said quickly, seeing my expression. "I shouldn't have brought it up. Can we forget I did?" She put her hand on my arm. "Please don't be mad." My arm felt hot where she touched me.

"I'm not," I lied. While I wasn't angry with Jemma, I was suddenly aware that the hot, sour feeling I'd been carrying around in my stomach was rage. I was furious at the way people were choosing sides at school like it was a popularity contest. I was mad at Spencer and the rest of Knox's stupid friends for how easy it had been for them to humiliate Summer. Most of all, I was furious at my brother for the dark, unreachable person he'd become; the way he'd made it impossible to trust him because I didn't know him anymore. I felt sick about the doubt inside me that had turned into something bigger. I knew whose side I was on and it wasn't the one I was supposed be.

I took a deep breath as I turned to face Jemma. "Or maybe I am mad, but not at you. Everything's so confusing right now. I just wish the whole thing would go away."

"I don't think that's going to happen," Jemma said.

"Yeah, I guess not."

She took a deep breath and cocked her head as if considering something. "OK, I wasn't sure if I should tell you but now I think you should know." The words came out so fast I had to strain to understand them.

"Tell me what?"

"So, earlier today I was in the library during my free period and I peeked at tomorrow's edition of the *Watermark*."

"Peeked?" I asked.

"They keep the final version in a protected folder on the shared drive we use—Violet doesn't want anyone getting access before it comes out. She's the only one who can access the final version. Like, even though I write for it, I don't get to see the final edition until it's in my inbox. No one does." She gave a guilty smile. "Except I *do* have access. I always have." She gave me a guilty smile. "Someone set up my permissions wrong at the beginning of the year and I just never told Violet because I like getting to read it early."

"OK," I said, still trying to figure out what this had to do with me.

"Anyway, usually there's just one file in the folder, but today there were two." She tapped the marker she was holding on our poster like it was an extension of her nervous energy. "One was marked as *Final—Approved by Lang*. Ms. Lang is our advisor, she always signs off on the edition before it goes out. But there was another file with a different name and a more recent timestamp." I started to interrupt with a question but she waved my hand away. "I'm getting to the point, I promise. So, the version approved by Ms. Lang has a front-page article about the senior class's community service projects. But the *other* file was also a full version of the edition..." She paused and bit the inside of her cheek. "Except the front page was an article about what happened between Knox and Summer. Written by Summer."

I stared at Jemma, still trying to make sense of her words. "What kind of article?"

"Like an account of what happened. Her side of the story. Not just about last weekend, but also of other times when she felt super uncomfortable and pressured by him."

I sat back, my head spinning with possible scenarios. "But that's not the version Ms. Lang signed off on, right?"

She shook her head. "No, but I'm pretty sure it's the one being published tomorrow."

I blinked, willing the thoughts swirling through my brain to settle into something that made sense. "Why are you telling me this?" I asked.

She sighed. "Because I like you, Archie." Her face was open

and her tone was frank. "And you know I'm Team Summer, but, well, he's your brother and I thought you'd want to know."

"Yeah." I nodded, the crank in my brain starting to turn again. "Thanks. Can you show it to me? Like, can I read it?"

Her watch beeped. "Ugh, that's my mom," she said. "She's outside."

"Please," I said. "I need to read it."

She paused, uncertainty written on her face. She bit her lip again. "I'd have to log on through the student activities portal, which takes forever because Westwood runs a software program from the Stone Age. But I could do it tonight and send it to you."

"Thank you," I said. "Seriously."

She nodded, then looked down at our project. "So I think we're basically done, right?"

"Yeah," I said, disappointed we'd finished so fast. Now I had no idea when I'd see her again.

"But... how about I come by tomorrow to help with the finishing touches?"

"Yes!" I said, too quickly, my stupid grin making a reappearance. "And thank you," I added. "For telling me."

Our knees bumped as we stood up. I wanted to hug her, but at the last minute I awkwardly thrust out my hand to shake.

"See you tomorrow," I said. Ignoring my hand, she leaned forward and wrapped her arms around me for a brief instant. Then she grabbed her backpack and darted up the stairs.

# FORTY-SIX

## LORRIE

### *Wednesday, 7:30 p.m.*

On Wednesday night I stared at the sad cheese plate I'd created from the scant leftovers in my refrigerator. Normally in the days leading up to book club I went to the gourmet grocer up the street and took my time reading over the neatly lettered placards next to each cheese, texting the most ridiculous ones to Eden.

*Creamy and balanced, with light notes of glacial air and Icelandic ponies.*

*Silky and oozing, imparts a gentle aroma of cooked broccoli and decaying leather.*

All week, though, I'd avoided my usual neighborhood routines, worried about who I'd bump into. I'd wanted to cancel the whole thing, but when I mentioned this to Ed he didn't listen, and just insisted I carry on.

It bothered me. "I've never seen you so enthused about my book club," I said. "Usually you moan about how loud we are and how late everyone stays."

"Look, Knox is in the clear with the attorney general," he

said. "But Beau mentioned there could still be a civil suit, which I wouldn't put past Witt. We need to do everything as we normally would, not like we're hiding."

"But I do want to hide," I said, exasperated. "Possibly forever. Things just keep getting worse. First the accusation, then the fight at school, then Mr. Ellison removing me from the Parent Boosters. It's all such a mess."

"Exactly. Which is why we need to act normal so people take our side if there is some kind of legal action." His tone was matter-of-fact and he didn't even bother to look up from where he'd clicked open the ESPN app on his phone.

"But there shouldn't be any sides; these are kids we're talking about!" But even as I said it, I knew it wasn't true. While Knox had yet to experience any of the traditional rites of passage of early adulthood—college, his first apartment, first job —the events of the last few days had forced him across the threshold prematurely.

"Please, Lor, trust me on this one." He put down his phone and flung his arms out in exasperation, like he couldn't believe I was so dense.

"Why should I? What makes you such an expert on the situation, anyway?" I felt a familiar prickling of suspicion on the back of my neck.

"I'm just taking my guidance from Beau." Ed held up his hands.

"You never did say how you know him." I lifted my chin in challenge as I held his gaze, refusing to look away first.

Ed's eyes darted to the side. "I told you, he's worked with some of the players who've gotten into... uncomfortable situations."

"Yes, but how do *you* know him?"

"Mom?" I turned to see Archie standing at the bottom of the stairs. "I finished my homework. Can I go play video games?"

"Sweetie, you're suspended," I said, repressing a sigh. "Besides, don't you have the whole week of schoolwork to do?"

"It's mostly done," he shrugged. "It's the end of the school year, there's not much going on."

"He's suspended for defending his brother," protested Ed. "We're not punishing him for that!" He nodded at Archie. "Come here, kiddo." Archie approached him with a wary look on his face.

"You did a great thing." Ed wrapped an arm around his shoulder. "You stuck up for your brother when he needed you. That's what family does—we stick together."

"Thanks," mumbled Archie. "So, I can go play?" He looked at me.

"Absolutely." Ed clapped him on the back and Archie stumbled forward toward the basement.

"Dinner in ten minutes," I called after him, curling my fingers into fists as I glared at Ed.

"What? What was he supposed to do?" asked Ed. "Stand there and do nothing while his brother was attacked?"

"First of all," I said through gritted teeth, "Knox wasn't there during the fight. And even if he was, he can take care of himself. Second, we shouldn't be rewarding our children for violence, whatever the motivation."

Ed shook his head. "Even if Knox wasn't physically attacked, his reputation was—which I'd argue is more damaging. Sometimes you've got to stand your ground."

I forced myself to turn away before the torrent of angry words that had flooded my throat could escape.


Caroline rang the doorbell promptly at seven thirty. As the clock crept toward eight o'clock, we were still the only ones seated in the living room, the cheese plate untouched. We made pleasant conversation, avoiding the obvious topic, until my phone dinged. I frowned, reading the text.

"Natalie's daughter has a fever," I said. "She can't make it."

"Poor thing," Caroline said. Then there was another ding, and another.

"Kristen is out too," I said, referring to our neighbor down the block. "Family emergency."

"I hope everything is OK," Caroline mumbled, her eyes on her lap.

"And Melinda isn't feeling well," I sighed, reading the text from another Westwood mom. "Well, then I guess we're just waiting on Danielle. But she's always late, anyway." Danielle lived two streets over and had a daughter in Archie's grade.

"Mm, too bad." Caroline said, fiddling with her napkin and not looking up.

"Caroline," I said, suddenly aware of her discomfort. "What's going on?"

She sighed and flung the napkin down on the couch. "Oh fine, I suppose you might as well know. There was a side text with everyone trying to figure out whether to come or not."

"What? Why?" I felt the air go out of my lungs as if I'd been punched in the chest.

Caroline gave me a look. "You *know* why. We're all still on your side, of course, I think some people just figured it would be better steer clear until the dust settles a bit." She forced a weak smile.

"Steer clear? Let the dust settle?" I asked. "My friends shouldn't need the *dust* to settle." But even as I said it I knew the truth was they weren't really my friends. They never had been. They were relationships of convenience, built around small-talk dinner parties and kids' birthday parties, designed to give us all a surface sense of belonging but nothing deeper. I'd only ever had one real friend.

"I'm sure we'll be back on track for the next meeting," Caroline reassured me. "I'm hosting."

I leaned back in my chair and closed my eyes, the world falling away for an instant.

Caroline's phone dinged. "Let me guess," I opened one eye. "Danielle can't make it either."

Caroline looked up from her phone and pursed her lips. "It's just Jackson," she said, "telling me we're out of milk when I guarantee there's a carton in the fridge staring him in the face. How that child is going to survive on his own at college is a mystery to me."

I sat back up and pulled my knees into my chest. "Was he... there yesterday?" Neither Caroline nor I had mentioned the fight yet. From Archie I'd gleaned that Violet was involved, but he hadn't said anything about Jackson, who was a good friend of Knox's.

Caroline sighed. "No. He had a dentist appointment that morning, thank goodness, or likely I'd have two teenagers stuck at home this week driving me crazy."

"So Violet was suspended? Archie was, too," I offered. "I've been trying to piece together what happened but in typical Archie fashion he doesn't have a lot to say."

Caroline stayed quiet with her eyes downcast, picking at a thread on the couch pillow.

"Caroline," I continued. "Did Violet say anything? I know she and Summer are close."

"Lorrie, please." Caroline's tone was pleading as she looked up at me. "I'm in a tough spot already, what with Violet being friends with Summer and Jackson with Knox. My own children aren't even speaking to each other right now."

"But surely they've told you something," I pressed. "I mean, for Violet to get suspended for fighting like that—she never causes any trouble. There must be a good reason."

"You already know why," Caroline said, looking down. "She

thinks Knox raped Summer." The word hung between us, expanding until they had taken up most of the oxygen in the room.

"Do you?" I asked.

Caroline uncrossed and recrossed her legs. "Look, Violet's not an overly-emotional kid—Jackson's more of a crier than she is—but she's been devasted about the whole thing, absolutely beside herself all week."

"So you're sitting here in my house telling me you think there's a chance my son raped someone?"

Caroline looked up, startled by the sharpness of my tone. "Lorrie, this is hard for all of us. Did you know the police interviewed both Violet and Jackson? They've even talked to me, for God's sake, because the kids were at our house earlier that night."

"I heard that's where the party was," I said, crossing my arms over my chest. "You might want to rethink the appropriate level of parental supervision for teenagers."

Caroline's face hardened. "You know, I almost didn't come tonight for this reason. I didn't know what to say to you. It's so confusing. But I also know that you're my friend, so I wanted to show up. And look"—she gestured to the empty living room—"I'm the only one who did."

# FORTY-SEVEN

## ARCHIE

**Wednesday, 9 p.m.**

I sat on my bed, rereading the article Jenna had sent over as a screen grab. YOU DIDN'T GET THIS FROM ME!!!!!!!! she'd written in the subject line. I'd immediately saved the file to my desktop and deleted her email, then emptied my deleted items folder.

I'd lost track of how many times I'd read it, hoping for something different every time. But each time was just as much of a gut punch as the last.

I was used to reading about coverage of my brother's heroics on the pitching mound, but those articles never stuck with me like this one. Even after the first read certain phrases had already lodged themselves in my brain.

My palms itched as I sat there staring at my laptop screen, my brain bouncing back and forth between reading the article and trying to figure out what to do about it. What would happen if it went out to all of Westwood? Did Knox deserve that?

Earlier I'd tried to keep from groaning when I saw my mom

setting out cheese and wineglasses. I hated book club night, when her friends took over the house with their loud voices and cackling laughter. Even when they thought they were being quiet and discussing top secret things I could still hear them. Not that they ever had anything interesting to say. I mean, who cared that Mrs. Doyle wanted her husband to go on Ozempic or that Grace Kinley's daughter had been wait-listed at every school she'd applied to. Not me!

Tonight, though, it was weirdly quiet downstairs. I forced myself up off the bed and stretched my legs, which had cramped from being frozen in my cross-legged position for who knew how long. My mind still spinning, I let my legs carry me down the hall to Knox's room.

His door was open and he was stretched out on his bed, his eyes open and directed at the ceiling. Shifting my weight in his doorway, I cleared my throat. "Hey," I said.

He turned his head by a degree to register my presence. "Hey."

All the things I wanted to say to him stuck in my throat. That I missed him, the old Knox. That I didn't want anything bad to happen to him. But that I hadn't wanted anything bad to happen to Summer, either. I couldn't tell him about the article, I just couldn't. "Do you want ice cream?" I was all I could manage.

He rolled over and propped his head up on his elbow. "Isn't mom's wine club down there?"

"Book club," I corrected.

He snorted. "Yeah, right."

"I don't think anyone's down there."

"Oh, OK. Then, um, sure." He sat up and looked at me like I might spook if he moved too fast.

Sure enough, downstairs the living room was empty, though the cheese plate and glasses remained on the coffee table. It reminded me of the scenes from Pompeii captured in ashes when everyone was taken by surprise. I got out bowls and Knox scooped ice cream into them, the silence between us awkward.

"Are you, um, excited for graduation?" I tried.

He shook his head. "I don't even want to go."

"Mom would kill you." I raised my eyebrows. "Like, literally kill you. Old-fashioned matricide."

He laughed. "I know. But I just, like, I wish I could just fast-forward right now. Or maybe rewind, I don't know."

I nodded. We ate in silence, but this one was more comfortable. After, I rinsed out our bowls and Knox turned to me. "I think I'm gonna go shoot some baskets. Want to come?"

I laughed. "Absolutely not." We both knew I was hopeless at basketball.

"OK. But Archie, thanks for—just, thanks." He gave me a smile that was almost shy.

I nodded and watched him walk outside.

Heading back upstairs I felt better. While I still didn't know what to think about everything else, or what to do about the article, at least I knew I still loved my brother.

Rounding the corner into my room, I froze. There, sitting on the edge of my bed staring at my open laptop screen with Summer's article still pulled up, was my mom. Her mouth had dropped open and her eyes were wide as her pupils scanned the text. My knee cracked as I stepped forward and her head jerked up. "What the hell is this?" she demanded, her tone so sharp I felt like it would slice my skin if I got any closer. "And why do you have it?"

"I can explain," I said.

"Then start now."

# FORTY-EIGHT

## LORRIE

### *Wednesday, 9:30 p.m.*

It was a good article, objectively. Well written and compelling. Weighty yet succinct. Vivid without being gratuitous. I had to resist pointing this out when I showed it to Ed.

"What is this shit?" he yelled, gripping Archie's laptop. "This shit filled with *lies*! About my *son*! Where did you get this?" He whirled to face Archie, who cowered behind me.

"I just found out about it, I swear," he said.

"I'll repeat myself. Where did you get it?" Ed spoke every word separately like you would to a child, his voice laced with fury.

"Someone sent it to me." Archie stared at the ground.

"Who, goddamnit? Who sent it to you?" Ed gripped the laptop so hard I worried he might hurl it at the wall.

"I don't know." Archie raised his chin now and met Ed's eyes. "It was an anonymous email."

"Let me see the email."

"I deleted it."

"The hell you did," growled Ed, taking a step forward. I shifted so that Archie was directly behind me.

"It doesn't matter who sent it, it matters that we have it," I said. I was also upset about the article, but seeing Ed's rage had scared me into playing the role of the calm, reasonable adult.

"What's going on? Why is everyone being so loud?" Chloé rounded the corner into the room, still in her dance leotard from practice. The innocence of her question made me want to weep.

"Nothing, sweetie," I said, trying to defuse the tension. "We're just talking to Archie about something."

"Oooh, is he in trouble?" She executed a perfect pirouette and looked delighted at the prospect.

"No—" I began.

"He's in so much trouble that he'll—" snarled Ed.

"Let's all take a deep breath," I interrupted in my best tantrum-calming voice. "Chloé"—I looked at my daughter, who was now doing a series of jetés around the room—"can you give us some privacy?"

"All everyone around here wants lately is privacy," she said, putting her hands on her hips. "It's so *boring*!" She stomped out of the room but I didn't have it in me to go after her. We had bigger problems.

"Were you ever planning on telling us about it?" Ed turned back to Archie.

Archie looked to me for help. "Go to your room," I instructed in a low tone. "We'll talk about this more later." He nodded and scurried toward the door before Ed could say anything else.

"Goddamn lies," Ed muttered, one fist curling and uncurling as the other continued to grip Archie's laptop.

"Who else has seen this?" he asked.

"Archie told me it hasn't gone out yet in the *Watermark*," I said. "But beyond that I don't know anything. I'll call Mr. Ellison first thing in the morning."

"Call him tonight."

I raised my eyebrows. "He doesn't give out his cell number to parents, clearly."

"Then I'll call the police."

"Look," I said, biting back an annoyed sigh. "As upset as I am about this, I'm not sure an article for the school paper warrants a call to the police."

"Then I'll call Beau," Ed said. "See what he thinks."

I paused. "Why don't you let me call him?" I tried to sound casual, like it wasn't a test. "I can talk to him lawyer to lawyer."

Ed shook his head. "I deal with Beau."

"Why?" I crossed my arms, ready to call his bluff. "I have a right to know what's going on in this family."

"What's going on is that we're paying Beau a lot of money to handle this for us—money that I work my butt off for—so we're going to let him handle it."

I narrowed my eyes. "Are we playing the who-works-harder game? Because I guarantee you'll lose. Who do you think makes your entire life possible?"

"You really want to do this?" Ed's eyes narrowed.

"I really do, Ed." My heart was beating fast now, sending rushes of near boiling hot blood through my body. "Because while you're off palling around with a bunch of professional athletes, I'm doing everything else."

"You mean playing tennis and having lunch with your Parent Booster girlfriends?" His face looked mean in a way I'd never seen before.

"I mean raising your children! Doing their laundry—and yours, for that matter. Volunteering at their schools, signing them up for summer camp, booking the math tutors, driving them around to dance and baseball and the million other activities they do. Cooking dinner every night. When was the last time you did any of that? You're not even here half the time!"

"Because I'm working, goddamnit!" He slammed his fist on

the desk. "Working to pay for all the things you just listed, the fucking tutor and dance classes, and now a lawyer to keep our son's name clear."

"A lawyer I'm not allowed to talk to?" My voice rose in anger.

"Control yourself," he spat. "The kids will hear you."

"I don't care! Why are we being so secretive? They deserve to know what's going on, just like I deserve to know."

"You have no idea how this works." His tone held a warning but I pressed on. We hadn't had it out in a while.

"And you do? Remind me why you're such an expert? Oh, right, because you work with a bunch of overpaid narcissists who can't keep it in their pants and need someone despicable like Beau to make all their problems go away."

"Get the hell out." Ed pointed to the door.

"Gladly." Storming upstairs, I slammed our bedroom door so hard the house shook. Then I waited. It took him nearly an hour, but when he came in, he locked the bedroom door behind him. He grabbed me and we clawed at each other like animals, pulling each other's clothes off and wrestling on the bed, up against the wall, then finally on the floor, where he pinned me under him and pulled my hair as he entered me from behind, calling me all the dirty names I loved to hear as I came. After, we lay wrung out and panting. Usually this was the moment when we whispered apologies to each other, doing our best to erase the harsh words we'd released into the air. This time, though, Ed got up, pulled on his clothes, and left the room without a word.

I showered, shaking with rage that refused to abate and scrubbing my body so vigorously I cut a long gash in my arm with my fingernail. Smoothing moisturizer onto my face afterward, I had the sudden urge to hurl the small glass jar at the mirror in front of me. Better yet, to smash everything on Ed's side of the counter. I pictured his aftershave, his cologne and his expensive electric toothbrush all shattered into pieces on the floor.

I laid rigidly in bed, willing the clock toward morning and the minute I could call Mr. Ellison about the article. When I heard Ed come in later I almost got up to storm out and sleep in the guest room, but instead rolled over and pretended to be asleep as I shoved a pillow between us. Why should I be the one to give up our bed? But once his breathing settled into the light snore I'd learned to live with, I gave up on my own slumber. Easing my feet onto the floor I felt my way through the darkness to the door.

I let my feet propel me back toward Ed's study. This time I felt no hesitation, only angry determination. Inside a maddening sense of order prevailed, with no hint of the earlier conflict that had taken place. The books on the shelf were arranged alphabetically and a pad of paper and pen sat square with the edge of his desk. I flipped through the pad briefly and was disappointed to find it blank. Sitting down in the leather desk chair, I jerked open the drawers and rifled through the contents with little thought for the careful order Ed had put them in. What I found was uninteresting: a stack of golf score sheets clipped together, a folder labeled *Tax/Legal*, and half-used bottle of Rogaine.

Closing the drawers, I ran my fingers over his laptop. To my surprise the screen sprang to life without a password. Guilt rose sourly in my throat as my eyes began to scan the screen but I didn't stop. I clicked on a message near the top of his inbox. The sender was Beau Sykes; the subject was "Per our conversation."

Spoke with the atty gen office. They're not filing charges, so I wouldn't worry too much about empty threats from the girl. Also, Christi signed the NDA. Go celebrate, just not with her, ha.

Christi?

I typed the name into the email search field and was flooded with messages about building hours, hot water outages, and weight room upgrades from Christi Bell, the baseball stadium's facilities manager. There was nothing unusual in any of them. Next I typed in Beau's name and was rewarded by two emails, both with the subject, "Time Sensitive" and an attachment.

The first had been sent on Sunday and contained no text. The attachment was a legal form from Sykes & Associates, outlining "Attorney services related to representing Mr. Knox Keller." It listed a retainer fee of ten thousand dollars. I swallowed hard. We had the money, but to spend that much on Beau's services felt like an unsavory trade. I clicked on the second email, which was from less than a month ago. The body contained only one sentence.

Please remit payment immediately.

It contained the same legal form attachment, only this one read "Attorney services related to representing Mr. Edward T. Keller." The fee listed was twenty thousand dollars. I sucked in my breath. Had Ed spent that kind of money without telling me? What kind of legal services cost that much? I handled the family bills, so I'd seen the invoices from our family lawyer and they were nowhere near that amount.

Painful goosebumps rose on my arms as if someone had suddenly cranked on the air conditioning. I reopened the desk drawer and dumped the contents of the folder labeled Tax/Legal on the desk. There, near the bottom of the pile were two pages clipped together. The first was a hand-written police report, dated February of the current year. The filer was listed as Christine Frances. Sentence fragments jumped off the page as I scanned through it:

*Sexual intercourse... office party... intoxicated...*

*Unwanted sexual contact... multiple instances... coercion...*

*Accuser feared loss of employment upon reporting...*

The second document was a lengthy legal form titled "Non-Disclosure Agreement." The signature at the bottom of the last page belonged to Christine Frances, witnessed by Beau Sykes III. In it Christine forfeited her right to further legal action against Edward T. Keller and agreed to cease all contact with him in exchange for what was referred to simply as "the settlement". She agreed to delete all previous instances of contact with him from her electronic devices, including text, videos, sound recordings, and photographs. The agreement endured in perpetuity. If she was found in violation of it she would be subject to repayment of "the settlement" and possible legal action.

A chill spread throughout my body as I read the documents a second time, laboring to keep my brain focused on making sense of the words. I tried to order my thoughts but they kept sliding every which way in my brain like they were covered in oil.

I typed the name Christine Frances into Google. The third search result was a link to a bio and head shot of Christi Frances, an Atlanta-based physical therapist who listed the baseball team as one of her clients. Though young and blonde, she wasn't as pretty as I'd expected. Her hair looked bleached and damaged and the cheekbones in her round face appeared to be mostly the work of heavy makeup contouring. Under the photo her hobbies were listed as yoga and being a "dog mama."

I sat staring at the screen, my body weighted down like concrete.

What was forgivable in a marriage?

I'd always considered myself to have a strong moral compass, to be someone adept at judging right from wrong. After the events of the last week, though, I had increasingly less faith in that ability.

# FORTY-NINE

## EDEN

### *Thursday, 7 a.m.*

I stayed in the shower an extra-long time, letting the hot water scald my skin pink. I'd just woken up but I felt exhausted. I'd spent the last twenty-four hours in a frenzy. I'd texted Violet for assurances that, even though she was suspended, she'd still be able to switch out the edition of the *Westwood Watermark* at the last minute. I'd also forced myself to read what Summer had written. As I did I could feel the bile coming up in my throat, but I kept it at bay long enough to hug my daughter and tell her how proud I was of her for using her voice. Then I locked myself in the bathroom and retched into the toilet bowl, as if doing so could somehow keep the awful things I'd read from searing themselves into my memory. As I clutched the sides of the toilet all I could think about was how thoroughly I'd failed my daughter.

Now there was nothing left to do but wait until the *Watermark* came out later in the day. When I finally got out of the shower and dressed I headed down to the kitchen, Witt stood at the stovetop whistling, spatula in hand.

"Pancakes!" I said. "How can you do this to me? You know I'm trying to eat paleo."

"That's the one where you only eat dinosaurs, right? Wait, watch this!" He flipped a pancake high in the air and caught it on a plate with his other hand.

Summer giggled from the stool she'd pulled up to the kitchen island.

"Good morning," I said to her, trying to sound natural. "How are you feeling?"

"Hungry." She smiled at her father, and when she turned toward me, for once the smile didn't fade.

"Breakfast is served." Witt placed the plate in front of her with a flourish and then looked at me. "Can I offer you a plate of nefarious carbohydrates?"

"Fine," I sighed. If I was forced to eat pancakes so as not to ruin the strangely sunny mood everyone seemed to be in, so be it.

When Summer was little, Witt was the one to get up with her on the weekends when she padded into our bedroom carrying her increasingly ragged favorite blanket. He'd scoop her up and carry her downstairs while I rolled over and snuggled back into bed until the smell of coffee became irresistible. Those lazy mornings ended as soon as I realized other moms had their pre-verbal toddlers signed up for a battery of weekend activities designed to give them a head start on their résumés. Now it hit me in the gut that I hadn't savored those moments enough. I hadn't known those years would feel so short.

"Honey, you OK?" Witt asked, and I became aware of the wetness in my eyes.

"Fine," I said, looking up at the light fixture and blinking rapidly.

"You sure?" Summer cocked her head and looked at me. "You look like you just saw that Humane Society PSA narrated by Sarah McLachlan."

"I wouldn't bring that up if I were you," said Witt. "Mom will give them your whole college fund."

"Very funny." I rolled my eyes and reached for the syrup. It was a running joke between Witt and Summer. Today, though, I didn't mind watching them share a laugh at my expense. It felt for a minute like everything was normal. I sipped my coffee and cleared my throat, dreading the words that were about to come out of my mouth. Witt and I had agreed it was time to tell Summer that there would be no charges filed by the attorney general's office. I'd asked him to hold off for a day, not telling him the reason—that I wanted to have everything in place for Summer's statement to come out first in case the news hit her hard.

"Summer," I said. "The attorney general's office called."

"I know, Dad told me."

"He did?" I put my fork down and looked at Witt. He gave me a small, sad smile and I knew he'd tried to protect me from the conversation.

"Yeah," she said. "It's OK." She looked at me. "I mean, it's not OK, but I understand now. It's a broken system. And I think I'd feel a lot worse if I we didn't have the other plan." She frowned. "Though I'm still kind of nervous."

Witt frowned and set the spatula down. "Nervous about what? What are we talking about here?"

"I wrote something," said Summer. "And Violet's going to publish it in the school paper."

I watched Witt's face turn pale and then flush scarlet as she filled him in.

"Absolutely not!" he said before she'd even finished. "That's not happening. You need to call Violet and tell her you changed your mind." He grabbed Summer's phone off the counter and thrust it toward her. "Tell her!" He turned to me. "We can't have this out there. We could get sued for defamation."

"It's not defamation if it's true," I said, trying to sound calm despite the adrenaline beginning to course through me.

"Are you crazy?" Witt asked. "What if this gets back to Princeton? Not to mention all the other potential fallout."

I shrugged. "If this gets back to Princeton then we've gotten much more than just the local media coverage I'm hoping for."

"The media?" The vein in the center of Witt's forehead throbbed.

"I was thinking of sending it over to Patty at the *Atlanta Journal-Constitution*, and maybe Leyla at WSBTV," I said. Both were former Westwood moms whose kids were now in college.

"Summer," Witt said through gritted teeth, "your mom and I need to talk for a minute. Alone."

Summer eyed the two of us, confused. While I hadn't explicitly asked her not to tell her dad, I'd done what I could to make sure he didn't catch wind of it. "Um, sure," she said, grabbing her plate and fork and scooting back from the table.

Witt waited until he heard her feet on the stairs and her bedroom door closing. Then he leaned toward me, his body tense with adrenaline. "This is insane, you have to pull the plug on it. It could blow up in our face. And it would definitely complicate filing a civil suit."

I set my jaw and turned away from him. "I said no civil suit."

"But why?" he pressed. "That's our best option for justice."

"I don't want justice," I said. "Now that everyone knows everything anyway, I want revenge."

"Revenge, Eden?" Witt winced and rubbed his forehead. "Don't you think that's a little dramatic?"

"No, I don't." I turned to face him. "I don't think it's dramatic to want something better for my daughter than to be at the mercy of a legal system that's not set up to protect women and girls to begin with, waiting around for some judge to decide whether what happened to her was wrong. And if we don't win the case—which is likely—I don't want her to spend the rest of her life feeling alone, believing what happened to her is just how things go. I refuse to watch that happen, Witt. My baby girl is going to know the world is on *her* side, for once."

Witt was quiet for a minute as I gripped the counter to control the rage that had swelled inside me. "This isn't really about Summer, is it?" he asked.

I didn't bother to brush away the tears rolling down my face. "It's about all of us," I whispered hoarsely. "It's about every goddamn woman who's felt how I feel right now."

We stared at each other in silence for a long minute.

"Have you thought about Lorrie?" he asked finally. "It's Knox's name you're putting out there, too."

I felt a sharp tug in my chest at hearing her name, which constantly hovered just below the surface of my thoughts. In this moment, however, my rage was more powerful than my sadness. "Of course I've thought about it," I said. "But it's time Knox Keller got what he deserved."

# FIFTY

## LORRIE

### *Thursday, 7:30 a.m.*

It was the most curious feeling. No matter how hard I tried I couldn't lift my head from the pillow. Trying again, I sent the command from my brain to the muscles and tendons of my neck, *Ready, lift*. Nothing. My head remained weighed down as if someone had swapped it out for a small boulder.

"Lorrie." Ed's hand was a gentle pressure on my shoulder. "Lor, your alarm went off a while ago. When are you going to call Ellison?"

"Five more minutes," I mumbled, trying and failing to flutter my eyes open.

"Are you sick or something?"

*That's it*, I thought. *I must be sick.* "Yes," I said.

"OK," he said after a long pause. "I'll get the kids to school before I head to work. But can you still call him? Or do I need to do that, too?"

"I'll do it," I said, rolling away from him. The sound of his voice was sending a surprising rocket of rage through me. As the bedroom door clicked closed behind him, I struggled to make sense of why. Wrenching my head from the pillow, I sat up. A wave of dizziness followed as an explosion of words detonated in my brain.

*Affair. Coercion. Non-disclosure agreement.*

My stomach roiled and I flung the covers off and stumbled to the bathroom. I retched into the toilet boil, then rinsed my mouth and pulled my hair back in a headband, a look I normally reserved for the gym. Staring in the mirror, I examined my face, the lines on my forehead and around my mouth, the age spots dotting my cheekbones, and the newly sagging skin around my jawline. When had I gotten old? How had I failed to notice it happening? What else was I unaware of? That my husband had cheated on me with—and possibly sexually assaulted—a blonde physical therapist might only be the start.

I waited until I heard the garage door rumble shut and quiet descend on the house. Wrapping myself in my favorite terrycloth bathrobe, the one I'd had since college, I went to sit at the kitchen island, grabbed my laptop and dialed the number for Mr. Ellison's office.

"Hi Jane," I said. "It's Lorrie Keller. I'm wondering if he has a minute?"

"I'm sorry," said his assistant after a pause. "He's in a meeting."

I pressed my lips together and struggled to remain calm. A week ago she would have put me right through. "Look, Jane," I said, my tone sharper than I meant it to be, "he's the last person I want to talk to right now. So I wouldn't be calling if it wasn't incredibly urgent."

There was another pause, longer this time, then the beep of my call being transferred.

"Are you sure?" Mr. Ellison asked once I'd outlined the situation.

"I just emailed it over to you," I said.

"Well," he said after a minute in which I assumed he was

reading. "This is highly unusual. I'm certain the *Watermark*'s faculty advisor wouldn't have approved anything like this. Let me touch base with her and get to the bottom of it."

"Good," I said. "Please do."

My energy somewhat renewed, I walked with purpose back into Ed's study. Methodically I opened drawers and emptied files. I piled papers on the floor as I sorted through them, taking no care to put them back where they'd come from. After an hour of searching, I discovered nothing beyond the police report and the non-disclosure agreement I'd read the night before. I took pictures of both, unsure of what I'd do with them. Sitting cross-legged in the middle of the piles of paper, I laughed. That after twenty-five years of marriage I should find myself sitting in my bathrobe on the floor of my husband's study trying to dig up evidence to suggest our whole life together was a lie seemed absurd.

"Mom?" I looked up to see Archie standing in the doorway.

"Sweetie, what are you doing home?"

"Um, I'm suspended, remember?" He scrunched his face up in concern. "And you and Dad are really mad at me... aren't you?"

"Right, of course." I shook my head. "Sorry. Come here, sweetheart." I extended my hand to him. He approached warily, taking in the disarray of Ed's normally immaculate study with alarm.

"What are you doing?"

"Just a little spring-cleaning," I said, rising to my feet. "And I'm not mad at you." My eyes filled with tears as I regarded him. I felt suddenly overwhelmed by all I had been given in life, despite all that had just been taken away. "I love you so much," I said, my voice breaking.

"I love you too, Mom," he said, eyeing me with concern. "Are you, like, OK?"

I laughed and wiped at my tears. "It's been a rough week."

He nodded. "Yeah." He shifted on his feet. "So what's happening with the, um, article?"

"Mr. Ellison's taking care of it."

"But you read it? Like, the whole thing?" I nodded, his unasked question lingering between us. He shifted on his feet again, his eyes traveling back to the piles of papers on the floor. Then he looked back up at me. "Can I go play video games?"

"Sure," I said. "I'm just going to finish straightening up in here." I grabbed Ed's sport coat off the back of his chair and folded it over my arm as though I were tidying.

"OK." He turned away, already heading for the basement.

Sighing, I leaned against Ed's chair, still holding his coat. I felt something in the inside pocket and pulled out a leather monogrammed checkbook. The checks were inscribed with his business account, Dr. Edward T. Keller, LLC. I began flipping through it. Most were made out to his insurance company and accountant. All except for one. Dated two weeks ago, it was made out to Christine Frances in the amount of thirty-thousand dollars.

I sank back into the chair. My body went cold. Closing my eyes I willed myself to breathe.

What did one do after such a discovery? Pack my bags? Pack Ed's? I pulled out my phone and stared at Eden's contact. She would know what to do. I wondered if she would answer if I called.

I scrolled through the rest of my contacts. There were my three closest college friends; we saw each other once a year for a girls' weekend where we drank wine, talked about our kids, and lamented the challenges of modern motherhood. We had a long history; still, I couldn't imagine calling one of them about this. After all these years I felt more connected to them as a group than I did individually. And clearly calling anyone from book club was out. Whether or not they were truly "on my side" as Caroline had claimed was debatable. What's more, every one of them and their husbands socialized with Ed and me us as a couple. Though I was the keeper of the relationships, they existed primarily as part of our social network of couples, built carefully over time because, like all women since the dawn of time, I recognized the safety and security of belonging to a group.

The uncomfortable truth was that while I'd built a tight-knit community for my family, we were a package deal. Things were bad enough already, but without Ed, the best the kids and I could hope for was a place on the outskirts, fighting for scraps. It wasn't that people were mean-spirited; it was that they lacked imagination. They didn't know how to coordinate car pool with two different parents or handle an odd number at a dinner party. Most of all, they held an unspoken fear that you would contaminate their own marriages with whatever plague had decimated yours, as if coming into close contact with you could cause an Ebola-like outbreak of divorce.

I sat rooted to the chair as I ran through the list of options, waiting to land on the obvious next step. When it didn't appear, I placed everything back where I'd found it as best I could and closed the study door behind me.

# FIFTY-ONE

## EDEN

### *Thursday, 3 p.m.*

My thighs burned with effort but I sank lower into my squat. "Lower, lower still, you've got this!" commanded the voice on my screen, belonging to Tyler, a chipper, smiling man in athletic shorts and a tight shirt that showed off a set of sculpted abs to match his chiseled cheekbones. "Are your legs shaking yet?" he asked, a blindingly white smile on his face. "They better be, baby, 'cause that's when the magic happens! That's when you transform into your best self, when you find your inner light and peace and achieve your highest purpose."

"Seriously, Tyler?" I muttered. No one was in this for inner peace. We just all wanted our asses to look good in jeans.

"Close your eyes and picture what you want," he demanded. "Whether it's that winning lottery ticket, meeting Mr. Right, or your own reality show, you have the power inside you to make it happen!"

"Oh, fuck off, Tyler." I stood up from the squat and slammed my laptop closed. I hated working out at home, but I'd found it impossible to leave the house while Summer was there, as if my presence was somehow keeping her tethered to the Earth, like without it she'd just float away into space. And after spending the morning stress-eating a bag of peanut butter pretzels, though, I was willing to try anything to keep me from thinking about what was about to happen.

Violet had said the *Westwood Watermark* was programmed to land in everyone's email inbox at 3 p.m. on the dot—the final edition of the school year. So after abandoning overcaffeinated Tyler I drank a glass of water in the kitchen and stared at my Apple watch like a crazy person until the numbers read 2:59. Then I bolted upstairs and knocked on Summer's door. She sat cross-legged on her bed, staring at her phone.

"Is that the email?" I asked, my breath coming fast. "The *Watermark?*"

She raised her eyes to mine in a dull gaze. "There's not going to be an email," she said.

"What do you mean?" I crossed the room to her bed, resisting the urge to grab her phone and look for myself.

"They found out," Summer said. Her shoulder slumped and her voice lacked any intonation. "I just heard. I think Violet's in serious trouble."

"Who found out?" I demanded.

"Mr. Ellison. Mrs. Doyle had to go to the school. They might suspend Violet from graduation."

"Oh my God," I sank down next to Summer in disbelief. "But how? Who?"

She gave a defeated shrug. "I should have known it wouldn't work," she said. "And it wouldn't have mattered anyway. No one believes me." She started to cry.

"That's not true," I said in a forceful voice. "Lots of people believe you."

"But more of them believe Knox," she said, her shoulders shaking. "And they always will. And I'll just be stuck with this feeling. This awful feeling like I failed—at everything."

I wrapped my arms around her and pulled her to me, wishing I could absorb her pain into my body. "You didn't fail at anything. This is not your fault."

We sat like that on the bed until her tears subsided into slow, hiccup breaths. When she laid down I curled up next to her, stroking her hair. It took a long time, but her shaky breaths eventually evened out. After that I stayed a few minutes more. Then when I was certain she was deep in sleep I slipped my arm out from under her just like I'd done when she was little and couldn't fall asleep without me there. Back then I'd sometimes roll onto the floor and army-crawl to the door lest she notice me leaving. Today I tiptoed and closed the door gently behind me.

I grabbed my phone to call Witt at the office, then hesitated. We hadn't spoken more than necessary since my refusal to call off the *Watermark* plan. Halfway down the stairs I froze, cold sweeping through my body.

Could Witt have called it off himself?

I nearly stumbled down the stairs as I typed a text to him.

> Did you do this??

Then another:

> How could you do this? How could you do this to her?

I lowered the phone, my hands shaking. Witt and I had had fights before, of course, usually sparked by my temper and resolved by his calm ability to wait me out. But in all our years together there had never been anything unforgivable, nothing that threatened our stability.

Was this forgivable?

I stalked through the house with my phone, calling Witt for what felt like the millionth time. As with every other call I'd made, his voice came on after the fourth ring. "This is Witt Van Doren, please leave a message."

"Pick up already, damnit!" I yelled, hurling the phone onto the couch. Eight increasingly hostile texts and twelve unanswered phone calls later and I still hadn't heard a word from him. Who did he think he was, going behind my back to sabotage things and then *ignoring* me?

Tears of frustration filled my eyes and I sank to my knees, pummeling the couch cushions with my fists as I bit back a scream.

"Mom?"

I jerked my head up. Over the back of the couch Summer was staring down on me, her eyes wide. "Oh, hi baby," I said, sitting back on my heels and blowing a piece hair out of my face.

"Are you OK?"

I wanted to laugh at the absurdness of it all, but I didn't have the energy. "No," I said, leaning forward so that my forehead rested on the couch. "I don't think I am." Taking a deep breath I sat back and looked up at my daughter. "I think your dad might have been the one who told the school Violet was planning to publish your statement."

Dismay rolled over Summer's face, quickly giving way to confusion. "But Dad didn't know Violet got caught—I was the one who told him that."

I stood up so fast I knocked my knee on the coffee table. Wincing, I asked, "Told him? When? You talked to him?"

She shook her head. "No, he sent me an email this morning, telling me he forgot his phone and to tell you to call him on his office line if you needed anything because he knows you're terrible about checking your email, and—oh, oops. Sorry, I guess I forgot to tell you, didn't I?" She bit the side of her lip.

"An email?" I rubbed the pain in my knee and tried to keep my voice from coming out as a shriek, with limited success.

"He called just now from his office to check on me. I told him what happened with Violet getting caught."

I felt a manic smile spread across my face. Witt hadn't betrayed us. I'd been texting and leaving voicemails for him over an hour, demanding to know how he could betray our family—and God knows what else, my rants were now all blurring together in my mind—while really *everything was fine*.

"Anyway," said Summer. "He was worried so he's coming home early. Sorry I forgot to tell you about the phone thing earlier."

"It's OK," I said, really hoping it would be. "Hey," I said, suddenly recognizing the significance of her being downstairs after a full day sequestered in her room. "Are you OK? Do you need anything?"

"I just wanted a snack, that's all."

I sent up a silent prayer of gratitude for the normality of her statement. *If you're there, thank you God.* "Can I make you—"

"I can do it." She held up her hand and headed for the pantry.

As soon as she turned her back I began searching the coffee table for Witt's phone, looking under books and magazines. When my search revealed nothing I pulled up the couch cushions and thrust my hand into the cracks. I had to find Witt's phone before he could listen to my crazy messages.

"Mom?" Summer asked. She peered at me from the kitchen, a box of cereal in her hand. "What are you doing?"

"Just looking for your dad's phone. Did he, um, say where he left it?"

"No," she shrugged. "But sometimes he leaves it on the Peloton."

"Great idea," I said, stumbling over the ottoman as I turned to sprint to the sunroom where we kept the Peloton and Witt's free weights.

"Mom?" Summer said again, her voice suspicious. "What's going on?"

"Oh fine," I sighed, looking at the ground. "I may have left your father some voicemails. I, um, thought he might have been the one who sabotaged things for Violet. It would probably be better if he didn't listen to them." I twisted my mouth in guilt and looked back up at Summer.

"Mo-om!" she said, shaking her head. It was amazing how many emotions she could convey with just that one word. "Don't be the crazy voicemail person."

I gave an embarrassed shrug. "Yeah, well, it's a little late for that. Can you just help me find his phone?"

Together we searched the main floor and then I hunted through our bedroom, pulling back sheets and looking under nightstands.

"Shit," I muttered when I heard the garage door rumble open. I walked downstairs to see Witt wrap Summer in a hug and kiss the top of her head.

"How are you going, pumpkin?" he asked.

With her slight frame wrapped in his arms she looked less like a teenager and more like the little girl who used to hurl herself at Witt each night when he walked through the door.

"I'm OK," she murmured, her head still buried in his chest.

I waited until Summer had gone back upstairs, then tried to sound casual. "So, I looked for your phone for you but I couldn't find it," I said.

"It's right here," he said, picking it up from next to, nearly under, the toaster oven. "I was using the flashlight this morning to try to fish a crumb out." Unlocking it, he glanced down.

"You called me twelve—"

"Yeah, maybe don't—" I began at the same time. Witt looked at me. "Maybe just delete those messages," I said. "And any texts I sent today." He looked at me, his eyes wary.

"I have a feeling I'm in trouble for something I don't know about," he said.

"It's all fine," I said. "It's just, well, maybe just delete the messages. And, um, the texts, too. Please?" I gave him a pleading look.

He nodded and held his phone up, showing me that he was swiping right on each one. "Gone," he said.

"Thank you," I said, the words feeling altogether inadequate to express my gratitude at having married someone who was a better person than I was.

He nodded. "So, Summer told me what happened with Violet."

I stiffened. "I'm sure you're relieved," I said.

He sighed and rubbed his eyes. "Eden, nothing any of us do will change what happened."

"I wasn't trying to change anything," I said, my voice choked with all the emotions that were wrestling inside of me. "I was just trying to even the score."

Witt regarded me for a long beat, his expression a mixture of anguish and tenderness. Then he opened his arms and I fell into them.

# FIFTY-TWO

## JULES

### *Thursday, 3:30 p.m.*

It wasn't until I turned back onto my own street that Audrey finally fell asleep. *Of course,* I thought, sighing. I'd been out walking her around in the stroller for the better part of an hour, desperate for her to nap so she wouldn't turn into what Paul called "our personal banshee" an hour before bedtime. She'd fussed and fussed in the stroller, but now that I had to pee and home was in sight, she'd conked right out.

I gritted my teeth, wondering how long my bladder could hold out. I knew from experience that any hint of the motion of the stroller ceasing would cause her eyes to pop back open. I also knew that my bladder wasn't what it used to be. I mean, the things they don't tell you about childbirth.

Distracted by the mental gymnastics of nap strategy, I didn't notice the voices until I was almost on top of them. They came from Summer's front yard, loud and caustic. I paused, jiggling the stroller back and forth under the shade of a large magnolia tree one house away that stooped low to the ground and mostly shielded me from view.

"... they banned her from graduation! Her own high school graduation, a once in a lifetime experience. You had to know this would happen!"

"Caroline, I'm sure you understand I couldn't ignore what she was planning to do."

I recognized the heated, accusing voice as Caroline Doyle and the flinty, cold one as Lorrie Keller.

"But you could have come to me first! I would have taken care of it. Instead you had to run to your best friend, Mr. Ellison, and now Violet's missing out on the pinnacle of high school. And what if Vassar finds out about it?"

"Well, perhaps Violet should have thought about that before—"

"You should have come to me!" Caroline was full-on yelling now. I could see their figures through the magnolia leaves enough to make out Caroline's arms waving around wildly and Lorrie's crossed over her chest.

"I told you; I didn't know Violet was behind it when I went to Mr. Ellison, and I had no way of knowing he would—"

"What did you think would happen? Oh wait, you weren't thinking—at least not about anyone else but you and protecting *Knox*." Caroline spat his name like it had defiled her tongue. "I read Summer's article, you know. I made Violet show it to me. And I can see why you wouldn't want it to get around." Her voice grew even louder and Lorrie looked around.

"For God's sake, Caroline, keep your voice down. You're out of control."

Caroline gave a bitter laugh. "Me? I'm the one out of control? What about your son?"

"That's enough!" Lorrie's voice rose to match Caroline's. In the stroller Audrey stirred and I jiggled the stroller faster. The loud crack of a stick came from under one of the wheels and both women jerked their head my way.

"Um, hi." I raised my hand in a weak greeting as I pushed

the stroller toward them, hoping it looked like I'd just walked up.

"Just ask her," Caroline said, pointing at me. "She knows. She was the one who took Summer to the hospital."

Lorrie glared at me. "Did you need something?" she asked. The coldness in her eyes caused a shiver to go through me.

I shook my head and pushed past them. When I'd almost reached my driveway I looked back in time to see Lorrie disappearing back into the house, slamming the door behind her.

As I turned to push the stroller up to the house Eden's garage door opened and her Escalade backed down the driveway so fast I had to leap out of the way. She braked hard and opened her window.

"Oh my God, I'm so sorry!" she said. "I was in a hurry and not looking—" She was on the verge of tears.

"It's fine," I said, though my heart was pounding.

"It's not fine. I almost hit your stroller!" She put her head in her hands and shook her head. When she looked back up at me her face was wet.

"Are you OK?" I asked.

"Oh, just great." She laughed and wiped her cheek with the back of her hand. "I'm out of Xanax, my dog's out of diapers and the whole world is one giant fucking booby trap if you happen to be born female. So yeah, I'm fucking spectacular." She laughed again, sounding close to unhinged.

"I'm so sorry," I said, meaning it.

"You think it's hard when they're that age," she said, pointing at Audrey. "But just wait until she's older. You think you can protect her from everything, you know? I mean, that's your job, right? But then puberty happens, and middle school, and all her friends turn into petty little shits. And then high school and all of that fucking drama. But you get her through it all, and you think, we're almost there, I did it! I fucking did it. And then Knox fucking Keller comes along." I nod, trying to follow along. "And then I think, this is it, people are finally going to know what a shit he is, you know? But then that goes to hell and it breaks her all over again. Fuck!" She shouted the word and slammed her fists on the steering wheel. Audrey whined. "Oh God, sorry again," Eden said, eyeing the stroller. "Did I wake her up?"

"It's fine," I said. "Anyway, I was about to have to wake her up anyway because I really have to pee and she apparently only naps when she's moving."

"Here," Eden said, getting out of the car and reaching for the stroller. "Go pee. I'll stroll her right here."

"Are you sure?" I asked, surprised.

"Go," she ordered.

When I came back Eden was walking slowly back and forth between our driveways. The flush of adrenaline had left her face and her body seemed less like a tightly coiled spring. "Thanks," I said.

She nodded. "Summer never slept when she was a baby. It's like, I tried for so long to have her and then sometimes I was so exhausted I wondered why I'd ever wanted a baby in the first place."

"Sounds about right," I said. Then I cleared my throat. "Hey, um, you said something about people finding out about Knox. Does that mean they're pressing charges?" I eyed Eden with caution, unsure how far to probe.

"Of course not." Eden's shoulders slumped. Then she gave me a long look, followed by an exhausted, resigned sigh. "Sure, why not," she said, seeming to give in to something. She continued to push Audrey back and forth as she told me about what it had been like to read what Summer had written and what had happened. "And now she's left hanging again," she said, "just like with the fucking police and the attorney general and all the rest. And now she thinks her voice doesn't matter, that she doesn't deserve to be believed. And I want to tell her that's not true, that's not how the world works, but the truth is, I'd be lying." Her voice turned bitter. She stopped jiggling the stroller but I no longer cared whether Audrey woke up or not. My body felt hot with indignation.

"And there's no other way to get the truth out?"

Eden shook her head in anger. "I'm mean, I'd hire a fucking skywriter if I thought it would work." She gave a short, mirthless laugh and the pinched expression on her face made her look much older than I'd ever seen.

Audrey opened her eyes and squirmed. I stared down at her, then back up at Eden, grasping at the thought drifting through my brain. Maybe, just maybe, I could help. Or at least, I knew someone who could.

# FIFTY-THREE
## ARCHIE

### *Thursday, 4 p.m.*

Jemma and I sat on my basement floor, our finished frog poster between us. I'd been so worried I'd never hear from her again after my mom found Summer's essay on my computer and called Mr. Ellison that I hadn't been able to sleep.

> I'm so so so sorry

I'd texted her, my fingers trembling as I told her about my mom discovering the article on my computer. I'd spent the rest of the night inventing horror stories about what her lack of reply meant, not knowing it was really just because she had to turn in her phone to her mom every night at nine.

> Not your fault

she'd written back the next morning at 7:34 a.m., and by then it was too late anyway. I'd already overheard my mom talking to Mr. Ellison.

> Do you still want to work on Bio later?

I'd asked, but there had been no reply the rest of the day.

I tried to tell myself it didn't mean anything since students technically weren't allowed to use their phones during the school day, though there were plenty of teachers who didn't enforce it. Still, by the time lunchtime rolled around I'd already talked myself into the need to switch schools so I'd never have to face her again. So when my phone finally dinged in my pocket around lunchtime, I jumped to pull it out.

> Hang after school?

My body deflated to see Tadpole's name on the screen instead of Jemma's but I sent back a thumbs-up emoji. At least I still had my best friend.

When the door rang in the afternoon I was still in my sweat-pants and the black T-shirt I'd slept in, expecting to see Tadpole. But there on the doorstep stood Jemma. Her mom waved to me from their car as she pulled away from the curb.

"You came," I said, frozen.

"Of course I came." She gave me a strange look. "I mean, is that OK?"

"Yes!" I said, too fast, the loudness of my voice startling both of us. "I guess I just thought—I mean, with the whole *Watermark* thing, I thought like, maybe you wouldn't want to, you know, hang out anymore." I looked down and pretended to be very interested in a scuff on the wood floor.

"Ugh, it really sucks," she said, making a face. "But it's not your fault. So of course I still want to hang out. That is, like, as long as you do."

I nodded, worried my relieved smile might swallow the rest of my face. "After you," I said, gesturing to the basement door.

"I think Violet's in a lot of trouble," Jemma said once we'd settled onto the floor in front of our finished poster.

"Wait, are you?" I asked, suddenly panicked that someone had seen through my story about the anonymous email.

"No." A guilty expression crossed her face. "No one seems to know I was the one who sent it to you. Thanks, um, for that. My mom would kill me. I'd literally be locked in my room until graduation, possibly longer."

"Phew." I breathed out a sigh, but my relief was steamrolled by a truckload of guilt. "Jeez, I feel bad about getting Violet in trouble."

"Yeah well, comes with the territory." Jemma shrugged. "Violet's like, not afraid to take a stand." The admiration in her voice was clear. "I *loved* her exposé last fall on the girls locker room conditions compared to the boys. I cannot believe you guys have *vending machines* in yours." She wrinkled her nose. "And we barely have enough showers; there's always a wait and then you're late for class." I vaguely remembered the vending machines. The noisy, jock-filled locker room was somewhere I tried to spend as little time as possible.

"I don't remember that one," I said.

"But you definitely read her article tracking the origin of our cafeteria food, right? Talk about disgusting." She shuddered.

I gave a weak smile. "I must have missed that one, too." I wished I knew how to tell her that until a couple of months ago, I was too deep in my dark fog to notice much of anything. I had to give Dr. Frank credit, between hanging out with him once a week and the small green pill I took every day at breakfast, some days I almost felt excited to get out of bed. Mostly those were the days when I knew I'd see Jemma, but still, it was a nice change.

"Archie!" Jemma chided. "You have to be more informed." She sighed. "But it's OK, I still like you."

My heart fluttered to life. "You do?"

"I do," she said, her face growing pink. We were sitting cross-legged next to each other on the floor. She shifted so that her knee touched mine and I felt heat spread through my body. We turned toward each other at the same moment and all of a sudden our faces were nearly touching. In one quick move she leaned forward to close the gap, touching her lips to mine. They were smooth and warm. The whole thing only lasted a second, and then we sat blushing and grinning at each other.

"Helllooo!" Tadpole's voice echoed from upstairs. Jemma and I sprang away from each other as Tadpole's feet thundered down the stairs.

"Crap," I said, "I forgot she was coming, I'm so sorry!"

"Let's get ready to rumble!" Tadpole burst into view. She paused, surprised. "Oh, hey Jemma." Then she peered at our agitated state and flushed faces. "You guys OK?"

I avoided looking at Jemma while I swallowed a laugh. I hadn't felt more OK in a long time. "All good," I said, doing my best to wipe the huge smile off my face. "Just finishing up our Bio project."

"Ni-ice," Tadpole said, eyeing the poster. "Do you game?" she asked Jemma, who shook her head no. Tadpole cocked her head. "Wanna learn?"

Jemma looked at me. "Sure," she shrugged.

A few minutes later I found myself sitting on the couch, watching in near disbelief as Tadpole showed Jemma how to play Mortal Kombat. How was it possible that I, Archie Keller, was hanging out with my best friend and my... maybe girlfriend? On top of that, I'd been so excited to hang out with Jemma that I hadn't once thought about deforestation in the Amazon or whether my suspension would go on my permanent record. Was this what it felt like to be normal?

"Wow." Tadpole sat back when she and Jemma had finished their first game. "I thought you were going to suck way more than that."

"Um, thanks?" Jemma rolled her eyes but she was smiling. Her watch chimed. "Oh, my mom's in the driveway." She frowned with disappointment. "Thanks for the lesson," she said to Tadpole. "I'm definitely beating you next time."

Tadpole snorted. "I'd like to see you try."

Jemma looked at me. "OK then, well... bye."

"Text you later?" I tried to sound casual but I knew my face had turned bright red again.

"Yeah, OK. Sounds good." She flashed me a megawatt smile and then bounded up the stairs. I watched her go, then turned to face the full power of Tadpole's gleeful eye-roll.

"O.M.G.," she said. "You and Jemma, I knew it!"

"Careful," I said, grabbing the other video game controller. "Don't make me beat you."

"As if!"

I couldn't remember the last time my face hurt from smiling so much.

# FIFTY-FOUR

## LORRIE

### *Friday, 7 a.m.*

I watched Ed drink his coffee at the kitchen island. The gentle slurping sound he made with each sip was a noise I'd lived with for years, but today it was unbearable.

"Can you not do that?" I asked, narrowing my eyes.

He looked up from his phone. "What?"

"Can you just drink your coffee like a normal person?"

He rolled his eyes. "You're in a mood this morning." I shot him a look and glanced at Knox and Chloé, who were eating cereal at the table. We never fought in front of the kids. But neither of them had even looked our way. Knox was scrolling through his phone and Chloé was glued to the morning news show Ed had turned on. I was so restrictive with her screen time the poor girl would have watched anything.

It had been just over twenty-four hours since I'd found the check to Christi and the email from Beau, and I was no closer to knowing what to do.

I looked at my husband, noticing for the first time the fine lines around his eyes. What had happened to us?

When we'd met back in college Ed had fallen for me first. I'd written him off as a skinny, good-natured guy who made me laugh with his dumb jokes and helped me with my organic chemistry homework. He was the kind of guy who cheered you up when you got your heart broken, not the one who broke it. Somehow over the years I'd missed his transformation to a pseudo-celebrity doctor who would have looked at home on the cover of *Men's Health*. I'd also missed my own decline from energetic career woman to joyless stay-at-home mom.

"I have some dry cleaning that needs dropping off," Ed said.

"As if I have nothing else to do today," I retorted, feeling a swell of anger mixed with self-loathing. How was it that today, of all days, these feelings were consuming me? Knox's graduation was less than twelve hours away. I should be enjoying the sweet nostalgia of the day and basking in the glow of my accomplishment. I'd done it. I'd gotten my oldest child across the finish line and nearly launched into adulthood, the culmination of eighteen grueling years of motherhood. People should be throwing me a goddamn party, not the other way around.

I walked over and set my own coffee mug in the sink. The loud clang of the ceramic on stainless steel caused Ed to jump. "Jesus," he said. "Easy."

"Can we talk?" I said, crossing my arms. He glanced at his watch.

"I need to leave for work in five minutes."

"It's important," I snapped. Both Knox and Chloé looked up at me, and something resembling fear flickered through Ed's eyes.

"Sure," he said, following me out of the kitchen.

In his study I closed the door and put my hands on my hips. "I know," I said.

He arranged his face into a confused expression but his face had paled. "What do you mean?" he asked, having the audacity to look me in the eye.

"I mean, I *know*." My voice rose. "About—her." I couldn't bring myself to say Christi the dog mama's name.

"Lor, keep your voice down," he said, his eyes darting away from mine. I fixed him with a glare, staying silent to force him to fill in the lines.

"Mom?" called Chloé. "I can't find my tie-dye shirt!"

Ed let out a long breath, then squared his shoulders and narrowed his eyes. "You really want to do this now?" he asked. "With the kids in the other room? On Knox's graduation day? You'll ruin everything for him."

"Oh, you're funny, talking about me ruining everything," I said, a sudden rush of ice hitting my veins.

"Mo-om!" Chloé's voice was insistent. "Mom, I need my tie-dye—"

"Wear something else, Chloé!" I called, my voice sharp.

"But it's tie-dye day!" she wailed.

Ed glanced at his watch. "The kids are going to be late for school." He looked at me, his face no longer pale but flushed with anger.

"Mom!"

I glared at Ed, wishing I had something to strangle him with. "We're not done here," I said, then stalked out of the room.


I had no memory of dropping Chloé off at school, but once I pulled back into my driveway with an empty car I assumed that's where I must have been. Poor Chloé, I felt like I'd barely registered her presence for the last week. I made a silent promise I'd be a better mom to her while there was still time.

Back inside the quiet house I sank onto the couch. I wanted to cry, to let the tears overwhelm me, but they wouldn't come. I felt oddly detached, like I was watching a movie of my life narrated in the same hushed, even voice as a nature show. *And now Lorrie is loading the dishwasher. Now she's checking her watch to see if there's time to squeeze in a workout before her dentist appointment. Now Lorrie has just discovered her marriage is a sham. Also, her son may have—*

I shook my head to rid myself of the voice. Then I picked up the phone and dialed Eden's number.

# FIFTY-FIVE

## ARCHIE

### *Friday, 3 p.m.*

I tried to stay focused on the zombies that kept appearing in front of me. As soon as I vaporized one with my ray gun, another popped up out of a manhole and staggered toward me. I eliminated him, then spun around to aim at another as she crashed through a nearby store window and lunged for me. It was a near miss, but my victory was short-lived as I was tackled by the child zombie hiding in the tree I passed. It dropped down on top of me and devoured my brains. Game over.

I threw the controller down on the couch, annoyed. Normally I'd never let myself be defeated so early in the game, but the voices upstairs had gotten so loud I'd lost focus. I walked to the top of the stairs and paused before opening the door.

"Those are my private documents! They have nothing to do with you!"

"Nothing? Really? The fact that you slept with another woman has nothing to do with me? And that she filed a police report accusing you of sexual misconduct?"

"She's crazy, obviously, and I should have realized that before—"

"Before you fucked her?"

"Please watch your language."

"Oh shut up, Ed. No one else is here; there's no one to perform for and pretend you're the model husband and father."

*I'm here*, I thought, huddled behind the basement door. Why did everyone always forget I was in the house?

"Look, I made a mistake. One mistake. It was wrong, I admit. I was under a lot of pressure at work and I had a weak moment. She initiated everything and it didn't mean anything, I swear. Please let's not make it into anything more than it was. I've already paid the price for it, believe me."

"And by price you mean thirty thousand dollars?" There was a silence, and then my mom's voice got quiet. "Tell me the truth; did you pay that woman to silence her?"

"I did what I had to do to save our family." My dad's voice was tense. "She went crazy when I ended it. She threatened me, my career, our family. She wanted to destroy everything we have. I was protecting us."

"That's not what the police report says. It says that after the first time she was the one who wanted to end it. And that you pressured her into doing it again and told her you'd tell everyone she was cozying up to several of the players, as well. That you were the one making the threats."

"I can't help it if she was a slut." There was pause, then a sharp, cracking sound like a palm hitting skin.

"What the hell!" my dad yelped, and there was a loud crash.

My head bursting with everything I'd just heard, I pushed open the basement door and ran into the kitchen. A stool had tipped over onto the floor and my parents were glaring at each other on opposite sides of our large granite island, my dad holding his hand to his cheek, my mom with her eyes blazing.

"Archie!" My mom's eyes widened and her face went pale. "I forgot you were—"

"No one ever remembers I'm here!" I yelled. "I'm sick of it!" My blood was thudding in my ears as I ran over to the door and jammed my feet into my shoes. Outside, I strapped on my helmet and grabbed my bike. I was already at the end of the driveway before my mom ran outside, waving and shouting for me to stop. I pedaled as fast as I could, my legs blurring together when I glanced down. I kept that pace until I felt like my lungs might explode. I didn't slow down until my house was long gone out of sight.

I rode with no destination in mind, up and down the winding neighborhood streets until I found myself in front of a popular bike path that led out of the city. I imagined myself following it as far as it went, camping at night and fishing in streams along the way to feed myself while my family sent out search parties and went on the news to plead for me to come home. That would teach them to forget about me. Except I had no tent, no idea how to fish, and no actual desire to sleep outside by myself in strange places.

I felt for my phone in my pocket and thought about calling Dr. Frank. He'd always told me I could call anytime if I needed to. Lately, though, I didn't feel as much like talking to him. I was feeling better for one, and also he wasn't the only person in my life anymore. Glancing at the screen I saw three missed calls from my mom plus a series of texts. I couldn't face reading them right now.

> Hey

I typed. Jenna responded immediately:

> hey! perfect timing school just let out. woohoo last day, hello summer!!

> what ru doing?

omw home

I checked my watch. In less than three hours I was supposed to be sitting with my parents and Chloé watching Knox collect his diploma. I knew from driving by the school with my mom yesterday that they'd already put up the stage on the football field and started setting up rows of folding chairs in front of it.

My stomach churned thinking about sitting there at graduation with my dad. It didn't take a genius to figure out he'd done something bad.

> would it be cool if I came over?

I held my breath as I waited for Jemma's response.

when?

> now?

cool! home in 10

I pedaled to the address she sent me, a street on the edge of Mountaindale where the houses were smaller and original to the neighborhood. Jemma's brick house had bright blue shutters and a tidy hedge. Unclipping my helmet, I parked my bike next to the front steps before ringing the bell. Somewhere inside a dog barked and its paws skittered on the wood floor.

"Jasper, down!" yelled Jemma as she opened the door. A fluffy Pomeranian strained to get around her legs. Looking me up and down, it barked and let out a low growl. "Sorry, he thinks he's, like, a German Shephard," Jemma said. She opened the door wider and I stepped into a small entryway with a row of neatly arranged shoes. Jasper sniffed my leg and then wandered off, unimpressed.

I followed her down a long hallway that smelled of fresh, lemony cleaner into the living and kitchen area. Jemma's mom stood at the counter chopping vegetables.

"Hello, Archie." She waved.

"Hi, Mrs. Lee," I replied.

"Would you like to stay for dinner later?" she asked. "I'm grilling pork chops."

"Oh, thanks," I said. "Maybe, yeah. I'm supposed to... be somewhere later but I'm not sure if I'm going." I glanced at Jemma, whose smile made my legs feel like Jell-O.

"Well, there's plenty of food whatever you decide," Mrs. Lee said. "Now you kids enjoy your first hours of freedom now that school is out."

"Can we go upstairs? I want to show Archie my sneaker collection," Jemma said. "I'll leave the door open," she added when her mom hesitated.

"OK then, sure," her mom nodded.

In Jemma's room the walls were covered in photographs of what looked like graffiti.

"I took most of those myself," Jemma said when she saw me looking. "I'm kind of obsessed with street art."

"Cool," I nodded, trying to keep my eyes away from her unmade bed where a set of white sheets with pink hearts on them peeked out from under the blanket.

"Wanna see my collection?" she asked, crossing the room to a large bookshelf that held at least twenty pairs of Vans, in all different colors and patterns.

"Wow," I said, impressed. "It's like a museum."

She gave a modest smile. "It's not much compared to some of the sneakerheads I follow online, but I only started a few years ago. I use my babysitting money."

"They're amazing," I said. *You're amazing*, I wanted to say.

We stood in silence for a minute.

"So, um," I said, trying to think of something to say. "What're you doing this summer?"

"Babysitting a bunch," she said. "And taking a photography class at the High Museum. What about you?"

"I'm supposed to go to camp." I grimaced. I hated the musty, mosquito-infested cabins, the freezing mountain lake I was forced to swim in, and not being able to play video games for an entire month. "But maybe before I go maybe we could, like, hang out?" I rushed to get the words out before I lost my nerve.

Jemma smiled. "Definitely."

Somehow we'd drifted closer to each other, and without thinking I leaned forward to kiss her. This time lasted longer than the first and felt like I'd fallen into some beautiful time warp where there was only me, Jemma, and her graffiti pictures.

"Jemma!" Mrs. Lee's voice at the bottom of the stairs startled us apart. "Do you and Archie want to help me make the *oi muchim*?

"That's spicy cucumber salad," Jemma explained, blushing. "Sorry, I've never, um, had a boy over, so I think she's freaking out a little about us being up here."

"No problem," I shrugged. Then I surprised myself by reaching out to take her hand. "Let's go see what this evening's Top Chef challenge is," I said.

Jemma giggled. "Coming, Mom!" she called.

Mrs. Lee showed me how to cut the cucumbers into thin slices and mix them together in a bowl with the scallions Jemma had chopped. Then she had me mix vinegar, soy sauce, and a pinch of salt and sugar and pour it over the cucumbers. Last she added sesame seeds and a big douse of special Korean chili flakes. It was delicious.

As we cooked I kept glancing at the clock, watching the hands creep slowly toward six o'clock. The last thing I wanted right now was to be around my family. But I pictured my mom's face as the chair next to her sat empty. I pictured Knox scanning the crowd for me and realizing I wasn't there.

"Are you going to go?" Jemma asked in a low voice as her mom rummaged in the fridge for more cucumbers since I'd eaten most of the salad already.

My chest felt like someone had zipped me up in a jacket that was too tight. I closed my eyes and shook my head. "I don't know."

# FIFTY-SIX

## LORRIE

### *Friday, 6 p.m.*

Chloé was still wearing her tie-dye shirt, paired with jean shorts that were far too short now that she'd had a growth spurt and sparkly high-top sneakers, but I'd been too sapped of energy to argue her into something more suitable for Knox's graduation. After our fight that afternoon Ed had stormed out of the house and I'd mostly laid on the couch, taunted by the rotating reel of family pictures in the digital frame across the room but unable to move to go turn it off. I clutched my phone, waiting to see if Eden would call back. She never did.

When five thirty rolled around and Ed still hadn't returned home I directed Chloé into the car.

"Where's Archie and Daddy?" she asked.

"I don't know," I said. My head felt too thick to come up with anything but the truth. Ed would either meet us there or he wouldn't. Either way, I was surprised to find I didn't much care.

After I'd texted and called him repeatedly for an hour, Archie had finally written me a one-line message.

at a friend's

When he didn't respond to my follow-up texts I gave up. He was safe somewhere, that's all that mattered. I just had to get through tonight, through Knox's graduation, and then I'd figure everything else out.

Everything else. As in my entire life, which had just been leveled by a wrecking ball that had been aimed at me for months—years, maybe—but that I'd never even seen coming. I was the person who finished my Christmas shopping in August and planned the kids' camp summer schedules in January, yet I'd failed to see what was happening in the present moment right in front of me.

"When is this gonna be over?" Chloé looked up at me from her phone, then out over the sea of chairs on the high school's football field. We'd gotten there early enough to get good seats, in the center and only a few rows back from the stage.

"Chlo, it hasn't even started yet."

"Well, then, when is it gonna start?"

"Soon." I surveyed the crowd and locked eyes with Jules, sitting two rows in front of us. She stared as if she'd been waiting for me to look her way, daring me to say anything or even point a finger at her. I shot her a cold look and turned my attention back to the stage.

"Excuse me, sorry, excuse me."

I looked up to see Ed squeezing past people to get to the empty seat next to me. "Hi," he said as he sat down, his eyes straight ahead.

"Hi Daddy," Chloé said, eyes still glued to her phone. At home it remained locked in a cabinet except for one hour in the evening after homework was done, so her eyes had lit up when she'd gotten into the car and I'd handed it to her.

"Archie's fine, but no, I don't know where he is," I said without looking at Ed. "Thanks for asking."

"I was about to—"

"Mm-hm."

"Look," he said in a low voice. "Can we just try to enjoy this? For Knox's sake."

"Oh, don't worry," I said. "I'm planning to enjoy every second of it. For my own sake."

The school band marched onto the field playing the West-wood fight song and everyone got to their feet to clap and sing along. During the whistling and clapping that followed the last, sustained note of the song I looked up to see Archie making his way down the row of chairs toward us, his face flushed and his hair flattened from his bike helmet.

"You're here," I said when he reached us, my voice trem-bling. He nodded and sank into the seat on the other side of Chloé. I reached out and squeezed his hand.

The crowd quieted as Mr. Ellison took the stage. I stiffened and imagined my gaze was a sharpshooter's scope fixed on his large forehead. Tuning out his empty speech I scanned the chairs until I found her, three rows up and a few seats over.

Eden's hair, loose down her back, gleamed in the sunlight. Shame washed over me thinking about the desperation I'd felt when I dialed her, like I'd had too much to drink and called an ex-boyfriend. What had I been planning to say to her? "I know your life just fell apart but now mine has too, please help me?" I felt stupid just thinking about it. I felt stupid thinking about so many things.

The speeches droned on, important old white men in suits, then a student speaker, then another. I couldn't focus on any of it. Finally they began to call the names, Mr. Ellison urging everyone to hold their applause until the end. Most people obeyed. At least Keller was in the first half of the alphabet. Maybe I could just leave after that.

They reached the Js, then the beginning of the Ks. Jules twisted her head to look back over her shoulder, at what I couldn't see. A murmur went through the crowd, starting as a whisper and growing into a noise like the hissing of a faulty radiator. People began to point at the sky. Something floated into the upper corner of my vision field and I craned my neck to look up along with everyone else. High above the stage buzzed what looked like a giant insect, black with four appendages that seemed to be spinning, holding the creature aloft. Below it hung a wide black banner with large, white block lettering. I furrowed my brow, confused. Was this part of the program? A final congratulatory message for the graduates?

A few people had risen out of their seats now. On the stage they'd ceased to read names, and one boy had stopped awkwardly in the middle of the stage. Knox stood on the side of the stage in the on-deck position. Both of them stared up at the creature as it made a slow descent toward them, but I still couldn't make out what was written on the banner it held.

There was movement on the stage again now. Mr. Ellison and a couple of teachers ran toward the device as it hovered in front of the stage. I gasped as one of the teachers lunged for it, but the device was positioned far enough in front of the stage that it remained out of arm's reach.

"It's a drone!" someone shouted.

"What the hell?" Ed's voice cut through the noise of the crowd. The large letters on the banner came into focus, now easy to read.

NO MEANS NO WHOEVER YOU ARE
EVEN FOR WESTWOOD'S BASEBALL STAR

I gasped and leapt to my feet, my hands clawing the air as if I would somehow be able to reach the banner. People had their cameras out now, pointed at the drone.

"Get that thing down, goddamnit!" Ed was also on his feet now, pushing past people and even climbing over an elderly woman, knocking off her stylish hat, forcing his way into the main aisle and toward the stage.

From the side of the stage it must have been hard to read the banner because I saw Knox moving from side to side to get a better angle. Then, as he took a step forward and leaned out to read the sign, his posture changed. His hand froze at his face where he'd been shading his eyes, and his head whipped toward the crowd, searching for someone. Before I knew it, I was out of my chair heading for the stage, my heart hammering in my chest.

The drone began to move again, staying at the same height but turning in a slow circle, the banner moving with it. The students on stage, in their caps and gowns, were pointing and holding up their phones. The drone stopped halfway around, revealing a second message on the other side of the banner. I squinted to read it.

LEARN THE TRUTH ABOUT WESTWOOD'S RAPIST

Under the letters was a QR code, the kind of code that when viewed with your phone's camera, would take you to a website.

"No," my voice rasped, pushing people out of my way. Ed had reached the stage now. Scrambling up onto it, he made a running leap toward the drone, nearly catching hold of a corner of the banner. The drone rose back up with a sharp move, avoiding Ed's hands. I looked around wildly, wondering who was controlling it.

"Knox!" My son's name escaped my mouth in the form of a high-pitched wail. Knox was still standing on the side of the stage, rooted to his spot, staring open-mouthed at the drone.

"Get off me!" roared Ed as an off-duty police officer acting as security threw himself on top of Ed where he'd fallen and held his hands behind his back. "I'm not the one who did this!"

The drone receded back up into the air at a fast clip and sped off toward the parking lot on the other side of the school building. I catapulted out of my seat and pushed through the chaos. I'd reached the stage and was nearly touching it when I stumbled over someone's leg and went flying down onto the grass. All around me people were climbing over each other to film the spectacle of Ed lying on his stomach, screaming at the police officer. I shook myself off and tried to stand up.

Mom!" I looked up to see Archie, his face pale, pulling me to my feet. With his other hand he gripped Chloé's arm. Craning around, I could see Knox climbing down off the stage and heading toward me. I grabbed his hand and pulled my three children toward the parking lot, or maybe they pulled me, the four of us falling through the crowd until we reached the rows of SUVs parked outside the stadium. I stopped and drank in a deep gulp of air.

"In the car, all of you, now," I said, pushing them forward. Archie gripped his phone and stared at the article on the screen, which, with a stab, I recognized. "Put that away," I said, reaching for it, but Knox was faster. "Don't read that!" I begged him as he grabbed Archie's phone.

"Read what?" Chloé asked, her voice high and frightened. "Mom, what's happening?"

"It's going to be OK, Chlo," I said, trying to sound like I believed my own words as I pushed Knox into the front seat. He refused to relinquish Archie's phone and his eyes moved back and forth across the text as I started the car, his face pale. I drove in silence until, a block from our house, Knox gripped the dashboard.

"Stop the car," he said in a strangled voice.

I turned to look at him. His face was a greenish color. "What—?"

"Now!"

I pulled over to the curb and Knox fell against the passenger door, pushed it open and vomited onto the sidewalk.

"Oh my God," I exclaimed. "Sweetheart, are you—"

"Mom!" wailed Chloé. "I want to go home!"

Knox held up his hand for everyone to stop speaking, then sat back up, wiping his mouth. Dropping his head back against the seat, he closed his eyes.

"Please," he said. "Just take me home."

# FIFTY-SEVEN

## SUMMER

### *Friday, 6 p.m.*

I didn't see it at first. With Van Doren as a last name I was in the back of the senior section, off to the side awaiting my turn to walk across the stage. Then everyone started talking and I thought, *Rude.* I mean, I know it's boring to have to watch everyone shake Mr. Ellison's hand and claim their diploma (which, I'd learned, was just an empty case anyway—the actual document came in the mail later, talk about a letdown.) But like, people, just shut up and let everyone have their moment.

Then it came into view, a black robot-looking thing descending from the sky.

"It's a bomb!" one kid shouted.

"It's murder hornets!" another yelled, eliciting laughter.

But I knew what it was right away. And I knew where I'd seen it before.

The message on the banner made me gasp along with everyone else. But, unlike everyone else, I didn't pull my phone out and point it at the QR code to see what it linked to. Because I had a feeling I knew what that was, too. And then there it was, over the shoulder of the girl next to me, confirmed. My words on her iPhone screen; my story there for everyone to read.

I didn't tell my mom, and I definitely couldn't tell Violet after all the trouble she'd gotten in for me, but I'd felt weirdly indifferent when she'd gotten caught and what I'd written didn't get published. I mean, I felt awful for her, obviously. But while I thought I'd wanted everyone to read what I'd written, to know the truth, while I was writing it I realized it actually didn't matter, because most people had already decided what the truth was. Hearing from me wasn't going to change that.

The only thing that really mattered was that I knew the truth: that it wasn't my fault.

Realizing this, a nice kind of quiet came over my brain, like the loud staticky channel I'd been tuned into for the past few days had suddenly switched off. But then when I saw the drone and the banner floating down toward the stage, the static roared back into my ears again. The buzzing of whispers started back up and everyone craned their necks to look at me. So I did the only thing I could.

I ran.

I ran without thinking about which direction I was going in, heading around behind the stage and across the football field. "No, this way." Someone caught my arm and I turned to see Ari. "The parking lot's over here." He jerked his head in the other direction. I nodded and let him pull me along until we reached the rows of parked cars, our blue graduation robes dragging along the ground. My mortarboard hat had fallen off somewhere along the way but I didn't care. No way I was walking across that stage now.

As we reached the parking lot he paused to scoop something up from the pavement and thrust it under his robe. Then he opened the backdoor to a familiar-looking Subaru Forrester and shoved me inside. Mr. Shulman sat in the passenger seat and Jules turned around to look at me from the driver's seat.

"Hi," she said, surprised to see me.

"I thought we could give her a ride home," Ari explained, sliding in through the back door on the other side, squeezing me in between him and Audrey, who gave me a drool-soaked smile from her car seat.

"Of course," Jules nodded.

"What's going on?" My words came out low and gravelly, like they were stuck in my throat.

"I keep asking the same." Paul's face was stormy and he gave Jules a stony look.

"I'll tell you later," she said, a determined look on her face. "Right now we need to get out of here."

Ari struggled to buckle his seat belt, and from under his robe a black robotic arm and a piece of the banner peeked out.

We made the drive in tense silence as if there was an unspoken agreement that whatever was about to go down between the Shulmans could wait until I was safely out of their car.

Jules pulled all the way up my driveway and Ari got out with me. "I'll be home in a minute," he said to Paul and Jules.

"You damn well better be," Paul said, his face dark.

They pulled back down the driveway and Ari stood facing me, his face like a puppy expecting a treat.

"Why did you do that?" I put my hands on my hips.

Ari's smile slipped. "I thought, I mean, she told me you wanted—"

"Who told you?" I interrupted.

"My stepmom. She said you were trying to—"

"But no one asked me!" I scrunched my eyes closed in frustration. "Which seems to be a pattern in my life." I opened my eyes to see Ari's stricken expression.

"Oh, God," he said. "I'm really sorry." His eyes flickered to the ground and then back up at me. "I just wanted to help you.

What happened to you was..." He trailed off and I could see there were tears in his eyes.

"Oh my God, it's OK," I said, reaching out to touch his arm. "You didn't know."

We stood there for a minute, the silence surprisingly comfortable. Then I sighed and shook my head. "I just really, really want to this part of my life to be over, you know?"

He gave a short, sarcastic laugh. "Yeah, welcome to the last four years of *my* life. College can't start soon enough."

I looked at him then and thought about how many times I'd passed him in the halls without really seeing him. And about how many people had done the same thing to me. "I'm sorry it's been so rough for you," I said.

He gave me a half-smile. "For what it's worth," he said. "I thought what you wrote was really good. Your thesis statement was clear and eloquent, and your syntax was sophisticated yet accessible."

I laughed in spite of myself. "Thanks," I said.

Inside, my house was quiet. After my mom called me a fifth time I turned off my phone and went upstairs and shed my graduation robe, letting it fall into a blue puddle on the floor. My guitar was on the floor next to the bed and I pulled it into my lap. I strummed the chords of the song I'd been working on. It was about falling in love for the first time, what it felt like and what it meant. I hadn't written the end. Or rather, I had, but it wasn't quite right.

I picked out the melody on the strings, trying different notes here and there. I adjusted the key. Something was still off.

I wondered what Knox was doing right now and if he'd read what I'd written. What he thought of it. What he thought of me. If he thought of me. I hoped there would be a day when I didn't think about him. I was ready.

Setting the guitar down, I walked over to my dresser, pulled out the soft, gray T-shirt and held it up to my face. Any lingering smell of him had disappeared. I ran my fingers over the letters, *Property of Westwood Baseball.* Then I tossed it in my trash can.

I did the same with the framed photo of us from winter formal that was face down on my desk. And the sheet of notebook paper I'd kept that he'd folded and slipped inside my locker. It read, *Will you go to prom with me?* Under which there were two check boxes, one for *Yes* and one for *Hell Yes.* I'd drawn a heart around the second one before showing it to him.

When everything was in the trash can I carried it downstairs and walked outside to empty it. I dumped it all out in our big green bin and watched it hit the bottom. It hurt, but not as much as I'd thought. I set the small trash can down and pulled out my phone.

There was one last thing to do.

I pulled up our texts. I stared at them, remembering the fantasy I'd had of adding to them throughout college, then printing them all off for him into a book I'd give him on our wedding day. Now I swiped left, took a deep breath, and pressed delete.

Then I turned and walked into the backyard, and lay down on the grass. It was still warm from the sun, though the light was starting to fade. I watched the clouds drift by overhead and listened to the cacophony of birds. I hummed the chords I'd been playing upstairs. My fingers strummed imaginary strings in the air.

And then I found the right chord.

Of course. I should have known. The major chord progression I'd been using was all wrong, too shiny and optimistic. But by including a minor chord progression the song suddenly had depth. It was still hopeful, but rounded out with a hint of loneliness.

It was perfect.

# FIFTY-EIGHT
## EDEN

### *Friday, 7 p.m.*

Witt pushed me into the house ahead of him, glancing over his shoulder as though we were being chased. Everything had happened so fast it was like watching a movie on double speed. The drone appearing in the sky. Witt turning to me in confusion. Jules craning her neck to watch my reaction. Ed climbing on the stage. Archie pulling Lorrie up from the ground. Me looking around for Summer, and the panic of not finding her. Calling my daughter over and over.

I was pushing through the crowd and about to dial Summer again when Jules's number appeared on my screen. "I just took Summer home," she said when I answered.

"Oh, thank God," I said. My relief was accompanied by a twinge of jealousy as I thought of another mom helping my daughter instead of me. It was followed by the realization that it was the first time I'd thought of Jules that way—as a fellow mom instead of an interloper. Then the reality of what had just taken place hit me. "Do you have any idea what just happened? Or how it happened? I mean, did Summer and Violet somehow...?" My voice trailed off into the silence on the other end.

Jules cleared her throat. "So about that—actually, can you hang on a sec?" I heard an angry voice in the background that sounded like Paul's. "I'm so sorry," Jules said to me. "I have to call you back." Then the line went dead.

"What's going on? Where's Summer?" Witt put his hand on my shoulders and nearly shook me with his urgency.

"At home. Jules just dropped her."

I let Witt propel me toward the car, his hand gripping my shoulder like he was afraid to lose me. Once home we stumbled into the living room like drunk teenagers—a thought that, as soon as it passed through my brain, made me wince. And there on the couch sat Summer.

"Oh my God," I cried, running over to her. "Are you OK?"

"Are you hurt?" Witt sat next to her and began looking her over for injuries. She shook her head.

"I'm fine." But then she leaned forward and buried her head in his chest. He pulled her close. Bailey hopped over and licked her ankle.

The three of us plus the dog sat frozen on the couch like some kind of fucked-up Norman Rockwell painting. Finally Summer inhaled deeply and sat back from Witt.

"Sweetheart, how did—did you and Violet?"

She shook her head. "It was Ari."

"Shulman?" Witt's forehead creased with confusion.

Summer nodded, then hesitated. "And I think also maybe—Jules?"

"Jules?" Witt repeated, looking like an English major who'd stumbled into Advanced Physics.

My thoughts whizzed in circles, trying to connect the dots. Ari. Jules. The conversation we'd had at the bottom of our driveway. Had she—

"Mom?" Summer interrupted the pinball game going on in

my brain. "I don't want to fight this anymore. I just want to move on. I'm sorry if that's letting you down."

Everything else fell away. I took her hand and pushed her hair behind her ear. "Oh, sweetheart," I said. "You could never let me down."

# FIFTY-NINE

## JULES

### *Friday, 8 p.m.*

I rocked Audrey an extra-long time after she fell asleep, doing my best to delay facing what I knew was waiting for me. When I finally slipped out of the nursery and headed downstairs, Paul was pacing the kitchen while Ari sat slumped on a stool at the counter.

"I mean, what the hell were you thinking?" Paul's face was creased in anger.

"I was just trying to help," Ari mumbled.

"Help?" Paul barked. "Help who? Help get yourself kicked out of MIT before you even start?"

Ari straightened up, alarm shooting across his face. "What? No! They can't—"

"It's not Ari's fault," I cut in wearily. "I asked him to do it."

"And you!" Paul whirled to face me. "You're supposed to be the grown-up! The rational adult. How could you let this happen? It's insane!" His hands were balled into tight fists as he continued his path from one end of the kitchen to the other.

"Summer deserved—" I began.

"Summer Van Doren is not our concern," Paul snapped. "I told you to stay out of it! I mean, let's face it, we're not exactly the most popular house on the block as it is. But this," he gave an exasperated laugh. "Well, this will just add fuel to the fire."

A cold calm washed over me. "Stay out of it?" I said. "When the girl—the woman—who cares for our child on a regular basis is raped? When it happens in *our* neighborhood? When it involves our *neighbors*? I should just stay out of it?" I took a deep breath, and shook my head. "No. Just, no. I refuse to believe that's the right thing to do."

"Jules, listen—" Paul interjected.

"No, you listen." All the puzzle pieces of thoughts that had been floating around in my head the past few weeks clicked into place. I pointed to Paul, my voice strong and steady. "You brought me here. We could have lived anywhere, but you wanted to live in this house, in this neighborhood. But now you're telling me I don't get to be a part of it? That instead we should just keep to ourselves so we don't make anyone uncomfortable?" I laughed and crossed my arms over my chest. "Absolutely not. If we're going to live here, damnit, I'm going to *live* here. And the neighborhood I want to live in, the community I want to be part of, isn't one where you stay out of it when something bad happens. You do something, Paul. You act like a grown-up and you help." I threw his words back at him.

I realized then that Ari had gotten up from his stool and was standing next to me. I turned and saw him, his shoulders squared and nearly touching mine, his gaze fixed on his father.

"Jules is right," he said. "It's like we've been hiding out, Dad." He looked sideways at me and gave a small nod. "It feels good to be a part of something for a change."

The fight drained from Paul's face and he looked taken aback at the sudden alliance between Ari and me. He cleared his throat. "I, uh, didn't know you felt that way, buddy. I'm sorry."

"You never asked."

Paul rubbed the bridge of his nose, then looked from me to Ari. "Look, this isn't over. And I should probably still ground you or something." But his voice had lost its fire. Ari groaned and I squeezed his arm.

"I'd vote to overrule that," I said. "But we can discuss it over ice cream." Then I turned to the cupboard to get out three bowls.

# SIXTY

## KNOX

### *Friday, midnight*

I hadn't meant to break up with Summer that night. Things had just gotten so intense. I loved spending time with her because she made me feel better about myself. But then after we started having sex, being with her just made me feel worse. Each time it happened I hated myself a little bit more. No matter how hard I tried not to, I always ended up closing my eyes and picturing scenes I'd watched the night before. I'd say things to her that made me feel sick after. It was like for those few minutes I became this other version of myself, one I usually kept hidden. I hated that she got to see it. She always did and said whatever I wanted and acted like it was fine, but it wasn't fine with me. I was tired of feeling so fucked up.

I didn't want to go to the party that night. I didn't like hanging out with my old friends and Summer together. It made me feel stuck between the person I'd been during high school and the person I was ready to be.

I already thought about Spencer, Jackson and Mackenzie in the past tense, knowing I was about to leave them behind. And

Summer... well, I wasn't sure where she fit in. There were moments when I wanted her to be part of my future—a better future—where I wasn't so messed up about so many things. We were stuck in the present, though, where I was defective and didn't know how to fix myself.

All that stuff was running through my head when we left Jackson's house that night. I was pissed off by then. The whole night felt like such a waste of time; just the same stupid people crammed into the same stupid basement having the same meaningless conversations. I was officially over all of it. But Summer was having fun and wanted to stay. Finally I said she could do what she wanted, but I was leaving.

It was her idea to go to the park. I was so exhausted from acting like everything was fine I just wanted to go home. I felt like I'd been pretending for as long as I could remember. I knew from the start it was a bad idea. Like so many things in my life, though, it felt set in motion, and I was too tired to stop it.

When I found out the attorney general wasn't pressing charges I thought I'd feel relieved. I expected my shame to evaporate, like when I was fourteen and scraped the side of my dad's car with my bike as I wheeled it out of the garage. He grounded me, not because I scraped his car but because I lied about it, claiming it hadn't been me. I spent one night so consumed with guilt that I couldn't sleep, and confessed the next day. He rescinded the grounding and instead took part of the repair cost out of my allowance and Christmas money, telling me we were square and could close the books on the whole thing. Knowing it was over and done with was like having a giant barbell removed from my chest. After hearing from the attorney general, though, I didn't feel any lighter.

I'd tried to push it out of my mind, but after everything at graduation, well, I knew it was time. I wanted to hear—I *needed* to hear—what she had to say. I just didn't want it to be in front of the whole school. I would have given anything to go back in time, tell Dad's sleazy lawyer friend to go to hell, and go find her. To sit and talk and figure out what happened and how to fix it. How to fix me.

What she'd written hit me like a line drive to the gut. It opened a door in my brain I'd been trying my hardest to keep locked. I tossed and turned in bed, her words buzzing through my head.

*"Blurry lines are still lines..."*

*"... part of a club I never wanted to join..."*

*"... when you love someone, no still means no."*

They whirl around in my brain, kicking up a tornado of questions I'm too scared to answer.

Is it possible...?

Did I...?

What now?

# SIXTY-ONE

## EDEN

### *Two months later*

Two half-packed suitcases took up most of the floor in Summer's room. I'd been stepping over them for days as I delivered clean laundry and collected the empty cans of seltzer she left lying around.

"You know she's going to have to learn to do that on her own, right?" Witt asked when he saw me headed for Summer's room with an armful of folded clothes. "Like, really soon." I shot him a look. We had an unspoken agreement not to talk about Summer's departure for college. Lately every gripe I'd ever had about her cluttered room and overflowing clothes hamper had been replaced by a painful feeling of nostalgia that followed me everywhere like an animal stalking its prey, pouncing on me when I least expected it.

I'd walk past what used to be the playroom but had long been repurposed as Witt's home office and be struck by a vision of toddler Summer in pigtails, busy dressing and undressing her baby dolls. Or I'd see eight-year-old Summer in the yard, shrieking in her rainbow tankini as she ran under the sprinkler.

Or twelve-year-old Summer in ruby slippers and a Dorothy costume with Bailey tucked into the basket over her arm, the last year before she was too cool for trick or treating. Then I'd blink and the real Summer would be before me, scrolling through her college packing list and asking where we kept the extra toothpaste.

All summer I'd been watching her and storing her up in my heart as only a mother can. There were days when she seemed so grown up, the tilt of her head and confidence of her stride positively womanly. Then there were others when she seemed to still be a girl, her legs tucked under her on the couch, scrolling through her phone alternating between giggles and eye-rolls.

She was at that in-between stage when you're too young to fully understand the consequences of your choices, but old enough to be responsible for making life-altering decisions. Knowing this, I should have been terrified to send her off into the world, but I wasn't. She'd already survived the worst.

The morning after graduation we'd woken to local reporters —none of whom I'd called—camped out at the end of our drive-way, hoping for a comment on the news story making the rounds about the Westwood rapist. We stayed in the house for two days until they packed up and moved on to the next salacious story.

I'd wanted to take her away. I'd suggested Paris or Italy, promising shopping and Michelin-starred restaurants.

"No thanks," Summer shook her head. "This is my last summer with my friends. I don't want to miss it." Instead she spent her days at the pool with Violet, or babysitting next door —a point of contention between Witt and me. He was still furious about Jules's role in the graduation fiasco, whereas my response had been more shock and awe. When my plan had failed, Jules had mounted a brute-force campaign to defend my daughter, something I never would have thought her capable of. But I shouldn't have been surprised. She was a mother, after all.

In between packing for Princeton, once a week I drove Summer to the therapist she'd finally agreed to start seeing. She'd complained about it before the first session, but never after that. Every so often she locked herself in her room and came out with puffy, red-rimmed eyes. When that happened she'd come sit with me on the couch and put her head in my lap while I stroked her hair. During those times we mostly sat in silence, but it was enough for me. I hoped it was enough for her.

The week before she was due to leave I heard Witt's car roll into the driveway in the afternoon, hours before he usually got home.

"Make sure you're putting those stickers I got you with your name on them on all your bedding," I said to Summer, surveying the disaster zone that was her room. She rolled her eyes.

"Mom, it's college, not summer camp. I don't think people label their stuff anymore."

"Well then don't come crying to me when those cashmere sheets you made me buy disappear from the dorm laundry room." I put my hands on my hips.

"Honey?" Witt called from downstairs.

"Just a minute!" I called back, focused on Summer. "Did you finish signing up for all your orientation activities?" She nodded. "And set up all the online banking stuff like Dad asked you to?"

"Mom!" Summer rolled her eyes. "I'm not, like, a child."

"Eden?" Witt called again. "It's kind of important."

"Coming!" I raised an eyebrow at Summer in warning.

Downstairs there was no sign of Witt. "Where are you?" I called.

"In the mud room."

"Why?"

"Can you just come in here, please?"

"Fine," I sighed, following his voice. He stood next to the pile of shoes in the corner, one hand on the door that led out to the garage. "What are you doing in here?" I asked.

"Honey, I know next week will be hard," he said, grinning at me. "And the house will feel empty."

"Stop it," I said, my eyes pre-emptively filling with tears. "We agreed not to talk about—"

"Shh," he held up a finger. "Just let me finish. I thought you might need something else to focus on, to take your mind off... well, you know."

I heard a scratching sound on the other side of the door. "What did you do?" I asked, widening my eyes. His smile beamed brighter than the fluorescent lights in the laundry room I was always complaining about.

"I got you... this," he said, flinging open the door.

In bounded a small black puppy, his large feet skidding on the tiles. His ears flopped around as he snuffled around on the floor and then licked my bare toes. Kneeling, I held out my hand for him to smell. He gave it a cursory sniff and then nuzzled into it to have his head scratched.

"But you said no more dogs!" I looked up at Witt, astonished.

"Things change," he shrugged, smiling. "I thought Bailey needed a friend."

I pulled the dog close to me and wiped my tears on his fur. "Thank you," I whispered.

We spent dinner trying out different names.

"Hamilton?" suggested Summer. I wrinkled my nose.

"Sir Shits a Lot?" said Witt. I threw a crouton at him.

"Though I do like the royal theme," I said. "Maybe Prince Harry?" Both of them groaned.

After we cleaned up I put the puppy on a leash and headed outside. Though the sun had begun to drop the humidity still hit me like a blanket that was impossible to shrug off. I felt the hair on my neck frizz and made a mental note to deep-condition that night when I showered.

Automatically my eyes wandered to the house across the street where I'd spent so much of my time the past fifteen years. I wondered if I'd ever again walk through Lorrie's front door without knocking, or sit propped against the opposite side of the couch from her, our legs stretched out toward each other, a bottle of wine between us on the coffee table. Would we ever again have a casual text exchange or an inside joke? Would anyone ever know me as well as she had?

Despite my pleas to Summer to let her feelings out, I'd spent the past several weeks burying mine under the endless to-do list of packing for college. But suddenly my entire body felt heavy with a sadness that had been waiting to catch up with me.

Prince Harry pulled on the leash and stopped to examine a threatening-looking pinecone, giving a tiny growl and nudging it with his paw. Looking up, I saw Jules headed toward me with her stroller.

"Hey," I said, dashing away the tears that had formed in my eyes. "Whew, steamy, right?" I picked up Prince Harry and patted his head.

"What in the world?" she cried. "Did you get a new puppy?"

"He was a surprise from Witt."

"But I thought he didn't want—"

I snorted. "Please, Witt doesn't know what he wants. Most men don't until you tell them." She laughed and reached out to scratch Prince Harry's head.

"Aw, he's adorable," she cooed.

"I know," I grinned. "And now I'll have an excuse to go on more walks with you. Oh, and don't forget about book club tomorrow—Caroline's hosting." I felt a twinge as I said it, knowing Lorrie wouldn't be there with her annotated copy, forcing us to spend at least a few minutes actually discussing the book.

Jules smiled. "Oh, I'll be there," she said. "I might even finish the book first this time." She held up her crossed fingers and I laughed. Audrey shifted in the stroller and let out a cry of impatience. Jules sighed and eased the brake off the stroller. "I should get her home," she said. "But are we still on for coffee tomorrow morning at Nan's?"

For an instant my vision blurred into a slide show of memories as I thought of how many times Lorrie and I had met at Nan's, and how her order was always a half-caf latte with one pump of vanilla. I wondered if there would ever come a day when my brain would no longer store that information.

Shrugging off the past, I refocused on Jules and everything that was to come. "We're still on for coffee," I said. "I wouldn't miss it."

# SIXTY-TWO

## ARCHIE

### *Two months later*

"I don't think you need to see me anymore," Dr. Frank said. I looked up from examining my hand of cards.

"What do you mean?" I asked. "Like, I'm fixed?"

A smile flickered across his face. "You know you were never broken to begin with, right?" he asked. "What you experienced was a temporary condition as you struggled to adjust to big changes in your life, like starting high school. As far as I can tell, for the past few months you've been feeling good. You're doing well in school. You've made friends. You even have... dare I call her... a girlfriend?"

I blushed and tried to hide a smile behind my cards. I'd talked to Dr. Frank a lot about Jemma; how we rode our bikes around the city looking for street art for her to photograph, how I'd taught her to play a couple of my favorite video games and now she was almost as good as me, and even how easy and natural it felt to sit with my arm around her and her head on my shoulder when we watched a movie in the family room, and to kiss her when no grown-ups were looking.

"It's been a good summer," I admitted, laying down a pair of sevens. One of the best parts was that I hadn't had to go to sleepaway camp. Tadpole had signed up for a summer coding class and Mom had agreed to let me do that instead of camp.

"What about Dad?" I asked when she'd said yes. I'd seen him a couple of times since he'd moved out into a shiny new apartment complex a few miles away, but mostly I'd been busy with Jemma. The house felt bigger with him gone, in a good way. Like I could spread out and be myself everywhere, not just hidden away in the basement. That realization made me feel both sad and guilty.

Mom gave me a half-smile. "Don't worry about your dad. I'll take care of it."

Tadpole and I met three other kids in our coding class who loved gaming as much as us. After class we'd get burritos or a slice and then bike to Tadpole's to spend the next few hours gaming and working on our projects. It was awesome. I'd never had a group of friends like kids always do on shows, but sprawling on the floor of Tadpole's rec room surrounded by people who wanted to talk about the same things I did made me realize maybe the problem hadn't been me—maybe it was just that I'd never found my people before.

"What about my medication?" I asked Dr. Frank. "What if I'm only feeling better because of that? Maybe those aren't real feelings."

"Archie, I assure you that the feelings you're having are all your own," he said.

"OK," I said. "But what if things get worse again? What if I get worse?"

"You can call me anytime," Dr. Frank said. "And, if it makes you feel better we can keep a monthly check-in on the calendar." I nodded, relieved. We agreed on a date for the next month and he gave me a small wave as I closed his office door behind me and stepped into the waiting room.

I saw her hair first, the red mess of curls pulled back into a half ponytail, spilling down her back. She was turned away from me, reading a magazine. I glanced toward the exit. I could easily make it across the room without her seeing me.

"Um, hi," I took a step toward her. Summer lifted her head from the magazine and locked eyes with me, surprise registering in them.

"Archie, hi."

The million things I wanted to say to her flooded my brain. "Uh, how's your summer been?" I managed. She shrugged and tilted her head. I stood there for a minute, unable to string together any of the other words in my head. "Well, OK," I said. "I should get going."

"See you," she said. For a split second her old smile spread across her face, then faded as she turned her eyes back to the magazine.

Outside I started to unlock my bike, then stopped. I had nowhere to be, so I left my bike in place and sat on the building steps. It was shady and the concrete was still cool despite the heat.

I checked my phone and saw an email from Knox. Since he'd been at the ranch he'd emailed me twice from the internet café in the nearest town. I'd thought it was weird that someone who spent so much time on his iPad would want to be disconnected like that, but he said it was where he wanted to be. He'd even talked to me about it, which was weird since we hadn't had a real conversation in months.

"Hey," he'd said, plopping down next to me on the basement couch.

"Um, hey," I said, pausing my game, surprised he'd even come down there.

"So Dad got me a job at a friend of a friend's horse ranch out west. I'm leaving in a couple of days."

"Do you know anything about horses?"

"Not really." He shrugged. "But I guess I'll learn."

"Well," I said. "Good for you." I turned back to my game.

"Look," said Knox. "I know what you think of me. But please don't write me off, OK?" There was a pleading tone in his voice I'd never heard before.

"Sure," I said, feeling something inside me shift and crack open a little. "So, a horse ranch, huh?"

"I need a change of scene. To get away from everything for a while."

"You mean from what happened with Summer?"

He was quiet for a minute, then nodded. "That, and other stuff too. But not you." He glanced up at me. "I just wanted you to know I'm not trying to get away from you. You're a good kid, Archie. I've been a pretty shitty big brother. But I'm gonna change that." His shoulders slumped. "I fucked up with Summer. Like, really fucked up. Sometimes I can't believe I—" His voice caught and he took in a shuddering breath. "But I did." His eyes met mine and I saw the tears forming in them. "I'm gonna change, Archie. You have to believe me. I'm gonna change a lot of things."

I stared at him for a minute, my big brother who'd been my best friend, my idol, and then my biggest disappointment. "I believe you," I said. And in that moment I really did.

Knox nodded and blinked away his tears. Then he grabbed the game controller from me. "For now, though, I bet I can still beat you in Mario Brothers." I smiled as he rebooted the game.

"Not a chance."

I settled onto the front steps of Dr. Frank's building and scanned Knox's latest email.

Hey little bro. So far ranch life is hard work but I like it. I do stuff like repainting buildings, fixing fences and working in the garden. I get up before the sun and after dinner I'm too beat to do much but go to sleep. I have one day a week off and they're letting me learn to ride the horses which is cool. I also started seeing this doctor in town, kind of like you did, I guess. He's pretty cool and it's nice to have someone to talk to about stuff. There's a pair of Swedish girls who are here for the summer working in the kitchen and dining room. They're pretty cool and we've gotten to be friends but I'm not looking for anything more than that right now, you know? Speaking of, how're things with Jemma? OK, my time's up, gotta go. Oh, be nice to Mom. She needs it right now. Love you bro.

Knox

I read it over, then wrote a reply telling him what I'd been up to with coding, Jemma, and that Mom seemed better lately.

After I sent the email off to Knox I pulled up a game on my phone. Time flew by, and just as I was starting to feel the need to stand up and stretch my legs the building door swung open and Summer stepped out.

"Hey." I scrambled to my feet. Her eyebrows shot up.

"Stalking me?" she asked. I could feel my face reddening.

"Yeah, kind of," I admitted. "Sorry to be weird. I just... wanted to see you."

She crossed her arms but made no move to go. "So... now you know I'm so fucked up I'm seeing a shrink."

"I don't think you're fucked up," I said. "Not that it matters what I think."

"Oh Archie." Her green eyes brimmed with tears. "Of course it matters."

I was quiet, aware that being near her didn't make me dizzy anymore. Instead of Summer's face in the back of my notebooks there were now sketches of Jemma, where I tried to capture her expressions in just the right way; her smile or the way she pressed her lips together in a small bow shape when she was thinking really hard about something.

"I used to be in love with you," I confessed. "I thought you were perfect."

"And now?" she asked in a low voice, her eyes on the ground.

"I think I was in love with the idea of you," I said. "Real people are way more complicated."

Summer laughed again, for real this time, and wiped her eyes. "You seem happy, Archie," she said. "That's nice to see. I thought maybe you weren't for a while."

"You noticed?" I said, surprised.

"Of course. Last year it seemed like you just kind of... faded."

"Yeah," I said softly. "I did. That's why I come here. Or came. Dr. Frank says I'm done now."

"Done? So he helped you?"

I nodded. "What about you? Is he, um, helping you?"

Summer was quiet for a minute as she nudged a piece of gravel off the step with her foot.

"Yes. Maybe. It's hard to tell if I feel better because I'm coming here or because I'm leaving soon."

"Leaving?"

"College. Princeton. Next week. Where no one knows me, thank God."

"Knox said that's the same reason he likes being out West," I said, forgetting myself. Summer glanced up at me sharply. "Shoot, I'm sorry," I said quickly. "I forgot—"

"It's fine." She cut me off with a wave of her hand and gave a sad smile. "I miss him, isn't that weird? After everything that happened, he's still the person I want to talk to sometimes." She paused, her cheeks flushed. "Is he happy?"

"I think so. Happier, anyway." My phone buzzed with a

text. Glancing down I saw it was from Jemma. "My girlfriend," I said, unable to keep the pride out of my voice.

"A girlfriend, wow!" Summer raised her eyebrows. "What's she like?" I told her about Jemma—her cool shoe collection, how she was teaching me some words in Korean, and how I was going to ask her to Homecoming when school started. After a while I realized I'd been talking nonstop for several minutes.

"Sorry," I broke off, embarrassed. "I'm rambling." Summer just smiled. We stood quietly for a few minutes.

"Archie," she said after a while, "things with Knox were so... complicated. How things ended between us... everything I wrote, I never wanted for him to end up—you know that, right? I'm not the kind of person who would do that to someone."

"Yes, you are," I said. "And that's OK. It's OK to stand up for yourself, even if it's scary. But you're also the girl who used to catch lightning bugs in the backyard with me and Chloé. And the one here today trying to figure it all out."

As I said it I thought about how my dad was the guy who cheated on my mom and also the one who ran up and down the street with me every night for months while I learned to ride a bike. And how my mom was the person who chose my dad, but also the person who'd now chosen us. And how Knox was the person who used to let me crawl in bed with him during thunderstorms and also the one who did something horrible to Summer. And me... how I was the kid who spent a year on antidepressants and now I was happy again.

"We're all complicated, Summer," I said. "Don't sell yourself short trying not to be." Her eyes met mine and I saw there were tears spilling down her cheeks.

"Hey," I said. "I'm sorry. I didn't mean to upset you."

"No." She shook her head fiercely. "You didn't." We stood for another minute, then she smiled and brushed her hand across my cheek. "How'd you get so wise, anyway?"

I shrugged and smiled back at her.

"I should go," she said. "I have a lot of packing to do." We stood facing each other for a minute before she reached out and caught me in a fierce hug.

"Stay complicated, Archie Keller," she whispered.

I got on my bike. As I rolled out onto the sidewalk I turned back to look at her one last time, standing on the steps and waving as I rode away.

# SIXTY-THREE

## LORRIE

### *Two months later*

Now that Ed was gone I still slept on my side of the bed. It was faster to make the bed in the morning with only half the sheets to smooth and one pillow to plump. Not that I was pressed for time these days. My phone hadn't exactly been ringing off the hook with invitations.

With Chloé at camp and Knox out west the house was quiet in the mornings. Most days I didn't even see Archie until the evening; he was up and out the door before I could peel myself off the mattress.

Standing in my bathrobe in the kitchen while my coffee brewed I threw open the French doors that led to the deck, hoping for birdsong or the faint buzz of a lawnmower, anything to fill the silence. The day stretched out endlessly before me; I had all the peace and quiet I never wanted.

I'd had coffee with Meredith Price a few weeks earlier; my attempt at holding my head high. To my surprise we'd hit it off. I told her I was considering restarting my career and she'd offered me some part-time legal work at her firm. I thought about it for a while, but decided I wanted to go in a different direction. After updating my résumé with all my volunteer work, I had two interviews lined up for development roles at non-profits.

Ed and I talked more often than I wanted to, mainly to figure out what to do about Knox now that his college admission for next year had been rescinded. All it took was one tweet by a teenager for the story about graduation to be picked up by the local news outlets and make its way to the Florida State Admissions director's inbox. He said he hoped we understood what a sensitive situation it was. That even though there were no charges pressed, he was sure we could appreciate what a "distraction" Knox's presence on campus would be.

Ed wanted to sue but Knox had refused.

"I'm eighteen and it's my decision," he'd said. "I just want this part of things to be over."

After I finished my coffee I went upstairs to get dressed and paused outside Knox's room, then stepped inside. My eyes traveled the room, thinking back to the last time I'd seen him in it.

The morning of his departure I'd knocked softly on his door, expecting to find him still asleep, but he was up and dressed, smoothing down the clothes in the suitcase that lay open on his bed.

"Do you have enough warm layers?" I'd asked. "I read it gets cold at night out there, even in the summer." I checked my watch. "There's still time to run to Target before your dad takes you to the airport."

He shrugged. "I'm good, I think."

I took a step toward him. "Are you sure this is what you want? I mean, Wyoming? Ranching is really hard work; you know that right?"

Knox smiled. "Because you've spent so much time on ranches, right, Mom?"

"OK, fair," I said, smiling in spite of myself. "But there's still plenty of time to look into one of those gap-year exchange programs—you could travel, go to France, or Ireland."

He shook his head. "I want to work, and Dad's friend did me a favor by hiring me with zero experience. Anyway, it's only six months, at least at first."

"And then you'll re-apply for college."

"Yeah, maybe."

He zipped the suitcase closed and heaved it onto the floor. I looked around his room, aware of how neat it looked without clothes spilling out of his drawers and toiletries cluttering the top of his dresser. His closet door was open and the empty hangers stared back at me like forlorn orphans. I'd spent the previous whole year anticipating how sad I'd feel when he left home, but this wasn't the way I pictured him leaving. I didn't feel sad so much as utterly destroyed.

"Mom?" He was facing away from me and his voice caught.

"Yes, sweetheart?"

"I've been thinking. About Summer, and... everything." I inhaled sharply. "And I realize I—like, how did I... I just never thought I could..." A raspy sob escaped from his throat and the tortured look in his eyes made my whole body ache. "Mom, am I bad?"

I reached out, caught his shoulder and pulled him toward me, wishing I could absorb his pain. "I will always love you, understand?" I said hoarsely. His cheeks were wet as he nodded and let himself be folded into my arms to be rocked like the baby he once was.

As I held him and bore witness to his anguish I was struck by the difference between my oldest son and his father. The only contrition I'd seen from Ed with his "oopsie" as he called it, had been one late-night phone call the week after he'd moved out. He'd obviously had too much to drink and babbled on about how much he loved me, and how he really hadn't heard

Christi when she'd said no, or at least hadn't thought she'd meant it. I hung up after that.

When Ed pulled into the driveway later to take Knox to the airport I stayed in the house. We hadn't seen each other in person since our first couples counseling session two weeks earlier when he'd asked me when I was going to come to my senses and let him come home. I'd canceled our remaining sessions after that.

Outside in the driveway where Ed waited the sky was gray and heavy to match my mood.

"You have your wallet? And your phone?" I asked Knox. "Do you need any cash?"

"You already gave me some, Mom." He rolled his eyes and was all teenager again.

"Text me when you land, OK? And when you get to the ranch."

"I'll try. But they warned me there's no Wi-Fi and cell service is spotty. So don't freak out if you don't hear from me, OK?"

I nodded and did my best to smile like he wasn't my heart walking out the door away from my body. Hidden behind the curtains I watched Ed load the suitcase into the car. When he finished he stared at the house for a long minute. I knew he couldn't see me but still I held my breath. When Knox drove away I felt my whole body deflate.

Now, months later I stood in Knox's empty room. I smoothed the comforter I still kept on his bed and brushed my fingers over his bare nightstand, picking up a layer of dust. I made a mental note to grab the Pledge wipes from the hall closet next time I was downstairs.

I checked my watch. Archie would be home soon and there was nothing for dinner. I pulled out my phone to order and saw that I'd had takeout delivered the last three nights. Guilt propelled me to find my purse, put on my shoes, and head to the market up the street where at least I could pick up deli food with actual nutritional content.

In the store I loaded my basket with chicken parmesan and roasted asparagus from the deli for Archie and a can of soup for me.

By the time I saw her it was too late to turn around and walk the other way. We were face to face; her green eyes locked on mine. I fingered the elephant charm I still wore around my neck.

"Hi," I said.

"Hi," Eden replied.

We stood there for a minute and I watched a parade of emotions flicker across her face so fast that anyone who didn't know her as well as I did would miss them.

"How, um, are you?" she asked. I raised my eyebrows. "I know," she sighed. "Stupid question."

"I've been better," I said, knowing it was pointless to pretend. She nodded.

We stood in silence for another minute. I felt a physical ache of longing in my chest as I breathed in her familiar musky perfume.

"OK then," I said, giving a small nod. I made it to the end of the aisle, where I abandoned my basket and walked out of the store.

It had begun to rain, a sprinkling of droplets that transformed into a heavy sheet of water by the time I reached my car. I sat inside and leaned forward to rest my forehead and arms on the steering wheel as the rain drummed on the windshield. Tears dripped down onto my knees. I wondered if a day would come when I didn't wake up feeling flattened by all I'd lost—my marriage, my son's future, and my best friend, all in the space of a week. Sure, to outside observers it might appear I was moving on, but would I ever feel that way on the inside?

I heard the click of the passenger door opening and jerked my head up to see Eden slide into the seat next to me. Her hair was dripping and a rivulet of water ran down the side of her face.

"Hi," she said. I regarded her in silence, unable to trust my voice. She bit her lip and hesitated. "Look, I heard about Knox and Florida State. I'm sorry, I didn't mean for that to happen."

I regarded her in disbelief. "Of course you did," I said. The longing I'd felt inside the store was replaced by a dull anger. It was muted by grief as if wrapped in a thick layer of cotton, but still, I almost laughed with relief at its return. I hadn't known I was capable anymore of feeling anything but desperately sad. "You couldn't have just left it alone?" I continued, gripping the steering wheel. "Why didn't you just leave it alone?" The harshness of my voice made us both flinch.

Eden's eyes were red, and there were droplets of water on her face, whether rain or tears I couldn't tell. She gave a small, sad shrug. "She's my daughter, Lorrie."

"And he's my son." My voice broke on the last word and I tipped forward again, pressing my face into the steering wheel as I let the sobs of anger and desperation overtake me.

"Lorrie." She placed her hand on my back, hesitant at first, then firmer as it rubbed slowly in a circle. Without raising my face to look at her I leaned to the side and fell into her. Her arms encircled me and the cool dampness of her shirt felt good against my hot cheek. She leaned her head against mine and didn't loosen her arms for several long minutes until my shoulders stopped heaving. As my breath evened I wished for a world where we could stay that way forever, just the two of us together protected from the outside world.

I took a last inhale of her scent and sat up, wiping the back of my hand under my nose. For a long minute the only sound was the rain on the windshield, softer now but with no signs of letting up.

Then we both began to speak, voices on top of one another.

"I really want to—but I can't—"

"I wish I could—but I know—"

We stopped and exchanged a teary smile. Then Eden opened the door, and stepped out into the rain.

# A LETTER FROM THE AUTHOR

I want to say a huge thank you for reading *Such a Good Family*. I hope you were as hooked on reading about Lorrie, Eden, and others as I was about writing about them. If you'd like to join other readers in hearing all about my new releases and getting access to bonus content, you can sign up for my newsletter—I promise I'll never send you nonsense.

www.stormpublishing.co/caitlin-weaver

If you enjoyed this book and could spare a few moments to leave a review that would be hugely appreciated. Even a short review can make all the difference in encouraging someone else to discover my books for the first time. Thank you so much!

As the mom of two boys, I think a lot about how to raise them to be kind and empathetic people in a world that can often force kids into rigid and sometimes toxic gender roles. I've spent hours talking to other moms (and dads!) who worry also about this, and while we're all out there doing the best we can as parents, quite often it feels like swimming against the tide.

The idea for this book sprang from many late-night conversations with mom friends about "are we doing this right?" and "what would you do if?" It forced me to wrestle with questions about who bears responsibility for the kind of people our children turn out to be—parents or the world at large. Because while we can control what is said and done within our families, the outside influences and pressures on our kids are vast.

I'm in agreement with Gloria Steinem, who said, "I'm glad we've begun to raise our daughters more like our sons, but it will never work until we raise our sons more like our daughters." It's my hope that this book might play a small role in reminding people of that responsibility—and also that it kept you turning the pages until the very end!

Thank you again for being part of this amazing journey and I hope you'll stay in touch—I have so many more stories and ideas to entertain you with!

Caitlin Weaver

www.caitlinrweaver.com/contact
www.threads.net/@caitlinrweaver

 facebook.com/CaitlinRWeaver
 x.com/caitlinrweaver
 instagram.com/caitlinrweaver

# ACKNOWLEDGMENTS

First, a huge thank you to my fantastic editor, Vicky Blunden, for sharing my vision for this book and for her countless brilliant suggestions that have made it better. Also to Oliver Rhodes and the whole Storm Publishing team for their invaluable support and enthusiasm along the way.

People often think of writers as working alone, but in my case that's fortunately not true. I'm incredibly grateful to the people who read part or all of this book on its journey to publication and offered their feedback. Specific thanks go to Amanda Vink, Hadley Leggett, Heather Meloy, Jen Craven, Kerry Chaput, Ojus Patel, and Renee Ryan.

Thank you to two organizations in which I've found wonderful connections and resources, the Women's Fiction Writers Association and the Toronto Area Women Authors.

They say that behind every successful woman is a group text cheering her on, and that's certainly true for me. Thank you to my ATL crew who show up for me on a daily basis: Angela Howard, Arden Rowland, Beth Barry, Cara Frattasi, Christi Feeney, Kelli Hadfield, Kristen Rajagopal, and Molly Carter Gaines.

Thank you to all my friends and family for your love and support, and for asking, "So when can I read the book?" from the very beginning. To Cari Galle, Kim Hagerty, and Lauren Gardiner, thank you for always picking up the phone and saying all the right things.

To Elijah and Sam, thank you for introducing me to the

wild and wonderful journey of motherhood. I've loved (almost) every minute of it.

To Marcus, thank you for everything, always, again and again. I love you more than chocolate milk.

And finally, a huge thank you to **you**, dear reader! With so many books in the world you chose mine, and for that I am very grateful.

Printed in Great Britain
by Amazon

43323864R00209